# Football

## Don Skiles

# Praise for Football

"In this beautiful novel, Don Skiles illuminates the life of a young man coming of age in 1950s Pennsylvania. Larry Simmons hasn't a cynical bone in his body, but just behind his eager embrace of his world hovers the dark side of small town America. This novel's great charm is its subtly contained melancholy, its fragile dreams modestly conveyed, its sufferings cast in the best possible light by a young man who always takes the high road even when there isn't one. Larry is one of the most lovable and heartbreaking characters in any book I've read in some time."

ELIZABETH McKENZIE, author of *Stop That Girl*

"Don Skiles' novel, *Football*, has the intimacy of a heartfelt memoir, nostalgic but clear-eyed, about an America of just yesterday. And boys, young men, like his protagonist are still to be found in today's America, we can hope."

HERBERT GOLD, author of *Fathers* and *Still Alive: A Temporary Condition*, reissued as *Not Dead Yet*.

"Don Skiles' *Football* certainly does capture the awesome power of the game and its collateral culture in 1950s small-town America. More than that—much more than it—it's an extraordinary evocation of a simpler place and time—but far from being a nostalgia piece, it puts the reader squarely inside that lost reality, body and soul. I find this novel weirdly irresistible."

MADISON SMARTT BELL, author of *Zig Zag Wanderer*

"'Football' is a euphemism for 'Making It' in Don Skiles' passionate novel about the manifold things Boomer boys dreamed about—sex, heroes, making the team, lettering, deer hunting, victory, movies, cars, being a man—in small town western Pennsylvania of the late 50s. This time tunnel owes more to Larry McMurtry, David Guy, and *All the Right Moves*, than it does to Tex Maule, Clair Bee, or *Friday Night Lights*. And Skiles is hip to the fact that while the trappings of adolescence may change the actual process never gets any easier, which allows him to drill deeply into the heart and soul of America."

RICHARD PEABODY, editor *Gargoyle Magazine*

ISBN: 978-1-938349-20-1
eISBN: 978-1-938349-21-8

Library of Congress Control Number: 2014908010

*Book Design by Mark Givens*

For information: Pelekinesis, 112 Harvard Ave #65, Claremont, CA  91711

First Pelekinesis Printing August 2014

www.pelekinesis.com

# Football

## Don Skiles

*For my sister, Gwen, and
my mother, Mary Elizabeth Canaan*

# 1956

By early August he was lithe and trim and had even managed to gain some hard-earned pounds in the endless days since school had finished, back on Memorial Day, which now seemed long ago. It would probably not be enough, though. When he looked at himself in the bathroom mirror he still saw a smallish boy, with some, but not enough real muscle bulked on his shoulders and arms and chest. The work-outs had helped, it was true; he no longer looked "skinny as a rail", as the phrase had it. His neck was bad, though; it looked like the fragile stalk of a long flower. His legs were certainly better than they had been back in early June. He had tried hard to build them up, especially the calf muscles. On real football players these bulged like biceps, heavy-veined, right below the cuff of the padded playing trousers. His were still too much like bony shanks - "chicken legs." They looked like they would snap easily.

What might save him would be speed. That, and agility. He was smart and felt he could easily learn the playbook given to players to study at night during the two-week Training Camp coming up in the last two weeks of August. But in the pit of his stomach he felt a churning uneasiness, fear. You could get hurt playing football, hurt badly - a broken arm or leg, or a head or neck injury, although the latter were rare.

His mother was puzzled by his set intention to try out for the team. She queried him increasingly on it as the day got nearer for reporting for the physical examination that preceded the two-week camp.

"Are you still thinking about trying out for football?" she had asked that morning, putting a bowl of cereal with freshly cut peaches in front of him.

"Sure," he said, nodding. "Couple a weeks, I'll be out there." He felt his stomach instantly knot up at the thought of it, and dug fiercely into his cereal.

"Larry…You know…you don't have to do it. You know that, don't you?" She eyed him closely.

It always surprised him how much his mother knew, understood. In this matter of going out for football, although she knew very little about the actual game itself, what she did know was that it was not simply about playing the game, or even making the team. It was somehow connected to proving that you were really a man, a guy, one of the real boys.

"I have to do it, Mom. You know what I mean." He spooned up the last of the fresh cut peaches, sweet and yet tart, and pushed back from the table.

She shook her head. "Just be careful. You mind what I say. You're a small boy. I wonder about those coaches even letting you boys try for the team at your size."

He grinned, and mimicked hauling in a pass, giving the stiff arm to a would-be snarling tackler at the same time. He had seen varsity players photographed in this pose, in the newspaper and in the school yearbook.

"We're small, but mighty. And fast. Fast!"

He had a set routine after finishing breakfast that was in a way his own training camp regime. After he left the old, rambling three-story red-shingled house, he walked over – it wasn't far – to the big green field where the sprinklers had been turned off, even though it was only 8:30. The sun was already a hot, heavy presence. It would be one of the "Dog Days" of August in Pennsylvania, when the humidity hung heavy in every particle of air but it stubbornly refused to rain. Sweat was already running down the middle of his back as he began his routine, sprinting up and down on the sideline of the big field, doing forty-yard sprints to improve his speed and breathing.

He did not go onto the field itself. It seemed to him some sort of sacred space, filled with an intensity and special light even when it was empty, and no one was there, as it was usually early in the day. Secretly, he liked it best when it was like this, with the wet grass sparkling in the morning sun.

Soon in the autumn months just ahead, the big field would be scarred – torn with the marks of the warfare, the battles, that would take place there every Friday evening. Large hunks of turf would be torn out, leaving muddy swathes that got larger, deeper, despite the efforts of the groundsmen; these parts would increase as the season went on, marking those areas of the field where the ball was most often in play. The end zones would remain almost pristine, greenly beckoning to the players like the oasis the parched cowboys staggered towards in the movies.

Most prominent, though, were the countless round holes that would appear in the field, the cleat marks from the shoes of the players. When he had been a small boy, he and other boys had combed the field after the practices to find these cleats, which had come free of the ankle-high black leather football shoes - they were hard, rounded pieces of rubber about an inch or so in length. There was something thrilling about finding the cleats, although they had no practical value. He kept an arrangement of them on his desk, like jewels.

He stood at the one end of the field and looked down it. One hundred yards. It was a distance he had run so often, trying to do it as fast as he could and marveling in his mind at the recorded fact that there were human beings who could run that distance in ten seconds. That meant they were covering ten yards in a second. He could not fathom such speed. He had asked his friend, Frankie Malone, about it.

"I wonder how it feels..."

"What? Feels what?" Frankie was walking with him after school, in the aimless scuffling meandering that often occurred after school. They had no money to go to Peter's, the restaurant where the school kids congregated after school, drinking Cokes and phosphates and some, who had money, eating the large cheeseburgers, which made his mouth water; he tried not to think of them.

"Running a hundred yards in ten seconds."

"Running a hundred years in ten seconds!" Frankie often quickly altered something he would say, so that it came out bizarre, fantastic, better. It was a trait he had, and yet he did poorly in Miss Evens' English class, staring idly out the tall classroom windows most of the time, to her consternation and anger. Now he shook his head violently.

"Fast! That's what it feels like. Faster 'n you or me'll ever know. I can tell you one thing, Larry, for sure. Frank K. Malone Jr, yours truly, will never be able to have that experience, because there is no way in hell that I could run that fast. Or even want to." He nodded vigorously.

"It must be something…"

Larry had never asked anybody to time him because it seemed vain. His mother was against vanity and he felt he was also. It was important not to be vain, although he could not say for certain why. Some people, it seemed, expected you to be vain, and even argued that to not be vain was vainer. It was complicated.

The markings on the field seemed to him almost magical, especially the larger stripes marking the goal line. To cross that was what the whole game was about - making the touchdown. He often ran the hundred yards between the large thick white stripes marking the ten-yard end zones doing a sort of interior timing. Was he even near the magic ten second figure? Of course, he could not be. If you could run that fast, it would be noticed. Any athletic ability of that magnitude would come out. Such abilities were much more noticed, looked for, than scholastic abilities, for example, although everybody always advised to study hard. There were always smart kids, but there were few who could run really fast. Or catch forty-yard passes. One of the coaches had said that - Mr. Barnes. He had overheard him in the hall outside the coaches' office.

When Larry ran these hundreds, he began to realize some of the true difficulties of running. It was easy, relatively, to burn the first thirty yards, but very soon after that you began to feel heaviness in your body; not just in your legs, but everywhere, a pulling, retarding, slowing down sensation; it resembled the feeling of trying to run in the swimming pool, which they often did in the summer up at the park, since it was said to be good for your leg muscles. At the same time, he had the sensation that he could not really control his legs, that they were without any power or even substance, and yet their jarring contact with the ground made him feel how easy it would be to lose balance, to trip, to sprawl and roll in a terrible fall.

At sixty or seventy yards, all these sensations intensified, especially that of running in a heavy element, like water, rather than air. That was the only way he could fairly characterize how it felt. You began to slow down, although now you wanted to run harder. But you simply could not do it, and the last twenty yards became a great distance, even a taxation.

Afterwards, as he would stand with his head down, chest heaving, gasping in the end zone, or trotting very slowly around the field, it was those last twenty yards he thought about. That was the area where the runners who recorded those incredible times increased their speed, their power, their momentum.

When he talked to Frankie about it, he had a phrase for it.

"You know those jet fighters, those Air Force planes? They got this thing, an afterburner, and they throw that on, and pow! Shit! Straight up! I saw one do that, over in Ohio? At the Dayton Air Show? Sounds like an explosion. There's a big flame spurt, and that plane is just gone... That's what those runners got - an afterburner, in their legs. They kick that in, in that last twenty, thirty yards..."

But as Frankie himself pointed out, playing football rarely involved running a hundred yards in ten seconds or even fifteen, for that matter. How long was the longest run he had ever actually seen in a game? About eighty yards. It had been in a late season game the previous year, a simple running play, an off-tackle slant, and suddenly the halfback carrying the ball had popped into the defensive secondary as if he had been shot out with an afterburner. And then he kept going, straight as an arrow, down the middle of the soggy field with a couple of the defensive backs gaining on him. But he had had something extra, something left, and angling over towards the sideline at about the thirty he had made it into the very corner of the end zone standing up, with the last defender taking a sliding, grasping, desperate last grab at his heels at about the five yard line, but not even touching him. Touchdown!

The crowd of some ten or twelve thousand erupted in a prolonged, wave-like roaring. High school football was a big deal in Western Pennsylvania, a very big deal, and the team, the players, were very good. Everyone said so, it was regularly noted by sports writers in the newspapers, even in the big Pittsburgh dailies - what players made the all-league team, where they were headed for their collegiate careers, their statistics. There had even been the case of a player, some years ago, drafted directly out of a local high school into the pros - and he had made the team, played several seasons. A fullback, a big kid who already weighed 230 pounds, nineteen years old as a senior. There had been some argument about whether he should be allowed to play.

He knew that he, Larry Simmons, was too small to be an effective running back, though, even if he were to somehow magically gain even more weight, muscle. If there was any chance at all for him to make such a run, it would no doubt be as a receiver, an end. But he was not tall, and – again – he was not large enough to be a good blocker, something ends had to be, in addition to their pass-catching role.

What position, then, could he play? That was the thought that had occupied him all summer, as he trotted around the small, quiet town in the humid heat, or swam in the placid Allegheny River wondering if it was true that he would come down with an earache, or something worse, from the pollution said to be in the river. In the early afternoons when the sun was high in the sky and he lay on a towel in the backyard listening to the Top 40, trying to get a deep, dark tan that would look good when he went back to school in September, he would hear the band practicing over at the field, already getting ready for the season.

In the worst heat, he lay in a dull, sweating stupor in his bedroom on the top floor of the old, crumbling run-down house he and his mother and older brother lived in, in the Lower End of town. A room where, at night, during the fall, he would see the great blaze of the lights from the football field as another Friday night game was preparing to get under way. That went as far back as he could remember, that blaze of lights in the chilly autumn night; that, and the sound of the crowd. Over twice the population of the entire town of Ralston - 5,000 - came to every game. It was the biggest thing in town, no doubt about it. You had to play.

# 2

There were no secrets about going out for the team. Ralston people seemed to instantly know about anything connected with football, as if there were a telepathic network. He had told the barber, Sam, that he was going out, earlier in the summer.

"Kinda small... Hey, but remember that Murphy boy? He was good! Went to... Lehigh, I think it was. Full scholarship. Played both his junior and senior years."

It was true. Jerry Murphy had been perhaps even smaller than he was, at least in height, but had played halfback on the varsity as a junior and senior, lettering both years, and the coach had seen to it that he received a full athletic scholarship to a very good small Eastern college.

That was part of the whole deal. The coach – and everyone in the town knew this, not just the kids at school – would get you a scholarship if you wanted to go to college and you kept your grades up. Of course the best players, the first string players, often got numerous offers from major, well-known colleges. One player had gone on to a major university team, Maryland, and become a first-team All American his senior year. Another had been the leading collegiate passer in the country as a junior. There were endless rumors in the town – in the barbershop, especially – that sooner or later the head coach, Coach Rossi, would leave to coach at a prestigious football college – Notre Dame and Pitt were often mentioned. In fact, it was difficult to see why he did not do this, but he stayed on for his own reasons – well-respected, loved by his players and the townspeople.

These colleges, the fabled names, seemed a very long way off to him, inaccessible, and this was painful. He could not imagine what it would feel like to actually attend such a place. In the summer when he was twelve he had nearly won a week-end trip to Notre Dame. The trip included a two-night stay on the campus and the Saturday afternoon game. Pictures of the great school were shown in a slide presentation to motivate the boys to sell more newspaper subscriptions. The thought of being able to walk around the tree-shaded campus, enter the impressive grey stone buildings, read the books students in the slides carried, made him giddy. That would truly be another world, and a portal to an even larger, richer world he could only vaguely sense. He imagined himself returning to Ralston at the Christmas vacation, going to one of the high school dances (held at the Odd Fellows' Hall), telling others as he stood there "I'm at Notre Dame…" He did not know anyone who'd gone to this university, he could not even recall any who'd taken or won a football scholarship there.

But he really wanted, for reasons he could not understand, to go to a school he'd never even seen. Princeton. When he was a boy, there had been a football player there,

Dick Kazmeier, who'd become a first team All-American; he could pass, run, or kick the ball, in the old-fashioned single-wing Princeton offense. He even remembered the name of the coach, Charley Caldwell. Maybe he wanted to go to Princeton simply because of that, the impression it had made on him.

No one in his family had gone to college, and certainly his mother had no way to pay the fees involved in going even to a state college, which were reputedly the cheapest. His stepfather had died, suddenly, of a heart attack. His mother had woken in the early morning and found him like that, next to her in bed. Larry remembered the white-sheeted body, the feet sticking up, being wheeled out to the fire department ambulance, although he was not supposed to see that.

So, even though he was smart and had his own considerable reputation in the school for it, he had a persistent, depressing sense that it would come to nothing, and that he would not go to college. It did not matter how much he wanted to or how smart he was. Going out for the football team represented, in his better moments, a slim possibility of opening that door. What if he actually made the team? What if he did well? After all, there was the case of Jerry Murphy - and there had been others. Well-coached, it was not impossible that he might join their ranks. He would gladly go to Lehigh or Carlisle (Jim Thorpe's alma mater), or one of the other small colleges.

To give himself this chance, all summer he had been eating as much as he could. He asked his mother to make him huge platters of spaghetti and meat sauce, and after eating two of these, he would eat a quart of ice cream. But his best discovery was in a neighbor's garage.

There he found, one humid morning when the door was left open, a set of rusted, red barbells. Old man Krebs, who owned the garage, was vague about where they had come from, but after some hemming and hawing he agreed to let Larry have them, if he toted them away. Larry got a wagon from a group of neighborhood kids, and with their help pushing, took the whole set back to his house.

Included with the barbells was a mouldy-smelling, black spotted binder notebook. To his amazement, in it were numerous photographs of a muscular, smiling man demonstrating sets of progressive exercises, for the various groups of muscles of the body. After some experimentation with too heavy weights, he began a daily routine of an hour or more, pouring sweat, puffing and groaning, following the diagrams and numbers of increasing repetitions like a religious ritual. In less than a month, he could see clearly - and so could others - the results. Since he had been so skinny to begin with, it all looked more impressive. His deltoid, bicep and chest muscles showed the most change, and even though he gained only ten pounds, it was all muscle. He had a different look, by early August, when opening of the training camp for the team was only two weeks away, and some kids had even journeyed to his house to see him "work out".

He felt increasingly stronger physically, and thought that this could only help him, give him confidence. He had watched many practices, from the wooden stands at the dusty practice field off to the side of the big green gridiron where the weekly games were played - that was never practiced on. In the practices, it was clear that confidence, or what some called guts, was a big factor with the coaches, and they yelled and slapped the players on the helmets and pads, exhorting them. The players, savagely grunting, ground into the tackling dummies, the blocking sleds, under these loudly yelled commands, some of them obscene.

One of the coaches, Mr. Barnes, assigned the specialty of the backfield players, was himself a small man, and Larry often wondered how he had managed to play football at the Big Ten school, Purdue, he had graduated from. He was the most fiendish of the coaches in his cursing and swearing. His face mottled red, veins in his neck standing out, he would seize the football and run directly into the line, cursing, snarling and spitting, stiff-arming and kicking, and when the players had finally brought him down, he continued to kick and punch them, telling them they were sissies, weaklings, "gutless wonders". He spat at their feet, shoved them, told them to get mad, to get mad, stay mad, to hit him when he came though. And then he would seize the ball again and start another run.

How did he keep from getting hurt? Larry wondered. He wore no pads of any kind – not even a helmet, which seemed especially foolhardy. Some of the varsity linemen weighed over two hundred pounds and were exceptionally fast. They were well-conditioned, experienced tacklers and it was routine in the regular season for players from opposing teams to be injured in playing Ralston, while Ralston players rarely sustained injuries, even though noted for their hard, bruising play. Not dirty. Just hard.

For some reason, he imagined that this coach would make him, Larry, run as he did, urging the biggest linemen to hit him, and they would, but he would not be able to spit and snarl and kick and lunge with the ferocity the coach did. It seemed silly, when he thought clearly about it, what the man was doing. What was the point? When he asked Jimmy Washburn, another boy who he knew intended to try out for the team, he had a ready answer.

"Barnes? He's nuts, that's what it is. Look at him out there. He was probably nuts when he went to Purdue, got his fat head kicked around there, and got even nuttier."

Maybe it was so. But Larry felt it had much to do with Mr. Barnes' size. The much larger Mr. Kowalski, the line coach, who had played at Pitt, was a slow-moving man who often smiled and spoke in a low voice, rarely yelling. Although he spoke intently to his players, he never swore.

Then there was the Head Coach. Mr. Rossi (his first name, in the yearbook, was Vincent, but nobody ever called him "Vince", as far as Larry knew) always wore a baseball cap, which Larry found unusual since he had nothing to do with baseball. It was so much a part of the man it was hard to think of him without it. There was no team insignia, nothing, on the cap; it was a simple white cap with red stripes running down from the crown with a matching dark red brim. It was true he was balding, but

Larry did not think that this was why he wore the baseball cap.

He was an exceptionally intense man with piercing black eyes. Larry was afraid of him, although he did not think he would even be noticed by him, because the Head Coach did not pay much attention to the younger players – those at Larry's level – who would, if they made the cut, end up on the Junior Varsity, the JV, which Mr. Kowalski coached. But in the summer training camp, Coach Rossi would observe the drills carefully so Larry would inevitably come under his gaze. He felt nothing would escape those eyes.

Coach Rossi was very different from the assistant coaches. His wife was a physical education teacher at another school, and for him, the game seemed to exert a continual pull. It was obvious that he placed great weight on the playing of it. He always carried a large playbook and a small portable blackboard, on which he would quickly chalk play diagrams, showing them in intense conversations with his starting players especially. Football was serious business for him. He quickly detected those for whom it was not serious, not a matter of passion, of the heart, which he spoke about often. A good player, a good team, was one with heart, in his words. Losing a game was not shameful if the team had played with heart.

Coach, as he was always called, imparted these same ideals in his Health classes, where he spoke often about having heart and the importance of it. And respect. That was another word he spoke in firm and stressed tone - you had to have respect for yourself. Larry had found him not an especially good health teacher, but on the philosophy, on his ideas about Life, he was strong. This was really what he taught.

If he were to actually make the team, Larry wondered what lessons he would receive from Coach Rossi. Because it was said that he taught all his boys, those who played for him, important things - about being a man, for example. This was often noted in the conversations in the barbershop; Larry had heard it many times. Being a man was a big topic there, and also in the community, and playing football for Coach Rossi was said to be an infallible way to learn what it meant to be a man, to become a man.

When Larry thought about this, as he did in his long, looping runs around the town, day and evening, he wondered if this was something that could, or even should, be taught in school. What kind of a subject was it? The game of football, it was held, was the real teacher, and men in the barber shop assured him, passionately, that they had never forgotten what they had learned on the football field.

But what was it they had learned? When he tried to formulate this question specifically, he found he couldn't. Something about the look in their faces stopped him, or made him rephrase his questions.

Maybe he would find out when he went out for the team, in the training camp, on that green, long field, which seemed to hold out some indefinable promise to him that he had to pursue. He set out to run his five laps around the big field, before it got too hot. Maybe he would go to the pool in the afternoon, rather than the river. Swimming was good for you, although he had heard the coaches thought it loosened the muscles too much, and wasn't good for football conditioning.

# 3

Guinta's was a fruit stand at the junction of the old main road and Highway 28 running south to Pittsburgh and up north to the county seat, Kitanning – an old Indian name. As long as he'd been alive, Guinta's in the summer had been a place to sit in the evenings after they had been swimming in Buffalo Creek, and watch the cars pulling in to buy from old Mr. Guinta, who some said was an Italian - a "dago" - but others maintained was Portuguese. Larry knew of no Portuguese people at all in Ralston, so he'd always thought the old fruit vendor was an Italian. Frankie Malone called them "guineas", which he said was what his father called them.

He certainly looked like one. Short and squat, bandy-legged, wearing an old, stained pair of suspenders, he had thinning hair, going gray, combed straight back over his balding head, something no one did. A hairstyle from "the old days", as his mother put it, although when exactly that was wasn't clear. Maybe after World War I, Larry thought. Mr. Guinta also wore a thin moustache covering only part of his upper lip, another oddity; no man in Ralston wore such a moustache - or *any* moustache. They, too, were a thing seen only in photographs of the past - "the old days". Larry associated them with photographs he'd seen in history books, particularly of men in uniforms, who invariably wore moustaches. Why? It seemed useless, a moustache, and probably not easy to keep clean.

Old man Guinta. That was how everyone referred to him, and everybody knew him. His mother remembered his older brother had hauled a cart around the town collecting scrap metal, calling out "Old iron! Old iron!", and now had a large scrapyard outside Natrona Heights that his sons managed. She said he still could not speak good English, although Larry wondered how she knew that to be a fact. His name was Giuseppe; his younger brother with the fruit stand was named Tot, but no one ever called him that.

From May on through into October, the long, rambling wooden stand, painted green, was open from early morning until past ten at night. Guinta had put up large floodlights on the stand's ends, so it was clearly visible from the top of Mile Long Hill. Its bright illumination reminded Larry of the football field's tall lights, which would be on in summer for the night games of the Ralston Merchants, a semi-pro baseball team that was quite good and had won several of the league championships in recent years. Reputedly some of the Merchant players had had tryouts with the Pittsburgh Pirates, and the team had played 6-inning exhibition games with them in the spring, but Larry had never seen one of them.

Everybody stopped at Guinta's in the summer. He also sold cold sodas, ice cream, and candy. But the chief draw was his fruit and his corn in season. It was the best, and Larry and his older brother Carl sometimes sold him blackberries that they'd picked on the big steep hills that rolled lushly right down to the river's edge. Carl preferred to sell directly to the people in town. There was one guy on Fourth Street who bought twenty baskets every year, if they could harvest that many. Carl never tired of telling his name – Mr. Berry.

Old man Guinta's melons – cantaloupes, honey dews, Persian, watermelons – were his greatest pride. He liked to show them to customers, urging them to feel them, for weight and proper degree of ripeness. And to smell them, for this was a critical measure of ripeness, the smell, the intensity of it. Mr. Guinta would beam at his customers, nodding his head, as they did this. He would offer samples, which he'd cut up and had arranged on dishes, in the middle of each melon display. "Try! Try!" he would urge.

For Larry, there was something about this display – the heaped up, plump, rounded melons – that literally meant Summer. More than lemonade, or fresh mint iced tea, or popsicles and Eskimo Pies and roasted hot dogs – weenies. Mr. Guinta's melons meant it was really summer.

He and Ducky Estes and sometimes Jimmy Washburn had sat over at the end of the bridge, watching the fruit market, many summer evenings. You would see all kinds of things, people, there. People – and cars – you'd never see in Ralston. Out-of-state license plates, "hot" cars, or "hot rods" as they were called, with vivid customized paint jobs, gleaming chrome grilles, and tail pipes that growled low as they drove off and ran up Mile Long Hill, or across the bridge. Some were convertibles, really sharp, and they'd seen an occasional Thunderbird, a fantastic car, and some Caddies – Cadillacs – the best, the most expensive car. None of them had ever ridden in a Caddy and didn't know anyone who had. A Buick Roadmaster was the best any of them had done.

And it was at Guinta's, in late July, that'd he'd first seen the cherry red 1955 Chevy with, of all things, a girl driving. The car had peeled in smoothly, and Ducky, who had the great vision, had seen it wasn't who they assumed it would be – Jimmy Caye, the son of the town mailman, owned such a car, although he did not fit it. He wore heavy, dark-rimmed glasses – a four-eyes.

"It's a girl driving," Ducky said, as they all looked even more intently.

"What? You sure? Not Jimmy Caye, that four-eyed creep?"

"Mebbe he got some girl and let her drive, so she'd go out with him... he's so ugly, nobody would if it weren't for that '55 Chevy. Damn! That's one hot car!" Jimmy Washburn shook his head appreciatively.

But when the driver's side door opened, they could plainly see it wasn't Jimmy Caye, or any girl he'd picked up somehow.

"Jesus!" Ducky said softly. "Look at that. It's Cameron Mitchell."

The girl that exited the car had long, flowing dark hair, and even though it was evening, she was wearing sunglasses. Later, Larry would remember that first time he had really seen Cameron. Her. He knew who she was, a junior, but he'd never seen her car, although he had heard about it.

Jimmy Washburn whistled softly. "You know, she's a girl – she's different. You know what I mean."

Ducky laughed, and shook his head. Cameron was already inside the stand, and the Chevy remained, as if just waiting for her.

"Out of our league. Out of our league."

When he was laying up in his muggy room later that night, before sleep, he thought about her. Who knew much about her? She didn't go with any of the boys at Ralston – maybe another school, down the road? He would probably see her in the hallways at school, he thought. That would be it. How would you talk to such a girl, he wondered. Was it even possible?

The first week of practice was about to start. He fell asleep thinking about the field and how hot it would be out there all day long. For two weeks. Few other football teams in the entire Valley area had such Training Camps. The Ralston Raiders would arrive at their first fall game, with the Glassers, with really three entire weeks of practice and more important, conditioning. There would be many laps of the playing field in the dust and glare and dry heat of the August dog day afternoons. It would make him think of walking up in the coolness of the woods, on top of River Hill, which you'd see from down on the practice field, far away in the shimmering summer haze. There was always a breeze up there, coming from up the river, where the nights were already growing cooler. Up as far as Brady's Bend, where the big river bent at such an angle that it nearly doubled back on itself.

He fell asleep finally thinking about the Training Table that some of the mothers of players ran during the camp. One thing was certain; they would eat well. Maybe he could even put on a pound or two. It would help. He was still too skinny. He would look funny in the uniform... and Cameron Mitchell, the girl getting out of the red Chevy. Was she down at Eat N' Park even as he was going to sleep? Where did a girl like that go, alone, anyway?

# 4

After so long a wait, it seemed the first day of the summer Training Camp arrived suddenly. In the gym, Larry stood in a long line of semi-naked boys, and finally passed the physical examination given by the old town doctor. He listened long to Larry's heart and looked at him closely.

"Sure you want to do this, little man?" the doctor had said, clapping him on the shoulder. It was an embarrassing moment. But more was to follow.

In the humid dressing room, rank with the sweat of over fifty young boys, Larry clearly saw what he was up against. Some of the older players, who were at the camp to assist the coaches, were already obviously young men, with heavy genitals and mats of dark body hair. The developed, packed musculature of the chest, upper arms, and the especially powerful looking legs made him realize how difficult the task he'd set himself up for would be.

These boys were of a different order and breed. The slight looks they gave him showed this clearly. He was not one of them, not likely to become one of them, and he was not to be taken seriously. Even the coaches, with their omnipresent clipboards, expressed this when they looked quickly at him, and then their eyes flicked away to a more promising candidate behind or to the side of him.

To succeed at football, to make the varsity - for even one year - to receive the large, blue letter "R" with the raised, gold football on it; these were probably the most thrilling, exalted achievements possible at the school. The special assembly where these letters were awarded was the most eagerly awaited event of the school year, other than the Junior or Senior Proms in the spring.

Not only the school followed these matters intently. The town, the entire valley, all the way down to the big metropolis of Pittsburgh, where the League Championship game would be played just before Thanksgiving, took notice of the Ralston players and their exploits. The fall months, the season, belonged to them. The local newspapers followed the fortunes of former players at the college they were at. People in the town could easily recall great games, fantastic plays, and the players who made them. Players could do no wrong, and they were already acknowledged to be "men" by the locals. They had proved it by making the team, by playing each week, by "beating the shit" out of the rival team, another barbershop phrase echoed even at pep rallies, although no profanity was supposedly allowed at the school.

Inside the high school's buff brick building, they reigned as kings, princes, dukes. Each of the starting eleven, the fabled "first string", glittered when they walked, and they walked wherever they liked. Nobody messed with football players. Coach Rossi taught, and demanded manners, decorum, from his players, that they be gentlemen, an odd word rarely heard in the town, or the valley for that matter, but they knew they could get away with quite a bit - who would talk?

A girl asked out by a player could not refuse, especially if he was one of the starting team. It was a duty, an obligation. It was unheard of for a girl to turn one of them down, even though Larry had seen looks that troubled him on the girls' faces.

There were stories about what the boys did to those girls, in the back seats of cars or in rooms of cabins out on the creek where private parties were held. There was bragging by older boys which he had heard in his gym class, in the dank locker room where they seemed to relish talking about how they had made such and such a girl cry. He wondered if the things they claimed they'd done were true, and when he saw one of the girls named, he felt a conflicting welter of emotions. He had thought at times that if he were larger, stronger, he would challenge some of the stories, but he knew what the result would be if he did. It made him feel bad. He knew he could never be one with these boys.

They finished suiting up in the humid gym, many standing in the bleacher seats where people sat to watch the basketball games in the winter. All the boys wore white athletic supporters, jock straps. Some older varsity players had taped their ankles and wrists, and stood calmly higher up in the gym, looking down, surveying as it were. Another boy helped him with the bulky shoulder pads.

The thigh pads were encased in the dirty brown practice pants. Last to go on was the white practice jersey. If you survived the two week camp, you would get to keep this and pass it on to your girl, who would wear it, washed white as she could get it, over her small frame. It was the height of fashion in the school for a girl. Or you could wear it, with a pair of Levis... They began to file out to the field, and he could hear the odd sound of all the cleats on the bleachers, a clattering and pounding.

Out on the large practice field it was glaring, the light and the dust rose with every move made. Mr. Barnes lined them up, and they started a drill of calisthenics, first side-straddle hops, then running in place - "Pick 'em up, pick 'em up!" - Barnes yelled, over the noise of their stomping.

The pads and helmet quickly became hot, and Larry felt they constrained him, and he would have to somehow get used to them. Then they were dropping down for twenty push-ups. Already some of the boys panted, and two were not able to do the full push-up count. Barnes stood over them as they wriggled and heaved in the rising dust, flopping like caught fish.

"My, my! Wadda we got here, eh? Couple of mummies boys..." He kicked one of the boys in his shoulder, and yelled at the top of his voice.

"COME ON! MOVE IT - GIMME TEN MORE!"

Somehow the two boys managed this and were allowed to rise. Their eyes were fearful, peering out of the helmets that looked much too large and wobbled on their heads. Larry wondered if he looked like they did - their legs looked pathetically thin in the big padded football pants. The large black cleated shoes felt unnatural on his feet.

Although it was still only mid-morning, the sun was already glaring hotly in the dull whitish sky. His mouth was dry and tasted sour, his chest heaved under the loose fitting shoulder pads, which he was sure were too large to really protect him. After they completed the first exercise drill – Barnes told them with relish it was only the first – they set out on a run around the practice field. This was traditionally the way a practice ended, in Larry's experience, so he was not sure why this was being done, but he duly lapped the field with the others. As they ran, the purpose of the run became clear to him; the same two boys, those who had been forced to do ten extra push-ups, lagged badly. By the time they had all formed up in the one corner of the practice field, these boys were obviously feeling bad, weak. Larry wondered if they would make it through the first day of practice.

Much more was asked that morning. Under Barnes' fiercely barked commands, they ran out of a long line, while he threw them passes, sometimes overthrowing them by five yards or even more; sometimes hitting them with a viciously hard-thrown bullet. One boy was knocked down by the force of his pass. But he held onto the ball, and received Barnes' praise.

They took turns hitting the tackling dummy, which proved much heavier than Larry could have imagined; there was a flat metal disc weight suspended from a rope connected to it that you had to pull up as you tried to drive the dummy back, and then down, into the ground. The dummy, to Larry, resembled a hanged man, and he felt an odd sympathy for it.

"Hit'em, hit'em, hit that sunuvabitch!" Barnes screamed, flailing his arms. He threw down his clipboard, charging the dummy himself, driving into it with a hit that was audible, grunting and spitting, his feet throwing up clouds of dirt, dust. His mottled red face contorted, enraged, he turned to them, breathing hard, nodding.

"Do it!"

By the time they had run a set of wind sprints, it was already time for the morning practice to end. And this would be how it would be; there would be the rest of the week, and then the following week, and then there would be the cuts. A cut list would be posted the morning of the second week listing those who were not to continue in the second week. In some ways, this seemed unnecessarily cruel, because the home room and class listings were posted the same day, which meant many students knew who'd been cut.

The first week, to his surprise, went quickly, although other boys said they thought it would never end. A few quit voluntarily, walking dejectedly off the field, with the coaches turning away from them. But he got no clear indication of what position he might play from the drills and laps and exercises of the first week. It came to an end on Friday afternoon, finishing with the dreaded one-on-one tackling drill. In these drills, two lines of players faced each other, about ten yards apart, enough distance to get up a good bit of speed. One player ran directly towards the other, and into them; the other player charged forward to hit and drop the runner, as hard as he could. The sound of the hits was what was noted, commented on. It was a drill that some relished, but not many, especially those in the line designated to be "ball carriers". You were not allowed to swerve, or make any evasive move, but were to charge directly into the oncoming tackler, driving hard, trying to, if possible, break his tackle, knock him aside, or over, backwards and continue running through him. If this happened, the tackler had to return to the front of the line and face the next runner.

The drill ensured that you would come away bruised and perhaps even bloodied. The coaches watched this drill closely, seeming to particularly relish it, grinning as the players charged and collided, dust exploding in clouds from their pads, and swirling up as they crashed to the ground. Larry noticed that they had picked a very hard packed bald patch of the practice field for this drill. Grass, especially if there was a good cover of it, softened the fall, but there was no grass where they drilled, and hadn't been for some time.

He survived the first round of the drill, drawing as his tackler, a boy only slightly heavier than himself, an awkward boy named Jason Phelps who had no athletic ability, and ran heavily, plodding, in the pads and helmet. His tackle was grazing, almost from a side angle, and Larry wondered if he had been afraid. Coach Barnes had snorted derisively as he watched them.

"You two should go to the prom together - dance real good."

As he worked his way to the front of the line in the next round, he tried to see who his opponent would be. Some of the varsity players had suited up that morning and participated in drills, and there had been some in this drill. As he came into the third from the front position, Larry could see clearly who it would be - Berton Jones, a junior, a potential first-string tackle, who weighed over two hundred pounds. He felt his throat go dry.

There was no turning back. He was there, at the front of the line, facing Jones, who looked across the distance with a serious set face, and then went into a three point lineman stance. He would be the tackler. It meant that Larry would get smeared; Jones was a formidable tackler. Coach Barnes blew his whistle and Larry moved forward instinctively, covering the space between them quickly, trying to piston his knees high, and then, as they closed, lowering his shoulder for the impact he knew was coming.

As Jones hurtled into him, Larry drove forward as hard as he could. Surprised, he could feel Jones move backwards, for an instant. It was enough for him; he kept driving, and although Jones had gotten his powerful arms wrapped around his middle and immediately reversed the momentum, driving him backward, and down, he had not done too badly. He had done better than he or anybody else could have expected. As Jones ran back to the end of the opposing line, he looked to the side, and then back, for only an instant. He had been surprised, too, Larry sensed.

The force of the tackle had still been punishing. Would he be able to stop Jones if the roles were reversed in the next round? Already his back felt sore where he had smashed down, with Jones on top of him, on the hard ground. It was amazing how hard that ground was, something he had never really thought of as a force in the game of football. The ground!

Jason Phelps plodded past him, and turned, smiling wanly.

"Not bad, Larry. Not bad."

He looked up, above him, and could see the large curved bowl of summer blue Pennsylvania sky. It was hazy lower down, above the big river; directly overhead the sun beat down, and he felt the sweat stream on both sides of his face; it made his skin raw. The water they gave them to drink had salt in it, and some of the players were encouraged by the coaches to take a salt pill. He could not help wondering why they did not practice in the evenings, when it was cooler, the sun less harsh. There was plenty of daylight left, or they could turn on the lights, for that matter. Almost all of the actual games played would be under the lights, at night. By late September, it would be cold, chilly, on the field. Why practice in these furnace conditions?

But he already knew the answer to his question. What was going on in the Training Camp was a testing to see who would tough it out, who would keep coming back in the morning (if they did not quit, or were taken aside by one of the coaches, and let go that way). And, in terms of the conditioning of his players that Coach Rossi was famous for, the twice a day practices in the August heat would mean that an actual game, played in the evening, would feel much cooler, no matter what the humidity was.

By the time he had reached the head of the line again, he could see that it would be another player who would draw the big junior tackle, not him. In fact, he drew Jason Phelps again, who, compared to Jones, was a feather. They drove into each other with the thick, satisfactory smacking, thudding sound of pads, and his nostrils were flooded with the heavy smell of Phelps' sweat-soaked jersey, greasy with dust, as they crashed to the ground and then rolled heavily. Barnes' voice came through the cloud of dust they had raised but he could not clearly hear him. He noticed Barnes was looking closely at his face, and then he felt a trickle of sweat running down from his lip, and raised a finger to it. It was a thin rivulet of blood and he pulled it away, looking at it - some abrasion of the helmet, maybe. Looking up, he saw Barnes grinning at him with his gap-toothed grin; there was a noticeable division between his two front teeth that the players often mimicked, sticking their teeth out as if they were buck-toothed.

The coaches called a general break, and allowed players to remove their helmets. Although he could not see it himself, he saw others looking at him, and knew the blood was there, but he could feel no pain. Sweat ran down into his eyes, stinging, and he noticed the others' eyes were red, inflamed. There were heat waves dancing and surging at one end of the field, around the white goal post. It seemed a long way off, as he stared.

The water buckets were brought out onto the field, and some of the varsity players took salt pills. The practice was nearly over, and in fact they drifted over to the sidelines, where he sat down immediately, with several others, on a narrow worn wooden bench, the type used on the side- lines in regular games. None of them looked like they would make the upcoming cuts, and their faces, streaked with sweat rivulets and caked with dust, looked tired, and older. He wondered if he looked as they did.

One was a boy named Mike Hawkins, who lived only a block away from his house. Now, looking out at the field in front of them, Hawkins started talking about the majorettes, gesturing with one hand down the long field.

"Yeah - you know they'll be out here tonight, when it gets cooler, practicin'. Around seven. March around and all that stuff - you know, like they do at half-time at the games." He rubbed his crew cut head, and rolled his neck. "They sure look good - wearin' those short-shorts, tanned legs..." His voice trailed off.

"Fat chance any of us lame asses got with them," another boy said, from down near the end of the bench. He spat a large hawker on the ground. The phlegm quivered and shone like an egg yolk. "That's varsity stuff."

There were only ten majorettes actually chosen to march with the school band at games, twirling and throwing their sparkling batons high into the night air. They were among the most envied girls in the school. Holly Burris, the captain of the majorettes, had perhaps the highest status of any girl in the school. She was a senior, and went steady with Fred Lucas, the varsity fullback, a dark haired boy who rarely spoke. She was especially good at twirling a lighted baton, throwing it very high in the air, spinning, and then catching it deftly, even, amazingly, behind her back. Larry had always wondered how this custom of twirling batons had originated, but had never found an answer. He had been stunned when he had seen, on television, the Notre Dame marching band, led by a male majorette. Or, as he heard the announcer say, a drum major. In Ralston, it was inconceivable that any boy would be seen strutting in front of a band in that way. Yet, after all, this was the Notre Dame band.

Earlier in the summer, in late July, there was a week-long carnival sponsored by the volunteer firemen. Rides and booths were set up, and on one evening, a large and very popular parade was held, of fire engines from even surrounding states. Many high school marching bands marched in this parade, and there was no doubt they were as big an attraction as the gleaming fire engines. And they all were led by majorettes.

Tanned in various shades, from a light honey tone to a rich, dark chocolate brown; weeks of swimming and sunning at community pools and in local streams had them in perfect physical condition, and the excitement, running like a live current in the big, responsive crowds lining the main street the parade marched down lighted them up, charged them even more, so that they twirled and spun and high-stepped and smiled with contagious, wonderful energy. The extremely short skirts they wore (several bands had majorettes who dispensed with these, and wore tight shorts) flew up and down like flashing flags, and some clowns would always make as if shielding their eyes, saying they were being blinded.

Larry thought they were not far wrong. There was something perfect about the majorettes and he had a confused sense they would somehow never be like they were then, at those moments, and that that was what was really going on in the whole performance. Some were so beautiful he had in fact looked away, or down at the ground. Often they marched by within a few feet, and he was mesmerized by their vitality, their fresh, cheerful vigor. But there was also something else; from time to time he would look away to the crowd lining the opposite side of the street and see the looks on older mens' faces, in their eyes. This always gave him a sick feeling. He wondered how the majorettes felt being looked at that way. Was he looking at that them in that way, was he any different?

"Maybe they're gonna let us go," Hawkins said, shielding his eyes and looking towards where the coaches now stood in a small knot, talking.

"Mebbe so. It's gettin' late. Friday afternoon..." said the boy at the end of the bench. Larry felt sure he would be one who would be cut, and in fact maybe he even desired this, strongly, he thought.

He felt worn out, dog tired, and hoped that the coaches would call it a day, a week.

"Awright, that's good enough for the week...shower up! Go on, get the hell outta here!" Coach Barnes banged loudly on his clipboard, and they turned and began to trot tiredly off the field. Larry wiped the blood on his white practice jersey, observing with satisfaction that it looked right smeared there with the dusty grime and his own sweat and that of the others. When washed, it would fade, but there would remain a faint discoloration, a rusty stain mark.

# 5

The big field now lay quiet as if sleeping, parched and dusty around its borders under the still punishing late afternoon sun; the players had finished their practice at 4:30 or so, limping into the stifling locker/shower room, for a much-looked forward to shower. There was a pleasant tiredness after the work-out exercises, the practice, and the concluding laps around the big field. Larry felt a satisfying sense of accomplishment even though he could not remember ever feeling so used up, without energy. It was no doubt the punishing heat and humidity, working out in that. When they played their pick-up games, for instance, they never played in the heat of the mid-day; everybody knew you could get heat stroke.

When they emerged from the gym's side doors into the slanted rays of the August sun, already a thin scattering of kids was spread out in the stands above the field, lounging or drinking sodas; some horsed around down on the sidelines, tossing a worn football back and forth, copying plays they had watched in the earlier day's drills. They were waiting to watch and hear the evening band practice.

As Hawkins had predicted, in the early evening, around 7 pm, the field was taken over by the marching band, a completely opposite group from the sweating, struggling players of the Training Camp. The Pittsburgh Steelers maintained their summer training camp at Latrobe. It was said to be a grueling, punishing, brutal experience, getting through the Steelers' camp. The Ralston high team's "camp" was reputedly modeled on the Steelers' and was one of the very few high school summer football pre-season camps in the entire area.

Some players would return to see these band practices, and since he lived so close by, it was a quick, easy walk for Larry. The high school band members arrived in groups of three or four, and gradually an odd medley of sounds – tootings of brass, staccato drum rolls, shrill woodwinds doing some sort of scale exercises – rose like a mist from the field where earlier in the day dust had swirled up from the scrimmages. Platoons of band members executed marching maneuvers, looking like small military units drilling.

It was the arrival, the appearance, of the band majorette corps that everyone - or nearly everyone who was male, at least - was really waiting for. And they never arrived – the ten of them, evenly matched tandems of two, and the Head Majorette – until nearly 7, when the band director, Mr. Krause, would begin the evening's practice.

Several wore the prized, oversized creamy white letter sweaters of varsity members of the team. All wore trim-fitting shorts, with amazingly clean white tennis shoes.

How did they keep their shoes so white? In their full marching uniforms, they would wear short, tasseled white boots. The majorettes did not fraternize much with the actual members of the band. There was a strong sense they were not really part of the band. They were of another order.

Larry was embarrassed by his inability to keep from staring at them. They filled him with a sense of awe and a vague, dazed fear. It was unbelievable how good they looked. These were all girls he had known as a child, not too long ago; they had been in grade school together, chasing each other on the playground behind the elementary wing. Now, in the space of a summer, they had suddenly become like another species, different, even remote. They looked dramatically different.

But the majorettes were unattainable, he felt, and this nagging sense bothered, perplexed him. Their connection to the football team was so strong that sometimes he thought one wasn't possible without the other. They must always be together; it was fated to be that way.

It was undeniably a great and thrilling moment when "the Team" burst through a large paper banner held by the cheerleaders onto the field before a home game, and then the band came on behind them, wheeling out from under the goalpost, out of the end zone, brass blaring, with those ten girls out in front, way out in front, so proud, stepping high, twirling and throwing, up into the lit-up night sky, their flashing batons. Smiling at the crowd, at everybody and nobody and probably, he thought, at *their* player, they moved regally down the field creating a glittering aura around them that was not just the reflections of their sparkling, sequined uniforms. The crowd roared nearly as loudly as when the team burst out onto the field, or a score was made. No; you could not have football games without the majorettes, that was certain.

What they created was a potent magic and even if one missed a baton, losing it momentarily in the glare of the big, saucer-shaped night field lights glaring down from seventy-five foot high towers, or dropped hers while twirling, it did not matter. They were perfect, and part of what they made you feel was that they would never be like that again. There was an undertone of melancholy in their marches and pirouettes, their knee-down salute to the crowd, with batons pointed high.

In the summer evening band practices, with the dog days heat of August still thick in the air, the majorettes were more casual, more themselves. They joked, laughed, even pranked around a bit - not too much; horseplay was for the cheerleaders, who, after all, stood on each other in pyramids, performed cart-wheels and leap froggings, and were grass-stained, red-legged, and sweaty by the end of a game. Majorettes did not do that sort of stuff.

In the girls' implacable hierarchies of the school, the majorettes' captain, Holly Burris, was the trend setter of all fashions, the girl most of the other girls (a few hated her intensely) looked to to see what to do, what to wear, how to act.

Larry had once actually spoken to Holly Burris, been that close to her. That moment was sealed in his memory. Holly had come around a sharp, blind corner near the music room, late in the day – 7th period had just ended – and they had collided, with an audible, solid sound. He had been surprised, in fact, at how firm she was. Her dark eyes had flashed angrily, but then she had quickly smiled, flashing perfect white teeth.

"I'm sorry!" he had blurted out. She was wearing her majorette's captain jacket, with the large letter "R" above one pocket, and her name, "Holly", and "Captain", in small blue scrolling letters on the left.

She shook her head. "My fault, I think…"

And then she had hurried on down the hall leaving a sense of the impact, the vivid, felt imprint, of the collision on his body, and a light, pleasant smell of some cologne, perfume. How close had he been? he wondered. Did she even know his name? Probably not. That night, he fell asleep seeing her face, close up, flawless.

Holly Burris' steady boy friend Fred Lucas, the fullback on the starting eleven, was very different from her. Dark-haired, muscular, but not particularly big, he was not in the mold of the other great Ralston backfield players of past years. Still, he played with an intense fierceness and no doubt he would receive scholarship offers to good small colleges, like Lehigh or Muhlenberg or Carlisle or Lafayette. Lucas was a quiet boy – or was he already a man? Larry had no communications with Fred Lucas, other than occasionally seeing him on the practice field or in the locker room. Lucas, like Holly, probably did not even know his name. Why should he? Like Holly, he roamed the halls of the school wearing his football captain's jacket, with a crisp white tee-shirt invariably underneath.

He would see Fred and Holly walking in the halls, or talking intently, outside a classroom. What would it be like to actually go out, regularly, with such a girl? The two captains; they were a match in more ways than one. Larry thought Fred Lucas might be in the best time of his life, even though he was only seventeen years old. He knew glory, was admired, kept company with a beautiful girl, a goddess. It was scary to think that maybe it would not get any better, but worse.

The band practice began after Holly Burris arrived about ten minutes late; they had waited for her. Larry watched for a half hour or so, marveling at their maneuvers and the easy, yet ordered, calm way they moved about the field. The band itself was not sounding bad. It was rumored that a horn player, a girl, would make State Band this year, and that would be quite an achievement if she did. He could see Terry Malone, Frankie's older brother, flailing away at his snare drum. He wondered if Malone would end up having to tote the big bass drum which had a large blue "R" in the middle of one side, and a rearing horse, for the team mascot, the Mustang, on the other. This was a position he had always found somehow funny. The drum was strapped onto the drummer's back with large leather straps, forming an X behind his shoulder blades, and it jutted out in front of him like a huge belly. He wondered how someone learned to play this instrument. What a job, to march around, pounding on that! Maybe it felt good, though, beating the hell out of that drum.

# 6

He walked towards home in a meandering way, thinking that he might go down and look at the river. He had done that since he was a little kid, it was something that always calmed him, to just look at the big river rolling by out there. A half mile across, then the raised high-bed railroad tracks on the other side. Soon it would be completely dark, and the boat fishermen would go out, drop their lines, and hope for the big catfish to take hold, lying down there on the bottom. His brother had told him about a diver who had been sent down to examine the state of the channel in the middle of the river, where some said it was nearly one hundred feet deep. The diver had come back up and refused to go down again, saying he had seen giant catfish at the bottom so large they frightened him. There were tales of men hooking into one of the big catties and their boat being towed down the river, until the huge fish broke the line. Catfish had to be hoisted up off the bottom; when hooked, they invariably went down and tried to stay down, using the weight of the water and their own weight. They were not a spectacular fighting fish, like a large-mouth bass, which would leap clear out of the water when - and if - hooked. The thought of the monster catfish, down on the bottom in the deepest part of the river, was scary and at the same time mystifying. The fish, to him, seemed to somehow be the soul of the big river. It made him recall the Bible story, of Jonah and the Whale. Why should he be disturbed?

He saw Kathy Ferris's mother at the window of her house, and waved to her; she waved back, quickly. He wondered how she was doing. Kathy's mother was a remarkable looking woman to be the mother of a 16-year old, or nearly 16-year old, daughter. But then she herself was only 37; she had had Kathy when she was 21. That was the age of legality, or whatever it was; you could sign for yourself; you could legally drink. But to have a child, all that responsibility! He did not think he wanted to have children, from what he saw around him.

Kathy Ferris was a really nice girl. Everybody said this. Thus, it had come as more than a shock when his mother had told him the news earlier that summer; it had seemed plain wrong, it could not be. He had thought about it for days.

"You know Kathy Ferris, that nice girl? They live down on Water Street, by the river?"

"Sure I know her. I've been going to school with her since the first grade, Mom. You know that."

"Yes… Well, I hear she's…she's pregnant." She shook her head with vigorous disapproval, pulling her lips together.

He had felt an electric shock go through him. It wasn't possible, not Kathy. He had often walked with her back to her house on Water Street from school; he knew the house practically as well as his own. Kathy Ferris and the house she lived in represented to him a kind of goal, which he thought might turn out to be unattainable, although he could not say why he felt that way. The house was large, and full of types of furniture he'd never seen before. It always smelled good in her house, there was often classical music playing; it was the first place he'd heard that type of music. At Christmas, the Ferris's tree was always a wonder – tall, perfectly and fully shaped, packed full of ingenuous ornaments he saw on no other trees, and more strings of lights than anyone else had. It took Mr. Ferris an entire day, working on into the evening, just to string those lights the right way and hang the densely packed ornaments. He could have stayed in Kathy Ferris's house forever, he had often thought, but especially at Christmas, when there was a never-ending supply of candies and cakes and all sorts of food set out to eat, as often and as much as you liked. The huge refrigerator was loaded with soft drinks. There were bowls of freshly popped popcorn, even caramel corn.

"Kathy's pregnant? Who told you that?"

"Never mind who told me. It's all over the town, I can tell you that. Poor Mrs. Ferris. I feel sorry for her, I really do. What can you do when something like that happens?" She shook her head again, and heaved a sigh. "What are things coming to these days? I just don't know."

He had not asked what he wanted to ask, who the father was supposed to be. But he found out soon enough, from

Jimmy Washburn. It was a kid named Paul Thorpe, he had often gone fishing with him at the creek when they were younger. Even then, Paul had been talking continually about girls, asking him if he played with himself. He had described a unbelievable device to Larry, as they sat on a dock fishing one afternoon.

"Clyde Jones, you know him? He told me he made this outta a cigar box, you know? One a them Dutch Masters boxes. His father smokes 'em. We stole a couple from him, too." Thorpe had grinned, showing large horse-like ugly yellow teeth.

"Anyway, he took this box, put a round hole in the end of it? Little bit bigger than his dick." He laughed, and grabbed himself between the legs. "Course, you gotta hope yer dick gets biggern it is now, don't you?"

Larry had said nothing, watching the float on his line. This was going to be another sex story, like the ones told endlessly by the older boys hanging around the garage/ gas station on the corner near his house where they never seemed to talk of anything else, and it was said there were certain kinds of magazines in the back room.

"Yeah, well he takes this box, see, puts this foam rubber inside it. Just packs it with the stuff, as much as he can get in there. You get the picture?"

He did. Thorpe was going to tell him how Jones used this box to play with himself. Jack himself off, they called it.

"He greases up his prong, then, real good, with the Vaseline, or you can use cold cream, too, he told me, works real good, real smooth. And he sticks his dick in that box and starts to fuck the shit outta of it! Goddamn! Ain't that the damnedst thing you ever heard? Says it nearly drives him crazy, he's doing it alla time, can't wait to get home and shoot his load off innit... Ya gotta be careful, though. It'll take the skin right off yer dick!" He laughed uproariously, spewing a fine spray of spittle.

How old had they been when Thorpe had told him that story, of Jones's cigar box? Thirteen, maybe even twelve? Now Thorpe was sixteen, now he had gotten Kathy Ferris pregnant. It was a painful thought - Thorpe with his yellow horse teeth, braying laugh, the spittle - and Kathy Ferris. How could it have come about? Maybe he had raped her, forced her. It would not be surprising. Most of the stories he heard, increasingly, from older boys seemed to indicate a point was reached where almost all girls said "No," but you had to go ahead and do it in spite of their saying "No." They actually wanted it, but could not say this, because that would make them a slut. Only a slut said, admitted, that she wanted to do it.

He found it troubling, the whole idea. He did not want to force a girl like Kathy Ferris, or any other girl, treat her like Jones's cigar box, "fuck the shit outta her," as he so often heard older boys say, smiling knowingly, rubbing themselves.

As the summer had gone on, the story turned out to be true. Kathy Ferris was pregnant, Paul Thorpe the reputed father. That was not the end of it, though. Thorpe was said to be the father of the child a second girl, Shannon Brunell, was pregnant with. Two girls, at the same time. This was unheard of, and Larry wondered what would happen to the two girls, to Thorpe, to the children. The girls would not be allowed to continue in school, for one thing, and although he knew little about Shannon Brunell, other than that she was known to go in for heavy necking in the back of the movie theater - she had reportedly jacked off a boy there once, another story told and re-told in the school - Kathy Ferris was an "A" student, bound for college, certainly. This would be a heavy blow to her. Would she keep the child, or would it be born in the home for unwed mothers he had heard about, down near Pittsburgh, where the girls went to stay for the last couple of months of their pregnancy, and then delivered the child, which was immediately taken from them, and sent out for adoption?

He had not seen Kathy since early in the summer. He felt very sorry for her, and wished that there was something he could do for her, but could think of nothing.

Kathy Ferris was a pretty girl, but he had never found himself attracted to her, and Frankie Malone, who did find himself attracted, joshed him about it all the time.

"She's your girl, Larry! Can't you see it? It's as plain as the nose on yer face! I mean, you gotta be blind, I swear."

"We used to play horse together… She's like a sister to me." He was surprised to hear himself say this, because Kathy really was not like a sister, and in fact he had had feelings, but had simply not known what to do. After all, they had been in the first grade together. Besides, he was not ready to have any girl be "his girl". What did that mean, anyway? That they would allow you to do certain things, go farther than others? What had Thorpe done? But if he had gone out with Kathy, maybe the business with Thorpe would never have happened, not had a chance of happening...

By the time of the Training Camp, the rumor was that Kathy could be in school, that her mother was working out some sort of deal with the principal, but Larry could not believe that this would happen, and hoped it would not. The shame attached to being pregnant was so severe that to subject a girl like Kathy to it was unthinkable. She would not be able to bear it, it was too much.

Then it came out. Paul Thorpe had run away from the town, joined the Navy, lying about his age, getting falsely signed documents. Some said his parents signed them. After all, they lived on The Island, a part of Ralston where low types lived, bums like Smick Smead, a man who spent all of his time when he was not drinking or lying in the town jail sleeping it off, down at the river fishing. No one knew where Paul Thorpe was, and nobody on The Island was saying anything. But he had left not one, but two, unwed girls in the town, carrying his children. It was a scandal, the biggest in Ralston he could remember since the time when two telephone operators had been revealed to be lesbians, a word he had never heard before.

Other boys, it was true, had got girls pregnant, run off, and managed to join one of the armed services. The Navy, for some reason, seemed to be the favorite. The Marine Corps was too hard; everyone feared, although they would not say so, the famous boot camp at Parris Island, South Carolina. Few mentioned the Army. A small number of boys went into the Air Force, reputed to be the hardest branch to get into. Although he knew of the Coast Guard, he had never heard of anyone trying to enlist in it, and did not even know if they accepted enlistments; he had never met anyone who knew anyone who'd even been in the Coast Guard.

If it were true that Paul Thorpe had joined the Navy, wasn't there some way he could be forced to admit that he was the father of the girls' children, and have to pay them money, something? But when he asked his mother about this, she was not much help.

"If he denies it, then …then it's his word against theirs. Sometimes girls get pregnant, and try to get someone to marry them. Maybe he isn't the father, think about that. What if that's true?"

This did not make much sense to Larry. "Why would they name Paul Thorpe? Both of them?"

Now Training Camp was in its second week, school was about to start the day after Labor Day, the first game was that Friday. He had not seen Kathy Ferris' name on any of the home room lists posted. No news of Paul Thorpe, either. Or even Shannon Brunnel. Somehow, with the onset of the fall and the opening of school, it all seemed already to be fading, even as it happened. Nothing could take the place of football, and its time, the season.

# 7

His stepfather Al (they never spoke his name in the house, Larry noticed, nor did anyone coming to visit) probably would have had some answers on the situation, but he was not going to be able to help Larry. He often thought of him, especially when he went down into the cellar of the house and saw his workbench, all of his tools still hanging neatly arranged on the wall behind it, arrayed in boxes on the floor, some even laying on the bench itself. His mother had never touched them. A man had come to the house at one time and told his mother she should sell off the tools, that they were worth a good bit of money. There were two large power saws, and several smaller power tools - a lathe, and a plane. His stepfather had been able to fix almost anything, and was a skilled carpenter, who had built several houses, including the one they lived in now. But he had unexpectedly had a heart attack on his job on the railroad, where he operated a large crane, a very well-paying job for a working man, as he called himself. He had never been able to regain his job on the railroad; the railroad's doctors would not certify him, although his own doctor did.

"I think your stepfather died of a broken heart," his mother would say, ironing at the tall ironing board he so often saw her at, looking out the back window, towards the garden plot he maintained, year in, year out, growing especially large, dark red beefsteak tomatoes that were his pride and the envy of his competing neighbors, especially old Mr. Letto, an Italian from "the old country", who still wore a funny brimmed hat, and a greasy blue bandana knotted around his leathery neck. Mr. Letto also made home-made wine in his basement, although this was against the law. The lone policeman in the town, Constable Stroup, knew about it, too, Larry was sure. He had often seen him talking with Mr. Letto's wife – Mr. Letto spoke very little English, and conversed with his stepfather in an odd mixture of Italian, broken English, and gestures. Especially the gestures, which Larry associated with Mr. Letto as being as much a part of him as his name and the bandana always knotted around his darkly tanned neck. There was no mistaking these gestures, their inclusiveness, their anger, their force. He had gained Mr. Letto's favor by trying to speak a few words of Italian himself, which made the old man beam and nod approvingly.

When he was eight, his real father had died, a stone-broke alcoholic who had been reduced to living with his aged mother in her old house across Buffalo Creek. He could not recall very much about his father, a small man who he remembered for some reason as often going around the house in long underwear. He did recall his father's assaults on his mother, once with a knife, the constable coming to the house, his brother, Carl, crying. The time seemed very long ago, remote, far-off. He could not have explained how it made him feel.

His stepfather had been dead for only two years. He felt an enormous loss of something very important, that there was no way of getting back, recovering. Although his mother seemed to handle Al's passing quite well, Larry knew differently. He heard her muffled and choked sobbing at night, alone, in her bedroom, long after he had gone to bed and was supposed to be asleep. He was unable to think of anything he could do to stop her sobs - he knew if he went to her room, this would only alarm her; she did not want him to know. He could not speak about it to other friends, seek advice; he felt unable to, even embarrassed.

It would be a great thing to have a father one could talk to about the whole football thing, the Training Camp, the coaches, people like Coach Barnes, and Coach Rossi. His stepfather had been a wise man, Larry felt. He had taught Larry a great deal about a number of things, although Larry had never been able to learn much about the tools in the basement, and in fact did not really want to. They never talked much about it, but Larry sensed his step-father knew he was not eager to learn to work wood, or make things by hand, something Al assured him would give great satisfaction, last a lifetime, as he put it. Larry had been content to occasionally go down in the evening, after supper, and watch his stepfather work at the big workbench, the overhead light shining brightly, the smells of the wood and the grease on the tools and a faint aroma of sweat creating an atmosphere he liked. He did not like the noise of the big power saw, and was fearful of amputation by it. A boy in one of the shop classes at the school had taken off a thumb in just such a saw. The image of the boy's thumb laying on the flat metal plate of the saw, with blood jetting out of his hand, was one Larry could not get out of his mind. That was something that was irreparable.

He disliked the shop classes, which were mandatory for boys, and did not do well in them. He envied those boys who did do well, and it was undeniable that some had real abilities, talent, making beautiful tables, gun racks, lamps. In the Advanced Industrial Arts class, a senior had made a large table with chairs - cabinet making, his stepfather had called it when he'd told him.

"A good cabinet maker'll never be out of a job," he had said, nodding, as he planed a large flat piece of wood. "And if he's really good, he'll do very well. Very well indeed. Maybe have his own place and all. That's the way to do it."

Having one's own business, owning one's own place, was given high esteem, Larry noticed. Then you worked for no one but yourself, or so it was said. You could even take off, go fishing or hunting or just lay around, if the urge took you. Close up your shop for the day, or a couple of days. That would be the way to live. There was a great dislike of the work routine among the working men in the town, the unvarying getting up at four or five am, winter and summer, rain or shine, and returning home at five or six in the evening, tired out, worn. Eat supper, maybe sit on the porch and have a smoke - in the summer, people listened to the baseball games on the radio. Watch television, and fall asleep there.

This had been the case with his stepfather, who would sometimes be downstairs, sleeping in his chair, with the television screen casting its glare, at one in the morning. Especially after he had lost his job and had not been able to get back to work. Watching that - Al had gone down to work in the basement less and less - Larry had felt that to lose one's job had to be one of the worst things that could happen. It was something to be avoided, at all costs, if possible. It was also terrible that the job had such power over your life. His mother talked about that a great deal and he believed it, but did not know what to do about it. But it made him angry, and he was certain that he would do something about it.

As he walked up the alley to the school in the warm early fall mornings, he would think about the oddity of his life, that he was not yet sixteen and had had both a father and a stepfather, and now had neither. There were no other kids in the school who had experienced such a thing. What was he to make of that, do about it? He thought about writing to Carl down in North Carolina, but he had his own problems. He could not expect Carl to offer him much help with such a large problem. It weighed him down, and he sometimes wondered if he were stooping, already, as he walked up that alley hill, looking at the individual bricks in the street, which he had looked at already for years. At those times, he felt old, and knew that it was not good to feel that way. Maybe playing football, the game, doing that, would help. Maybe that was why he had gone out in the first place.

# 8

The town – to him every place and everything – nestled in a small valley on a triangular piece of flat land. It had been there since the 18th century; before that there had been Indian massacres on the location, scalpings, several early settlers killed, their cabins burned. The broad, slow-moving, deep river had brought the coming of trade and commerce. Like Pittsburgh, 30 miles down river, Ralston (named after a prominent early settler, who had run a ferry service further up the river) was at the convergence of a smaller stream and the much larger Allegheny River. In the summer, stern paddle wheelers – like those he had seen photos of plying the Mississippi, in a book about Mark Twain at the school – passed down the big, smooth Allegheny, and the strongest swimmers would swim out to meet the large waves their wakes produced. His older brother, Carl, who was in North Carolina finishing his hitch in the Marine Corps, had dived off the bottom of the dark iron bridge spanning the river, going over to Garver's Ferry, the ultimate test. And since he and his brother Carl used to pick blackberries in the summer and sell them in the town, going house to house, he knew every block – every foot of it.

He had lived in the town his entire life – going on sixteen years. His mother talked of coming there as a very young girl, riding in an old car with her father (Larry was said to resemble him remarkably) An Irishman, a house painter, he died at 43 from injuries sustained in a fall while working. James Cavanaugh, his name was – his grandfather, whom he'd never known. There was only one photograph of him, which his mother had saved from a devastating house fire before Larry had been born. His grandfather James had fallen onto the spiked top of an iron decorative fence surrounding the house he was working on – his mother had described this many times.

Falling like that, onto a set of spikes, was an awful image – he had often imagined him impaled, bleeding, struggling. But maybe the fall had knocked the wind out of him, he was unconscious… How long had he taken to die? His mother never spoke of that.

About his grandmother he knew only that she had been a tall woman – five foot eleven, his mother said, nearly six feet, very tall for those times. She had died of cancer not long after her husband James fell and died. There were no photographs of her, so he had to try and imagine how she might have looked.

"Your grandfather could've talked to anyone. The President of the United States! He would have been right at home. He was comfortable with everyone – and read! He read all the time, even when he was working, he'd take a book – that's where you take after him, loving to read."

This was true, he loved to read, but it was not something he felt necessarily proud of. He knew most of the football players, for instance, did not like to read. Some claimed it damaged your eyes, your vision. He had heard Bradley, the big first string guard, talking in the dressing room about this.

"My father says it's as bad for your eyes as playin' with yourself. Has the same effect. Worse."

"No good havin' your nose inna book all the time, that's for sure," agreed Vitale, the starting end. Several others grinned, and nodded, toweling themselves vigorously.

He was embarrassed by his love of reading. It was part of his lacking of some essential quality the coaches were looking for, that was the thing. The best coaches, such as coach Rossi, had an instinctive sense that a boy, a player, had this quality or lacked it. But what was it, exactly? It was not just physical strength, size, or even athletic abilities, for there were boys who possessed these qualities, but often they did not make the starting team, or even the second string, and spent perhaps three years "pickin' splinters outta their asses." On the bench. If the team were well ahead, in the fourth quarter, then they would be put in, their clean uniforms an embarrassing sign of their real status.

No, the real players had this competitive drive, or force, that added to their abilities. The more he thought on the mystery, the more Larry felt *this* was the essential quality – competitive drive – that made all the difference. Some players naturally thrived on it, enjoyed it; these were the ones who played varsity ball two, three, or in rare instances, four years – like Harry Gibb, the center – for Ralston.

Once a player was identified by one of the coaches, they stuck with them, that was another thing. They played regularly. If they had a bad game, or even several, this was waited out, the boy was patiently talked to. It was part of the process of forming the player. They inevitably gained in confidence and experience and almost self-predictively became better players.

Larry was left, though, with a nagging unanswered question; if one did not get such a full, extended chance to play, how could one become a better player? And the converse was true also, he thought. It was really his first exposure to a type of selection process, a picking out as it were, which was inherently and unsettlingly unfair, unequal, one which locked out those not "picked" from any real chance of developing their abilities; in fact, of even getting picked. The power to make this selection – residing with the coaches – made him feel uneasy about them in a way he had not felt before.

The night before the beginning of the second week of Training Camp, he walked over to the field, even though he had made a vow he would not go near it over the weekend. His mother had asked him repeatedly if he would need to go to the second week.

"Sure I need to go. It's the second week. This is the week the cut list comes out."

"The cut list? What is that, the cut list, then?"

What was the use in telling her? he thought. "It's the list of those players that aren't invited back for the second week of training. So they're cut. Let go."

"Well, I hate to say it, but it might be better for all concerned if you were on that list, whatever it is. You're too small for football. You're going to get hurt out there. And it's going to get hotter this week than it was last week, it was in the upper eighties every day…"

The cut list would be posted early Monday morning in front of the main gymnasium entrance. Larry wondered if somebody, one of the coaches, did not actually put it up very late at night the evening before. It was typed neatly on a single sheet of crisp white school stationery. There would be a large number of names on it, perhaps as many as twenty, out of the original fifty to fifty five boys who'd made it through the first week. Some preliminary cuts had been made even during that week, some by self-selection and some by the coaches, who would take a boy aside, or speak to him when he came from the shower room and was dressing.

Although he would not tell his mother, Larry was surprised he had not been cut during the first week – he hated to admit to it but he had fully expected, at times, it would happen. And it was not dishonorable to be let go from the squad in such a fashion. You had tried out, hadn't made it; no shame in that, and you avoided the much more trying second week of Training Camp, when all the varsity players returned, working out with the new players.

"You're gonna take some hard hits, no two ways about it," Ducky Estes said.

Ducky was a Lower End kid, who lived two blocks up from Larry's house, in a small frame house that sat alone in the middle of a dirt alley, across from the big field. They had played touch football, and then tackle, for as long as he could remember, back to when they must have been six, seven years old, and the ball itself had been almost too large for them to handle. A small, wiry dark-skinned boy, Ducky achieved such a dark tan during the summers that he was the envy of all the others kids in the school, acquiring the nickname "Burn". (Some said his other nickname, Ducky, was from a duck's ass, a DA haircut, but Larry had never really seen him wear this popular style, although his hair was long.) His tan was so heavy that even in November, you could still see the dark rings around his upper arms where the short sleeves of his tee-shirt stopped. In the shower room, you could see the even darker ring around his waist, where his shorts went.

His other claim to distinction occurred during the yearly eye exams, the reading of the lettered chart the school nurse administered each year, from which some kids invariably came away demoralized, having been told they had to get eyeglasses. In this test, Mrs. Craig, the nurse, discovered Ducky Estes had 20/10 vision. She exclaimed loudly over it, the other kids waiting in line outside the testing room heard her, and it was not long before it was all over the school, generating yet a third nickname for him, "Hawk". It was a remarkable fact –he could see clearly at twenty feet what people with normal 20/20 vision could see clearly only at ten feet. His eyes were twice as sharp as anybody's in the entire school.

Estes was really a much better basketball player than football – probably the eyes had something to do with that – and Larry wondered why he went out for football, but he realized that "Hawk" did it for the same reason he did, to prove that he was not afraid to, gain some sort of admittance to the circle of approved males.

He and Ducky had played basketball about as long as they had football, but there were fewer boys who did that. For one thing, there was the matter of finding a basket to shoot at. Those in the playground facilities were often in use, so he and Ducky, in their intense enjoyment of the game, had often played there late at night, by the light of a single streetlight across the street. They played year-round, even in winter, when there was ice on the hard-packed dirt, wearing gloves to keep their hands warm. Ducky would say "If you can make this shot with gloves on, think how easy it'll be up in that warm gym…" When he thought about it, he could not remember a similar devotion to football.

Varsity football players made up the majority of the twelve players on the varsity basketball team. Coach Rossi had a well-known philosophy, that a good football player made a good basketball player, and since he had just gone through a season, he would also be in top physical condition. A boy who played only basketball was likely to be less "physical" – smaller, lighter-framed, less muscularly developed. The football players made a more imposing appearance and presence on the basketball court, too. With stubbly crew cuts and bulging arm and leg muscles, they looked hard and tough. Just seeing such players coming onto the court had to affect the opposing team.

Ralston never had a great basketball team, however, but that seemed acceptable. Ducky had a theory about it all.

"He plays them, the football players, in basketball to keep them in shape and keep them out of trouble during the winter. That's the reason. You ain't got a chance a playin' basketball unless you play football, see? It stinks."

When he went over to the football field the night before the posting of the cut list, Larry stopped at Ducky's house, but he was out at a movie, up at the drive-in on the pike. Movies were supposed to be bad for your eyes, too, they said. Nevertheless, Ducky loved movies, and would go at any opportunity. He did not believe movies were bad for your eyes - and in any case, that whole business, he said, was about baseball players. Neither of them seriously played baseball. In fact, hardly anyone in Ralston did. It was the forgotten sport. You could letter in baseball but not much was made of that achievement.

He walked over to the big field that lay dark and vast in front of him, almost like a lake. Although it had been hot in the day, now in the evening air there was a noticeable coolness. That would soon change, by the third week or so of September, to a damp, foggy chill coming off the big river, that meant Fall. The crushed grass on the big field had a particular night smell, unmistakable, rich. It would not be bad to be tackled and fall into it, roll, and rise, with green smears on your jersey, and as you trotted back to the huddle, hear the roar of the crowd, coming from the steam it sent like a vast breathing up above the field. Driving down into the town on a Friday night when there was a home game, you could see that glistening patch of green, with that hovering mist, like a fog, over it. And that scene was repeated in how many towns like Ralston all the way down the river into Pittsburgh, and beyond, down on the other side, where the big Double AA schools like Aliquippa and Taylor-Allderdyce fielded truly awesome teams. One school down there, Braddock, had fielded a starting team the year before completely made up of black players. Their picture in the newspaper startled him. They had won the Division A championship, the same division Ralston was classified in. An all-black team... Braddock was known to be a tough town, a real steel town. He had learned in American History that it was named after a British Revolutionary War general, which seemed odd.

The field always strongly affected him. He wondered if it were so for others – other boys, other people. Standing near it, he would often imagine previous players for Ralston he had only heard about, running out on the great field, breaking away for a winning touchdown, mud flying from their cleats as they streaked around end, or ran clear with a pass coming in perfectly over their shoulder. Yet he had not seen these events, they existed only in his imagination.

His mother often said he had too active an imagination. Why should that be so bad, though?

"You need to calm down, Larry! I don't know why you come up with the things you do – unless it's your grandfather! He could make up stories you wouldn't believe. But people would listen to him, believe him. You take after him…"

Would he then, taking after his grandfather, dreaming away, fall on spikes and die, as he did? Why did he even have such a thought? Probably his mother was right; his mind was too active, it ran too fast. If he could run as fast as his mind, he would easily make the team, he thought. But such an imagination – he had made up stories sitting in the bathtub when he was a very small child, four or five, and his sister and mother used to stand outside the bathroom door to hear these, trying not to laugh and give themselves away – was not useful in football. Or, if it was, he was not able yet to see how.

Looking up and across the field, he could see the cars' headlights coming down Mile Long Hill into town. On the night of a game (always a Friday night) there would be a solid string of lights all the way up that hill. People came from Pittsburgh, it was said… When he was a child, still sleeping in the same bed with his older brother, a tanker truck had gone off the road coming down that hill, crashed through the guard rails, falling over two hundred feet straight down onto the railroad tracks below, exploding in a billowing fireball and huge plume of dense, black smoke. The explosion he could still hear, and feel, in his mind; it was unlike any sensation he'd experienced. The driver had been "incinerated", the paper had said, a word he had previously connected only with the incinerator at the school, where they burned waste paper and debris. Trains had not been able to run on the tracks for three days; the heat of the burning truck had twisted the rails in both directions so badly they had to be taken up and replaced by work crews.

He wondered if his name was already printed on the cut list. He felt strong, conflicting sensations. A sense of relief, he could not deny, took hold of him when he thought his name might be on the infamous list. It would solve many problems for him. Did he really want to play for an entire season with all the attendant practices, the endless drills, the slogging around the field in colder and colder weather? Pounding into the blocking sled, and the damn tackling dummy, while the coaches raved at him? What would he learn from such work?

In the barbershop, Sam's, they said you learned how to work from playing football, that work and life were hard, and you had to keep going, not quit. Quitters were despicable, and he could remember a grizzled old farmer with tobacco stained teeth and very red lips screwing his face up in a grimace at the word there in Sam's.

"Ain't nothin' comes a quittin'. Nothin'. No sir, not a damn thing."

All the other men had nodded approvingly. It puzzled him, though; why was there this unending emphasis on how hard life was? Couldn't it be any other way? He felt traitorous when he thought this way, but could not help it; there had to be another way, or ways, to live.

But you couldn't quit, once you had gone out for the team; you had to finish the job. Of course, if you showed up on the cut list, what could you do? It was unheard of for anyone to appeal to Coach Rossi, ask for another chance. Everyone accepted it; it was the word.

When he thought of how long the season ahead was, stretching into the middle of November and beyond, to near Thanksgiving if they made a playoff game, he grew faint. It was a long time, a long time of taking those punishing hits, tackles, hard, jarring falls into the dust, the ringing in the head and the constant possibility, likelihood, of pain. There was a lot of pain in football, it was hard, even after only a week of Training Camp he felt he could say that from experience. It wasn't like pick-up games, where you could chose your position, your team, and quit when you felt like it, or if you twisted your ankle or got a cut. No, real football was pain; that was it. When he looked at his body in the bathroom mirror, already he could see several blue-black bruises, red abrasions. His hands were cut in several places, but he had not been "cleated" yet. People talked of having your face stepped on with those cleats. If you played into college, or the pros, you would be marked for the rest of your life, like a convict or a sailor with their tattoos. One boy had had his nose broken the previous season in the first game of the year.

Tomorrow he would find out, and he would discover what home room he would be in, since that listing was posted,too. He would find out if Sandy Stevens was in his home room, find out if she had indeed become a majorette although only a sophomore. And that, that was something big. What had she been doing all summer? Practicing with her baton, no doubt. Getting her legs tanned, in those short-shorts that drove the boys nuts. She would also, no doubt, probably not even notice him.

# 9

The next morning, as he walked by the big river, it had changed color already and seemed to be moving slower, as if it were heavier, another sign of oncoming fall. The odd, ringing sounds of the locusts – there was no other sound that he knew like that one - had been heard back in late July. His mother said it meant an early fall and a cold winter. The caterpillars had unusually dark and heavy coats, too, another certain sign of a long, cold winter.

How many times had he walked up the steep-hilled brick-paved alley leading to the buff brick school? He had gone to this same school since he was in the first grade. With the school consolidations going on, it was becoming increasingly rare for a student to have attended the same physical building for all of his academic life, yet this was going to be the case with him. He could remember his first grade teacher, Miss Clements, a young – twenty-one or two, maybe? – dark-haired woman he had fallen deeply in love with. He and another boy had finally asked her, standing in the hallway outside the first grade classroom, if she would kiss them. She had, smiling. That was his first kiss…

The low slung, two-story school itself sat facing Fourth Street, a quiet street in a town that did not have a noisy street, even on weekends. Fourth Street was lined with large chestnut trees, maples, and a few pine trees; he had always wondered, how had they gotten there? The big pines were trimmed at Christmas time with lights, as was the school building itself. He had been walking up the hill (as he used to call it; now he called it what it was, an alley, paved in the middle with the same buff-colored bricks as the school was built of) to this school for nine years, going on ten. In only two more years, he would march in cap and gown down its aisles and graduate. It made him feel strange, how much of his life he had spent inside this building, inside its rooms. He knew the old school as well as his house, the streets of the town. This was another of his feelings he never mentioned. He loved the school; the smell of it, the feeling of just walking around in it, especially when classes were in session and the halls were nearly empty.

The first grade room, Room 101, was still there, on the ground floor, right next to the dark wooden paneled principal's office. Here the home room lists would be posted, lined up on the wall, with seniors on an opposing wall of their own. Students would congregate here all morning, checking to see what room they would be in for the entire next year and who the home room teacher was. You would be with this teacher for an entire year; it was important, vital information.

The cut list was certainly up, and Ducky met him outside the main door of the school, before he had a chance to look at it himself.

"You made it! You're not on there. One more week!" Ducky cawed, slapping him loudly on the back.

"What about you?" he asked.

Ducky shrugged deprecatingly. "I never thought they'd keep a real good basketball player, with twenty/ten vision..."

Larry did not know what to think. For one thing, it meant he would immediately have to go to the gym, and suit up for the morning's work-out and drills. This would be embarrassing, because with so many kids around to check the listings for classes and home rooms, many would take the opportunity to look at the players as they filed out and down the long stairs to the field, and some would watch practice, until it began to get too hot in the open stands, and they drifted off to Peter's, or home, for lunch.

He went in himself to double-check the listing – maybe Ducky had overlooked his name in his haste. While he stood examining who was on the list – he noticed Jason Phelps' name – several kids came up to congratulate him, and wish him well, slapping him on the back, shaking his hand, smiling. Indeed, he had gotten farther already than he thought he would.

When he went into the big gym, it was still cool from the weekend. A large, thick new rope was hanging from a beam, high up in the rafters… This was the famous rope, the one Coach Rossi insisted every member of the football team had to climb, and eventually climb to the top, and then come slowly back down. Many students had the rope burns to show for their efforts. Larry looked at it – it was swinging slightly; already someone had been trying. It was amazingly difficult to climb the rope, although those who regularly did it made it look easy.

He had told his mother if he did not come home by 9:30, that meant he was not on the cut list, and would be remaining at practice for the day. He began to suit up; his jersey smelled heavily of sweat and soil and a drier, grassier odor. Other players were coming in, bantering around, slapping each other affectionately on the back, or mock-fighting. The big gym was cool in the morning, and as he looked at the shining highly polished floor Mr. Dempsey, the janitor, took such high pride in, he thought about the upcoming dances that would take place in the gym. It would become a very different place then… He could see the young girls down on the floor, milling about in the clusters they seemed to invariably get into, talking excitedly, while the boys bunched up around the exit doors, almost as if they did not really want to be in the place. The girls would be wearing their frothy gowns – these came in an amazing variety of colors, and the girls looked like walking flowers on the nights of dances. What he most remembered were the first times – it had been in the eighth grade, not that long ago really – he had danced with a girl wearing one of these dresses, and how wispy the dress had felt contrasted to the firmness of the girl's body underneath it. It had been amazing, and he had gone home that night feeling light-headed from dancing with Judy Wilson, a girl he had not really noticed before. Close up, though, in her light blue dress, her eyes and hair and her smell had made him feel like he had never felt, and he realized in a flash why the dances were such a big deal, why such a fuss was made about them.

"Hey, Nipsy! Lookit!" someone called out, breaking his reverie of the dance. He turned and saw the equipment manager, who was also the biology teacher, Mr. Bigelow, moving in a sort of exaggerated dance back in the last rows of the gym. He looked like he had a large white bandage on his face.

"Fucking Bigelow got a jock strap on his nose!" said one of the varsity players, who was standing, stripped to just his own jock strap nearby. By the time he had turned back and looked again, Bigelow was walking down the seats, and if he had had a jock strap over his nose, it was gone. That was an odd thing to do, but then Mr. Bigelow was known to be odd. He had a reputation for clowning around in his biology classes, where he kept, among other things, a large white plastic container holding a foul-smelling fish. Sometimes during one of his classes students would open the container and the smell would quickly spread through the corridors of the school. Mr. Bigelow seemed to derive some sort of entertainment from this, although he always quickly and loudly expressed what was supposed to be anger and condemnation of the students who'd opened the fish container. There were other rumors about him, too. But there were always rumors about the biology teacher, whose classes were often chaotic, which he seemed to enjoy. Certainly no other teacher had a large, dead, completely white fish in his room.

But there was always good natured horsing around in the locker room and in the gym in general; it was a place where strange things happened. Strange objects – condoms, Kotex boxes - were put in people's lockers; guys grappled in mock fights in the showers, cursing and yelling so loud they could be heard outside in the halls. Then there had been the incident the previous year. A new teacher, a math teacher – he couldn't even remember his name now – had been discovered with a junior varsity cheerleader, going at it on a mat in the darkened gym. He had been gone by the end of the week, and nothing more was said of the incident; it was never clear which cheerleader, even.

What really happened, he wondered? Coming back late at night to pick up something from his office, Coach Rossi discovered them. He punched out the math teacher, who appeared the next day with two blackened eyes and a swollen lip. The girl had run away during the ensuing fight, and Coach Rossi would not or did not reveal her name... Had she been naked, Larry wondered, again staring down at the expanse of the gymnasium floor? And where had they laid down the mat they used? Out in the very middle of the floor, for instance? Something about that idea tickled him, that that was in fact what they'd done – or they had just utilized what was already at hand, and that was it. In the middle of the floor, in the dark gym. And then bang! Rossi throws on the overheads, and suddenly they are bathed in blinding white light, going at it. That was the expression. Going at it. Sometimes people added, "like rabbits." Once he had heard a man turn to a woman in a crowd at a baseball game and say "I'm going to really give you a grinding …"

As he finished dressing for practice, he noticed that the blood on his jersey from the previous week had already turned a dark shade of brown. Looking around the gymnasium, he saw a number of the varsity players were already in full uniform – some wore not practice jerseys but the regulation dark blue team jersey, those worn for away games. This was a sign of their favored status, that they were allowed to wear these jerseys. Later in the morning, some of them would assemble with the coaches and have some early yearbook photos taken. Without their shoulder pads or helmets on. It was odd that they had their pictures taken like that, since nobody played in a game actually looking that way. But it was a sports, a football, tradition. Backs were photographed stiff-arming a tackler, mouth determinedly set, or with the ball tucked securely into their stomach, as if they had just taken a hand-off. The quarterback, of course, was always posed poised to throw, arm cocked, the ball back behind his head, looking downfield for his open receiver.

Over in one corner, talking together and smiling, were the starting quarterback, Dick Atkins, and the right halfback, Robert Henderson. They would be photo-graphed later that morning for sure. Fred Lucas, Holly Burris' boyfriend, was talking with Coach Rossi, who had said at a rally the previous year that he thought of him "like a son." He had his arm around Fred's shoulders as they talked. Henderson, who wore number 21, was reputed to be the fastest man on the team, and was said to be hoping for a full scholarship to the University of Pittsburgh, a big football power. Why would he want to go to a college like that, right in the middle of the city, Larry wondered? And then there would be the stiff competition, the certain difficulty of even making the team. Did you lose your scholarship if you didn't make the team? But Robert Henderson in some odd way seemed to Larry to already be in college. He did not pay much attention to class – Larry had two classes Henderson was in – and he did not even really relate that much with the other students. He was friendly enough, and he dated a string of girls. He had a rumor in Sam's about him, even.

"Yeh. That Henderson boy, he's gonna be something, you mark my words. He's the best damn halfback I seen in this valley for more'n thirty year."

"That ain't all he is. I hear tell he gets more ass than any grown man in the town."

"Well … I don't know about *that*. You hear a lot of stuff."

"These kids today don't know no restraint. They do it soon as look at you. Ole Barenekkid Stroup can tell you some tales, I tell you what. Out in them cars, back some damn ole dirt road out there in the township... unincorporated area. He caught one, he called her daddy, too!"

This was Dick Atkins' senior season, and he was King. He might receive as many as a hundred – or more – scholarship offers, people said. A hundred different colleges – it was a phenomenal idea to Larry. Even as early as October, Atkins would be taking weekend trips to some of these schools and once the season was over, in November and early December, the trips would increase. His parents would even accompany him on some trips, hosted by the college recruiting their son. On these trips the boy got a free car, a brand new one, to drive while there, and a number of social events were planned for him. College girls were made available for him to date if he wanted to. It was hard to imagine being treated that way.

He laced up his practice shoes tightly and stood up. He felt out of balance somehow, like a large puppet or robot, in his uniform; it did not seem to fit him the way Atkins' uniform fit him – it seemed part of him, a second skin. Number *12* on the jersey. Everybody knew that number.

He rinsed his mouth at the gym fountain on the way out. Someone had pasted a photograph of James Dean over it – probably one of the cheerleaders. Dean had died in a car crash the previous September. September 30th, the last day of the month; he could recall the date, and even the time of the evening, around 8:30, when he heard the news. He had been listening to his favorite, four-hour, 8-midnight disc jockey show from Greensburg, doing his evening's homework, and the network news announcer had broken in to report the actor's death out in California, in a bad car crash. He was only 24 years old. Larry felt a connection to the actor but could not explain it clearly, even to himself. Bonnie Evans had asked him about it in the library, and he had stumbled around badly. She didn't know what she thought about James Dean, she said, but Larry thought she probably did. She said "You know what? He's one of the gods – that's what it is. That's some people's fate, like in the Greek books?"

There was a mirror placed in the side of the wall on the tunnel-like hallway leading out to the field – maybe for girls to check their appearance in at dances, he thought. Now he looked at himself, briefly. His helmet looked too big, there was no doubt about it. It rode down onto his eyebrows, wobbled when he moved his head quickly. He took it off; he would carry it. All in all, he did not really look like a football player but like a kid who was trying to look like a football player. How did one get to be the real thing?

When he came out into the morning light, now spread over most of the field below, sure enough, there were some students standing near the stairs. Head down, not looking at them, he broke into what he hoped was a suitable jogging lope. He heard somebody call his name – it sounded like Frankie Malone – but he kept going, not looking back, down the steep wooden stairs that clattered, shaking slightly with the sounds of the cleated shoes in front and behind him. He could scarcely believe he was really doing it. He had watched this very scene so often, as a kid, just as the students now were. And the cleats' sound – that was special.

The second week of Training Camp would be more serious. They were assembled at one corner of the field by the coaches, after a set of warm-up calisthenics – side straddle hops, push-ups, drop downs, running in place. Coach Rossi was there in his baseball cap, holding his ever-present clipboard. He looked serious, yet smiled at them.

"You boys have made it to the second round," he said. "Congratulate yourself. It's an accomplishment in itself." He nodded affirmatively, and looked off to the side of the field, and then spat a stream of spit on the ground, a habit he had. Larry wondered if he had ever chewed tobacco, for he spit like a tobacco chewer did – an arcing, copious spit, relishing it.

"This week'll be harder. You all know that. Two a day, every day. This is your chance, so make the most of it – give it all you've got!" He made a fist, smacking it into his palm as he spoke the last sentence.

No one said anything, and there was a silence, a pause. A serious undertaking was about to commence, Larry sensed. Several of the players around him took deep breaths. He felt a light puff of breeze in his hair – that was something to be thankful for, it might help later in the day.

The drills in the morning were more squad-oriented, although they worked on the blocking sled furiously, with Coach Barnes screaming in his customary fashion. In teams of two, they pushed the blue-painted metal sled around the practice field, dust clouds rising, choking them, stinging their eyes where the sweat ran down. Their faces flushed dark beet-red. It was all about work, working hard, Larry thought. Yet he did not feel as tired as in the first week – the conditioning drills were having their effect already.

Lost in the straining exertions of the blocking sled and then a set of wind sprints, followed by a lap around the field, before he knew it, it was time for the lunch break, and they walked slowly back up the steep stairs. In the gym itself, out on the basketball floor, women of the community had set up tables and generous helpings of hot food were served out to them. He sat at a table next to Walter Gibbons, a junior, who had been on the junior varsity the previous year. He knew him from hall patrol – a friendly kid who did not fit Larry's idea of a football player. But, then, neither did he. They were all caught up in the same mystery, he thought.

He was starving, and tried to control his eating. Gibbons was munching away, nodding furiously. "Good eats," he said, his mouth half full. He took a large gulp of milk from his glass leaving a white moustache on his upper lip, which he wiped off with his jersey sleeve.

"Hey, I saw the home room lists, Larry. You're in Turner's room – and Sandy Stevens is in there!"

"Yeah?" Larry muttered. He did not know what to say. Mr. Turner was an English teacher, known for his walking absent-mindedly – at least it seemed that way – up and down the aisles of his classes, stopping suddenly by your desk. He had an uncanny sense about whether or not you had done your homework, your reading, the previous night's assignment. He never said anything when he made these brief stops, but would simply walk on. He seemed always to be carrying, or reading, a book, and when he walked around in the classroom, he would have his book open, and often read to the students. He was a large man, whose clothes were always somewhat rumpled, the trousers never pressed sharply like some of the other male teachers. He wore large, black-framed glasses which went oddly well with his coal black hair. His wife, a neatly groomed woman with a short haircut, his exact opposite, taught typing classes, for those students who were in the business curriculum. Larry was in the college prep curriculum – and there was the general studies one, which everybody else was in, those who didn't know what they wanted to do, or be, after graduating, those who did not, or could not, go to college.

There was not much time to take in the news of the room assignments. They finished eating and filed into a large room off the main floor of the gym, where the coaches had set up chairs. Here they were to have the first of the "skull sessions" as the coaches and varsity players called them. Playbooks were duly taken out, and Coach Rossi walked to the front of the room. He had a pointer in his hand and a diagram already drawn on the chalkboard beside him.

For the next hour, fighting off drowsiness while their food digested, the players were subjected to explanations of various kinds of blocking maneuvers, connected to a basic series of plays they might run in an actual game. They had already tried some of these out on the field, in opposing groups of only the front lines. This second week, the backfield players on defense would be added. Towards the end of the coaches' talk, Larry realized the defensive players must have to learn something more each week, for each team played, whereas those who played primarily on offense had a much easier learning chore. It was strange that it might be more demanding to play defensive positions. Of course, the defensive team rarely got any glory – occasionally a defensive player would recover a fumble, or intercept a pass. "Dago" Paretti had run one back the previous year for a score. But he could not remember many times when a defensive player had scored a touchdown. He did recall an odd game in which a big defensive lineman had smeared the opposing quarterback in that team's end zone, thus garnering a safety – two points, a score more appropriate to a baseball game.

It had been hard for him to concentrate during the skull session. The Xs and Os on the board were often erased suddenly by one of the coaches, and often became covered up by a series of drawn arrows, sweeping one way, or the other, or "straight up the middle", as Coach Barnes liked to say loudly. "Up the gut!" he would say, thrusting his fist forward fiercely. "Right up their gut!" He relished those plays. Power plays, they were called.

Larry was thinking of Sandy Stevens. The idea that he would be in close contact with her – perhaps even seated next to her – for an entire year, for home room assignments were for an entire year – was overwhelming. He would not be able to hide his attraction, he was certain, and what would come of that? In his freshman year he had fallen head over heels in love with a cute girl named Mary Ann Patton. He had waited for her outside classrooms, so she would let him carry her books. When he thought of it now, he could feel himself turning red. Would he become a figure of ridicule among the girls, who knew everything and would laugh and look at him as he went to his wall locker between classes? Worse, Sandy might simply treat him as if he was not there. It was powerful, how a girl could do that. They could look right by you, or even, it seemed at times, through you, walking haughtily past, laughing with another girl, or simply doing it, with their mouth set and their books clasped in front of them. Who could figure them out? He felt a sense of hopelessness already about his attraction to Sandy Stevens.

The skull session was finished, and they filed out of the room, across the corner of the gym, being careful not to walk on the wooden floor with their cleated shoes, a terrible infraction. He glanced up at the big wall clock above the gym floor – 1:30.

When they hit the top of the stairs, the heat from the field hit them. The air was thick and warm, and he began to sweat immediately. The sun was high in the sky, glaring. Some of the varsity players, he noticed, had smeared dark patches underneath their eyes – where had they got that stuff, anyway?

They began with two laps around the field, and then he was assigned to a group that was lining up at the tackling dummy. Why was it that he seemed to get in this drill more often than others, or was it his imagination? Was he being targeted for a defensive position, was that it?

The tackling dummy was a contraption he disliked the more he had to work on it. For one thing, unlike a real player, it could not move, although often the coaches would stand beside it, moving it rapidly from side to side, as a player rushed in. Sometimes they would even hurl the dummy directly into the charging player. He had seen several players knocked backwards like this, while the coaches grinned. For some reason, the dummy reminded him of a hanged man, swinging in the wind, and although he knew it was only a padded thing made of cloth, it began to take on a personality to him in some vague way. How would you like to be hit like that, over and over again, days on end, the whole season?

Some players grunted audibly as they hit the dummy. "Keep your head up!" Barnes yelled. "Drive, drive, drive!" the coaches would chant as the chain clanked and ground and you lunged against the increasing weight and thrust with your shoulder and legs, cleats churning the ground.

Coach Kowalski was brought over to demonstrate tackling. He was smiling and spoke something to Barnes that made him smile his gap-toothed grin, which always also made him salivate; a dribble of spit remained on his chin. Coach Kowalski looked to Larry like one of the players pictured in the sports magazines that he leafed through at deNicchio's by the train station. These were always featured in the August and September issues, especially, with the various sports writers picking their All-America teams, and also the top 20 national teams. Pittsburgh had been in this ranking often, and Kowalski had played there – an offensive tackle.

Now he got into his three-point stance. Looking up, setting his jaw firmly he suddenly lunged forward, accelerating towards the lightly swinging dummy. He moved amazingly fast for a man of his size – it was said he weighed 230 pounds or more, an incredible weight. Larry could not imagine what it would be like to have such a huge man smash headlong into you, running full tilt like that. That was football – it seemed mad. Standing near the dummy, Larry could see his concentrated eyes, a fierce expression on his face. He slammed into the dummy so hard the frame of the apparatus rocked, swayed, and without any apparent effort he tore the dummy all the way back as far as it would go, with the metal weights clanging loudly at the top of the frame when they struck it, like the sound of a huge hammer hitting a rail.

"Yeah, yeah, that's the way ya hit it!" Barnes said, nodding enthusiastically. "Let me at it!"

He quickly took up a three-point stance, and ran, uttering a loud cry as he started, and hit the wildly swaying dummy. Spittle sprayed out of his mouth, his face was twisted into a terrible contorted look, he looked as if he were out to murder the dummy.

"Scare the shit outta the other guy, huh?" said Gibbons, who was standing next to him, grinning.

Larry nodded. There was something scary about Coach Barnes, an intensity that was extreme. Maybe you had to be that way to be his size and play in the Big Ten, though. Larry wondered what he had studied at Purdue – probably physical education; that was what many of the coaches had their college degrees in. It was said to be an easy major in college. He could remember, though, that one of the All-American first stringers, in the College Football magazine, had been written up as being a physics major, and a straight-A student. As he had read it, he had wondered if it could be true. The photograph had shown a huge young man with a blond crew-cut, bursting towards the camera with his arms raised in a blocking pose. Had Barnes confronted linemen like that in the games he'd played? Maybe that was the explanation of his fierceness. How else would a little guy like him compete?

They continued at the tackling dummy for another half-hour or so – "the salt mine", Gibbons called it. The sun seemed nearly directly overhead, but it was really on into the afternoon. Coach Rossi conferred with the other coaches on the sidelines while they did side-straddle hops and rolling drills on the ground, yet again; then, surprisingly, the practice was terminated.

It was called off for heat, apparently, and humidity. It was still early, so after taking a longer shower than usual, a luxury, cooling himself off, he dressed in the emptying gym, and decided he would walk around the corridors of the school. Most of the other players had left the gym quickly, although Dick Atkins and some of the other first stringers went to Coach Rossi's office for a meeting, after some horsing around with Bigelow and the student equipment manager, a junior named Danny Vincent.

He noticed it was not yet four when he glanced up at the big clock in the main hall.

He headed first for his posted home room to look at it through the square panes of glass in the wooden door, which would be locked, of course. It was. He looked in at the rows of empty desks, and the highly waxed floor. Mr. Dempsey had been at his work. A new flag hung over the blackboard, and there was what looked like a new teacher's desk in the room. Mr. Turner had probably complained about the old wooden desk that had been in the room the previous year; Larry remembered it. It was said to date back to the opening of the school, in the 1920s, when everything had been brand new. The old desk, made of scarred, worn blond wood, had smooth, worn curved drawer handles, with tarnished brass covers. They probably did not make desks like that anymore, at least not for schools. The replacement desk was noticeably smaller, made of metal, with a top that looked like wood but was obviously not. Fake wood. As he looked at it, he thought that Mr. Turner was too large to sit comfortably at it, and would in fact look out of proportion at it. He would not like that, he felt sure.

It gave him a strange thrill, an excited feeling in his stomach, looking at the empty classroom, imagining all the possible things that would happen there in the next year. Some kids never came to the school to even see what home room they were in, but he had always wanted to know as soon as possible, the day it was posted, and he had always tried to go and see the room, like today, when it was still empty, unoccupied, waiting.

He wondered where he would be seated. It was strange to think that he would spend a year – nine months – in that place, that location. What had been there before? he wondered. Before the school itself was even built? Probably no one would be able to tell him – he had never heard anyone ask, for that matter.

When he had been a little kid, he had played many summer afternoons - long, long afternoons they seemed, longer than even the ones in the Training Camp now – in a small wooded area he could see out the windows of the home room. They played children's games there, including the making of a slide in the dirt, from the top of the hill to the bottom, which made his pants so dirty his mother had gotten very mad, tears in her eyes. Once, they found a small wooden box cast into the brush; it contained rifle shells, which he'd taken to his brother Carl. They would not even go home to go to the bathroom, he remembered, but would shit back in the high grass, laughing. When they got tired, they would climb to the top of the hill and sit, looking down over the hugeness of the great green field, with the summer clouds rolling high in the sky above them. Inevitably, they would begin to talk of the football games they would see there that fall, who would win, who was on the varsity. When would the big lights be turned on for the first time in the fall?

When he thought about those times, he realized how different he was, and yet it was not that long ago. Could time move so quickly, as his mother was always complaining? It was true. Those days of his childhood summers seemed long ago to him now. How long past they must seem to adults.

He looked up and down the long corridor, thinking that someone might have seen him standing there, looking into the room. Where would Sandy Stevens sit, he wondered, looking back into the room, and then he could see her sitting in a seat at the front of the room. When she would smile, he felt light-headed. That wasn't good. You couldn't let on how you felt. He wished that he was not so interested in her, and in girls; it was an embarrassment, although everyone talked about nothing else around him, when they were not talking about cars or movies; something like that. Nobody talked about books, though, except for one or two other kids, and they were thought to be "weird".

He would have to watch his step, he thought. Otherwise, he'd make a complete ass of himself. A fool. You could not be a fool, that was a terrible fate. It was going to be a long year ahead, and he would just have to take it carefully. Maybe it would have been better had he not been in Sandy Stevens' home room. Or vice versa. But so it had happened. What was it that they said in Sam's barber shop? "You gotta play the hand that's dealt you. Yessir. That's the way it is."

# 10

When Friday of the second week of Training Camp arrived, Coach Kowalski called Larry aside on the field. They walked slowly over to the bleachers that were already set up in anticipation of the first regular season game, the Friday night after Labor Day the following week.

"Sit down," the coach said, gesturing. He tossed a football back and forth, slowly, from hand to hand. It looked small in his hands, easy to handle. Coach Kowalski taught shop. He had spent the summer out on a big knoll above the two-lane blacktop highway going through some lush green farm country, where he was personally building his house. Larry was impressed by that, that he was able to do such a thing. His stepfather had built a cabin up north, near Erie, almost completely by himself, except for the laying of the foundation, and even some of the wiring. And then he had never gotten to really use it.

The big coach was deeply tanned from working outdoors all summer. He was married to the math teacher, formerly Miss Clevenger. She had a disconcerting habit of sitting with her legs crossed on the front of her desk, while she taught. Her legs were beautiful – she liked to run her hand over them, often, stroking, and Frankie

Malone, among others, had nearly slid down out of his chair trying to see as far up her skirt as he could when she crossed her legs like that. She always smiled when she did. Larry respected her marriage to the coach, but didn't think her stretching and preening, like a cat, on the desk top was right. But certainly the boys in her classes all looked forward to math class where they learned little math.

Girls did not generally like her. She was not the only teacher who did this; the librarian, Miss Vukovich, also had the habit of perching on the edge of a desk in the library, and crossing her legs back and forth.

Now Larry wondered if Kowalski was going to cut him, on the very last day of the camp. He felt he had done well. There had been a full contact scrimmage the previous day in which he had made two tackles and assisted on a third. Coach Rossi had observed from the sidelines, with his omnipresent clipboard. He had worked hard.

"Don't worry, kid." Coach Kowalski had a habit of calling everybody, even varsity, "kid." He always grinned when he said it, as if to take the edge off. With his size, nobody was going to call him on it. "I'm not going to tell you you're being cut..." he shook his huge crew-cut head, as if to emphasize the point. "No. . . what I wanted to do, see, is ask you a question. At this point."

Larry nodded, looking intently at him. He felt small, puny, next to Kowalski. What was his first name – George. George Kowalski. He had never heard anyone except

Barnes and Coach Rossi call him George. Probably his wife did, though.

"Okay," he said, and it came out a bit squeaky, to his dismay. His mouth was dry; he wished he could take a drink from the big metal water bucket, but it was all the way across the field. He could see it glinting dully in the humid sunlight. He could taste the aching coldness of the water, going down, hurting the place between your eyes. Don't drink too much! Spit it out! The coaches would yell. He had never known water to taste so good, even with the metallic tang of the big bucket, and the dust that accumulated in your mouth, on your lips and face…

Kowalski nodded, and stopped tossing the ball back and forth, laying it gently on the ground. "Why do you want to play football, Larry?" he asked, in a serious tone. "Tell me. Your reasons."

He did not have time to think about it, and afterwards he realized that it was better he hadn't.

"I want to win a scholarship, so I can go to college. A good four-year college." He nodded his head vigorously as he spoke, and then heaved a sigh.

"That's the real reason? To get a scholarship? You're a smart kid in academics. You might win one that way, don't you think?"

Larry shook his head. "No – I'm not that good in math. I don't like math. You have to be good in it to win any kind of decent scholarship. I need a full one."

"You haven't been getting good teaching from my wife?" the coach asked, grinning.

Larry shook his head. "I just don't like math."

Coach Kowalski looked at him, and reached down and spun the football with his big forefinger. He wore a large graduation ring, from Pitt, Larry assumed.

"The way it is, I think we're going to put you in the JV squad," Kowalski said, looking across the field, squinting his eyes against the glare. "What do you think about that? The JV?"

The junior varsity had a regular schedule of games, played on Saturday afternoons. But it was not really making the team. You could be asked to suit up for regular games, but it was likely that you would play very little, if any; perhaps only in those games where Ralston had a two or three touchdown lead, and it was in the last quarter.

Still, it meant some practicing with the regular squad – and some players did move up from JV to full varsity. Chad Lewis was third string quarterback, for instance. Larry would get some letter time in the season - maybe, if lucky, even letter. Yet he felt hollow in his stomach. He had not realized how much he wanted to make the regular squad, as unrealistic as it was. He knew that now, after two weeks of the training camp.

"You're pretty small, Simmons. Not that that's necessarily bad, don't get me wrong. Look at Coach Barnes, huh? Played for Purdue – Big Ten. But you might want to think about all this some more." He looked closely at Larry, still shading his eyes.

"You got a lot of heart, kid. If you were fifty pounds heavier, you'd be All-American material." He slapped him firmly on the shoulder pad. "Take a hike now, over the other side, and get in the scrimmage over there. With Coach Barnes." He pointed down towards the far corner of the field, where Larry could see a mass of players moving around.

When he duly had trotted to the far corner, Barnes told him to stand by, while the first play was run. It was a scrimmage of the second string varsity, and a group of players Larry guessed would be mainly JV material, like him. Barnes stood in the middle of the defensive formation, behind the line, near the middle linebacker, dancing back and forth on the balls of his feet. A routine running play was faked, with the quarterback dropping back and throwing a short pass to the right. Barnes nipped in front of the lumbering kid the pass was intended for, adroitly picking it off. He ran directly into several startled offensive linemen, stiff-arming one vigorously. The quarterback stood stock still, his mouth open.

Barnes was not fully stopped by the linemen, but he threw the ball down so hard it bounced wildly, hitting several players. He pointed his finger at the quarterback, Tommy Phelps, Jason's older brother.

"You think you're too good to tackle me, Phelps? Huh? Huh?" He stood now, arms akimbo, leaning forward, glaring at the unfortunate Phelps, around whom a space had cleared as if by magic.

Phelps shook his head rapidly. "No…"

"NO? Then what the hell you doin' there, with your finger up your ass?"

Phelps said nothing, but looked down, obviously embarrassed.

"Ahhh!" Barnes spat out, shaking his head disgustedly. "Don't wanna get your uniform dirty, Tommy?" He turned then, and beckoned to Larry and the boy beside him. "You two! Stop gawking, and get in there. On defense. You, Simmons, in at middle line backer!"

Middle line backer. Larry wondered if he had heard correctly, even as he quickly cinched up his helmet and ran in, passing the boy whose place he was taking.

Middle line backer was a strong and important defensive position, often played by the most aggressive player on the entire team. It required a great deal of quickness, speed, and strength; you were expected to be in on every play, according to Barnes.

He looked over the defensive lineman in front of him, a fat kid named Paul Dobbins who was in at nose, or middle, guard. Dobbins was slow and moved clumsily; he was not effective at rushing and often fell down when blocked. Over the second string's center, he could see Tommy Phelps in the familiar quarterback crouch, calling out a signal, waiting for the snap. He felt Phelps was looking directly at him, but he also knew that his eyes were roaming up and down the line opposite him.

The play this time was a running play, for real, a handoff to the fullback, who came off-guard. He saw Dobbins fall in a cloud of dust and then the runner was there, and he went into him, charging forward hard. The back went down cleanly; he had hit him from the side, so he still had some forward momentum, but it was a single solo tackle.

Barnes was clapping his hands enthusiastically. "Yeah, yeah, that's the way! See that! See that little guy do that? He hit him hard, he goes down like a bowling pin!" he smacked his hands together. "Boom!"

"Phelps!" he called out over his shoulder. "Take a shower. Lewis! Get your bony ass in at quarterback for Tommy so he don't get his uniform dirty today."

Chad Lewis was also, like Larry, only a sophomore, but there the comparisons ended. Larry watched as he pulled his helmet on, and went into the offensive huddle as if he had belonged there all the time. He took charge; you could see it. He was already a poised, accomplished passer, and he had heard him being talked about in the barbershop as no doubt becoming the starting quarterback the next season, as a junior.

Chad Lewis was different. It seemed he could do almost anything he wanted athletically; he was good in basketball, a sharp outside shooter who could also go to the basket, and he excelled as a pitcher in baseball. It was possible he would be a three-letter player, a very rare accomplishment. And it did seem like he did it all without a lot of effort. "Gifted," as they said knowingly at Sam's, nodding their heads in unison.

When he brought the team up to the line of scrimmage, they already looked different. They were crisper – that was the word that came into Larry's head as he looked over at them. Chad looked as if he had been crouching behind the center for several seasons. He barked a set of short signals, and Larry moved instinctively forward, toward him. He sensed, rather than clearly saw, a large player coming at him, and then he was down, in a jarring block, rolling, hearing a muffled roar somewhere behind him.

Lewis had completed the first pass he'd thrown, to the left end, a gangly kid named Jesse Wheeler, whose father was an unpopular and disliked teacher about whom numerous messages had been scrawled in the boys rooms. "Wheeler sucks donkey dicks!" one read, over an accompanying drawing.

Wheeler had run another ten yards, after he caught the ball, and Coach Barnes was now raging at the defensive team, as they straggled into a formation down the field.

"You guys been playin' with yerselfs too much again!" he shouted. "You sure as hell ain't playin' any football here."

Lewis already had the team back up to the line. Another short signal called out, he turned, and a quick hand-off to the halfback, who looked like he meant to head for the far end. A hole was open in the line, and Larry sprinted forward and through, and, to his own amazement, lunged and caught the back's legs sufficiently hard enough to send him sprawling, behind the line of scrimmage for a loss of several yards.

The play – in fact, the plays since he had been in – had all happened so quickly that he was dazed by it. He looked around the field, wondering what he should do. Another of the linebackers, Cappelletti, was slapping him on the behind, telling him "Way to go!" Coach Barnes had said, strangely, nothing, but had made an entry on his clipboard, Larry noticed.

On the next play Lewis threw another pass which was deflected by one of his own lineman, tipped, and then caught by the big defensive end, who was almost immediately smashed to the ground by three big offensive players, in anger, Larry thought. They had had something going, and this stopped it. Barnes signaled for the defensive unit to take over the ball, with Richie Harris acting as quarterback. Then he pointed at Larry, and waved him to the sideline. He would not be in for the offensive series.

He stood on the sideline watching the scrimmage proceed, thinking that he had been in for what – three, four plays? It was something, a positive development. He wondered what he would tell his mother. She had begun to talk again about the conflict between playing football, the time devoted to practicing and studying the playbook, and his school classes. It was obvious which she thought was the more important. The thought of his mother made him think of the dinner table where they usually held their discussions, and he realized he was very hungry.

He went in for one more series, again with Lewis quarterbacking on the other side. The tipped and intercepted pass seemed to have affected his poise, his concentration. Maybe he was just disgusted. But the unit did not have that crispness in its stance and its execution – the word Coach Rossi often used – that it had had the first series with him. How quickly the tide could turn, Larry thought. That was part of the fascination of the game, too, how the feeling of the game could change like that, so quickly and so suddenly.

The practice ended early that day. He returned to the gym to shower with the realization he had survived the two-week training camp, and had probably made the JV squad. It meant he sometimes would practice with the varsity players, although the JVs were usually handled by Kowalski. It was not what he had planned – he really did not know what he had planned, if that was even the word – but it did mean that he would be closer to the real games than he had ever been before, and that he would be learning about the way the game was really to be played. Coach Rossi had a reputation for teaching his players a very high level of skill and execution. His teams had been singled out in newspaper articles the previous season by some other teams' coaches as being "over-coached", having a level of play more appropriate to a collegiate team.

As he dressed slowly, he heard a junior, a guard named Metzger, talking to another player. He was talking about a guy he knew who played ball for a small college, Bucknell, up in the north-central part of the state.

"They're called the Bisons ... it's a Little Ivy League school. You know, kids that can't make it in the Ivy League itself go there."

"He got a scholarship to this place?" Dago Paretti was the starting safety, a feared player, a hard hitter. "Really? Those places are usually expensive, those kinda colleges."

"Oh yeah – full ride, the whole thing. He says they got great food in the dorms – each one has its own dining hall. White table clothes. That kinda stuff."

"Bullshit! Come on, now!" Paretti slapped at him with a towel; Larry could hear the sharp snap.

"Hey! That's what he says. He doesn't want to leave the place to come home. Says his dorm is better than his house."

Paretti laughed. "I can believe that. Some of the dumps around this town..."

"He's the one told me this stuff about getting hit. Did I tell you that, Dago?"

"What? No, I never heard it."

The story Metzger told then was not so much odd as unexpected. The college player, a lineman, told of being in a game where the defensive lineman opposite him smashed him repeatedly in the face, forearming him. His nose bled, and he saw stars.

"What about the fuckin' ref?" Paretti asked "He didn't see this shit?"

"I don't know...I guess not." Metzer lowered his voice. "But get this. He said that by the third quarter, he realized he was starting to *want* this guy to hit him like that. He started looking forward to it, he liked the pain. A numb pain, he called it."

"Horseshit!" Paretti exclaimed, spitting loudly on the cement floor. "That's crap, you ask me. He was just messin' with you. He's been up at that fancy school too long already, gettin' too smart. Thinkin' too much, you ask me."

"Maybe," Metzger had said. "Could be. Still..."

The conversation had distracted him; he had sat in front of his locker, frozen, straining to hear it all. When he then finished getting dressed and was taking his gym bag from his locker, he realized the big oversized practice jersey was now his to keep. Already he had gotten a sign of his accomplishment, something that would mark him among the other students. If he had a girlfriend, he could give it to her to wear. He imagined Sandy Stevens wearing it, and his mind spun. That there was a connection between football and girls was always evident, but it was becoming a deeper connection the more he became actually involved with the game.

As he walked out of the gym, he draped the practice jersey around his shoulders, as he had seen varsity players do, like a sweater or jacket. It smelled ripe, as his mother said – he would have her wash it this weekend. When the school year began, he would be a real football player, something he would not have thought possible when the last year had ended, just a few short months ago.

When he passed by the fence looking down on the field, he stopped and looked down. There was a lone figure, Coach Rossi, standing at about the forty yard line. He could not be mistaken; the beige baseball cap was illuminated by the late afternoon sun. The coach often was seen like that, after practice standing alone looking out over the big field. Other players had mentioned it.

Soon the field would be marked off in the dazzling ten-yard white limed horizontal stripes – that would happen the coming week, getting ready for the first game, Friday night. Only a week away. He could feel the cold excitement churn in his stomach.

# 11

The first week of school in the autumn – his mother always called it the fall, he noticed; most people did, but he liked autumn, it was a richer word, more appropriate – was exciting. Coming back to the high school as a sophomore was better than coming back as a freshman, much better. There would be a dance devoted to his class, the Sophomore Hop, early in the spring; the first in the series of annual class dances. Many kids complained of returning and vowed they longed to get out of school, when they would never have to return, but Larry did not feel this way. He had always looked forward to going to school, but you couldn't say this, of course. Why not, though? He had asked Frankie Malone about it once as they walked down in the River Park and Frankie was amazed. "You are probably one of the very, very, very few who does like school, Larry. Don't you ever see it that way? Think about it! People *hate* school. They *hate* the teachers. The books, the homework. All of it."

"But why?" he persisted. He could do this with Frankie, he even expected it.

"Why? That's your favorite question, isn't it? Maybe I should turn it around and ask you – why?"

He laughed, nodding. "Okay, I get it."

Frankie was in two of his classes; his health class, for which he had Coach Rossi as teacher, and gym, where Coach Kowalski was the teacher. They went to the latter class after coming from study halls, a class Frankie enjoyed. He had somehow managed to get two of them into his schedule for the autumn.

In the gym class, Frankie pointed at the big rope that always seemed to be swaying slightly whenever you looked at it, even if no one had been near it.

"Thing reminds me of a damn big snake of some sort," he said. He turned to Larry. "You been able to climb up it, yet?"

"No. Not yet. Not all the way, at least. It's hard to do."

"I'd shit my pants if I got up that rope." Frankie began to laugh. "Grease my way down!"

It was true what he said. Larry had gotten about three quarters of the way up the rope so far, and when he had looked down at the gym floor below, it had seemed a very long way down and he had felt suddenly light-headed. Vertigo, they called it. It could make you fall, even if you did not want to. Again, he wondered at the wisdom of climbing the damn thing.

"You made the JV, it's said. Ducky didn't – too bad." Frankie noted, as they laced up their gym shoes. "So what position they got you playin'?"

Larry shook his head. "I don't know yet."

"You don't know what position? What position did you go out for, then?"

"You don't go out for a position. You just go out. The coaches put you in the position."

"Oh yeah. Sure they do... well, are you playin' offensive or defensive?"

"Mainly defense, so far."

"No glory there." Frankie raised his hands over his head, as if catching a pass. "You gotta get on offense, Larry. Make the play! Catch that fifty yarder with ten seconds left in the half. Then every cheerleader in the school will worship you. Hero!"

Kowalski motioned for the class to come out onto the floor, and space itself in intervals of about five feet apart. He looked them over. Dressed in the same blue gym shorts and white tee shirts, the class of about twenty-five boys looked ill at ease and uncomfortable, as if they did not know what they were assembled for, although they all knew in fact.

Kowalski was dressed in his grey sweat pants and his white practice jersey, looking very much the coach. What would he teach them today, Larry wondered. But he knew that in gym class you did not learn anything, you exercised. It was important for youth to exercise, and so you had gym classes.

Suddenly he realized Kowalski was beckoning to him. He pointed a finger at himself, at his chest, inquiringly. The other students were looking at him.

"Yeah, Simmons, you! Come on out, and lead us in some calisthenics here. This group looks like they could use it."

When he got in front of the class, the coach patted him on the back, and said, "They're all yours, kid. Give 'em a good work-out. I'll be over here in the stands." He pointed over his big shoulder.

After a few seconds of indecision, looking over the class facing him (Frankie was grinning at him), he nodded, and said, "All right. Side saddle hops. Begin!"

They did a rapid twenty five of the hops, an easy exercise, to warm up, and then he had them do upper body twists, to limber up, as the coaches called it. He followed that with fifteen toe touches. As they did the latter exercise, he could hear some of the students' breathing had increased and gotten ragged. A couple overweight boys were already red in the face, and struggled to touch their toes. He heard Kowalski snicker behind him; it was an unexpected sound from such a big man, and surprised him.

"Give 'em twenty of the best, Simmons," the coach said, in a loud voice. "Twenty push-ups! Huuup! Down! Huuup! Down! Huuup! Down!"

This exercise, which he found easy unencumbered with pads and uniform and the cleated shoes, which were also heavy, was too much for some of the students, who flopped on their bellies, groaning.

"Come on!" Kowalski roared. "Get up! What's wrong with you – you should be able to do these easy, at your age.

Whatta ya been doin' all summer, eh? Lookit Simmons—he ain't even breakin' a sweat!"

It was true. Larry was mildly astonished at how effortless, so far, the exercising had been for him. His body felt light, springy and taut, ready to do what he asked it to. It was a good feeling, he decided. If you got nothing else out of playing football than this feeling, that was a good bit more than you started with. What would he feel like in four or five more weeks, he wondered?

They did a series of sit-ups then, on the big mats, and then some knee curls and knee lifts followed by squats. The squats were a difficult exercise, both in terms of effort and balance. Many students fell backwards. Again, Kowalski laughed, shaking his head.

"If I was in that bad of shape when I was your age..." he said, implying that he had not been. But now, Larry decided looking at him, his belly was getting larger and maybe the coach was really not in that good of shape. But he was the coach. Coaches did not have to be in shape, apparently.

"Take 'em on a couple laps around the floor, Simmons," Kowalski ordered, waving his hand in a circular motion. "Do you all good to run it out now."

Accordingly, he led the group around in a fairly quick stride, but not running hard. They needed to loosen up to run properly, he thought. Running on the highly polished wooden gym floor, where it seemed it would be easy to slip and fall, was totally different than running on the big practice field. Frankie Malone fell in beside him, breathing hard.

"You been kissin' his ass?" he asked. "Where do you get off, leadin' and all?"

But he knew and Frankie knew that this was one of the rewards for being a player – a jock, as they were called, but not to their faces. Already he had been singled out favorably, and the others had been put on notice he was different. He was in better physical shape than they were.

They ran two laps, and he started on a third, noticing how far back some of the students were, stringing out in a wavering line under the opposite basket at the other end of the floor, closer to walking than running. It gave him an odd feeling he had not experienced before, seeing them like that and being so far out in front of them, not really being taxed in terms of effort. Kowalski sat with his arms crossed in the first row of the stands, above the gym floor, tapping his one foot slowly. Larry wondered if he could run a lap and was seized with the idea of calling to him to join them, do a lap with them.

Frankie was keeping up with him, but was laboring hard. "You know what I'm thinkin?" he gasped out.

Larry shook his head, smiling. He knew it would be good.

""How come they call these shoes tennis shoes?" He looked down momentarily at their blurred feet running. "Nobody in Ralston plays tennis. Never has. Tennis shoes!"

Coach Kowalski told them to go on into the showers after they finished the lap, and that was the end of the class. In the shower room, which stank of sweat and other odors he couldn't clearly identify, the students did not talk much, and some sat down immediately on the low wooden benches, leaning their heads back on the wall lockers. Others threw their gym clothes onto the benches and went immediately into the showers. There were always a few who changed hurriedly, without showering, not caring apparently about how this would affect others sitting near them in their next class. The gym teacher was supposed to monitor the showering, to ensure that this did not happen, but they never did.

"You the King Shit now, Larry," Frankie said, pulling off his shoes. He held a shoe up, sniffed. "Ummmm! Tasty!"

He had home room after the gym class –a nice break, those two classes together. It was apparent that the gym class would not be taxing for him. Maybe he could even make attempts to climb The Big Rope. He saw himself spinning on it, one hand up in a greeting gesture like a circus performer, up near the big iron rafters. He had seen a couple of the varsity players do that, and not once, but several times. It was impressive, especially if the cheer-leaders were practicing down on the mats.

In home room he found that he wasn't seated too near Sandy Stevens, but then he wasn't totally on the other side of the room from her either. She was like a powerful light in the room, even with the full day sun shining in and the dark green school issue blinds up. Mr. Turner liked sunlight, and often did not pull the heavy, dark blinds down as other teachers did. It got hot in the room as a result, but he always looked cool, as if he had just taken a shower.

Larry did his best not to look at her too much. It was uncanny how girls could know you were looking at them, even, it seemed, before you looked at them so that they were looking right at you – caught you! – when you made your look, and you had to quickly look away, or up, or down, or out the window. Or grin, and say something to whoever was next to you, or lean forward, and tap the person in front of you, and think of something to say to them. Cover up…

Sandy did not have a loud voice, but somehow he could always pick it out of the babble, the elevated beehive hum of the classroom, before Mr. Turner cleared his throat, his signal for them to stop talking. You were not supposed to be talking in home room; you were supposed to be studying or doing your homework. No sleeping, either, even though some students tried. Turner was severe on the latter. Again, Larry was struck by how he could walk so silently up and down the rows of desks, and suddenly be standing right beside you, without you hearing him.

He had Mr. Turner for his sophomore college prep English class. He taught all the college prep English classes – sophomore, junior and senior; one for each class group. It was a distinction even to be in his classes; you had to be recommended by your English teacher of the previous year. Mr. Turner himself would not automatically pass on a student into his next level class; he was a strict and severe grader with very high expectations. He could fix you with a baneful stare over the tops of his dark, horn rimmed glasses, saying nothing. The look was enough, and spoke volumes. There were no disciplinary problems in his classes.

The book they were using in his class was a large anthology of English Literature. He loved the heft, the weight of the book - the very smell of its glossy pages. It was bright red, easy to see at a distance. Just the fact of having this book, being seen carrying it, was status; you were in college prep classes. Frankie Malone, somehow or other, had gotten into the sophomore English class with him, a mystery if there ever was one. Jason Phelps was in there, too, but he was no longer on the squad. There was Jesse Wheeler, the skinny kid who caught the ten-yarder the other day, playing on the second string line. Although ungainly and awkward appearing, Wheeler was proving to be a real surprise on the field, probably even to himself. His father was already bragging about him to other teachers.

But that was it; no others from the team. Football players, it was generally known, did not do that well in English. It was a difficult subject for them, both the reading and the writing, but especially the writing. Many seemed to have an intense aversion to writing, and you could not really do well in English without writing. It was hard for them to get out a couple of paragraphs, they complained, holding up the blank paper to show that it was so.

Although he had not talked about it, Larry wondered how these players would be able to make it in college if they were unable to write in high school. But he had heard that they received tutoring help in the higher levels. It was said that several colleges housed all the football players in their own dormitory, and there they were helped with any studies they were having trouble with.

It took time, though, to write a good paper, and here again he found himself perplexed. Practice at Ralston was held every school day afternoon, except Fridays, from 3 until 5 or so. By the time you got home, you had been at school since eight in the morning. Practices in college would be longer, or there would be more of them.

Mr. Turner made no distinctions for anyone in his classes, and it was said that he was like a college level teacher in his demands and amount of work assigned. So Larry thought it would be a good indication for him; if he did well in sophomore college prep English, that would be a very positive sign. Mr. Turner himself said the most frequently failed subject at the collegiate level was freshman English, a required subject for all students.

The English class was held in a corner room on the second floor, next to the Library. It was smaller than most rooms on the floor, and did not have desks fixed into the floor, but instead a large, long, wooden table with chairs around it, where they all sat. It was interesting how this changed the entire feeling of the class. Larry had never been to a college class, but he had the intuition they would be more like this class. Mr. Turner sat at the middle of the table, not at the head, and this was an interesting change, too; initially, students had thought it would mean that Mr. Turner would not be able to walk up and down the aisles of desks as he normally did. Frankie Malone made a point of sitting next to Larry – since the table was round, there were not seating chart required slots. Mr. Turner took his roll without any apparent difficulty.

In the first week, he was looking forward to this class. Just leafing through the big, fat anthology book was exciting; he recognized some of the names, famous writers, poets, playwrights. They would read these works and discuss them, Mr. Turner told them. He would fill in background and literary history. They would take notes, that was required, and he would expect to review these notes, at anytime.

Mr. Turner always had a small, green, cut glass vase of flowers on his desk in home room. The flowers changed with the seasons. His wife gave them to him, and Larry wondered what it would be like to have a wife who gave you flowers, since it was always the other way around, in his experience. Like her husband, she was impeccably tailored, and supposedly she made her own clothes and those of her husband – "a very accomplished seamstress," his mother had said when he had told her this. Marla Turner had dark black hair, exactly like her husband. Larry thought they easily could be taken for brother and sister. They had met at college, the story went. That was really why most girls went to college, to find someone like Mr Turner and get married.

Watching the teacher seated at his desk, reading a book (Mr. Turner was always reading a book during home room, and Frankie Malone said he did the same in study halls he oversaw), turning the pages slowly, with one hand held to the side of his face in a gesture special to him, unique, Larry wondered if he would meet someone like Mrs. Turner when he went to college. Marriage was inevitable, sooner (probably) than later. If a man could wait the impossibly long time until he was past thirty, people said, he would make a sound marriage. But who could wait that long? And it looked like not too many made a good thing of it. "The ball and chain" or "the old lady", they called their wives at Sam's. It was hard to think of Mr. Turner referring to his wife like that.

What would it be like to be a teacher? That was another thing he thought about, even on the practice field, watching the coaches. You got paid for it. You could earn a living, for your life, doing it. Teaching was not the kind of work most men in Ralston did. Work was physical work, using the arms, the back. Labor, they called it. Hard labor. Real work "where you got your hands dirty!" as the men in town said. Somebody at the barbershop had once told a story about the revolution in France, where they had judged people in front of the court by feeling their hands, whether they were soft or hard, calloused with work. If they were soft, you went to the guillotine. Was teaching, being a teacher, real work? What was it that he could do to "earn a living"? He was too young to be thinking seriously about these things, his mother would say.

"You're living the best time of your life. Right now. Enjoy it. Believe me, you'll know what I mean in a few years..."

That was how she talked, how other adults talked. A scary prospect when you thought about it, that the best time came so early in life and the rest was worse. That couldn't be what they actually meant.

Mr. Turner assigned a lot of reading, even the first week. "I am not fooling around in this class, as you well know," he announced, striding around the room, hands clasped behind his back. "You will work. But this is nothing compared to college. Think of it that way."

So college must be brutal, very demanding. Not many made it through to a four-year degree. A college degree seemed so remote it was like Mt. Everest, the Himalayas, a part of the world he felt sure he would never get to. In fact, he realized, he knew no one other than his teachers who had a college degree.

The first week of classes was a blur, like a train. The autumn was already moving quickly. It always seemed like autumn, fall, went quickly, while the summer hung heavy, went slowly. He plunged into his studies, not liking the algebra class for which he had Mrs. Hills (instead of Coach Kowalski's wife), a teacher who had been at the school for many years. She was reputed to be the best math teacher "for miles around." She had taught generations of Ralston students "the higher mathematics," as she called it. He did not know how old she was, but her graying hair was frizzy, in a permanent wave, and she wore odd-colored dresses from another era, along with very small old-looking metal framed glasses which slipped down her nose. She constantly pushed them up with a forefinger, and he began to watch to see how often she did this. She would cover the entire blackboard with numbers and equations in an hour's class, during which you could hear a pin drop in the room. No one spoke, or even chewed gum, in Mrs. Hills' classes; if they did, they received not a verbal rebuke but a piercing, withering, prolonged stare, in silence, reducing the perpetrator to midget size. The whole class shrunk into their seats.

She moved methodically around the classroom, limping. The story was that she had fallen, years ago, on a smooth sheet of ice out in front of the town bank, broken her leg in two places and it had never healed properly, so that it was shorter than the other. She pointed at the figures on the blackboard with a long, wooden staff, which she also used like a cane. No one was exempt, except for Patsy Herbst, the genius, whose father was an inventor. Patsy read novels in class, one after another, like a reading machine. Occasionally, out of frustration or anger, Mrs. Hills would suddenly call on her. Patsy would look up from her book, briefly scan the board, and give the correct answer every time. Students feared Mrs. Hills, hoping not to get in her classes, yet Larry felt she would be better for him than watching Coach Kowalski's wife move around on the edge of her desk. "Mrs. K!" boys said, grinning.

Although he knew he needed to follow closely in Mrs
. Hills' class, what he was really thinking about was the
upcoming junior varsity game. It was the second week of
the season and the varsity had already played one game –
their opening game – at home against Glassboro, a hated
rival Ralston had always defeated for as long as Larry could
recall. They were known as the Glassers, since there were
two large Pittsburgh Plate Glass factories in the town. It
was an unfortunate name for a football team – "Smash
the Glassers!" "Break 'em!" and other tags were routinely
put on signs around the school that very first week. To
the Principal's annoyance, students were dragged up and
down the echoing halls in "The Little Red Wagon", yelling
and whooping. It was a tradition and he couldn't do much
about it.

The Friday afternoon before the Glassboro game there
would also be the first Pep Rally of the year. This would
pack the auditorium, and be led by the student body president, a bespectacled senior, Charlie Hibbing. Despite
his glasses, Hibbing was the most popular boy in the
school. He always had a smile for you; he seemed to know
everyone in the school by their first name. Unkindly,
Frankie Malone suggested he had a great career ahead of
him as a politician.

"He can't lose – you know, Charlie likes people to like
him. That's the whole thing with him. A complete phony."

Like many of Frankie's observations, this one felt pain-
fully close. Frankie often seemed to be smart beyond his
years, but Larry could not tell why this was so. It just was,

and always had been since they were growing up as little kids. Other kids were careful of what they said around him, saying "Ohh, Frankie's here..." rolling their eyes.

In the hallways, moving between classes, he fell back quickly into the rhythms of the school. There was still the special, unmistakable beginning of the year school smell – wax and washed blackboards and chalkiness – a smell he connected with no other place in his life. It was an intense, distinct smell, like that of leaves burning in the autumn; the two smells were connected in his mind. School meant autumn.

In Scheer's Men's Store, an autumn-themed display was up in the big front window – a half-dozen richly hued sweaters, laying fanned out; the new "Ivy League" buttoned-down collar shirts stacked neatly on a dresser whose top drawer was half-open and had several striped and solid colored ties hanging out of it. The mannequins wore tweed sports jackets, with leather elbow patches – Mr. Turner wore jackets like that. One mannequin wore a white Ralston cardigan letter sweater with two blue rings around the arm. Whose was it, Larry wondered?

He always looked forward to seeing the autumn displays at Scheer's even though he couldn't afford to buy the clothes. This was a store which had opened in 1831 – and been in the same family ever since. It would be wonderful to walk in there, buy several shirts, sweaters, maybe a jacket even. It would make you feel good, even if you didn't when you went in. He had once bought some socks, entered a drawing because of his purchase, and won a beautiful flannel shirt. "Clothes make the man." He had read that; maybe in the big English literature anthology. Men were not supposed to be interested in clothes – women, girls, were. But Scheer's window proved this wasn't true. Even so, he felt some twinges. It was a type of vanity, of calling attention to oneself. And this wasn't supposed to be good. But he felt sure you would be more confident if you looked good. That had to be important.

He was pleased to be acknowledged by other football players. They moved through the halls with an easy walk, seeming to walk on air, looking to be a head or more above the other kids although this was not always the case physically. Some varsity players already wore their letter sweaters. Harry Gibb wore his often; four blue rings around the left sleeve – four varsity letters, in football. You couldn't do any better than that. But, although as center Gibb handled the ball on every offensive play, it was nearly impossible for him to be a real "star" player. Larry had never heard of a center scoring a point in a football game. It could happen if they doubled as the placekicker, but this was never the case; the center specialized in snapping the ball to the holder for such scoring attempts. No, center was an odd position. How did you became fitted to it, "go out for it"? Maybe it came from sheer chance, the player having been the one who centered the ball in endless neighborhood pick-up games.

He had never even spoken to Harry Gibb, but as he passed him in the hall that first week, Gibb nodded slightly to him. Gibb would supposedly get nearly as many scholarship offers as the quarterback, Dick Atkins. He wondered if Atkins, or Gibb for that matter, would get scholarship offers from Princeton. But they would probably not go there even if they did. Princeton wasn't a serious football college, like Notre Dame or Pitt. Syracuse was a college he heard some seniors were considering. Another was Duke, in North Carolina. A former coach had starred at the University of North Carolina, four or five years back. All the football and sports magazines reported that teams in the collegiate conferences in the south played a tough brand of football. Maybe Gibb and the other "stars" would go there, the Southeast Football Conference. He knew the name from the football magazines. One thing was certain. He would not go there.

# 12

In the Problems of Democracy class, which he had been placed in as an accelerated student, which meant he was in the class with juniors, Mr. Ferris talked about the dignity of work in America, the first reading in their textbook. Larry daydreamed while the heavyset man droned on in the early afternoon class. He could not understand the business about the dignity of work. If you looked around at the grown men in Ralston, you would see many with part or all of a finger missing. Some had more than one finger missing; old man Carlotti, for instance, had chopped off his thumb in the butcher shop one Christmas Eve. Many men were ruptured, and wore trusses, or had such bad backs that they had braces or walked with a cane, in a permanent stoop. And hadn't his own grandfather, James, fallen onto the house railings and died?

He thought of the job he had for one day earlier that summer, in June, not long after school ended. His mother had received a phone call from another mother, and early one morning a few days later he found himself in a pick-up truck with a smoking tar wagon bumping behind, heading into the countryside above Garver's Ferry to a farm where he was to help tar the roof of a barn. He knew nothing about tarring or roofing, but his mother had been impressed with the offer of five dollars for the day's work.

The man, Gary Morton, was known to his mother through the acquaintance who'd phoned. He was an out of work railroader who had taken to doing roofing work and other "odd jobs" to make money. He said little as they drove to the farm, except to comment that it was better to get started early, because it would get hot on the roof in the afternoon.

"You ever work on the roof of a barn?" he had asked. Larry had shook his head.

"Haven't worked much, have you?" the man had said, and Larry knew that they would not get along and that it would be a long day.

It proved one of the worst days of his life. He didn't like to think too much about it. He found himself on a very large, steeply pitched, slippery roof – his only aid to keep from falling or sliding off a rope thrown over the top of the roof that Gary assured him it would not "let go". He mixed various elements in buckets, heated up the tar wagon, and then ascended to the roof himself. The work was dirty and in an hour's time he felt like simply leaving. He did not care if the roof got tarred, or if he even got paid. Several times he slid dangerously, once getting down to the gutter spout running around the edge of the barn's roof, which clattered loudly and shook as his foot hit it. It looked at least fifty or sixty feet to the ground from there. If he did fall, he would be badly injured, perhaps even killed. He felt a fierce anger at Gary Morton for even suggesting to take a kid like himself on such a job – yet this was common, many boys worked through the summer on roofing jobs or doing construction work.

When the lunch break finally arrived, he sat exhausted and miserable, leaning against the shady side wall of the barn. No matter where he moved, he could not avoid the raw stink of the tar wagon. He had burned his hands with it several times. Dejectedly, he went into the dark barn to urinate at a place Gary had directed him to. He was no sooner there than Gary came in, coming over, standing right next to him. Grinning, he unzipped his pants.

"Lookit this. Huh? Ever see one that big? Huh?"

The man had a full erection, and Larry felt himself get dizzy, his mouth going dry. As far as he knew there was no one near the barn; the farmer had earlier driven to Ralston, and hadn't returned. They were alone in the barn, on the entire farm, as far as he knew.

"You ever see your brother get a good hard-on like this?" Gary said. He gestured with his head, smiling, looking down at himself. "Go ahead – touch it. See how it feels." He moved his own hand back and forth, slowly.

Larry shook his head, and somehow managed to walk away – although his legs felt weak and shaky – out of the barn, and on out into an apple orchard surrounding the barn, trying to think of what he could do. He felt cold, with a sickening fear in his stomach, and again a mounting anger. He knew with certainty that what had just happened in the barn should never have happened, that it was a profound wrong. Why had the man picked him?

When he finally returned to the barn, Gary had gone back up on to the roof and resumed working, as if nothing had happened. He looked down and asked Larry to begin passing tools up to him, and he finished up the afternoon working on the ground, hauling the tar bucket up to Gary. He did not go onto the roof again and knew he would not if asked. When they quit working at five, Gary went into the house to see the farmer, who had returned in the middle of the afternoon, and then came out. They got in the truck. Gary handed him a five dollar bill.

"Your share," he had said. That had been all he had said, dropping Larry off as soon as they got into Ralston. Larry had not looked over at him once during the drive in, thankful it was summer and he could keep the truck's window open.

That had been "work." Later, as he laid in his room thinking about the day, he realized he could have fallen off the barn roof and died, emulating his grandfather's death. He never told his mother about the incident in the barn with Gary, but he did tell her that he would not go on such jobs again. She had never asked him to.

He worked for a week at an Islay's ice cream store, filling in for another student who had gone with his family on vacation. The five gallon containers of ice cream were rock hard. You were allowed to eat as much ice cream as you wanted, but he found he did not want that much. It was hard initially to keep from breaking the soft cones when you pushed the scoops of ice cream down on them; there was a trick to it, and the trick lay in not pushing too hard, gauging the feel of the cone and the pressure of the scoop, the consistency of the ice cream. Several times he had handed a cone to a customer, only to see the scoops fall off. The customers demanded a new cone. But he had gotten the hang of it by the end of the first day.

There, he had worked with an old man, over sixty, who seemed to have the attitude that you could have fun on the job, and with whom he worked smoothly, after the first day, in a team. Dave, the old man, seemed to sense when things needed doing, and would do them, whether or not they were supposedly "his job" or yours. In return, Larry quickly picked up tasks that had been assigned Dave, but that he could not get to. Together, they had the place running "like a ship" Dave said. He had piloted a mail boat somewhere in Maine for many years, making runs to an island and back, and brought a nautical chart of the island area to work one day for Larry to look at. He and his wife, now dead, had lived "year round" on the island, he said. "Best years of our lives, that was."

That week had gone very fast. He almost felt it an afterthought that he got paid at the end of the week. Dave said he was sorry that he would not be coming back the next week.

Then there had been the job selling newspaper subscriptions, door to door. That had really been the first job where he had earned money of any real amount. He had been twelve years old that summer – it seemed a long time ago now. A math teacher from a high school nearby had taken a group of six boys his own age – the crew, he called them – to the numerous small towns, and larger ones, in the area of about thirty miles' radius from Ralston. They would fan out and walk through a neighborhood, ringing doorbells, knocking on doors, trying to persuade people to buy an eight-week subscription to the Sunday newspaper, and if possible, a weekly subscription. To sell both was a real coup; you were paid a commission of a dollar for that.

In some ways, the newspaper job had been very interesting. You learned to quickly "read" a neighborhood – the state of the lawns, the ornaments outside or on a house, the sizes of the homes themselves, the cars in the driveways. Then, there were the customers. Younger women were the easiest to sell to, to convince. The "hook", as the teacher smilingly called it, was telling the perspective customer that you were working to win a trip to Notre Dame in the fall. You would go to South Bend, Indiana, with other prize winners on a special train, be housed in a dormitory on the Notre Dame campus, and best of all, see a football game in the famous stadium. This was the big prize you were working so hard for, trying to sell so many more subscriptions.

Very often, the approach worked, if you were allowed to really get into it. And it was critical to actually get into the customer's house or apartment; it was almost certain that you would not make a sale if you were kept outside, talking through a screen door, or a door that was partly opened.

Some boys told stories from this job. Several told of seeing naked, or nearly naked, women who hurriedly threw on clothing as they came to the door, not realizing (apparently) that they could be seen – not caring or, in the most interesting variation, wanting you to see them. They were all of an indiscriminate age, right on the borderline between being boys and being teen-aged boys, which was much different. Apparently, there were some women who wanted to go with teen-aged boys, or so some of the boys vehemently argued.

One boy, Alan Samuelson, claimed he had been "seduced" by a young woman, on a Saturday afternoon trip they had made to Vandergrift, a near-by town somewhat larger than Ralston. Alan said the woman had invited him in to share a glass of lemonade, taken him into the kitchen, and sat at the counter watching him as he drank the cold lemonade.

"She had shorts on – really nice tan, too. She asked me how old I was."

"What did you tell her?" Larry had asked.

"I said I was almost fourteen…" Alan was almost thirteen, so he had stretched it a year. "She kept rubbing her legs with her hand, looking down at them, and then at me. I really got a boner, watching her do that. I was afraid I wouldn't be able to stand up – she'd see it." He gestured down at himself.

"Boner! Boner!" the others had yelled, grinning, making pumping gestures with their hands.

It was an accurate word. It did feel as if you had a rigid, hard bone in the middle of your penis, that ached. Your prick, as it was often called. Or joint, somebody had said... The boner was a development that was difficult to deal with, to know what to do; it had a way of happening at unexpected, unwanted times. He remembered being in the school library, late in the day for a class meeting. Cheryl Lake, Dick Atkins' girlfriend, had been leaning back, in her skin-tight Levis, against a big, long library table. He had gotten an erection, despite willfully trying not to. It was hopeless. You got them pledging allegiance to the flag in the morning.

Alan Samuelson went on to tell two different versions (Larry had heard both) of what had then happened. He wondered if either were true – or perhaps partially true. The stories other boys told of their sexual adventures were truly incredible, there was no end to their invention. And then there were the stories they relayed, ones they swore had happened, stories told in a loud voice in the shower room, after gym class or practice. If all that was told of was going on, there would be a lot of hell to pay some-where down the road.

He did not win the trip to Notre Dame that year, and the next year he felt too old somehow to go out with the crew again. He would miss the red-haired twins in the soda fountain where he went to buy milkshakes after they came back from the job. But the thought of walking around the hot streets did not appeal at all to him – that had been a summer he had spent in a deep funk, laying on his bed in his room, often with a pool of sweat under him soaking into the sheet, the room dark, listening to the rhythm and blues station in Pittsburgh, WILY. It came from the Hill District, a black area of the city above the Triangle. The music appealed to him deeply and he often lay as if in a trance, marveling at the sounds, the words which seemed as if written with his own woes in mind. One of the djs, PJ Chasen, was his favorite. He spoke as if he were your friend, talking to you, having a conversation. He would say things like "Here's Chuck Berry... "Maybellene"...put your foot down on that accelerator!" He would get up and, in the dim pooled light of a desk lamp, jerk around the room in an increasingly frenzied, improvised dance, until he was sweating heavily.

The music was in some way clearly dangerous. In those evenings of intense aloneness, he also began to form a crazy desire to be a disc jockey himself. He could imagine himself talking easily over the radio, sitting in some broadcast room, speaking into the microphone, out into the vast, hot summer night. He had never done this, but it seemed natural to him, and he wondered if it had something to do with what his mother so often told him about how his grandfather could talk to anyone, even the President. Thousands of kids – tens of thousands – would be listening, just as intently as he did, staring at the radio as if willing for some miraculous event to occur that would forever change their lives. For sure, it would come from here, from this music!

He often listened to the entire four hours – 8-12 – of the evening dj's show, thinking as he did that he could have done the show better, or at least differently. Why didn't they have a real kid for a dj? Sometimes he would pull in the big 50,000 watt station in Buffalo, New York, after midnight. The dj was a strange-sounding guy who delivered what sounded like private messages, or instructions, aimed at individual listeners. He had strange sponsors for his show – one was a wine company, owned by a "mother" something or other. Larry wondered, after listening for a while, if the company actually existed, or was simply an invention of the dj. The mix of music he played was as unpredictable as he was. You could hear a lot of rhythm and blues, what some called "race music."

Down in Pittsburgh, he had seen a disc jockey sitting in a glassed-in booth jutting out right on the street, so that passers-by could look in at him. The glass was very thick, no sound came out (or went in) but there were speakers allowing those who gathered outside the booth on the street to hear the dj's talk. He would often point at them, wave, or smile. Then he would play another record. Bill Michaels was this dj's name; he did the 1-7 show weekdays.

It seemed like a very easy job. Then there was the money - $50,000 was mentioned as the salary of Bill Michaels, the person he had seen in the booth in Pittsburgh. It was an inconceivable sum of money to him. What would you do with all that?

But the part that appealed the most, increasingly, to him was the music itself. You got all the records and you got to play them for people, and talk about them, about the recording artists, their life, the music itself. It would be endlessly fascinating and exciting, he thought. It was a job so far removed from those he was familiar with, and those he had done himself, that he could not conceive of how one even went about getting such a job. Obviously, though, you would have to go to college. But what would you study there? As far as Larry knew, there was no major in disc jockeying.

In the spring, he had gone to an R&B show at the Syria Mosque in Pittsburgh, having heard about it on WILY. He went to the first show at 8pm, since he heard there would be a riot at the late show which began at 10:30. He had been seated in the balcony, and sat transfixed as the acts came out, sang, and moved through their routines as they sang. The names of the groups, he wondered how they came up with them – The Penguins, The Del Vikings, The Turbans – he had hoped to hear his most favorite group, the Coasters, there were rumors they would appear (Chasen hinted it) but they were not in the show. Chuck Berry was the main attraction.

All of the groups sang their hit song, and some groups had only one. Often, it did not sound like the record, but Larry put it down to the noise of the crowd, who whooped and yelled almost constantly. He had heard that some kids would pull out switchblades and cut up the auditorium seats, but he did not see any of this during the show he was at. It did happen at the late show, where chairs were hurled into the aisles and fights broke out. The show was stopped, and there were headlines in the paper the next day about "Rock n Roll Show Riot!"

The story in the paper amazed him, for it made a direct link between the "wild rhythm and blues music" and the riot. Larry did not think this was accurate; a few people at the performance had probably come there with the idea of starting trouble, and had been the ones who had done most of the violent things. But the article labeled everyone who was at the show, it seemed. If you liked this kind of music, you were a bad kid. That was the clear implication.

Larry liked the music. He could run off the Top Forty for any given week by memory (when he was a child he had had a photographic memory, which had startled his stepfather). The names of the groups, the recording artists, fascinated him. Then, the songs themselves. In under three minutes, they seemed to combine so much that he was continually amazed. They were a kind of poetry, although the English teacher, Mr. Turner, damned them and said they were not even music. Coach Rossi was even more adamant in his dislike. Once, he found two players stripped down to their jockstraps, gyrating wildly in the gym to an Elvis Presley number, while other players yelled and hooted. To everyone's amazement, he had stepped in, silenced the music, and then gave a short and stern statement to the effect that they did not know what they were doing, and that it was just garbage. Garbage. That was the word he'd used, spitting it out loudly, his face dark

red. He had been "pissed," as the saying had it. Highly
pissed.

He could not have said, if asked, what his favorite,
number one group or singer was at any particular time.
Buddy Holly and the Crickets. The Platters, whose lead
singer's voice sent a shiver up your spine when he hit
the high notes. The Del Vikings, which was a Pittsburgh
group made up of four airmen serving at a base near the
city. Johnny and Joe. The Midnighters, who had a bad
reputation. Bo Diddley. Fats Domino. The Coasters! That
was a group he loved deeply.

About the great god Elvis, nicknamed The Pelvis, he
knew he liked most his early records that a dj in Pittsburgh had unearthed on a label named Sun. These were
recordings made before he had "gone commercial",
as the dj scornfully put it. The way Elvis sang on these
records seemed to span a whole range of emotions – he
had never heard the old Polish beer hall polka song, "Just
Because" sung like Elvis did it. "You laugh, and call me
old Santy Claus/ Well, I'm tellin' you/Baby, I'm through
with you/Just because…" Larry was not an old man, but
he sensed the song was real. Then there was "Blue Moon
of Kentucky." And "Shake Rattle and Roll", a song he had
heard earlier on a record by Big Joe Turner, a black singer,
on WILY. "Get out in that kitchen/and rattle those pots
'n pans/Well, roll my breakfast/Cause I'm a hungry man!"
"You wear them old dresses/The sun comes shinin' thru…"

But his all-time favorite, if he had to pick one – one
he could listen to time after time, and dreamed about

dancing on the gym floor with maybe Cameron Mitchell or Judy Wilson or Cheryl Lake – was "In The Still of the Night" by the Five Satins. He had never seen the Satins and did not know anyone who had. Larry wondered if they were one of those groups who never gave shows but only recorded. There seemed to be more and more of those around.

# 13

He had been daydreaming so much in Problems of Democracy – for that matter, in many of his classes – he could not recall much of Mr. Ferris's discussion. He went to his wall locker in a sort of daze often. What was happening to him? Maybe the football practices were tiring him more than he realized. How could he daydream so intensely, though? Was it normal?

"Smoke a fat one!" cawed a boy named Joe Labrador, banging his wall locker shut loudly. Sometimes kids called out, "Smoke a White Owl!" It was the saying of the year, probably. There was a new one every year, and it got old rapidly so that nobody used it the following year, except a lower grader, trying to be a big deal. That was always humorous. Shoes were the same way. Since he had been in junior high school, there had been a different shoe every year. When he was in the seventh grade, it had been a spade-toed shoe, and this had to be in a color called "oxblood." When he was in the eighth grade, engineer boots had been in, worn with tight Levis, with the legs rolled up to show the seam, fitted over the boots. As a freshman, but only at Ralston it seemed, white bucks came in, especially for juniors and even more so for seniors. These could not be white, though; no, they had to be a dirty white, scuffed, used, stained with grass stains. These were a big shoe in colleges - they were expensive, and he had not owned a pair. This year, the shoe was the blue suede shoe, after the song.

Joe Labrador was getting a lecture – a dressing down – from Mr. Sweeney, the mad science teacher who the kids all called (behind his back) "Dr. Sweeney" or "Frankenstein." Mr. Sweeney always wore the same suit – for most of the year, in fact – until it looked like he had slept in it and everything else in between. Stains of his lunches dotted it, along with small holes – burns from chemicals and acids in the laboratory room. Labrador had been caught by him trying to feel up Norma Sterns, a girl who had very large breasts for her age, as she reached up to take books out of her locker shelf. Norma had slapped and kicked Labrador while he laughed, holding his hands up to his face; the fracas had brought Mr. Sweeney out of his lab, where he reigned.

With a red, chapped face and equally rough-looking red hands, Norma Sterns was a plain-looking girl from a large farm on the Kelsey Pike. No boy would have paid any attention to her, but Norma had the misfortune to have "developed" early. The girls' current dressing trend of close-fitting sweaters accentuated her large breasts; it was hard not to stare, wondering what they looked like unconfined. Norma's heavy breasts stretched out her sweaters so tautly you were drawn almost magnetically to try and put your hands on her. Norma was alternatively embarrassed, walking slightly hunched over, or with her books held in front of her, or she would throw her head back, square up her strong shoulders, and in this mode, defiantly push her breasts forward, like cannons. The sight of Norma coming down a hallway like this was remarkable. Even other girls looked. Boys grinned, nudging each other; some made cupping motions with their hands at their own chests, pursing their lips. Joe Labrador would clutch himself, and stop.

"Hey, Norma! Ooeee! You gotta real set there. How about a squeeze? Gimme me a break!"

At Labrador's jibe, Norma Sterns' already red face would turn an alarmingly darker red and her mouth would tighten to a thin, pinched whitened line. Clenching and unclenching her strong hands, she looked like she was ready to slug Joe, to physically fight him right there, to pound the living shit out of him.

Labrador would then hold his hands up, palms outward.

"Hey, hey! No offense. Just kiddin'…"

Norma looked like she could take Joe, that was the thing. There had been discussion of that a couple of times in the locker room, where players generally said they thought Labrador would come off badly.

"She's liable to rip his nuts off, you ask me," Harry Gibb said. He rarely offered this sort of opinion, so everybody listened. "Serve the asshole right, too."

"He's a jerk," nodded Dick Atkins. "Guys like him end up pumping gas for the rest of their lives. If they're lucky, that is…"

"Pumpin' his bone, you mean," Berton Jones, the big tackle said, making the well-know motion. The locker room erupted in laughter and hooting.

Joe Labrador was disciplined by not being allowed to go to the Pep Rally that Friday. It was a warm September day, but the players still wore their letter sweaters over clean white tee-shirts. None of them wore the tee-shirts with the short sleeves rolled up, however, with a pack of Luckies or Camels in one sleeve, as Joe did. To smoke was forbidden. Coach Rossi included his lectures and cautionary warnings about smoking in with his talks about masturbation, which he referred to distastefully. "If you're a masturbator, you'll never accomplish anything in life. I assure you," he said, nodding. "Nothing saps your strength, your will, more than that." He looked slowly and evenly around the locker room. Some players hung their heads, obvious admissions of guilt. Others looked away, to the sides of the room, or up at the ceiling. Some blushed beet-red, and chewed their lips. The coach nodded again, noting this. "Remember what I say. Save it for the next game."

Pep rallies always took place on Friday afternoons, after the home room period, and the following two academic periods, 7th and 8th. This last period of the day, the 8th period, was in fact given over to the Pep Rally, and this was one of the reasons for its great popularity. It was a Ralston tradition, and the principal probably could not have done away with it if he had wanted to. The entire student body filed into the auditorium, where the Pep Band was already playing.

Always, the rallies followed a set, expected pattern that never altered. The big moment was the beginning of the rally, when the student body president, Charlie Hibbing, would bound out onto the stage and grab the microphone, grinning and waving. The assembled students, roaring, began rhythmically jumping up and down so hard the auditorium floor shook, quivered, like it was alive. He would gesture with his hands, getting them to increase the roaring noise - a cheer known as "The Ralston Roar", which he had in fact invented the year before. It, too, was rapidly becoming a Ralston tradition, for Charlie Hibbing would go out in front of the crowd at games and lead this roar, with the assistance of the cheerleaders, urging on the crowd, screaming themselves red-faced. The "Roar" was noted by several sports writers in their columns. They commented on the loudness of the Ralston fans, how their enthusiastic support had to be like "an extra player or two". Some hinted it was unfair, unsportsmanlike.

Larry knew how the rally would begin, he knew most of what would happen, but his heart was still hammering as he sat down at the end of an aisle in the sophomore section, with his home room. Hibbing, full of an inexhaustible manic energy, immediately ran out onto the stage, the great, swelling roar went up, and then the Ralston cheerleaders were right on his heels. Eight of them, wearing dark blue skirts and dazzlingly white sweater tops, with blue and white beanie caps. The two cheerleaders who anchored the line of eight – they were the tallest girls – were identical twins, Linda and Lucy Wood. Many jokes were made about their names.

Donna Charles, the head cheerleader, the Captain, was the smallest in height, and the other girls radiated out from her, to the Wood twins, the tallest, at either end. Larry often saw them practicing in the gym, and on the sidelines of the field. They were very athletic, and put in hours of extra time under the leadership of the girls' gym coach, Miss Lassiter. She had been a cheerleader herself at Penn State, and that was a very big deal. There was a framed photograph in her office in the gym, directly behind her desk, of her in her Penn State cheerleading uniform. She was young, still in her twenties, and still looked exactly like a cheerleader. She was a great favorite of the cheerleaders, who followed and clustered around her everywhere she went in the school.

Charlie Hibbing hushed the crowd with his hand held up. "Hey! Whatta we gonna do to Glassboro?" he yelled loudly into the microphone.

"Smash 'em!" yelled the students, and some immediately began fiercely smacking their fists into their palms. But that was discouraged; several teachers walked the aisles, looked sternly at offenders, wagging their fingers at them, pointing.

A series of loud, banging noises erupted from the rear of the auditorium, and a line of small red childrens' wagons came rolling down the two main aisles. Seated in them were members of the starting eleven - Harry Gibb, Berton Jones, Dago Paretti, Robert Henderson - and the great Dick Atkins himself, the quarterback. They reached the foot of the stage, jumped out of the wagons, and ran up onto the stage to take the cheers of the crowd. The wagons were brought up and set in front of them; they had paper banners on them, reading "We're Gonna Fix Glassboro's Wagon".

Larry wondered who had thought up the stunt. The sight of the large players, especially the linemen, in the small wagons was comical. Pushing the wagons were other players, which also looked comical. The front row, right below the stage, was filled with senior class boys, many of whom had made large paper cones out of notebook paper, which they now used as megaphones, making hooting and whooping noises, loudly slapping their legs. They were nearly out of control, but Coach Kowalski came down one aisle, behind the wagons, and stood near the aisle, so they did not go too far. Several of the boys took the opportunity to yell comments at the cheerleaders, who looked down at them with mixed responses. The Wood twins smiled broadly - they were always good sports.

Charlie Hibbing pointed dramatically down into the orchestra pit, and the Pep Band struck up the Notre Dame Fight Song. The cheerleaders accompanied this with a series of punching motions of their hands, standing straddle-legged, as they all faced one way, and then quickly the other, and then forward, and then towards the rear of the stage, and then back again. They kept perfect time, in an amazing synchronized unison. Larry wondered how long they had had to rehearse to do this. However long that was, this routine was always impressive.

The players stood ill-at-ease, their hands clasped in front of them, looking occasionally at each other. Dick Atkins looked comfortable, though, even relaxed, as he watched the cheerleaders' routine. He would probably not have to play the whole game that night, Larry thought, so the second string quarterback, Carl Bozeman, was probably the one who was really nervous. Rumor was that even Chad Lewis would get a serious chance to play, getting good time towards a letter, for any time played in a varsity game counted.

The loud playing of the Pep Band made a chill run down your back, there was no question. You couldn't help but get worked up. Frankie Malone had made a cone megaphone of his own and was shouting into it, but Larry could not make out anything, the noise in the auditorium was so loud. Pacing the stage like a cat, Hibbing was now in his element, totally in control. Even the coaches deferred to him at pep rallies. The past year they had awarded him a special letter, with a unique lightening bolt monogram, for his work leading the pep rallies. Coach Rossi himself had made the presentation; it had surprised everyone. No one had ever been awarded such a special letter. Hibbing himself - for once - had been momentarily unable to speak.

Once again, the student body president held up his hand. Almost immediately the students quieted down. "You'd never see a teacher be able to do that," Jimmy Washburn, sitting behind him, whispered.

"Okay! Okay! I see you're getting into the mood for this game. We're gonna go out there tonight, support our team! And now, here's someone you all know. And respect. The head coach of the Ralston Raiders, Coach Rossi!"

The band crashed into the Fight Song again as the head coach entered from the wings, smiling and nodding. Without his ever-present baseball cap, he was noticeably bald, but his face and balding head were deeply tanned. The hours on the practice field, Larry thought. The Fight Song died down, and Coach Rossi looked out at them seriously.

"This is the first game of this new season. Against Glassboro, our old rivals. I don't take them lightly. No." He shook his head, looking slowly around the auditorium, which had grown completely quiet, like a church. "No. When you do that, you often lose. You get surprised. Especially in the first game of the season, which may be the most important game of the season…"

He had a small piece of paper in one hand, Larry noticed. Notes for his talk.

"What I wanted to say, today, though, is that this is the last year, the last season, for some of the boys you see in front of you here today. I don't have to tell you who they are; you know them well. Some have played varsity now for four years. Four years."

This was an obvious tribute to Harry Gibb, who looked out over the audience towards the balcony, and swallowed. He shifted his hands, clasped them behind him. Taking a deep breath, he rolled his powerful, thick neck, as if loosening up for a game.

"Go, Harry! Kill 'em!" someone yelled from the back of the auditorium. The coach held up his hand; Gibb looked down at the floor in front of him intently.

"This has been a very special group, this team. We are close. Very close. And I know you are close to them, too. I just wanted you to be aware, be aware of how special this game, and this season, the whole season, is for us. For me, for the other coaches - and for them. They represent you on that field. Don't forget that. Yes." He nodded.

"But you never do. Your support is a big part of this whole team's success. Don't think we don't hear you out there. Any of the players can tell you, and will tell you - just ask them."

Larry wondered if this was really true. It was always said. But even in his limited playing experience, he felt what you could hear were the sounds of the players around you. These were loud, and often violent. How would you hear what the crowd was yelling? But as soon as he thought it, he felt guilty. Coach Rossi no doubt knew the truth.

Now Rossi was gesturing to the wings, and the principal – a tall, gangly man whose suits never seemed to fit him – came forward. This was Mr. Abrams. He wore odd wire-rimmed spectacles, which Larry connected with people from another era. His hair style, with his bushy hair parted near the middle, was also old-fashioned looking. But the most obvious thing about the principal was his very prominent Adam's apple, which rode strenuously up and down as he talked. His neck was extraordinarily long, his shirt collar fitted it unevenly, and the whole sight was unforgettable, one the students talked endlessly about. Larry wondered if anyone had ever talked to Mr. Abrams about his Adam's apple, but it was not likely. He was a stern, severe, humorless man, a disciplinarian, well-thought of, as the phrase had it, but not liked. His nickname among the students was Ichabod Crane.

As the gangly principal reached the microphone, a loud "Boo!" was heard from the balcony. Some students audibly gasped, for to boo Mr. Abrams was unimaginable. Who had done this? But the principal went on as if he did not notice.

"I want to commend Coach Rossi and the fine young men making up our team here today, as we start this season. I am sure – I am certain – that this will be another season to remember. Whatever the record at the end, on the field and off, I know we will always do what will make ourselves, and others, proud of Ralston High School." He stopped, and peered owlishly out at the auditorium, which was now again absolutely quiet. Pushing his glasses up on his nose, he continued. The stagelights reflecting in his glasses made him look even odder than normally, Larry thought. What a strange man he was. It was as if he did not have any blood in his gaunt body. Bloodless.

"…football is certainly emblematic of larger American values, like the good struggle, the good fight. It teaches the players, and us, the meaning of teamwork, the values of cooperation and friendship, even on the gridiron."

"The gridiron," Jimmy Washburn muttered behind in disgust. Coach Kowalski looked around sharply, frowning; he had heard.

Although Mr. Abrams had not been talking very long, it was already noticeable in the auditorium, there was a feeling in the very air, that he should stop and leave. He was not really part of football, the team, school spirit, all of that. There was a compulsion about having to listen to him felt by all. He nodded at the microphone, seeming to pick up on this.

"I know that this is your time - the Pep Rally is an honored Ralston tradition. So, without any further ado, let me turn this back over to your student body president, Charlie Hibbing."

Mr. Abrams turned and walked off the stage, while Charlie Hibbing simultaneously ran on from the other side. The two did not like each other; Hibbing had incurred the principal's considerable wrath - he had threatened to strip Hibbing of his office - when he had played a Little Richard record over the school public address system one morning. Hibbing grinned broadly at the mike, knowing everyone was aware of this.

"Thank you, Mr. Abrams. Yes sir! Has Ralston got a good principal, or what?" he asked, leaning into the mike so that the last words boomed out with a rasping hiss.

"YES!" roared the students back at him, pumping arms in the air, releasing the tension they all felt. "YES!"

"Go team!" he yelled. "Go Raiders!"

Pointing again suddenly into the orchestra pit, Hibbing jumped directly up into the air, seemingly possessed. The Pep Band crashed into "On Wisconsin!", playing at a frenzied tempo, the cheerleaders ran onto the stage, jumping and flipping all over the place. Larry wondered that Hibbing was not felled by one of their flying bodies arcing through the air. Pandemonium ruled. Everyone was standing, and he could feel the floor underneath him reverberating again.

"Smash the Glassers!" somebody yelled in a side section nearby, but this was lost in the general tumult of the band now marching onto the stage, getting ready to lead them all out of the auditorium. They would snake up through the aisle and out through the front hall, into the street, and then back down the side of the school, playing all the time. Meanwhile, the excited students would try to file in some orderly fashion back into their rooms and retrieve their books and other materials, before leaving the school. Already the big yellow school buses were lined up outside; Larry could see them out there through the opened big back wing doors of the downstairs floor of the auditorium.

There was a glow, a tingling all over his body, and he took several deep breaths. Everyone around him was flushed faced, he could smell the sharp tinge of sweat and odors of perfumes the girls wore. He made out Sandy Stevens' hair bobbing in a group of students moving up the aisle on the left side, and as he looked, she looked directly at him, and smiled. He felt dazed, and felt wonderful; she had smiled at him, and he was absolutely certain, it was a very special smile.

The Pep Band was now directly by their row, with Zeb Lewis, a saxophone player, cavorting and honking wildly. Zebulon. That was his full name, Larry recalled, looking at him going on, the horn honking and shrieking as he pulled it back and forth and then up and down. He had a very short crew cut on top, but had a classic DA, a duck's ass, pulled and slicked back on the sides. That was a hair style that had already started to "go out". Zebulon Lewis. A name from the Bible, his mother had said. He loved to play his sax, and lived for it, he said, spending an inordinate amount of time down in the crescent-moon shaped music room. You could often hear Zeb honking away down there, the saxophone sound floating out and down the long corridor.

Larry suddenly felt he was a very lucky person, going to a school that had such a band, such people as Zeb, and Sandy Stevens, and of course their great team. Even Charlie Hibbing. Although he realized, as he began to file out towards the big double exit doors, feeling the cooler air coming from outside, where a couple of maples were already showing some red tinted leaves, that he wondered about a guy like Charlie.

# 14

He was thinking a lot about his brother Carl. In the early autumn, as it was now, his brother, had he been home - and when had he not been home, before? - would have been preparing for the long hunting season that lay ahead, stretching all the way into the first two weeks of December, when deer season would come in and all of the state of Pennsylvania would become a hunting ground. At that time, there were some farmers who even painted their cows to try and prevent them from being shot by crazed, often drunken, hunters.

But his brother Carl was not a drunk, and would never have shot a cow, mistaking it for a deer. That was unimaginable, even comic, to think about. His brother was an expert hunter, who had even hunted with the bow. He brought home rabbits, grouse, pheasant, and sometimes a fat groundhog, shot with a .22 in the head so as not to ruin any of the meat, or some squirrels, taken the same way. In October, he would hunt wild turkey, perhaps the most difficult of game to actually take. Larry had eaten a lot of wild game, even possum, which his mother made into a tasty, strong stew (as she did with the squirrel, and sometimes with the rabbits).

Rabbit was good fried, too, like chicken, or roasted. But he found that he felt sorry for the creatures. His brother maintained shooting them - the rabbits were taken with a small-gauge shotgun - was the only way to effectively keep their population down, in control. Otherwise, they would ravage gardens and farms - everyone knew the phrase about how they bred.

The dead rabbits had beautiful pelts of fur. Indeed, many of the animals (and the birds) were extraordinarily beautiful in their colorations, the patterns of their markings, the blending of all this together, like an individual painting. The ring-necked pheasants' plumage was the most spectacular and vivid. But his brother did not get many of these. You needed a good dog, and the weather often seemed to set in against bird-hunting. Carl talked about how wealthy people would dine on pheasant in fine restaurants in the city and pay handsomely for it.

"Pheasant under glass. That's what they call it."

Larry pictured the roasted bird, sitting under a glass bell, being brought to a white tablecloth-covered table, with well-dressed people seated around it. Why the glass, though? That seemed odd; he could make no real sense of that. But it was simply the way it was done, and if you could pay to eat in such places, you would know the reason. When they had pheasant, his mother simply served it on a large, white dish, a platter, the same one she put the Thanksgiving and Christmas turkeys on.

His brother had never hunted duck or geese for some reason. He was not sure why. In the fall, the big Canada geese could be seen in the river; they were on their migrations. Some would stay there, in the river, the entire winter, however. They would clamber up onto the banks awkwardly, waddling at times even up onto the roadway. People fed them stale bread and other table scraps. Probably that was one of the main reasons they stayed there. The geese were large birds. It would take a blast to bring them down, Larry thought.

He had helped his brother skin out animals down in the dank basement under the house, or outside on a small wooden table Carl would set up under the old apple tree. He would also hang his deer on this same tree, in December, his buck (he never hunted doe). It would hang there and freeze thoroughly before they butchered it out. Venison was one of the best meats he had tasted, especially the steaks. Again, his brother called attention to the fact that they were eating meat which rich people paid a fortune for, in the big cities where they lived.

He had often gone out and looked closely at the hanging deer. Stiff and very hard to the touch, hung from a stained piece of rope, the deer had also filled him with a sadness. He had often spoken to the dead animal, although he never told anyone of this. He would pat it, and nod.

He had been taken deer hunting when he was twelve years old. This was a ritual in Pennsylvania which almost every boy he knew had gone through, and all the men he knew had long since experienced. Getting your first buck, it was called. The men spoke of "buck fever" – a possession, a shaking, even, a lusting after getting a deer that took you over completely. After a young boy killed his first buck, one of the older men would daub his forehead and cheeks with the deer's blood. He had been "blooded". It was said to be an old Indian rite.

They had gone to a camp his stepfather owned in northern Pennsylvania, near Clarion. The closest town of any size at all was about five miles from the camp and had the odd name of Leeper, which he never forgot. Leeper was really just a crossroads, with a post office/general store, and a garage/gas station, and three or four ramshackle houses, set back in the woods. Larry felt sure he would not like to live in Leeper. The people there seemed of another breed; shaggy and oddly dressed, they often had badly decayed teeth which they displayed when they laughed, and they drank a lot. The women were uniformly large, heavy-bodied women, who could often outshoot and outfish their husbands, or so it was boasted. They were suspicious of anyone who came from "the city", and if a person, for instance, was said to live in Pittsburgh, they seemed certain this person was up to no good. On the other hand, they often made fun of the lack of knowledge of their ways, the ways of the country and the woods, that the city-dweller showed. But Larry wondered how they, in turn, would fare in Pittsburgh, say. How would they make out in the noisy, bustling streets of the city?

He remembered his first deer hunt well. Although he was supposed to be eager for the event, he had not been, and had had to feign he was excited about it. In fact, he felt extremely ill at ease, and this – that his feelings were different from what he knew was expected – made him feel guilty. He was, in some way he did not understand, letting the other men down. This was clear to him, and painful, for he was certain they knew. He would not be able to hide his true feelings. He would not pass the test.

It turned very cold once they had reached his stepfather's camp. It was little more than an unfinished house frame, covered with basic insulation, set up on a cinder-block cellar. Inside, the wood floors were also unfinished, but his stepfather had already had a large fireplace built by a local stonemason, Lew Welsh, who was a particular favorite of his stepfather's. Lew lived with his wife, Wanda, in a run-down old farmhouse about a half-mile away, and so the Welshes were the closest neighbors. On the other side of his stepfather's property stretched Cook's Forest, a large expanse of state forest land, unsettled. This was prime deer-hunting territory.

The big thick forest always filled Larry with a confused mixture of wonder, anxiety, fear. When he had been eight, he had been lost in Cook's Forest with two other children younger than he was, for most of a long summer day. At first, the children had reveled in just exploring the deep, quiet, forest, going deeper and deeper into it without realizing what they were doing. But by early evening, hungry for supper, tired with their wild play, and scratched and bruised and thirsty - above all, thirsty - from the trek, they had begun to realize they did not know which direction to go in order to get back out.

What Larry remembered most was how dark it had been in the forest, even at mid-day, and how cool. As the night approached and the sun went down, it was already cold in the forest, and the smallest child had begun to cry, saying he was cold and wanted his mother. The other child was a girl – Patricia, Larry remembered. She was the daughter of a man who worked in a coal tipple - a strip mine; there were a number in the area. She had seven brothers and sisters. Her family was larger than most Larry knew in Ralston, except for the "dago" families in the Lower End of the town, who, since they were Catholics, had large families. His stepfather's family had had twelve children in it.

But Patricia and her family were not Catholics, and they lived in a squalor Larry had not seen even down by the creek in the Lower End of Ralston. They used a dilapidated outhouse – "three-holer", one of Patricia's brother's crowed, showing it to Larry – and the front yard of their ramshackle shingled house was covered with the strewn-about parts of cars and trucks, which Patricia's father worked on in his spare time. In fact, most of the time Larry had been at their house, the father, Lymon, had been working out in the yard, his dark, hairy, thick arms smeared in grease and motor oil. He smelled of gasoline so strongly that Larry wondered if he would ignite if someone threw a match near him. Yet he always had an unlit black cigar in his mouth; he never smoked the cigar, but chewed on it. Occasionally, Lymon chewed tobacco – Red Man was his favorite – and this was another feature of the house Larry noted, the brass spittoons that were in several rooms with Lymon's baccy juice in their bottoms. "Good for what ails ya," he would say, rolling his "chaw" around in his mouth and then shooting an amazingly accurate stream of shiny, dark brown juice into one of these spittoons. He was unerringly accurate, but sometimes the juice splashed up and out, onto the floor. Lymon took no notice of this.

It was Patricia who comforted the younger child (her little brother Fred), and told Larry that if they walked in the direction of the setting sun, she was sure they would come out of the forest eventually. He wondered if they should try to make some sort of camp in the forest for the night and try again by daylight, but he agreed with her and they had continued their hike, tired and frightened and very hungry. And, just as the sun was setting, with long, golden rays coming through the forest, they had suddenly emerged at the edge of a corn field, where there was a paved road. They knew they had made it, and began to troop in a straggledy line down that road, when a pick-up truck had screeched to a stop in front of them. It was a group of men, including Lew Welsh and Lymon, who had been out looking for them since six that evening, when they had not appeared for supper. It was quite a relief and the children returned home in the truck.

Lymon himself was in camp when they got there. He had brought a five-gallon jug of the home brew the men insisted on drinking in camp. Larry had not been in the camp more than a couple of hours when he began to wonder if the drinking was not the real reason most of the men were there. Faces flushed, eyes glistening, they seemed excited like children almost; they were very different from the way he normally encountered them, going to work, coming home tired from work, or walking slowly through the market behind their wives.

Almost immediately, he had been taken outside and the Remington .33 Special rifle he was to use in the next day's hunt was placed in his hands. Lew Welsh, who had been a sharpshooter in the Army, instructed him on handling the gun, loading it, and sighting it. Then he had pointed to a large, white, round paper plate he had put on the trunk of a large tree, about 100 yards away. Just about the length of a football field, Larry had thought.

Then he fired the rifle. It was the first time he had fired a gun. He recalled all the stories he had listened to, men who spoke of bruised shoulders, the kick of a recoiling shotgun, a woman knocked on her ass, and everyone laughing. He fired standing, leaning into the rifle, the butt snug into his shoulder, breathing in deeply several times to steady himself before he slowly (Welsh had said, surprising him, "like you're squeezin' a girl's tit") pulled the trigger.

But it was not the recoil, it was the sound. The sound, he knew instantly, as it cracked out across the long field towards the tree, the white plate, the forest beyond, was serious. The rifles themselves were serious business. They were one of the few things in the camp, in the whole area, Leeper included, that could be called beautiful, in Larry's estimation. They were beautiful to the hunters, who handled them and stroked them like a prized dog. There was endless cleaning of them in camp; Larry was assured many times he would learn this art fully "in the service". Yet another virtue a young boy would pick up in the military. All the men in camp had been in the various branches of the military, and joshed each other over these branches' relative hardness endlessly. They talked of guns they had fired; the qualifying marksmanship requirements with the rifle, the completely different requirements of firing a pistol with any degree of accuracy. The rifles the men favored were as varied as they were: .275, .280 Winchesters, the big .300 Savage ("too big a goddamn cannon fer huntin' deer, you ask me"), the .30-30, which Larry gathered was the caliber rifle used in the military, was probably the favored rifle, the most commonly seen. So it was unusual that he was being broken in with a Remington .33 Special which Lew Welsh said was a somewhat rare rifle, but a very good one, especially for deer.

"Nice rifle. Don't see many of them…handles nice, not too heavy. Gettin' a little hard to get ammunition fer it, though."

His stepfather was hunting this season with a .32. What was the difference, Larry wondered? But nobody talked about this. Instead, they ragged on old man Fitz, a toothless, shrunken-mouthed man who preferred to hunt with a shotgun, a .12-gauge.

"You lookin' for bear with that thing, Fitz", Lymon joked. He was sitting by the big fireplace cleaning his own rifle, a .30-30.

The old man nodded knowingly. "Thas' right. You never know what ya might encounter out there." He pointed out towards Cooks Forest. "I like it. Yessir. Suits me, and always has. Always will."

Early the next morning they set out, when it was barely light. It was so cold Larry did not think he would be able to go far. But there was no wind, which everyone said was a blessing. It was 15 below zero, with an absolutely clear sky; the day before a few inches of fresh snow had fallen.

"Perfect," Lymon had said, looking out the window by the fireplace. He was drinking a large, metal cup of coffee, into which Larry had seen him pour a good belt of the home brew. "Mebbe you'll get you one today."

They had tramped through a patch of forest looking for tracks and sign, and come upon what looked like a bloody pouch, hanging from a small tree's lower limb. The men in the party grinned, and nodded their heads; one tried to move it from the limb.

"Frozen solid," he said. "Here. Take a look at it."

The pouch turned out to be the testicles and penis of a male deer. A buck. After the kill, the hunter had done this as a mark, a sign. It was done often, apparently.

Later that morning, with the sun a weak, pale disc in the hard white-grey sky, he had stood waiting by the side of an open cut through the forest where the big power lines ran. Deer crossed this space, and would be in the open doing so, so he had been instructed to take up a stand, as it was called, and wait. Others moved through the forest, driving the deer in front of them, moving them towards crossing this space. Larry wondered if this was really a good idea - wouldn't it stand to reason that someone might get shot? One of those driving the deer? But he had been assured that the deer moved far in front of the men coming through the woods, and that this would never happen. Still, he found it made him uneasy. And what if one of the men fired at a deer driven out, from that direction? No one had spoken of that… they had sat around the fire in the fireplace the night before, drinking and telling stories of hunting, and of famous hunters - "Old man Washinski, remember that ole sunavabitch? Jesus! Now there was a hunter! Used to spot deer in the summer, back there on his place? Always had venison out there."

He had met old man Washinski at Lew's, when he was younger, and remembered a man with no front teeth who spat streams of dark baccy juice into a brass spittoon, which he also said he pissed in if the feeling took him. He had seemed like a person from another time or era – another century, even – and Larry had felt he would never be able to really communicate with him. Old man Washinski had said that he, Larry, would never live past thirty, "cause the boy's too smart. They never live long, the smart ones like that…" That was his observation, rendered with a healthy gob of juice splatting this time into the red belly of the kitchen stove, which he opened to spit into.

What did he mean, Larry had wondered? The gap where his front teeth were missing looked like a black cave when he grinned.

Finally, near noon of that first day - the First Day, it was known as, in fact - he saw a deer. Nothing had come from the stand, and he resumed walking back towards the camp with two other men. Coming over a small hill, he saw a gray motion to the side; at the same time, one of the men swung his rifle up so quickly Larry was startled. Looking towards where the rifle pointed, he saw then several deer, about fifty yards away, just near the dark, grayish line of the forest. Puzzlingly, they stopped, and looked around them.

"You take that one," one of the men had said to him, pointing. Larry had looked again, and seen, so clearly he felt like his eyes were focused like binoculars, that one of the deer was a buck, the horns visible as he moved his head slightly. He seemed a part of the landscape when he did not move, and Larry marveled at his ability to stand that still. Then, before he knew it, the two deer disappeared into the forest, and he was deafened by the crack of the man's rifle next to him. Larry had not even brought his rifle up.

Not much was said back at the camp; the man who had fired had not hit either of the deer, and they walked back the rest of the way into the camp, the only sounds being the crunching of their boots in the frozen snow. No one had gotten a deer that first morning, although one man was certain he'd hit one, but the deer had eluded him, he said, even though he'd followed a trail of blood for a good distance.

"Mebbe somebody else got him," one of the hunters said.

"Yeah. Probably so…"

After they had eaten supper that evening, his step-father had asked him if he wanted to return to Ralston, and Larry had said he did. There was no question at all in his mind, and he felt a strong sense of relief. He could see, in his mind's eye, the very first sight of the deer when they had come, unexpectedly, over the rise of that hill, and there they had been, standing, alert, amazing, in the field near the forest line. That image repeated itself during the drive back down the next day, when they passed cars with dead deer tied on the front, over the hood of the car, or on the back of trucks. Some were parked outside taverns, where beer signs winked off and on in the window, along with Christmas light decorations.

Carl had not said anything at all about Larry's hunting experience, although he had remarked, as they had looked out over the backyard of the house in Ralston, towards the next yard, where a deer hung from an apple tree, "Mebbe you're more of a fisherman, you know? That's the way it is a lot of times…"

# 15

It was Game Night. It was possible to believe the whole year led to this night. A definite, clear crispness in the air; a damp, unmistakable, sharper chill. That meant Fall. The crushed grass on the big field gave off a rich and particular smell; it had many associations, going back as far as he could remember. The big river, like the leaves, was changing colors, and seemed to move slower, as if it were heavier. In the autumn coming on fast now, the falling leaves of the huge elms and the sycamores and maples would mix in a pungent, cool scent, as much autumn as their smoky burning piles, later in October. He could remember jumping frenziedly into these piles before they were burnt; it was like doing a cannonball into the creek in summer. The town was composed of smells varying with the distinct seasons, the trees, the winds, their directions. In a late spring night wind off the Allegheny you could smell the catfish, the pike, even the huge muskellunge his brother Carl had hooked once, and then lost, after an epic battle he never tired of telling and Larry never tired of hearing.

By seven thirty, the crowds, with that curious, murmuring crowd sound, were beginning to file through the main gate and spread out over the field. They were careful not to walk, though, on the field itself, sitting quiet, green and white-striped, resplendent under the bright lights. The town, and the school, were justly proud of these lights. With quadruple banks, the metal light towers stood nearly one hundred feet high, and there were twelve of them ringing the field. When he had been a small kid, he had watched older boys climb up these towers, some to a very high level. It had made him dizzy, given him a crick in his neck. You could see their glow far out in the dirt back country roads – some said it looked like a place where a UFO had landed. In the summer, the big lights made it possible for a semi-pro baseball team, the Falcons, to play a full season of night games on the adjacent baseball field. Money from the gates of the Falcon games aided in maintaining the big football field, and those mighty lights. No other school in the Valley had such powerful lights.

For as long as he could remember, Larry had been mesmerized and excited by them. The fact that they were on meant that a game, an important game, was being played – all games were important, that was what he had early on come to realize. The town found its very soul – hadn't the minister, Rev. Forbes, said so in a sermon? – in coming together and rooting for its teams. Even more than in its churches, the real congregation worshiped at the field.

It was called Morris Field, after a WWII hero, born on a farm just outside the town. He had won a Silver Star, and been killed at Anzio Beach in Italy. It seemed a very long way away to Larry. He had looked up Anzio in the encyclopedia and read the account of the terrible battle that took place there, with the American troops pinned down on the beach by withering German fire. How had Sergeant Morris died, he wondered? It was not clear from the inscription on the dedicatory plaque, set in a large, dark, polished marble stone outside the Main Gate.

He also wondered if Morris had played football before he went to war. In the school library he went through the yearbooks for the early 1940s, and in the 1942 yearbook he found him. He had played end – number 82 on his jersey; the yearbook photo showed a slim, wiry, grinning young man with copious dark hair, making as if he had just hauled in a long pass. He was looking up in the air, although the ball was already securely in his outstretched hands. Had he ever caught such a pass, a long bomb as they called them, running full tilt down the field, stretched to the limit with a defensive back, probably the Safety, just a few steps off his heels and the sound of the crowd's roar encouraging him? Watching the dark ball spiral down from its incredible height, out of the lights' glare (what sort of lights would they have had then? Maybe it would have been a day game, on an October afternoon, Indian summer warmth), coming at just the right trajectory for him to catch it without breaking stride, floating amazingly into his hands with almost a soft fall – the quarterback had been stretched to his limit to throw one that far...

His mother remembered Charley Morris quite well, when he asked her about him.

"He was a nice boy," she said, folding the laundry carefully. How often had he talked to her like this, with her folding, always very carefully but automatically, whatever it was she had just ironed. For everything got ironed, even wash clothes and towels. His tee-shirts were meticulously ironed and folded, and reposed in his drawer in a degree of calm neatness that sometimes made him stop in his tracks, looking down at their incredible whiteness there in the dark wooden drawer.

"He was killed at Anzio... there were some other boys from that group killed there, too. Harlan Woods, and Paul Phillips, I think...one of them was a paratrooper. No – that was Dominick Cerna – they always called him Dom. He was killed in Normandy...later, it was, in the war." She had looked out the small window which faced down towards the creek. "They were all nice boys."

Ralston players who had become famous were sometimes seen at Morris Field, revisiting. Larry had been told about Lon Brueder, a huge offensive tackle who weighed 230 pounds his senior year. Brueder went to Maryland – the Terrapins, an odd team name – and became a first team All American his senior year there. Larry had stared, fascinated, at his photograph, which showed him down in his lineman's stance, in the Pittsburgh Sun-Gazette. "Brueder First Team All-American!" it had trumpeted in headlines on the Sports front page.

When he came to visit his parents, who lived on a small, secluded farm some miles from Ralston, Lon Brueder was invariably seen "down at the field," meaning Morris Field. And Larry had seen him, once. He had walked, slowly, along one sideline, and then stood still, looking for a long time out over the empty field. Then he had turned and climbed up into the green, tiered bleacher seats and sat there, hunched forward, looking out over the field. What was he thinking? Larry had wondered.

On another occasion, two former players, one an end, the other a halfback, were found late at night, running out in the middle of the darkened field itself. "Barenekkid" Stroup had taken them into custody and then taken them to their families' houses. It was said at the barbershop that they "had had a few..." But the halfback – whose jersey was "retired" in the famous Ralston trophy case – was achieving prominence at the University of North Carolina – the Tarheels – and they were not charged.

The retired jerseys of great Ralston players were one of the prominent features of Morris Field. During the football season, they resided in a heavy display case, known as The Trophy Case, which was laboriously taken down onto the field, near the Front Gate, and then back up to the gym, for all home games. Once retired, at a special ceremony held on the field at the beginning of the season, numbers were never re-issued to players on subsequent squads. Lon Brueder's jersey, 77, was in this case, along with eight others. A small, select group. Some said Harry Gibb, the four-letter man, would receive this honor

– that his jersey, 50, would be retired, but no one could say for sure. Larry was not even certain how the honor was actually voted on, or decided. Gibb was a lineman, and they were not so honored very often, in any case. Lon Brueder had been an offensive tackle, never scored a point in a game, yet had been selected. The other seven honorees were all backfield players, except for one end, Richard Pepi, number 43. His jersey had only been retired three years previously.

"Hound Dog" was blaring from the field's big PA system. You could hear it up in the middle of town, at Fifth and Market, it was so loud. Some citizens complained, but they were definitely in the minority. Charlie Hibbing was manning the PA booth, along with his trusted "spotter," Paul Lewis. Lewis would tell him the names of those who carried the ball on a play, made the tackle, caught the pass, and so on, in case Charlie did not see it clearly or did not know. The two formed an oddly effective team, since they had very different personalities. Charlie chose the music for the evening, and for every evening, and had even effectively overridden vetoes of the principal. "Nobody messes with him!" Frankie cawed, slapping his legs delightedly. He loved to hear of "the system" being subverted, in any way, shape, or form.

The collection of people streaming up into the bleachers, on both sides of the field, amazed him. Who were they? There were old men with peaked hunting caps on, men who had come to every Ralston home game for longer than he had been alive. He would hear them talk up at the barbershop, or in one of the old grocery stores that had a fading Salada Tea sign painted on its peeling wooden side. They had survived – work had not killed them – and they were fierce, intense, even scary, he thought. Maybe Barnes, the coach, would become like one of them in his old age. They all had uniformly bad, stained teeth, most chewed tobacco continually, spitting out the long, dark streams in a way that reminded him of somebody pissing, the famous pissing contests of young men.

There were rich people, too, well-dressed, with scarves even this early in the year, the men smelling of some expensive aftershave, their wives carefully made-up, wearing skirts and nylons, their hair "done", as his mother called it. Ministers of local churches were there, even the priest from the big Roman Catholic church up on Market Street, Father del Rosso, a florid-faced man, whose red cheeks seemed to burn; his eyes were always watery, and one "wandered", as they called it. He also had a "wall-eye", one eye where the pupil was off to the side, which made it distracting to talk to him and not stare at it. It made you nervous the whole time you talked to him.

Then there were the students from the two opposing schools. The visiting team was always accompanied by four or five buses, in addition to the players' bus; these formed a motorcade, the buses decorated with flags and school colors. At Morris Field they had high, nice bleachers to sit in, facing the school itself, across the field and up behind the near end of the field. Most of these bleachers would be filled before the game began at 8pm. The two opposing sides would roar cheers at each other during the evening, as the game progressed; you could easily tell how the game was going by this sound volume, or lack of it.

As kick-off neared, everyone was waiting for the appearance of the two rival teams. The Glassers' band and cheerleaders had formed up on the far side of the field, Larry saw, and at about 7:40 the team itself came sprinting down the big wooden stairs to the field. The Glasser band struck up their school song, and the majorettes formed a long arc-like tunnel through which the Glasser players ran onto the playing field itself, while the visiting side of the field cheered, and isolated hoots and catcalls and an occasional "Boo!" erupted from the otherwise quiet Ralston side of the field. The Glasser players looked immature to Larry, they moved awkwardly, unused to their helmets and pads. They did not look well-conditioned, what Coach Rossi called "football-conditioned" and for some reason, he felt some of them looked scared, but he could not have said why he felt – or sensed – that; just the skitterish ways some of them moved. They lacked a certainty, a purposefulness, that you could, on the other hand, instantly sense in Ralston's players.

The Glasser team lined up in rows, with two players facing them, and set about doing a series of warm-up exercises – side saddle hops, drop downs, push-ups, some side-to-side body rolls. Then they paired off and began light contact drill, hitting each other on the shoulders with their hands, bouncing off each others' shoulder pads, out of three-point stances. Some sprinted quickly for ten yards or so, in bursts of speed. A couple of the backs threw footballs back and forth.

A long drum-roll commenced from the Ralston band. The band had somehow filed unnoticed down into the end zone, flanking the goal post there. The Ralston majorettes set themselves apart, in two rows coming straight out from the twin blue and white posts, where now a large paper screen unfurled. "Our Team!" it proclaimed, and the cheerleaders, running, extended their line until it reached nearly mid-field. Then, there was a noticeable diminishment in the crowd noise, and all heads turned to look up to the head of the stairs. Suddenly the band erupted in the famous "On Wisconsin" – a favored number for this – and the Ralston players began pounding rapidly down the stairs and then running at a quick pace around to the end zone, where they burst through the paper banner just so recently unveiled down over the goal post, coming on up the middle of the field through the lines of majorettes and cheerleaders, who all went down on one knee as the players rushed past them. The majorettes thrust their sparkling batons up like they were presenting swords, and the home side crowd erupted in a tremendous roar of welcome and pride. Larry could remember hearing that roar inside their house; it sent shivers up his spine.

Coach Rossi, and the other assistant coaches, along with the trainer, team physician (who would also take care of any injuries to the Glassers), the equipment manager and his student assistants, and several waterboys, seventh graders honored by being selected for such chores, came in after the team, almost like afterthoughts, not noticed much. Unlike the Glassers, the Ralston team immediately separated into several squads and began running plays. Dick Atkins threw passes to several of the ends while the first team line crouched and rushed forward, ten yards or so at a time, down into the opposite end zone. The whole impression was one of a very well drilled machine, remarkable for high school players.

Larry could feel the tension, the thick excitement mounting in him, as the black and white-suited officials for the evening's game gathered the two teams' captains on the fifty yard line for the coin toss. The crowd was quiet, he could see the coin spiraling, flashing, and then falling, the players bending over slightly to look down. One referee turned and placed his hands on Harry Gibb's shoulders – Ralston had won the toss, and Charlie was already excitedly announcing this, while a loud, prolonged cheer erupted from the home side. The referee standing next to Gibb made the motion of catching a ball – of course, Ralston would receive the opening kick-off. The captains shook hands and broke away, jogging to the side-lines, where the two first squads had formed up. Now the entire Glasser team swarmed around their coaches, yells erupting from them and their side of the field.

But the Ralston first team stood quietly in a tight circle around coach Rossi, who was speaking intently to them. He put his hands down and towards them. They all leaned forward, touched hands, and then broke out onto the field. The home crowd roared. Dick Atkins stood rolling his neck, with his helmet in one hand, next to coach Rossi, on the sideline by the middle of the bench; he would go in after the kick-off for the first series of offensive plays. These had already been decided, dependent on the field position the team achieved returning the kick-off.

This was a moment – it really was only a few seconds – which Larry felt indescribable in its focus and intensity. He had often wondered how the twin deep kick-off receivers, standing on the ten-yard line, could maintain their composure. Some teams kicked low, mean line-drive style kick-offs, hoping for a bounce off a lineman (the on-side kick), or a fumbled reception; others kicked amazingly high, arching kick-offs, but these were often not as deep as they should have been.

The Glasser kicker looked small. He was one of those high school football players who looked as if he really did not belong on the field, his helmet looked too big and bobbed on his head as he looked up and down the line around him preparing to move forward and kick. Larry thought he might try a line-drive kick. But he fooled everybody with a long, deep, and fairly high boot which sent Robert Henderson back nearly to the end zone line. Robert (he was always called "RT" in school, although nobody knew what the "T" stood for), the starting right halfback, was a speedster who could run forty yards in just over five seconds. He now took the surprisingly good Glasser kick and angled back towards the other side line, then cut straight up back towards the middle, looking for an "alley". He made it nearly to the thirty yard line before he was pulled down by three Glasser tacklers. The game had begun. Dick Atkins sprinted onto the field, and with very little huddle time, the Ralston team was already lining up for the first play from scrimmage. Scrimmage – an odd word, Larry thought; it did not even sound like modern English.

With the kick-off behind them, already the big crowd relaxed, settling in for the night's game. Unless something really unusual happened, Ralston would win; Larry thought that that fact was somehow already acknowledged before the game even started, like it was in the air. The only real questions were *how* they would win – with a ground or passing game – and by how much? And would the Ralston defense shut out the inept Glassers, not allowing them any points, a type of humiliation often seen in early season games when teams had only practiced for a few weeks.

There was that all-familiar game smell of cut, wet grass and dirt and hot coffee and hot dogs and a steamy wooly smell of people in the air which Larry loved. People were walking around towards the refreshment stands already; some were opening large hampers of food brought with them. It would not get too chilly that night, but game nights later in the season, especially in early and mid-November, could turn bitter cold. A piercing, damp cold coming in off the big river. The majorettes' legs would turn a chappy red, men would build fires with old tires in fifty-five gallon oil drums which would burn for the duration of the game, and even afterwards, until the Fire Department came down and put them out. The cold at these games was bone-numbing, teeth-chattering, legendary. People argued about what the coldest game night had been. And how could the players stand it? To be tackled – or to tackle – to get smashed down onto the already semi-frozen field; this would hurt even more with the stinging cold. But these, everyone argued, were the real football games. These were the games where a team proved it had the stuff, was of the right calibre. Only real football players could play well in such cold. Larry had seen grown men shaking by the third quarter from this cold, their coffee splashing out of the paper cup or thermos cup it was in. Their wives usually sat huddled down in the bleachers, swathed in scarves and gloves and boots, tapping their legs up and down, waiting for the game to end. Because nobody left these games early; it would be noticed.

There was another reason, too. These games traditionally had been those where an entire season's fate was clinched; a win, or loss, meant the whole shebang, as they said. The rest of the season was as if it did not matter; it all was riding on that last game – often on the last quarter. It had been this way the previous year, when Ralston had defeated Bleisberg, 6-2, in a muddy game decided by a 75-yard touchdown run by Dick Atkins, on a quarterback sneak play. But Ralston, although undefeated, had been tied, 19-19, much earlier in the season by Plum Township, a mediocre team whose very ineptness had somehow made Ralston play poorly. And that score – 19-19 – was really odd. But because of it, Ralston did not go to the championship game. Ralston, coming into this 1956 season, had an undefeated streak of eleven games, going back to 1954. The tie with Plum Township was the only blemish on the record.

But the game now developing, unfolding on the bright green field, would not be a tie game. By the third series of downs, Ralston had driven deep into the Glasser territory, and on a first down play, Dick Atkins, looking calm and collected, like a collegiate quarterback, rolled out to his left on a "keeper" play (Charlie in the announcer's booth made sure everyone knew that), and lobbed a short pass to Robert Henderson, on the opposite side of the field, who sped untouched into the end zone. You could almost see him laughing, it looked so easy, that score. The Ralston band crashed into their touchdown music, the major-ettes pranced, the cheerleaders did cartwheels and then formed a Tower of Power, with feisty Donna Charles on top. Ralston was rolling, and they led the home crowd in the "Ralston Roll", a favored cheer emphasizing that word "Rrroooollll!"

The inept Glassers fumbled the kick-off, and Ralston recovered the ball on the Glasers' twenty-five yard line. The confident Atkins immediately threw a long pass into the end zone, which the Glasser safety batted in the air, but Emilio Lazzeri, the second string end put in to block for that play – he was a big kid – caught the deflected pass, scoring the second Ralston touchdown. The extra point conversion was automatic, and still in the first quarter, Ralston was ahead 14-0. Larry felt sorry for the dejected Glasser team. It would be a long night for them ahead, and a long trip back to Ford City. The Ralston third stringers – even a few of the JVs chosen to suit up, though Larry hadn't been one of them – would see some game time tonight, he thought.

In games like this, obviously decided early on, the big crowd often started to move around the outside of the field's perimeter in a steadily growing mass, to and fro, almost like some odd sort of army near a battlefield. As a spectator at a game, Larry often went to stand underneath the announcer's booth on the light tower, where Charlie could be seen gesturing and moving, as he took in all that was happening on the field, and acknowledging people in the stands, some of whom called up to him. He was in his element, almost as important as the game. Larry stood under the tower because it was a place nobody else preferred, so it was somewhat quieter. From there, he could watch what was happening, unnoticed, which he liked. He could think there, while he watched. He could scan the crowds in the bleachers, see who was there from the town and then from the school, what kids were with who, what the various kids were wearing, what the kids from the opposing school looked like.

The fashions were uniform, though, and that was amazing, like some sort of underground communications center telegraphed it out each year, what would be worn, how hair would be cut. There had been the year when they had come back in the fall and everything was white; white tee-shirt, white pants, white shoes, white socks. It was supposed to have come from all the way out on the West

Coast, a surfer look. There was no surf in Pennsylvania, that was for sure. The look did not last long, but then none of them did. An Ivy League look was coming in now, he heard; button-down collar shirts that were in geometric patterns and a number of colors. Pants that had a weird buckle on the back, that had no apparent use. Some said white bucks were coming back in, too.

And if the game was looking to be not much of a contest, as this one looked, his thoughts would turn to school, his classes. And the ever-present thoughts of girls. These thoughts were a welter of images he was often confused by - the rush of conflicting feelings overwhelmed him. What were you supposed to do? Maybe the whole Sports thing, not just football, was for that; at least in practice and actually playing the game, you forgot for a bit about them.

Sandy Stevens being in his home room just added to it all. He had sat the other day and just watched her moving around in her chair, wondering how anyone could be so pretty. Every move she made was wonderful. She seemed a type of girl not reachable, but he could not explain why. And there were others he noticed, increasingly. Cameron Mitchell, in two of his classes, was such a striking looking girl she did take your breath away. Even more unattainable than Sandy. He was beginning to look forward to just *seeing* Cameron – even passing briefly in the halls. Wanting to see her. It was confusing. And he could not figure out who the hell to talk to about it, either.

# 16

Cameron Mitchell. It was an unusual name for a girl – it could have been a boy's name, the type of name a boy who would go to one of those prep schools, in New England somewhere, would have – but there was no mistaking that Cameron was a girl. She was in Larry's third period world history class, taught by Mr. Traynor, and he had often been able to get through the slow crawl of a Monday morning, especially after a game, thinking about her, looking forward to Traynor's class.

Mr. Traynor was an older teacher, a war veteran. Due to war injuries, Mr. Traynor wore large white wads of cotton in one ear. Some said his ears were injured, but students liked to quip that it was his brain, that the cotton kept it from oozing out. This, and his official academic title, Dr. Traynor, insured him relentless hounding by the class smart-alecks, as Larry's mother always called them, warning him, in passing, not to become one.

"Nothing to admire. Nothing at all. Young smart-alecks, they think they know it all. And it's funny! Wait till they learn they know nothing, just nothing!" His mother could go on about it. Where had the word itself come from, he wondered, listening to her. Smart-aleck?

The Monday after a winning game the school was always charged, still aglow with the communal awe of Friday night, of the game energy, the feats of the various players, what the band did, who went where with whom after the game, what they did. Probably did, Larry always thought as he listened to these stories, because who really knew? But you had to admit the stories themselves were fantastic. Nobody wanted to go to class on these days and thought only of the next game, the upcoming Friday night, the next Pep Rally. If the school year, or at least the fall, could consist somehow of only the Friday night games, and then the celebratory, happy-feeling Mondays, no one would cut.

The entire football season, ten games, into the middle of November, would go like that, a wild roller coaster ride, especially if they had a winning season, which already looked like the case for Ralston. Then, by the time it got near Halloween, and the team remained undefeated – it was never mentioned, for fear of jinxing the team – the tension would be nearly unbearable, from week to week. Nothing else would be talked of, or thought of. The teachers would begin to give up hope, and there would be more and more signs up, everywhere you looked. Signs and banners. If this season the team was undefeated by then, there would also be that long stretch of undefeated games noticed in the papers, highlighted even.

A teacher like Dr. Traynor was not helped at all by the football fever, as sports writers termed it. Dr. Traynor gave real college-style lectures in his class, as he duly informed each class at the beginning of the semester. He forced his students to "take notes" in a type of spiral-bound notebook, which he examined from time to time and commented on. He claimed this practice would serve them well in college. But many Ralston students, realistically, did not plan on college. They could simply not afford it. Many would instead get a job, buy a car, get married, have a kid. Usually in that order.

Ralston, and every other town in the Valley, was full of former students who'd done this, and they could be seen at football games on Friday nights, some still wearing their school jacket, now bringing a two or three year old child to a game that they might have been cheering at as students that recently ago. Then there were the older men, thirty or so – an unimaginable age – who already looked used up. That was the only way Larry could describe it, when he saw them. The light had gone out of their eyes, and they looked dulled, blunted, old. They spent increasing time in Ralston's beer gardens and taverns. The girls they had married had become fat and bandy-legged, with mousy hair and puffed eyes; it was hard to think they had ever been pretty, attractive. They moved slowly, heavily, often pushing a baby carriage with a chubby, snot-nosed, red-faced infant crying in it. Their husbands hardly looked at them. They looked at the majorettes, the cheerleaders.

He couldn't imagine this fate happening to Cameron Mitchell. For one thing, Cameron already had her license and already had a car – the cherry red '55 Chevy, you couldn't miss it; a car exceeded in style only by the out-of-reach Corvette, T-Bird, or Cadillac, which no Ralston student drove.

Cameron was also so beautiful it was apparent no Ralston boy would attain to her. Other girls said that she wanted to be a model in New York. There was a famous modeling school there, in a hotel, and Cameron's mother, who was also beautiful, was rumored to have her already enrolled in this school. Larry had never heard of any girl wanting to be a fashion model. But he had no doubt that Cameron could do it, especially when he saw her walking down a hallway in the school. Because Cameron did not walk like other girls. That was the only way you could put it – you noticed her walk, and her.

Cameron's coal black long hair, dark brown eyes, and perfect pale white skin defined the word "striking"; the eyes seemed hypnotic and dangerous. He found it difficult to look her in the eyes for very long at all. The combination of the hair, the eyes, and the lustrous skin was powerful. He would lie in his bed thinking of kissing Cameron Mitchell, his hands in that thick black hair, so close to those eyes. Would she close them? What would it be like, to kiss Cameron Mitchell? Then the reality of how ridiculous his fantasy was would knock him down, and he would know bitterly he was a fool. "Fool!" he would say to himself. "Just a fool!"

"You ain't got a rat's ass of a chance, baby!" Frankie Malone replied when he had, hesitantly, revealed his thoughts about Cameron. Frankie raised one hand, as if in a benediction.

"Hey. No offense. No offense. But Cameron Mitchell! She's another planet... you know what I mean?"

What made it all worse was that she sat in front of him in Traynor's world history class. She would turn and smile, shake her hair, he would catch that definitive perfumed scent. She could be a name for a perfume, he thought, it was so distinct. There was a clearly defined space always around Cameron, a zone as it were. Something she carried as part of her. A presence. Something very few, if any, of the other girls he knew seemed to have. Once he had found himself in line at a hallway water fountain behind her; he felt a warm radiance from her, and thought, momentarily, that he might have to step out of the line, go somewhere else. It was troubling how she affected him, and he did not really know who he could talk to about his feelings. The thing was, she seemed to know how she affected him. She would say something to him – amazingly – and he would only catch part of it and have to hurriedly imagine the beginning.

As if to add insult to injury she was smart, a very good student, and history was one of her best subjects. She took to talking more frequently to him – about the class readings and assignments before history class started – and he found himself trying to anticipate her questions the night before. To be within a couple of feet of her, looking directly into those large deep brown eyes, see her smile suddenly at something you said – this made any day a lot better, quickly. She could save you, he had thought, standing outside Traynor's class one day. She really could.

It was supposed to be the other way around, wasn't it? In all the stories, the movies, the hero saved the girl. But maybe in reality, in real life, it was different, more often than not.

And then he accidentally ran into her in the library. She asked him to sit down and go over some notes she'd taken of Traynor's lecture. His heart beat so hard when he remembered this chance meeting that he got alarmed – maybe he had an arrhythmia, a heart condition coach Rossi had spoken of. Cameron had asked him a series of questions as they went over her notes. He lost track of time sitting there, lost track of anyone around them. He could not in fact remember a time when he felt so happy as being there in the library with Cameron Mitchell. Maybe that was how it was in college, you studied in a huge library, and then walked across the campus together, and she would kick a pile of leaves, and laugh, shaking her hair. If he got to go to college with a girl like Cameron, he could stay there forever. Marry her and become a professor… he didn't know a single adult man in Ralston who was a professor, though.

"Hey, Larry! They'll be all over the place in college, girls like her." Frankie had said. Then he had talked about how Larry had looked, sitting there in the library with Cameron. "You shoulda seen yourself! I'm tellin' you. I look in that little window, in the door? There the two of you are!"

"How did I look? What do you mean? Did I look… funny or something?"

Frankie laughed. "Naw. You looked like you were in shock. Oh, Cameron!" He made a swooning movement with his hands. "Your face is an open book! You better not be a poker player, huh? See what I mean? She musta been enjoying it."

He had blushed hotly, and nodded. And if this is what Frankie had detected, he thought, what had Cameron noticed? No doubt she knew everything, she was miles ahead of him.

Some of the first string varsity players were in Traynor's third period class, too. "Dago" Paretti was in the class, and Robert Henderson, the speedy halfback. Both sat in the back row. In an odd way, they seemed as if they were already in college. But they were uniformly mediocre students, at best. How did these same players remember all their assignments on all the various possible plays that could be called from the big white Playbook they all studied, guarded? Every player had a different assignment on each play – linemen had different blocking patterns, backs had fakes, or routes to run for a possible pass, or a blocking assignment.

It was all the more remarkable because many of these same varsity players who executed the plays repeatedly without error could not remember a date in history class, the name of a president, or a famous battle, even the names of other states. They treated such knowledge as if it was useless or worthless – some openly said so, but not to Traynor's face – and their contempt was obvious to the class. Yet, they could easily remember all those plays…

their contempt resembled that of men in the town he had heard often claiming that school was a waste of time, that they had learned nothing of use there. They would spit on the pavement, and look off into the distance, nodding as if at an absolute certainty.

Frankie had an explanation, as usual. "They get a lot outta football – look at it. Glory, all that noise and yelling on game nights, the girls. Praise from the coaches, maybe a big time scholarship – their name and even picture in the newspaper. How many of us are gonna get our pictures in the paper, huh? At our age, especially. Think about it! Whatta you gonna get if you know when Cortez made his expedition? Or when Pizarro strangled the Inca? I'll tell you – nothin."

Larry could not let him get away with it. "You get a good grade, though. That's not nothing."

Frankie snorted derisively. "A grade. Ole Traynor's grade book'll be moldy paper in the dump up there by the river in ten years. A grade ain't gonna get you no time in the back seat with Carol Bigelow, is it?"

Carol Bigelow, the sultry-eyed, heavy- breasted cheerleader, who looked like she was nineteen or twenty already. In the previous year, she had seduced the smartest boy in the junior class, Ray Sherry. In the space of six weeks, he went from a straight A student to a wise-acre who cracked jokes back at teachers, wore his blonde hair in a greased-back DA. He began to resemble Joe Labrador, sporting a cigarette pack (which had already been taken from him several times) rolled tightly in the upper arm of his tee-shirts; before, Ray Sherry had not even smoked. Or worn tee-shirts. He began dancing in the Elvis style in the corridors between classes, in front of lockers, or in the vestibules, gyrating, grinding his hips, curling his lips and throwing his hair back. He kept a large black comb in the hip pocket of his Levis; the handle looked like one on a straight-edge razor, and someone took to calling him "Razor"; the nickname stuck. Teachers were appalled at his transformation. Especially the Latin teacher, Mrs. Martin, in whose class he had once excelled, to her delight. Now, asked to translate, he said "Read it yourself, you know what it says."

Frankie called Carol Bigelow "the Siren."

"You know. Those women in that long-ass old Greek poem? They lured the sailors to their destruction. Oh, yeah! Hey, I'd go, if it was her. Lemme go, please! Oh Carol!"

The whole subject was troubling. Looked at in the ways of the players, the men downtown, even Frankie, studies in school were some kind of wasted effort, with little real, meaningful, immediate return. Whereas football gave you a lot back on your investment, right away.

Even beyond that was the question of the players themselves, who were getting an education certainly. But it wasn't the kind the teachers praised and held up as a model. If anything, playing football seemed guaranteed to turn you away, on a deep level, from such accomplishments — they were not really manly. It seemed to say there were better things to do with your life, especially your young life, that part his mother kept saying was the best part, only you couldn't realize it when you were young.

When he thought of it that way, it made a kind of sense. But he didn't like the feelings this gave him. He hadn't imagined going out for a team, playing what was supposed to be a game, would have all the effects it was unaccountably already having on him. Coming with the Cameron Mitchell crush, and Sandy Stevens – and yes, even Carol Bigelow, who'd smiled at him in the hall between classes and said "Hi Larry" in her throaty voice – he felt a rush of ups and downs that wore on him, distracted him badly.

Ducky Estes, known to be "cool," said it was all, or mainly at least, hormones. "I read it in the library. Some biology book. It'll pass. We all get it, the girls too. Like a disease – you just gotta go through it. A stage." He suggested they go and shoot baskets in the gym, although it was long before basketball season.

"Get it off your mind, like. Make a few buckets." He mimicked shooting a one-handed set shot. "Like old Bob Cousy. The Celtics."

Coach Rossi intensified this effect with every one of his talks. Usually out on the field itself, all the players – JV and varsity, dusty and sweaty – grouped around him in a large, tight circle. He compared the team to the military, saying that many of them would go into the Army or Navy, and they would find it easier, having played football at Ralston. Military service was a good thing, he vowed. Young men needed it. Hadn't they all noticed? The big

changes in brothers or other friends who'd gone in, especially after they returned from Basic Training? Hadn't
they all seen a wise-ass, a *smart-ass* – he gave this term
particular emphasis – shape up? Grow up?

It was undoubtedly true, and many nodded. It was a
fact well-known in the community; going into the service
made a man out of you. Typically, a young man joined
up right after graduation – maybe waiting for the end of
summer, a last sort of summer of unrestrained freedom.
Or they certainly would be in within a year or so. They
went away for three months, returning much changed,
physically and mentally. You would see them at games,
sometimes in the school itself, or outside, in their trim
uniforms, looking serious. They were no longer "kids."
Some had small tattoos on the back of one hand – an
eagle, or a set of wings, or an anchor. That meant you were
a man.

Boys who had gone away fat came back muscular and
fit; boys who were skinny as rails returned filled out (as
his mother called it), some having gained fifteen pounds
or more. All were in the best physical shape of their lives.
Other men nodded approvingly, recalling that they too
had been in the best shape of their lives after returning
from Basic.

The Korean War was not long over, but it already
seemed, in large part, forgotten, Larry thought. Yet a
large number of men had died in the war – two men from
Ralston, Marines, had been killed at the Chosin Reservoir.
The Korean War Larry knew about, for in grade school

he had collected a large scrapbook of the maps published every week on the front page of the newspaper, for the several years of the war. There had been a noticeable shift in the war comic books he liked at that time, too. Many more featured the mad yellow and brown-tinted "gooks," the slant-eyed, cruel North Koreans, the evil, treacherous hoards of Chinese, who attacked in the Human Wave attacks, wave after wave of soldiers. Names like Pusan, Chosin, Seoul, the Yalu, Inchon, Pyongyang – as odd-sounding as they were, they were familiar to him, he had a sense of exactly where they were on the snubby finger of land sticking out above Japan on the world map. A small place.

Larry had also the example of his brother, who had narrowly missed being sent to Korea. Many of the men he had trained with in the Marine Corps had been sent, and a number had been killed, or seriously wounded. Carl had in fact been on his way to the West Coast, for processing and embarkation, when his wife, who was pregnant, had become ill, and he had been allowed emergency leave. By the time his wife's illness had been cleared up, his unit had embarked, and he had been re-directed back to his original unit in North Carolina.

Carl had had the odd distinction of being drafted into the Marine Corps, which was known to be an all-volunteer service branch. But the war had already depleted the ranks, and they began to select a few men from each draft unit. Carl always said he had been selected because he was in such excellent physical shape, from his job in the factory. He had returned from Basic Training, at Parris Island, withdrawn, haggard -looking. Of the 80 men who began training with him, 53 had finished. He did not think highly of the Marine Corps, and said so. "I saw more good men broken down there than made." he affirmed, nodding.

Although it was incontestable that his brother was a Marine, and this was well-known in Ralston where it was a decided mark of distinction for a young man, when Larry repeated his brother's story, other boys did not seem to believe it. Or maybe it was that they did not want to believe it could be true, accurate. To be in the Marine Corps was an exalted status. No one ever said anything about it – after all, it was the Marine Corps! Everyone knew what that meant. But Larry, hearing his brother's stories, felt that everyone did not know what it meant, not at all.

His brother counseled him not to even consider joining the Marine Corps, and, if it were possible, to stay out of the military service altogether. "Go to college, Larry," he had written in one letter. "Get a deferment, for as long as you can. That's the thing for you. Believe me, I know what I'm talking about! Forget about the Army, all that stuff in the movies and all. Go to college."

He did not tell anyone of his brother's advice, and he began to wonder if he was in some way unfitted to live a regular life, since he seemed to already hold these different views which nobody in the town held, or at least spoke of. But, then, did people really tell what they believed? That was yet another unsettling, recurring thought he increasingly had, couldn't shake off. Or did they just say what they thought people wanted to, expected to, hear?

He thought of all these things, sitting in study hall or in his classes, where the voice of the teacher became a sort of background drone. His study hall, for some unknown reason, was held up in the small, cramped balcony of the auditorium, which the students called "The Peanut Gallery," or "The Shelf." Here Harry Humes had once poured a chemistry beaker full of warm piss down onto the students sitting on the first floor. Humes had been suspended for two weeks for this act, but it had gained him an undying fame. Later, in winter, along with the infamous Joe Labrador, he had put piss on the radiator in their home room. Frankie talked of that a lot, and it got imitated.

It was hard to determine why in fact "study halls" were held. There was no "hall," only rooms (or The Shelf), and no one, it appeared, ever did any studying. Girls, in particular, passed notes frenziedly, laughing and jostling about loudly, chewing gum, and, until the teacher called out angrily, they whispered relentlessly, in some deep conspiratorial scheme, looking over their shoulders, or across from where they sat. What were they looking for? Or at?

One of the things he found he could do in study hall that he liked was read books from the school library, directly across the hall. He had been reading books from the school library since he'd been in grade school, and they had had a tall glass case in the room where the books were kept. The teacher had a key, and if you were good, special, you could pick a book and read it, and even report on it to the rest of the class. In the fifth grade, he had read about Kit Carson and Buffalo Bill and Custer and the massacre, and also about Lewis and Clark's fantastic expedition, and the Indian girl, Sacajawea, whose image in the book had haunted him. He had been in love with the Bird Girl.

His mother worried about his incessant reading, and so even did Dr. Curtis, the town doctor, who told him he should not read "too much." But what was too much? Especially when you liked it so much? When he had found out that masturbation would lead you to become blind, he was terrified; certainly, he would go blind, and thus suffer a double punishment, no longer being able to read books.

Frankie Malone, whom he told everything to, had laughed loudly. "Sure. Beat your meat, and go blind. You can have braille books, and beat your dong while you read them, too! Once you're blind, you can beat it all you want, eh? Fuckin' bullshit, is what it is, Larry. You really know of anybody in town that's blind from beatin' off?"

He had to admit he did not. Still, the doctor had asserted that "self-abuse" was not good for you.

"No. See? What'd I tell you? It's all crap. Crap, and more crap. I tell ya what," he looked around as if to insure nobody would hear what he was about to say, "I beat mine every chance I get." He made the famous motion with his hand. "I figure, it'll make it grow. Exercise."

In the sixth grade, he had read more advanced and complicated books, and read them easily and eagerly, cleaning out most of the bookcase by Christmas vacation. When he had been around eight, his sister had given him a series of Tarzan books, and then similar books featuring the Phantom. And then, in an old battered trunk in the attic, he had found green, hard-covered books. Among them was *The Adventures of Tom Sawyer*. This book enthralled him – he fell in love with Becky Thatcher, who seemed as real as any of the girls he knew. She could have lived next door. He wanted her to live next door!

*The Adventures of Tom Sawyer* changed his life. Following its reading, and then a re-reading, he and another boy pushed the hated, fat bully Iggy Hill, into the creek. He had not bullied them afterwards. They had constructed a boat using old wood they found from a house that had been torn down, or fell down (it was hard to tell), and sides made from empty fifty-five gallon oil drums, of which there seemed no end in the town. Where did they come from, Larry wondered? There were no oil wells around that they knew of. Jimmy Washburn had said that there were oil wells up in Oil City, up north.

"That's where oil wells started," he claimed. "You don't know that? Everybody knows that! Pennzoil? Come on!"

They launched the boat made from the old wood and the oil drum out into Buffalo Creek with some fanfare, a rag-tag group of smaller kids watching in awe, although one or two who had inspected the boat before its maiden voyage said it would sink.

Larry felt like Tom Sawyer, the acknowledged captain of the flat-bottomed craft as it left the raft that served as a launch platform, moving smoothly out into the middle of the creek. It was a great moment – a kingfisher flew up with a great squawking, its brilliant plumage flashing in the hot July sun, and all sorts of thoughts went through Larry's head. Maybe they would just go on out into the big, broad river and on down it towards Pittsburgh, and keep going. Who knew how far they could get? A boat! It was a great, great thing they had made.

Then, rapidly, the boat began to go down. Buddy Fletcher, who was rowing in the front, had turned and said, loudly, "Hey! This thing is sinking. We're goin' under..." And it went right out from under them, leaving them glad they had learned to swim fairly well previous summers back, in the very same creek, diving from the very same raft they'd launched from. Only a few rising muddy bubbles now remained of their work, while the small kids were hooting and dancing with glee on the shore, pointing and laughing. He and Buddy had swum to the opposite shore, unable to confront their mockeries. Buddy received a prolonged whipping for his wet clothes. His mother claimed he could have drowned.

In the sixth grade library cabinet he found more challenging books, and discovered the first of the sports novels, written by a man named John R. Tunis. Tunis wrote books about baseball and football, set in high school. They were entirely convincing and gripping, and Larry read every one in the case. He wondered how the author knew so much about how it felt to be in high school, the atmosphere, even the way the kids in the books spoke. How had he gotten to write these books? And who was he – who was John R. Tunis? Was that his real name? He wanted to ask one of the teachers, maybe even the librarian, but he felt his question was unanswerable. He was afraid to ask it.

He had become, by this time, still in grade school, an inveterate reader. Nothing could stop him, even though there were more comments about how damaging it was to his eyes to read so much, for so long at a time. And then the idea of writing books took root in his mind. People actually did this, and made money, made a living. John R. Tunis, for example. He knew no one in Ralston who had written a book, other than the nervous, excessively skinny newspaper editor, now retired.

In the main school library, which he had access to once he had entered high school, he found many treasures, including more books by the prolific John R. Tunis – he'd written some good ones especially about football, but there were several on basketball that were also very good. He also came across a history of football, from its beginnings, which the book traced back to the middle ages, when playing football was considered an irreligious activity by many, apparently. That struck him as strange, that playing football could be seen that way. It was denounced as inciting young men to violence, and luring them away from the church, to play a game of football rather than attend services and prayers.

The descriptions of college football as it was played in the early part of the 20th century fascinated him. He discovered, reading about football at Princeton, where a particularly famous player, Hobey Baker, played right before WWI, that fatalities were fairly common in college football at that time. People were actually *killed* playing football.

Hobey Baker had been a fabled figure, the stuff of movies. He had gone from Princeton to fly in the First World War, and after the Armistice, in December, 1918, the unthinkable had happened. Hobey Baker was killed in a plane crash in France. How could such a demi-god die? Larry wondered if anyone had written a book, a novel perhaps, about this Hobey Baker, who seemed more of a fictional character even in the narration of his real life. And the name – Hobey. Nobody in real life had a name like that.

The first football game – between Rutgers and Princeton – had been in 1869, nearly a hundred years ago. Later in the book, it noted the highest football score ever recorded; in a game played at Atlanta when Georgia Tech defeated Cumberland, 222-0. It was unimaginable. What kind of an afternoon must that have been?

Then there was the Bronko Nagurski story. Nagurski had played at the University of Minnesota. He was a fullback, a bonecrusher of a man who weighed 235 pounds when this was an extraordinary weight for a fully grown young man to achieve. He turned pro with the Chicago Bears, coached by the legendary George Halas. Late in a game in the old Chicago Stadium, the Bears reached the opponents' one-yard line. Nagurski was given the ball and plowed through the line, and then the defensive linebackers, "blowing by them like the swinging doors of a saloon." Head down, he ran on, straight into the concrete retaining wall immediately behind the end zone. The force of the collision with the wall sent him reeling back, and then down; Coach Halas, looking on, was horrified at what might have happened to his prize back, and investment. His face was described as "blanched white" as he looked intently down towards the end zone, where Nagurski lay on the ground.

But the indomitable fullback got up, shook his head, and then trotted towards the sidelines, where Halas and the entire Bears team were now standing apprehensively, waiting for him.

"Bronko! How are you?" Halas inquired, peering closely at the big back's face.

"I'm okay, Coach. But that last guy – boy, he gave me a helluva lick!"

There were other stories in the book, about the legendary Don Hutson, the "Alabama Antelope," whose moves were so secret that practices of his team were closed to reporters and the public. There was Johnny Blood, who played for the Steelers, whose owner, Art Rooney, used to gamble to win the players' salaries while the team played. Rooney looked odd; he wore obviously heavy-lensed glasses, and looked like a guy you could find running a gas station in

Cheswick or somewhere. How had he gotten connected with professional football?

As he looked at the photographs in the book, he noticed that the players often did not wear helmets, and when they did, they were odd-looking leather contraptions which looked like they had no padding or protection in them at all. And there were no face masks on the helmets. What a different game it was then. Players stood to lose something - to be marked, like boxers, prize fighters. A real game, something that had been lost already? Why did he think that? He had unbidden thoughts coming all the time like that now. It was adolescence, as Mr. Turner had said in English class. That, *that* was a class he might learn something in. If he could only keep his mind clearly focused and not think about the girls in that class so much. It was bad enough with Cameron Mitchell, in his world history class. But there were, inevitably, other girls, in other classes; you would suddenly notice one, hadn't you seen her before? It was mystifying and embarrassing, looking at all these girls. And they knew you were looking.

Holly Burris was in that class. She almost always wore her majorette's jacket, the captain's jacket, hanging it sometimes on the back of her chair. It was white, a snow white that never seemed to have any dirt on it, anywhere. When she slipped into it, her face glowed and he thought he would fall through the ground. The cheerleaders' jackets were items with as much power as a letterman's jacket, and nearly as much force as those the majorettes wore. But the majorettes were somehow casual about their jackets in a way the cheerleaders weren't; they threw them off, onto the ground, and carried them draped over their shoulders. Sandy Stevens didn't seem to wear hers much. They used them, really wore them, in an odd sort of way, if they had them around at all; he had never seen some in one, although they all had them. You would never find a cheerleader missing an opportunity to wear their jacket.

How was he going to keep his mind focused on his studies – and would it get worse, so that by college it was unbearable? Because studies, that would be the only way out, he could see that clearly. But there just seemed to be more and more pretty girls, and they kept getting prettier. And they all went with football players.

"Bad news," Frankie quipped. "Hard times!" He hooted out his laugh so hard Dr. Test Tube – Mr. Sweeney – opened his lab door and glared at them harshly. Then he shook his head disappointedly and shut the door with a hard thud.

"Fuckin' Dr. Frankenstein," Frankie said. "Back into his nuthouse."

# 17

Due to the girls, when he got up in the morning for school he wondered what to wear. Clothes were vital in a way he could not have imagined even a year ago, so important they could make or break the day, and he was embarrassed that he felt they were so important. He tried to downplay them, even to himself – it was not right to be so involved with clothes. Yet everyone was. You couldn't be the age he was and not be. If you denied it, you were lying. And – of course – the girls noticed. Was there anything they didn't notice? Always, it came back to "girls." He felt a hot flash of anger at it.

If he ever got rich, he would buy all the clothes he wanted, and stand and survey them in a huge walk-in closet. He had read a scene in *The Great Gatsby*, assigned for later in the year in English, where Gatsby shows Daisy his clothes, his shirts, and throws them, one after another, onto his bed. She began to cry and said, "They're such beautiful shirts!" That scene had stuck out, and remained in his mind, as had the last sentence of the book, which he could not figure out, completely, to his satisfaction. "So we beat on, boats against the tide, borne ceaselessly back into the past." It did not seem the way most books, novels, ended.

In the summer, lying up in his bedroom in the late night, with sweat pooling in his bellybutton from the humidity and heat, he had read some Edger Allen Poe stories in an old book his mother had, and some Sherlock Holmes stories which he could not stop reading, feeling sad when he came to the end of the book. He mother seemed worried that he stayed up at night reading so much. He did not want to go and sit over at Guinta's fruit stand, though, and eat watermelon and talk about the girls that pulled into the stand in cars with their boyfriends. One of the usual summertime nighttime entertainments in Ralston. "Cunta's," some called it.

The reading jags he went on made him ask Frankie if he thought you could ruin your eyes with too much reading.

"I wouldn't know, you ask the wrong person. Hey! I already told you I don't think you'll go blind from strokin' off." He made the gesture of pulling at himself. "*That's* all horseshit."

"Yeah? Can you be sure? How do you know – you're not a doctor."

Frankie laughed. "Hey – come on. Every guy you see walkin' around is floggin' his dummy. How many are goin' blind? You tell me. Now, they do say you can get blind goin' to a whorehouse. I heard that. That's different."

A whorehouse was also called a brothel, or a cathouse, or a crib (down in Pittsburgh). He looked up the words in a dictionary one afternoon in the library. Larry had never been to a whorehouse but had heard numerous stories of where they might be located. Many said the nearest one was in New Kensington, a town about fifteen miles down the river, where there was a large aluminum mill which employed a lot of men. The whorehouse was said to have black women prostitutes. He often heard men at Sam's talk about it. They referred to the black women as "poontang," although when he had asked Frankie, he'd said the term referred to all women's sexual organs. Whatever it really meant, the word was strange, unlike any he'd heard, He was fascinated by "poontang," and took to saying it under his breath, just to hear it. He wondered how many others knew what this word really meant.

The thoughts of the women in the New Kensington whorehouse made him think of the dirty playing card photos Bob Goran had, and would show if you gave him money. One showed a man with an enormous prick, with a woman sitting on it. The man was squeezing her breasts. Both of them were not particularly good-looking, and Larry wondered how they got people to pose for such pictures, even assuming, as was no doubt certain, they were paid. In another card the man wore a mask, like the Lone Ranger's, and this Larry found funny, although Goran did not think it was so. A third photo had three people, but they were slightly out of focus, blurred, detracting from the picture. Another odd feature Larry noted in all the pictures was that the women all wore their nylon stockings and the straps and belts holding them up. Why hadn't they taken all their clothes off?

"It's better that way," Frankie Malone had maintained.

"What? What's better?"

"That's the way they always do it. I'm tellin' you."

"They keep their stockings on while they do it?"

They never resolved this question to his satisfaction. He could not imagine the girls he went to school with in such pictures, or such postures, or wearing the stockings, either. Yet Goran had several decks of these cards. (He claimed he got them from an uncle who lived in Detroit and worked on the railroad.) So there must be a lot of girls who were willing to pose for them. This thought discouraged him, and made him feel bad, and he could not have explained why, but it was so. The whole subject was impossible to even bring up with his mother. To make matters worse, Goran offered to sell him some cards.

When he got to school all the talk was of a crime that had occurred in Ralston on the weekend. No one seemed to know what had actually happened, but two men had ended up in a fist fight in an alley beside Adam's Tavern, a notorious place, and one man had either, in falling, struck his head on the curb of the street, or had had his head pounded on the curb by the other man – the story varied, according to who told it. Both men worked in a lumber mill outside Ralston which had a small stone quarry near it.

The man whose head struck the curb had died in the hospital on Sunday morning; the other man was arrested and charged with manslaughter. He had been taken to the prison down near Pittsburgh, apparently, awaiting a judge's ruling on bail.

Both men had apparently been at the football game Friday night. But it was hard to tell what exactly they had fought about. His mother maintained it was probably the result of drinking.

"Young men and drink, that doesn't mix well. They ought to keep those taverns under control..." She shook her head, biting her lip. Larry was surprised at how strongly she apparently felt. Did she know someone involved, he wondered. But then, as he thought of it further, he put it down to the general condition that existed in the whole valley with men drinking. They worked hard, so felt they were entitled to a little fun, and they went and drank, sometimes heavily, in the taverns. Then they came home and beat up their wives, for many different reasons. Larry had heard Sal Caferta, who lived in the house on the corner, beating his wife Julia frequently, and he had even asked his mother why nobody did anything about it. Even old Mrs. Pearson, who saw everything, kept her mouth shut.

She had looked at him for a long time, and then heaved a sigh.

"Well, what can they do about it? Call the police? What's old Stroup going to do about it? Nothing. Maybe put Sal in jail for a night. Then he goes home and beats Julia even harder, since she had him put in jail. No. You just have to live with it."

"Why? Why do you just have to live with it?"

"You're going to get in a world of trouble with those why questions of yours, Larry. You have to live with it because you can't change it. That's why. Plain and simple. There are a lot of things you're going to learn that you can't change, and you have to learn to accept them."

But when he would run into Sal Caferta, and the big man would smile at him and say "How ya doin', Larry? Playin' a little ball, I hear?," he felt anger, and a certain resolve that he would never beat his wife. He wondered how Sal could do it, being so much bigger and stronger. And why didn't his wife leave him?

What had the two men fought over outside Adam's Tavern? No one seemed to know for certain, but Larry had been startled to hear that the man charged with manslaughter, remanded to the big, gray, stonewalled state prison down in Aspinwall was Phil Leaver, who lived just two blocks away. Phil Leaver always wore Woolrich hunting shirts, plaids in green and blue, and he drove a late-model Mercury convertible, a very sharp car. But the most impressive thing about him was his wife, Janet.

Janet Leaver. She had light, golden-colored hair, light blue eyes, and the most beautiful skin (his mother always said "complexion") Larry had ever seen. He wondered how she had got such beauty. Noticing his interest his mother said, "all her family are good-looking." Larry thought Phil Leaver must be the most blessed man in Ralston, or in the valley, to come home to someone like that, every night. It would make you work hard, he thought. You wouldn't care how tired you got, if you knew she was waiting for you. Every time he saw her she smiled at him, as if she knew his feelings, and he wondered how this could be.

Women seemed to have extra-sensory perceptions men did not have; or at least, some seemed to. He felt certain Janet Leaver was such a person. Now her husband was in state prison, with every chance of being there for five years, which was said to be the term if he was convicted. What would happen to her?

Larry continued to work out religiously, four times a week, with the weights he had retrieved back in the early summer from the old geezer, Mr. Krebs. Everybody said Mr. Krebs had "gone soft in the head." He had been gassed in the First World War, and had no teeth. Sometimes, he would take his false teeth out and set them on the table, just to get a laugh; he liked to do this up at Sam's. His face, toothless, the sunken-in cheeks, with only the raw, naked gums, was awful looking, grotesque, although his mother thought it merely funny. She could even, amazingly, give a good imitation of him, gumming away, twisting her face and slitting up her eyes.

Sometimes he worked out in front of a mirror because this had been suggested in the yellowed manual that he'd found with the weights, although he had an uneasy sense about it, and did not want his mother to find him doing it. His muscles, especially those in the chest and upper arms, were well defined now, and his tee shirts fitted him tightly. The pimples were another matter; Clearasil did not seem to control them as well as it was claimed it would. Sometimes he went to school with a thick layer of it on certain parts of his face, feeling sure it must be clearly visible, like girls' make-up. Goran told of a guy who had been caught on a school bus in Arnold wearing rouge; he had been beaten by some men in the town. But what could you do? The alternative was worse. And there was the embarrassment of the certain knowledge that these eruptions, the sudden red rash, were an undoubted sign of masturbation. Boys who did not masturbate did not get pimples, this was a well-known fact. Even Coach Rossi had said as much.

"You can tell. It's apparent. Isn't it?" he had said in health class, while many boys looked down at their desks, wishing they could leave the room, hide, get away.

Frankie Malone, though (as he had said), masturbated "as often as I can," and he did not have any pimples, to speak of. As with so many other things, he laughed, and said it "was all bullshit, I'm tellin' ya, Larry. BS!"

The world was increasingly composed of BS, it seemed. But when he saw Janet Leaver, and her red eyes, which he had never seen red like that, and her puffy face, which might have been bruised, that was not BS. Something bad was going on. He felt a welter of conflicting feelings about Janet Leaver, which led him to both try to avoid her and wish that he would run into her. When he had met her in the summer at the pool, and she had invited him to sit on the big beach towel she had, he had been light-headed from sitting there looking at the smooth long expanse of her bare legs. He was sitting so close he could see the pores of her skin as she absently ran her hand over her legs. He felt a sharp jolt, and thought he would audibly start to breathe faster, since his heart had raced.

He wondered if he had a heart condition. After all, there had been that comment by the doctor who'd examined them before Training Camp, who'd listened longer than to the other boys (it seemed) to his heart. At night, in bed, his heart's thudding worried him. And there was the increasing frequency of erections, which came on at the worst times, like when they were standing pledging the flag in the morning. Semen stained his pajamas and the sheets of his bed – his mother said nothing, but must have seen, known. Was it the result of the weights and his physical conditioning? He had never been in better condition, heart thudding or no.

If only he could talk about these things with an older man, about all of what was happening so quickly to him – someone who *knew*. But his brother Carl was too far away, and he could not write of these things in a letter... He remembered finding a rubber – a condom – in his brother's room once, a few years ago. He had filled it with water at the tap in the bathroom sink, watching with amazement as it stretched but did not break.

Sometimes whatever was going on affected his digestion. He developed diarrhea, and did not sleep well at night, waking with a ringing in his ears, his heart pounding like a drum, shaking his chest cavity; he was covered in sweat. What was wrong with him? Did the other boys, the other players, experience these things? And how did you remain calm in the game itself? He had heard Dick Atkins talking in the locker room one day after practice, saying that the game, once it started, went so fast he could not believe it.

"It's waitin' for the damn game to start! That's the thing. All the stuff – running out onto the field, the introductions, the coin tossing, all that stuff – I'm sick to my stomach with the butterflies. But once you get hit out there, then it's okay. You know what I mean? I wait for that, to get hit – the harder the better! You need it."

Other than the manslaughter case, the pregnancies of Kathy Ferris and Shannon Brunell, from earlier in the summer, had been the big shock in the town, where people liked to say "nothing ever happens." But even if anyone at the school knew anything, they would not talk about it. Especially other girls. Girls feared pregnancy. It was an uncomfortable, loaded word for them, even though it seemed to loom with inevitability, not far away. There was no news of the two girls. Neither returned to school. What would happen to them? Larry remembered hearing about a 14-year old girl, Jeanette Bering, out on a farm in the country near Millersburg, who'd gotten pregnant by a 19-year old boy who lived on the next farm over. The couple got married, the girl left school. Fourteen – to leave at that point meant she would have an eighth-grade education. When he thought of Kathy Ferris, maybe somewhere in a special home that they had down in Pittsburgh, it made him feel bad. He had not seen Kathy around her house, and the blinds were now always down. His mother knew nothing further – or would not say. It was like a part of his life had already ended with Kathy gone. He heard her name mentioned among girls standing outside the girls' room, but not often.

The girls' room was a strange, slightly fearful place. What did they do in there? There were always some girls standing around outside it, it seemed.

"They have their periods," Frankie said. "Haven't you noticed?"

And he had. There was a rank, sharp odor from some girls that made boys hold their noses in exaggerated ways, making the girls furious. But he had to admit this smell was overpowering, unpleasant, certainly unattractive.

One teacher, Miss McCaferty, famous for her large breasts – even bigger than Norma's – was particularly bad. Frankie complained of having her for math class at these times.

"God! It's unbelievable!" He fanned the air in front of his face frenziedly. "I pity the poor bastard that's got to marry her."

Frankie had gone into one of the girls' rooms once on a dare.

"Well, I tell you what, they haven't got no urinals, see? Just stalls. The toilet, you know – sit down? And the Kotex machine! Yeah! You better believe it…and actually it's got stuff on the walls in there."

"What stuff?"

"You know. Shit written on the stall walls and all – I

didn't hang around to read it, get caught by the principal or some teacher."

"Nasty stuff? Dirty?"

"No drawings – at least, I didn't see one."

The main boys' room, on the first floor, was a different story. For months, in the spring semester past, there had been extensive drawings of penises, and then of womens' vaginas and then of couples "screwing," as Frankie always said. Where did the term "screwing" come from? "From screwing it in," he said, looking amazed. "Didn't you know that? Everybody knows that, for Christ's sake, Larry! You lead a sheltered life."

"It's because I haven't got any father," he had blurted out. "Nobody tells me these things."

Pecker Dolan was an infamous student, a senior who wore tight fitting, dirty Levis which bulged prominently at his crotch. As a junior, he had shaved his hair in a Mohawk cut and been expelled for two weeks because of it. He would sit in classes and rub his crotch slowly, and grin, especially if a girl looked at him. Dolan had been the one who discovered a teacher drawing the graffiti on the walls of the boys' room. The teacher, to everyone's amazement, was Mr. Hobson, a mild mannered, well dressed substitute history teacher.

"What will happen to him?" Larry asked his mother as they ate a late dinner of macaroni and cheese, which was one of his favorites. He put away two platefuls of the dish, and his mother smiled at him over the table, looking tired. She also looked sad – he wondered how old she really was, because it seemed things like she'd gone through would add to your age. This was what people meant when they talked about how "it's all written right there on his face.

Can't miss it, can you?" He could miss it, sometimes, but adults were evidently better readers than he was. It was like that other statement you'd hear people make knowingly, "he's so crooked he can't lie in a straight bed." That stuck in his mind. It was comical to think of such a person, trying to lie in their bed.

"Probably he will resign his teaching job," she said, running her hand absently over the table cloth. "Remember Mr. Burrell? That business?"

Mr. Burrell had been a biology teacher who'd had parties, it was discovered, at a cabin out on Buffalo Creek. He had been sent to prison for five years. Some members of the then football team had been incriminated, but nothing had happened to them, really, except that they seemed to play harder than ever that season, and won nearly all their games.

"Yeah, I remember him. He's in the state prison, isn't he?"

"So they say…"

He didn't agree with the punishment of Mr. Burrell, whom he'd remembered as a pretty decent teacher, although he had not had biology; you couldn't take it until you were a sophomore. But he had always seemed a good-humored man. He did not like to think of him in prison. And what would such a person do when they came out? His entire life would already have been ruined. How would you start over, in such a case? Go somewhere, where nobody knew you, or anything about your past, and hope that they could not, or would not, find out?

It was like what he had observed so often already. You could work hard, but you could have an injury, get laid off, things could go wrong, and you were finished. How could you get out of that? he wondered. People accepted it, did not say much. It made him feel bad, and angry.

He had seen Holly Burris and Fred Lucas, her steady boyfriend, in the hall, walking slowly, holding hands. She wore his class ring around her neck on a thin gold chain – that was what the girls were doing these days, after a long time of actually wearing their guy's ring on their own small fingers, having to wrap bulky additions of tape around the ring to keep it on. But that was part of the style, that bulky pad of tape that was so visible.

What did they feel? Because it had to be something intense and special and private. Holly and Fred had "gone steady" for three years, an incredible, unheard of amount of time. Was she giving it to him? This was how it was put – or, was he getting any? If a guy was asking it, it came out that way. Some were certain it had to be so.

"Are you kidding me?" Frankie Malone said. "Now ask yourself, put yourself in his position. Out on the Potsdam Road. It's a cold night, you got the heater on, and it's cozy, and you know ole Barenekkid Stroup ain't gonna be around. He's sittin' somewhere with his heater on, drinkin' his coffee. And she's already all over you. The girl likes you! Holly Burris! Come on! Can't you understand that simple fact of life? So, do you think this is gonna go on and on and on, like that, and no further, for *three whole fuckin' years?"* He threw his hands up, then let them fall with an audible slap on his legs.

He had to admit, it was hard to imagine it would. One thing would lead to another, and as everyone knew, once you went so far, you couldn't stop. Nature took over, and you did it. Maybe you regretted it afterwards, but you did it, and then, most likely, since you'd already done it, you inevitably did it again. What was to stop you at that point?

He would be no different, he had to admit to himself, especially with a girl as cute as Holly. She wasn't beautiful; not a Cameron Mitchell, or Sandy Stevens, they were beautiful, a force that made you stop, lose your train of thought, bang into people in the hallway, or into your locker door, but it was hard to imagine being in a car with either of them, to think they'd go that far, get into that sort of a situation, let you drive them down some dark back country road. Where were you going?

"A stiff prick has no conscience." Somebody wrote it on the bathroom wall in the boys' room. It was erased, then written again, with a large, fat exclamation point, looking like an erect penis, with drops of cum coming out the end. "Heh heh," Somebody else had put, right next to this, an arrow, and then written "Carol Bigelow Cum!" Under this, in a crude scrawl, yet another had written "Fuck Tadich." Mr. Tadich was a ninth grade English teacher who assigned "Research Papers" in his demanding classes and was roundly detested, although Larry actually thought him a good teacher. He knew a great deal about the Civil War, and had even published a small book of letters from members of a Pennsylvania unit that fought in the war. It was in the school library. You could learn a lot in Mr. Tadich's class if you paid attention, worked hard, and followed his rules, which were many and detailed. He liked to compare them to military orders.

With the football players and their girls, there was the whole thing about game nights, and how they both must feel on the Friday leading up to Friday night. Holly Burris would be there, cheering on the sideline with the cheerleaders, screaming her lungs out, crying, watching Fred Lucas play, getting tackled, maybe hurt, the whole thing. And he, knowing she was there on the sidelines, maybe catching sight of her when he came off the field, or even while running a play on it, a fleeting glimpse of her face as he ran by. How must that feel? Everybody else must be blotted out, he decided, and there is just the other person, just them, and what you are between yourselves.

So it was not what Frankie, and others, imagined, all the endless coarse talking in the boys' room, the showers. No. What it was, was what he saw when he saw Holly and Fred, her steady, walking in the hall and they did not know he was there. She leaned her head on his shoulder, just leaned into him, almost like she was going to fall, and he cradled his free arm around her, then draped his letterman's jacket over her shoulders. That was three years of going steady, being together. He had never been out on a date more than once with any girl. He knew nothing.

In Sam's they talked of the whorehouses, in "New Ken," in Pittsburgh, up in Weirton, West Virginia, and Steubenville, Ohio, which all the men said was a bad place, you wanted to watch out there.

"They say they got these young girls there…Not yer old, fat whores, ya know what I mean?" He made a sudden motion. "With their goddam tits hangin down, like this…" The man's eyes glistened, and he licked his thick lips. The others nodded, listening.

"But you got to have money. Just like always. Them that has, gets."

It was like a sermon in the church, and it had gotten quiet in the barbershop, so that when the bell on the door tinkled, they all looked in unison at who was coming in. It was the Burgess, as he was called, Ralston's mayor, with his huge stomach. Larry had suddenly thought, would he ever look like that, get that fat? It seemed impossible.

Fred Lucas and Robert Henderson and Dick Atkins were constantly talked of in Sam's. It seemed the men gathered there knew more about them – and their families – than maybe they did. They speculated endlessly about where they would go to college, and which of them would "make it."

"I think Atkins, that Atkins boy, he can do what he pleases. But the question is, what pleases him?"

"He's not a hard worker, you akst me… and that's significant. Yessir, it is."

"Mebbe he likes the girls too much?"

All the men hooted, slapping their legs and getting red in the face.

228

"Don't you worry, they gonna get plenty of that once they git in college. Plenty!"

He often came away from Sam's feeling that there was some essential thing about being a man he didn't understand, particularly in connection to girls. Of course, he was a virgin, and maybe it would all change when that did. He wondered how many of the guys he knew were like him. Virgins. Everyone talked of girls being virgins, but it was never said of a boy. Or at least, not very often. Yet he was certain most were just like him. The closest they – and he – had come was Goran's cards, in the boys' room.

What had happened to the girls who'd been gotten pregnant? He had heard no more, and it was as if they had disappeared. He knew there was a home – that was what it was called – down in Pittsburgh where unwed girls went to have their babies. Illegitimate babies. And then what happened? The babies were given away – adopted – and the girl would not see them again. It gave him a heavy feeling, of sadness and confusion.

"Yeah – that's what comes of messin' around," Frankie Malone said.

Carl would not be coming home for Thanksgiving, it seemed; his mother had already been talking about that. Or even Christmas. He would not be there, to read his mind, and with gentle questions and joking, bring out what was "eating him". Sandy, Carol Bigelow. Girls. Goran's cards. Football. College. On the latter, he already knew what his brother would say.

"Whatever you do, Larry, go to college. Do whatever it takes – you can do it."

If he could talk, over the kitchen table, with Carl, he could find some peace from the anxiousness that increasingly did eat at him, and even made his stomach upset. And if it bothered him now this much, what would it all be like in five or ten years? How did adults stand it?

When he saw Fred Lucas in the halls, he looked so intent it seemed he hardly saw you. The Glassboro game had been easily won, but Lucas had a bruise under one eye after the game. What was that from? "Game face," Ducky quipped. He could be sarcastic, a sharpness in him. Larry tried not to stare at Fred Lucas when he did see him. He wore his letter sweater over a white tee-shirt, which stretched tight over his chest.

"A good candidate for the Marines!" Frankie said one day. They were sitting in the cafeteria talking about Joe Labrador. His most recent incident had been one no one could have believed if it hadn't happened. Labrador had been scheduled to be paddled by two teachers, Mr. Bigelow, the biology teacher, and Dr. Traynor. Why these two had been chosen no one knew. Mr. Sweeney, the science teacher, was also somehow involved, probably as "witness" to the punishment.

Such punishments always took place right before the lunch hour, when all students were back in their home rooms. The doors to the rooms were purposely left open, so that the blows could be audible – the sharp, cracking sounds of the big paddle, and the crying out of the one being punished. This was only in the most extreme cases; usually, paddling was done in the principal's office with the door shut. But Joe Labrador had been asking for it, or so it was said.

At the time of the punishment, Larry and Frankie could clearly hear the whole thing, since room 102 was close to Mr. Hick's room, outside of which the paddling was to take place. It would echo in the big hall there satisfactorily. A hush fell over the room as they heard the voices of the teachers, and what sounded like a mild scuffling and pushing noise.

Then, suddenly, an uproar. There were loud thumping noises, and somebody banged against a wall locker, and then they heard the loud voice of Joe Labrador, breathing hard.

"How do you like it, huh? How do you like it?" Thwack! Thwack! "Huh? Huh? You like it?" Labrador was paddling the teacher, whoever it was (it later was said it was Mr. Bigelow, but no one would say for certain.) They were all informed the matter was not to be discussed.

Several teachers were heard running down the corridor, and flashed by the room. A louder scuffle, some more thumping and banging – "Hold him! Dammit, hold him!" from Mr. Sweeney. Finally, Labrador was subdued and taken to the principal's office, and later left the school. A three-day suspension was issued. This was bad, but Joe was a hero, to some at least. He had given them their own medicine, and the story quickly reached Sam's, giving the old timers a chuckle.

"That boy better watch out, though. Next thing, they'll expel him, for good. Kick him out."

"Mebbe they should – be good for the boy. He'll have to join up, then. They'll teach him a thing or two, he gets in the Army."

The coaches spoke of it as a "bad thing," and said the next time, they should be the ones to do the paddling.

It had brought to mind for Larry an incident from elementary school he'd never forgotten. Helen McFarland. A small, dark-haired wiry girl whose family lived up on The Island, in one of the long row of run-down – some were collapsing in front or back – clap board houses that ran along the Island Road. Helen raised her hand, twice, in Miss Higgins' third grade class, shifting and squirming in her desk. Miss Higgins was a famous old maid, who had taught the third grade for as long as anyone in Ralston could remember. She ignored Helen, but finally spoke sternly.

"Helen! Be still! This minute. Now!"

"I have to go to the bathroom."

Helen was surly, curling her small lips, which were very red. Her face was always dirty, and it was known that she liked to fight boys, if they would, rolling on the ground with them. Larry was somewhat afraid of her, and most of the others in the class were, too. She was not like Jane Pember, who sat in the desk across the aisle from him. He had shown Jane Pember the drawing of a naked cave man, in the history book, and Miss Higgins had caught him. But Helen, she was truly a bad girl. Miss Higgins said so.

Now, before the amazed stares of thirty two sets of eyes, while Miss Higgins wrote on the blackboard, Helen suddenly went to the side of the room, hiked up her small, dirty dress, and squatted over the wastebasket. A deep silence filled the room, along with unmistakable sounds, and a sharp smell.

Miss Higgins, turning from the big blackboard, stood frozen in shock, her mouth opening, but no words coming out. She stood as if rooted to the floor. Helen McFarland completed her act, pulled her dress down, and marched defiantly back to her small desk, turning then and sticking her very small, very red tongue out at Miss Higgins before she sat down.

She was taken immediately to the principal's office, and they never saw her again. He had wondered if she was one of the older girls he'd seen running in a wild pack back and forth sometimes, up on the Island Road. But no one seemed to know what had happened to her. She disappeared – like the girls who'd gotten pregnant.

# 18

September was a beautiful month, the most beautiful of the year. After the pressure of the summer Training Camp in August – and the pressure was there even earlier in the summer, after all – the daily JV practices were not so bad, as long as Coach Barnes did not participate too much. Coach Kowalski was more lenient and often had them do long runs around the field. "Conditioning." They would also run in place, hitting their knees as they brought them up on their held out palms.

"Lift 'em up! Up! *Up!*" Kowalski's eyes sparkled as he watched them, and he smiled. He seemed like a kindly man, even an older man than he was, Larry thought sometimes. He also wondered if anyone actually running in a game could keep lifting their legs that high. It was an odd running style to him. Kowalski surprised him by putting him in the second JV game, on a warm Saturday afternoon, against a Class "B" team, Hazelwood, that the varsity might play the following year, it was said.

Fred Lucas, the fullback, sustained a leg injury in only the second game of the season, against Wilson. There were rumors he and Holly Burris were "breaking up," that he was seen with Carol Bigelow. This was a serious development, especially during the season, and early on in it.

His mother told him Shannon Brunell had moved to someplace in Ohio – "Near Toledo, I think it is."

"Holy Toledo!" quipped Frankie, and then shut up, when Larry frowned. "Too bad. Shannon – she was a nice girl."

When September 30th came, it was the one-year anniversary of the death of James Dean. September 30, 1955. He could remember it precisely. Sitting in his room in the big old house, staring at the purple Motorola radio. He'd remember it as long as he lived, and told Bonnie that. But Dean was not that popular in the school – he was a "greaser," some said. Nobody wanted to be a greaser. Joe Labrador was a greaser. When winter came, and they turned on the radiators, he would put his piss on them to stink out the room.

Larry sat in his classes in a mild haze often, the teacher's voice far-off, like smoke itself. He was not really there, and he was not on the football field, either, despite Coach Barnes' demands that that be the case. No. He was hunting. With Carl, in the damp fall woods outside Ralston, near old man Symonds' farm, where the fading corn stalks stood rustling in the fields in long lines, like defeated but still standing soldiers. Carl said that hearing that noise, of the dead stalks rustling in the wind, made you colder. Made you shiver. It was true.

The hunt – rabbit or pheasant, grouse – this wasn't of much interest. It was walking through the woods, the late autumn colors, intense smells of leaves and rain and smoky pungency of the ground itself, the earth.

"Tilting away from the sun now," Carl said, pointing with his .20 gauge, which gleamed dully. The air itself had a rich tang of snow and winter sunlight. The time of buckwheat cakes (made from the crock outside on the porch), homemade sausage, and syrup. He had heard often about maple syrup, from Vermont, but never had it. The big buckwheat cakes "stayed with you"; you ate three or four of those, you could go all day on them. The deer ate buckwheat, too, they loved it.

If he could spend his life in the woods, he could be happy. But nobody wanted to live like that anymore. The Davy Crockett tv show had brought back the coonskin cap, and he'd read about Daniel Boone, who'd died alone across the Mississippi. Kit Carson and Crockett and Jim Bridger, all the way back in the sixth grade. Many had been killed, at The Alamo, in Texas... Maybe they just would not let you live like that, even then.

Mid-October brought some cold, squally rain down out of the north – in the country, farmers said they'd seen a few flakes of snow. The back practice field where the JVs worked out turned to greasy, slippery mud. Coach Barnes reveled in it, mud streaking, splattering his red face, forcing them to get down, take rolls in it – pushing you hard as you fell. Uniforms became smeared, stained. "That's football!" he yelled, panting; rolling over and over in the mud himself, until his jersey and gym pants were filthy. "Now you're lookin' like football players, not like you're goin' to that damn hop dance. Dirty! You gotta get dirty to play real football!"

Maybe an early winter was in store. The ground had not yet frozen but there was an unmistakable crispness in the air in the mornings, a thin rime of white frost appearing on the grass; jacket weather, and the lettermen had theirs out, sky blue with white arms and blue and white trim running around the collar and the snug bottom, their girls wearing them now. There wasn't too much that looked cuter, more fetching – that was a word his mother liked, *fetching* – than a girl in a letterman's jacket. Even a plain girl shone in one of them; it lighted them up. The trees turned shades of unimaginable red, vivid oranges and yellows, eruptions of fire around the streets leading to the high school. Looking down on the town from the top, the big curve of Mile Long Hill, it looked like a travel poster, the kind he'd seen in the big Penn Station in Pittsburgh.

It was time for the first Big Dance, the Autumn Hop, where the Harvest Queen and her Court would be crowned. Sitting on the tops of the back seats of shiny, new convertibles from Amstead's Chevrolet, the chosen girls would be driven around the football field at the home game with Clarksburg – not a big rival, but certainly always a good game. This year the Clarksburg game at mid-season had a little added significance, because Ralston was undefeated, and the news stories were already forecasting a possible championship for the team. That was a certain jinxing, the old guys in the barbershop lamented.

Clarksburg was a good academic high school nearer to Pittsburgh, down the Allegheny River. The town itself had as its prize attraction, running for a good half-mile along the river, the famous Alcoa Aluminum works. It was said three out of every four people in the town worked, or had worked, at Alcoa. Clarksburg was a company town, as they were called, which usually meant towns like the mining towns down in West Virginia, where people were locked in a hopeless cycle of work and debt. Tennessee Ernie Ford sung about them in "Sixteen Tons," with the deep refrain "I owe my soul to the company store." Coal miners and aluminum factory workers were different, though, Larry thought, so the famous song did not really apply to Clarksburg.

It seemed the sort of town that would produce good or even outstanding football teams, but Clarksburg didn't. What was it about a town, a school, that did lead to the good, the outstanding, the championship teams? Larry wondered, walking the streets, kicking piles of unbelievably colored leaves that seemed to grow of themselves there. They looked like the stained glass church windows, the history book illustrations of Gothic cathedrals.

Was it the players themselves? Ability? Or was it – as some at Sam's maintained, where the subject was frequently discussed – the caliber of the coaching, and in particular the leadership, the drive, experience, of the head coach? That seemed like it could be true, certainly. Winning coaches produced winning teams. But there was the choice rejoinder.

"Yeah. Mebbe so, mebbe so… But, you know, you all know, you sure as hell can't make a racehorse out of a jackass, now can you?"

Was it the fans, then? Or the *tradition* of football and football players, in family after family, in a town, no matter how small and poor? The large, well-equipped schools in the big towns in the valley, and especially in Pittsburgh itself, did not seem to produce great teams, famous players, unforgettable seasons, that were talked about, in awe, years later and became legendary. No, it was schools, and towns, like Ralston, and its arch rival Chester, that produced – year in, year out – teams that played consistently well, not just passably. They had winning seasons year after year, a losing season was a catastrophe, and they sent players to great college and university teams. They had full trophy cases in the front lobby of the school displaying old, signed footballs that looked larger and heavier, fatter, than the current ball, strange looking helmets that appeared like they could have been from the last century, numerous framed team photos, old programs of games, frayed school pennants, faded with age, some displayed photos of the early heroes of the game – Walter Camp, who wore a moustache and had his hair parted in the middle; Bronko Nagurski, who wore a jersey with the number 3 on it although he was a fullback; Red Grange, carrying one of the old-style fat, dark footballs; Ernie Nevers, with a shock of hair so blond it looked like corn. None wore helmets in the photos, except for a player named Jack Lummus, who was shown catching a pass; he had received the Medal of Honor in WWII. And at their arch rival, Chester, he had seen in a case in the gym a drawing of Hobey Baker, from Princeton. Reading the small card about him, he discovered he'd also been a hockey star.

In the great, running arguments in Sam's, some said it all came down to pride. And no one really understood that, or how you got it, held onto it, but pride was what made the difference. Larry felt he could understand that – it connected with the enormous "team spirit" at Ralston, evident in the pep rallies and on the sidelines and stands on game nights. It was in the loud, blaring playing of the band, the high-stepping marching of the always smiling majorettes (some of whom still had the summer tans visible on their legs), the leaps of the cheerleaders, Charlie Hibbing's mad running up and down in front of the stands with a blue and white Ralston beanie on his head. It was corny – another word his mother favored – but it was very real. The coaches spoke of it often, calling it "the magic." Coach Barnes called it "the grease," rubbing his hands. The players solemnly admitted at the pep rallies it made a big difference, that they could feel it, it helped out on the field.

Certainly the Autumn Hop, the election of the Harvest Queen (and her King), and the half-time parade onto the field that night were part of that spirit, that tradition, at Ralston. The previous year, George Spenser had been elected King. Although a varsity player, he wasn't one of the starting eleven, the First Team, the real football players. And while the game was important and the Harvest Queen parade was colorful and exciting, it was the dance, the Autumn Hop on Saturday night in the high school gym, that was the real event. Any dance in the gym was an event, but this one, where the girls wore special, frothy, wispy, pale pastel-colored chiffon dresses, was a big deal.

He went sheepishly to his first dance in the eighth grade. He could remember it vividly. A scary evening in some ways – as he had walked up the alley, the steep stone-cobbled hill he'd walked up in every kind of weather since he was in first grade – he could feel his heart hammering so hard; whatever girl he'd dance with would surely be able to hear it, or feel it. There would be many girls at this dance, there would be chances to ask a girl you really liked to dance. To hold her close – how close? It was one of the questions that bedeviled him, made his heart pound that way, his palms sweaty, hands ice-cold. Wouldn't the girl instinctively jump when he touched her with such cold hands? And there was something else, another problem.

"She's rubbin' up against you, you know your pecker's gonna get stiffer'n a poker. I guarantee it!" somebody said in the thick steam of the shower room. "Hell, they know what they're doin'. They like it."

For a long time, he had been hearing stories about what happened when you held a girl and danced close. What happened was you would get an erection. A hard-on, as everyone said, pointing down at themselves, grinning. There was no way to avoid it, even if you tried. Some even claimed you could come – "shoot" – in your pants, that some girls *wanted* to make you do this. And the imme-diacy of the girl, right there, unnerved him when they had held a sort of practice "hop" in the gym earlier in the eighth grade. The rich shininess of her hair, the smell of it, and even the texture, brushing your face – he thought of Cameron Mitchell's magnificent dark mane of hair. When he had mentioned this to his mother, by accident one night at dinner, she had smiled and said, "That's why they make women wear scarves over their heads, in the Catholic Church, at least." Something he'd never understood before. The whole, cumulative effect was something he hadn't counted on. It made you sort of deaf and dumb, as he told Frankie Malone.

"Yeah. It'll make you stiff, too." He grinned. Frankie always brought it back down to the ground.

The major dances of the school year (except for the two Proms) were always held in the gym. It was a place of strong, heavy, intense smells – rank, mingled sweat, pungent wool athletic socks, the soapy, wet smells from the showers, and a danker, cold smell, one like cellars had that had been through a flood, a thick smell of mud and brown, dirty water. There was a higher, sharper smell, the disinfectant foot baths you walked in and out of going to and from the showers. It smelled like Mercurochrome and was the same intense red color. The girls' side of the gym, really their locker room, had an even more amazing range of smells, including a sharp, acrid deep reek so strong at times it made you instinctively turn away, holding your hand over your nose.

Then there was the fresh, clean odor of the big wooden floor with the wax put on it by Mr. Dempsey, the janitor.

Moving his big broom in huge methodical circles, slowly and carefully – he seemed in a trance when he did this. Watching him, Larry thought it might not be a bad job, that of janitor. One thing was for sure, you were always warm in the winter. There were many jokes about what happened in the boiler room, which Mr. Dempsey ruled over, and some teachers descended to, to smoke cigarettes during the day.

But the most amazing thing about him was that on particularly cold winter nights, Mr. Dempsey sometimes let Larry and Ducky Estes into the gym to shoot baskets, for which he probably could have lost his job. Larry had always wondered why he did it. He kept the big lights over the court only half on, and he and Ducky tried to keep their dribbling down so there wouldn't be too much of the clearly audible pounding sound of a basketball on the wooden floor – you could hear that unique sound quite far away, you could hear it clearly outside the gym, even before you got there.

The gym on those bitter cold nights when Mr. Dempsey let them in became a place of fantasy for him. He filled the banked, wooden benches with a full crowd, yelling and screaming as he and Ducky drove down the court, passing effortlessly, and then driving to the basket for a score, the net whooshing as he passed. Or he gunned in a high, looping hook shot from the key, pivoting quickly, while Ducky watched, nodding in approval. The feeling of the difficult hook shot going down, going in, was a deep satisfaction he couldn't explain; it felt good, it was a completion. Sometimes they would try insane shots, from thirty feet or more, yelling in spite of themselves when they went in.

In the gym on those occasions, he often thought of his true heroes, the stars of the Boston Celtics, Bill Sharman and Bob Cousy. Both played guard, and both had outstanding types of shots that usually cleared the rim of the basket and swished the thick white nets of the baskets with a satisfying flourish and distinctive sound.

Sharman shot a two-handed "set" shot that was going out of style but that he shot with withering accuracy from the outside, launching the ball from chest level in a high arc, not using the bank board at all. Cousy had an amazing form and style moving the ball down the court, a smooth, effortless lope, dribbling the ball without looking at it – easier said than done. It was like he had been born dribbling a basketball. Cousy's patented move was a behind-the-back pass that he would make as he drove towards the basket to a player left open by one coming over to cover him. He also shot a good hook shot, which guards were not supposed to do. Only centers shot hook shots.

Larry worked for hours on his hook shot and got it down to where he could make a string of such shots from the top of the key, pivoting suddenly, throwing the ball in a high arc. There were few things as gratifying as the physical feeling he had when the ball sailed clearly through the hoop and net – two points!

The basketball coach, Mr. Pedjman, a dark-complex-ioned Armenian who had a small, neatly trimmed moustache and was sometimes called "Hitler Pedjman" by students who didn't like him, particularly disdained Cousy's moves. He lectured his team over and over that they had to learn "the fundamentals." It would be a long time before they could ever, if indeed they ever could, do the behind the back pass, or the infamous hook shot. That was "television stuff," as he put it. His players were drilled in the one-hand set shot, or the two-hand overhead set shot – those were permissible. The jump shot was not something he really liked, but he would permit it at times, grudgingly, never praising it. Larry thought a jump shot from either of the extreme side corners of the court to the basket was one of the most difficult, and most dramatic, shots to make, and Coach Pedjman positively hated this particular shot, hectoring his players never to make it. He emphasized team work, feeding the ball off continuously in an almost conveyor-belt like mode, taking clear lay-up shots, or close-in shots that could not easily be missed. And he insisted shots be banked off the backboard – that was what it was for, wasn't it? And endless dribbling drills, with folding chairs placed in long, looping lines down the court.

There was no esthetic to his game, his coaching. That was it, pure and simple. His teams played a kind of bland basketball, "hustle" (he loved that word), low-scoring games that really emphasized defense, working the ball ever closer in, taking an almost assured shot, playing for a foul shot. He insisted all his players shoot those under-handed, something that Larry had seen very few pro players do. It was the way girls shot fouls.

Larry finally came to the conclusion that Coach Pedjman did not understand, or love, the true game of basketball, which was really about movement, faking, and clean, high-arcing geometry. No. He was really using the game as a conditioning tool for the football players! It was obvious – everybody knew it. So, again, it was all coming back to football. He and Ducky Estes would never make the varsity basketball team, no matter how much they practiced their moves or their shooting. The whole thing gave him a sour sense of futility, made him angry. It was another disappointment of school, which always seemed to promise much which never materialized. Or, as Frankie would say, "School is just a big crock of class A shit, man! Except for football."

When he was dressing for practices, he could see that this year, for the Autumn Hop, it was looking like the old gym would be lavishly decorated. The signs up in the halls announced "An Evening In Paris" theme. There was to be a large *papier mâché* Eiffel Tower, made by the advanced art class. A cheese cloth sky with star-shaped holes cut into it, was going to be strung completely over the top of the dance floor, an amazing idea. Larry wondered who had come up with it. That would be a hell of a job, putting that up. A bunch of freshman and eighth grade girls would dance with each other underneath it while Pat Boone records played over the PA system… "April in Paris." It was a typical girl idea – it was October. Why didn't they use this theme for a spring dance? No one seemed to know, or even ask.

He did not think he wanted to go to the Hop – but then maybe he did and was trying to hide it. Certainly there wasn't any girl he could seriously think of asking. Cameron Mitchell, in her fire engine red '55 Chevy? Impossible, as fantasy even more remote than Cheryl Lake. And Sandy Stevens was out of the question. Too embarrassing, even asking her, for simply that act spoke volumes about you. The girls read every act taken towards them in complicated ways. Besides, no car to pick her up in – he would have to arrange some type of clumsy double-date, a notoriously unpopular thing with many girls. And, in addition, he was feeling tired from the mandatory after-school JV practices.

The JV season was turning out to be a grind. Too much practice, and few people, really, came to the games, so that you wondered if they were of any importance really, meant very much. The sound of the tiny crowds on the sidelines seemed almost pathetic to him, although he was glad they were there, for it would have been terrible if no one had been there. You needed the crowd, somehow, for the game to be real.

Then, an amazing thing happened. Cindy Shaffer, a red-haired sophomore in Larry's home room, asked Frankie Malone to go to the Hop with her. Frankie was stupefied and the news spread through the school like the proverbial wildfire.

"You know how it happened?" he maintained. "It was that stupid Sweater Thing. Sweaters! That was what did this to me."

The Sweater Thing was an idea dreamed up by some junior girls. Girls would ask boys for a sweater of theirs they could wear to the Clarksburg game, the Autumn Hop game. And, of course, by girl logic, if a girl wore your sweater, something was up between you. No doubt you were bound to actually go to the Autumn Hop together. Nothing could be clearer, no matter how it had been maneuvered. Cindy Shaffer asked Frankie for his sweater, a red v-necked one, and he'd given it to her freely, without a thought.

"Don't think it can't happen to you," Frankie said to him, as they walked in the hall outside the gym. "Hey, maybe big-tittied Norma'll ask you! How'd you like to have those cannons stickin' up in your face all night, huh?" He pushed his chest out, pouting his lips, licking them. "Ummmm!"

What would James Dean do in such a situation? Larry did not know how he had hit upon this idea at first -- maybe in that sort of dopey state before you fell asleep, when things slowed down and also sometimes became very clear. He invoked James Dean as an advisor increasingly, and thought how good it would be to actually be able to talk to him. He seemed to be wise, even though he had only been twenty-four when he was killed in the car accident. One of the disc jockeys had commented recently on the absurd name of the driver of the car that killed Dean – Donald Turnupseed. It was an unlikely name, a name that did not seem real, and yet it was, and Dean was dead, although it was claimed he really wasn't. But where would he be if he was alive? Frankie had said he was having extensive plastic surgery, he would never re-appear in public life. In fact, you might run into him at a gas station, a supermarket, or at a football game even, and not know it was him. He liked to think of that, that James Dean was roaming around America, in between having surgeries, unnoticed, anonymous. It was a thing he would do, too. You could sit in some roadside diner, one of those that was really a converted trolley car from Pittsburgh, or some Eat N' Park, and listen to what people said about you.

He told Bonnie Evans, the best-read girl in the class, about his James Dean fantasy, and she was enthusiastically in favor of it, could believe it, why not, she said, shaking her head intensely. Bonnie was very smart, her score on the IQ test so high they would not tell her parents, or her. Bonnie was constantly reading, books Larry hadn't heard of. She explained this by saying her parents read a lot. Bonnie would go to college, for sure – but she would never be Harvest Queen.

"I think football is stupid," she said to him. "Why do you want to play? You're going to get hurt – what's the sense in it? It's stupid, Larry, and I think you know it is. So the question is, why do you play it?"

He had been unable to successfully reply to Bonnie Evans, and she knew this, too, holding her books and large blue Ralston three-ring binder grasped firmly in front of her. He had looked at her notes in this binder in the library; they were amazing, scrolled on and on in a careful, small neat hand. A left-hander, he noted, watching her in class.

Was he playing, trying to play, football so he could go out with a future Harvest Queen? She'd gone on to ask that, really dumbfounding him. Girls' minds worked in ways you just could never predict. Why did she say that? He had a bad moment when it struck him that Bonnie Evans might ask him for his sweater, but she did not.

The upcoming big dance, the uncertainty of the Sweater Thing, his own essentially constantly wandering mind, put him in a daze. Now, at the midpoint of the football season nearly – the Training Camp weeks back in August already seemed a long time ago – the posting of the list on the board, the heat, the raging thirst for a Coke or a Nehi Grape or even a Seven-Up, the sun-filled daze of the long dog days afternoon, when the football would seem to hang in its lazy spirals forever, it would never come down. The heavy unmistakable "thunk" of the ball being punted downfield. But it all did not seem so important now. Although he had played in three JV games – true, only for a couple of series of plays, and only at the end of the game, when the game was already decided – he had that experience. It was then, actually out on the field itself, that he had felt it did mean something, it was real. It was in the game itself, as it was played. What would occur in a series of plays could not be predicted; no matter how often practiced, the players never knew how it would go. The practice was shit. It was the game that was real, and he could not explain that clearly, even to himself, but he knew it was true, and important.

He remembered that first game he had been put in against the Glassboro JV. The field was churned up, the grass torn, the players sweating heavily. Some cursed, and others grinned, happy. In his first series of plays, he had been on defense. He lined up across from a fat, red-faced boy playing guard who did not seem to see him. As the ball was snapped, he "submarined," a maneuver Coach Barnes specially favored. The fat offensive guard fell on top of him with a crashing noise of pads, more weight pressed him further into the ground, and for a few seconds it was dark, his nose filled with the smell of ground grass and black dirt, and even what he strangely thought might be worms. Then there was the referee's voice, far away. His "submarine" had resulted in a fumble by the back carrying the ball; Ralston had recovered. When he got to the sideline, there was some cheering by the small crowd and Coach Kowalski patted him on the back. "Fifty pounds more on you, you'd be All-American, Simmons!" he said. His eyes were moist, although Larry knew he could not have been crying.

They were two touchdowns ahead and there were only a few minutes left in the game. No doubt others would be put in now, but Coach Kowalski signaled for him before he had had a chance to sit down on the bench. He went in on offense, at end. The run back across the field seemed to take a long time, and he wondered if he would make it to the huddle where Chad Lewis, the third-string quarterback, called a pass play. It was not to be thrown to him, but to a back coming out of his halfback position. He would block.

The defensive players from Glassboro had very dirty, old uniforms that did not fit them and some appeared to have been crying, or it was perspiration, he could not tell. They looked very tired, and as they lined up opposite them, he felt they were already leaving the field, they did not want to play any more. But they knew they could not just walk off the field. It gave him a bad feeling, and he looked around, again smelling the distinctive tang of the crushed grass and mixed in earth, and the thick sweat smell of the players, his own team and Glassboro. Then the ball was snapped and he charged hard towards the linebacker who ran heavily into him – he saw his blue number, 44, in front of his face as they crashed down together, rolling in a tangle of legs.

He lay on the ground with the linebacker on top of him, struggling, and heard the crowd yell, and the linebacker, pushing at him, said "Shit!", and then he was off him, he could stand. Thirty or forty yards down the field, Gary Meakin was running hard towards the end zone, and as he stood looking, Meakin crossed the goal line into it and then trotted back towards them, carrying the ball high in the air with one hand, pumping it. Touchdown! Some of the Ralston players around him whooped loudly, hoarsely.

They had won the Glassboro JV game by three touchdowns, and his defensive play, on that one play, had led to the fumble directly resulting in a Ralston score. Although he hadn't played long, he'd affected the outcome of the game. It gave him a satisfaction he could not have expected; he stayed in the shower after the game longer than he usually did, accepting the congratulations and good words of other players, enjoying the sense of having won the game; he had been a part of that.

He wished there was a girl waiting to meet him when he got outside, as happened after varsity games. It was not likely any girl would wait for a replacement JV player, even a good-looking one. But he could imagine a girl, and imagine walking slowly with her down the tree-lined street, kicking through some of the leaves that were beginning to pile up. It was cold enough to wear a light jacket, and he would turn up the collar, like James Dean, that red jacket he wore in *Rebel Without A Cause*. The girl would have on black and white saddle shoes, a pleated tartan skirt, or maybe Levis, rolled up with that high cuff girls wore when they wore jeans. He thought of Cameron Mitchell. It wasn't likely she'd wait for anyone after a game. Cameron didn't seem to care about football, but she didn't have to.

He thought about this the whole way home, walking back down the steep alley, going past Ducky's house (he wondered if he'd seen the game; probably not, since there were really good college games on television now, and besides, Ducky was not a football fan). That was what the Autumn Hop was really all about, what he had been thinking about... He was home before he knew it, wrapped as he was in the fantasy, the imaginary walk, the imaginary girl. His mother had made his favorite dish, he could eat a ton of it - macaroni and cheese. The big dish gleamed on the table, steam rising from it, and his mouth suddenly watered. He was very hungry, he felt pleasantly tired, he felt good. Even if his mother did not understand football.

# 19

Jerry Schrader, a kid in the class who'd been among the first to see *Rebel Without A Cause*, and read nearly as much as Bonnie Evans, only very few people knew about it, lent him a book one day before American History class began, handing it casually but quickly to him – *From Here To Eternity*. It was a thick novel, about World War Two. There were a lot of novels about World War Two out, you could find them on the rotating, squeaking book rack down at deNicchio's, the tobacco store next to the railroad station. The lady down there would let him stand for long periods of time, reading the books – he did not have the money to buy all the ones he would liked to have bought. Some cost nearly a dollar. "A paperback book!" his mother exclaimed, shaking her head over the ironing board. "What are things going to come to?"

This novel was by James Jones, a writer who lived in Illinois. His photograph had been in *Life* magazine; he was an Army war veteran who had fought in the Pacific. He had the feeling that books like *From Here To Eternity* were too adult, there was a lot of sex stuff, which Jerry Schrader mentioned. Back in the spring, Schrader had lent him *The Naked and The Dead* by Norman Mailer, but he hadn't finished it. He did not know if he should be reading such books and tried half-heartedly to hide them from his mother, but felt pretty sure she knew about it and let him read them anyway. She was a great champion of reading, in any case. "Your grandfather, now, he would read anything. Anything, and everything, he just read all the time. Everybody talked about it." So he was following in his grandfather's shoes, with the reading, it was okay.

He could not put down the Jones novel. It was better than the Mailer. There had been long sessions of reading late in his room, until two, three in the cool summer mornings, and he felt he would always remember reading *From Here To Eternity* in the early summer, years later. He had wanted to go out and walk around the town after these sessions, he did not fell sleepy at all.

Once he had walked down to the creek and stood looking at it in the summer darkness, swatting at mosquitoes, thinking how far he was from Hawaii, where the novel took place. Actually, *From Here to Eternity* was not a real war novel, but took place immediately before World War Two started. But none of the characters in the novel knew that, and that somehow made it all much better. There was a lot of sex stuff in the book, and he knew that was something maybe he shouldn't be reading, he was not sure that he understood it all, either. Prewitt – a young enlisted man, the main character – he liked very much. He was a boxer who would no longer fight because he had once killed a man in the ring. He was also a terrific bugler, and a fine soldier, who liked the Army and what he called "soldiering." He thought of his brother Carl when he read of Prewitt. He also thought of himself. What kind of a soldier would he make? It was likely he would be drafted once out of high school, unless he could get into college; even then, you were eligible for the draft until you were the ancient ago of 26. Twenty-six! He could not imagine being that old, it was older than Carl was, even. Nearing thirty.

War novels reminded him of the comic books he once collected and read avidly. His favorites were the most exaggerated and violent, the World War II and Korean War ones, featuring buck-toothed Japanese, North Korean and Chinese soldiers, "gooks" and "Chinks," being machine-gunned down as they made a banzai charge or human wave attack, or being blown up by a well-thrown grenade. He also liked the crime comics, which invariably led up to the climatic scene of the tough guy being dragged to the waiting electric chair; some even depicted his shadowy figure straining in the chair as the current hit him, emitting a long capital-lettered scream. Other prisoners' bloodshot eyes started out of their sockets as they listened to his execution, gripping the bars of their cells, or cowering in their narrow cell beds… the cruelty of these comics was compelling, he could not deny it, it was awful and yet you could not take your eyes from it, and read on as if hypnotized.

Maybe he would escape, take off, take to hitchhiking. The interstate highways were going up everywhere, after all. Hitchhike across America! What would that be like, what would you see, who would you meet? Had anybody written a book about that? He could imagine James Dean hitchhiking, there was something necessary about it, almost like a ritual. You had to do it. He admired those whose stories you heard about in the barbershop. "That guy, you know, they say – after he got outta the Army – he hitched all the way across the country! Was a smoke jumper up in Montana, Oregon. I'd like to do that, once in my life. Just once!" Emphatically said, to everyone and to themselves.

But they had never done it, and probably never would. He was beginning to see Sam's was a place of "never done it and never would." The barbershop was like the village store they'd read about in history class, with the "cracker barrel" philosophers sitting around, endlessly whittling with their pocket knives. He knew he did not want to be like the men who seemed to always be in Sam's, lounging in a vacant chair with a magazine in their hand they never actually read, but used to gesture and point with or swat flies. The worst were the really old men, who constantly fell asleep, mouths gaping open, a black hole in their sunken cheeks. Some would even start snoring, and Sam the barber would laugh, snap out a towel or a cover, and they would wake and look dazedly around, swallowing and shifting in the same chair they'd probably sat in for years.

When he had been a kid, and they had been building the interstate highway through and around Ralston, he and some other kids would sit in the muggy summer nights over across the bridge at Guinta's Fruit Stand, watching for out of state license plates. That had been their summer game, their competition. He kept a list in a small black pocket notebook of how many states he'd personally seen. Some, like West Virginia, were common and nearby and meant little. He had even been there himself, to Morgantown, and some place where there was a big, recently built dam, and a lake that had a ton of bass in it, just waiting to be caught.

"Hell, you go down there, it's outside of Morgantown there, and them fish jist about jump outta the water onto your hook. I'm tellin' you!"

Driving down there in West Virginia too he had seen people sitting on the porch of a tilted, crazy-looking house. The roof looked half blown off, falling into the house. It was a shock. He could not believe that people lived in such a place. They had no shoes on and the men wore bib overhauls, which nobody wore in Pennsylvania. Their shriveled faces looked old, their mouths shrunken in as if they had no teeth – although they could not have been that old. Why did they look like that?

"Hillbillies," his mother had said.

At school, as the autumn had quickly progressed, suddenly, almost overnight there was the epidemic of "stuff" written on the walls. Frankie talked incessantly about the stuff he found seemingly everywhere – some even written in the mens' room of the train station, down on the cement Highgrade railroad bridge, and some was scrawled inside, on the heavy walls. In the Big Flood of 1936, the Allegheny River had come up inside the Highgrade, and there was a still visible, blackened marker of this famous high-water point. Every so often they would talk about it at Sam's, nodding seriously.

When a train went pounding overhead, it was a strange sensation to be in there, underneath the Highgrade. The noise was thick and heavy, it was dark, and Larry often thought it was the closest thing you could get to actually lying underneath a train and letting it run over you. He had heard people had done that, but he wondered if it could possibly be true. Wouldn't something on the underside of the train's cars snag the person? The full terror of having the big train, all that weight, hurtling over you – the noise would be unbearable, you would probably go crazy, berserk, right in that second, rear up, and be killed, your head torn off instantly. And what would you know, experience, in that instant, that fraction of a split second? Why did he think of such things?

There was a girl in the junior class, Kerry Stephens. She liked to run in front of the trains at night, at a crossing up by the Island, screaming as she did so. Frankie had not seen her do this, but had heard of it from someone who had, Bob Goran. Bob Goran had already been arrested by the truant officer twice. Goran's word was probably not that reliable, yet he knew a lot about things that went on in and around Ralston that it seemed many people knew nothing about. A few years back, he had been one of the first to know about the sex parties at the cabin where the biology teacher had been involved with every member of the first string football team. That had turned out to be true. Goran also claimed the two town telephone operators were lesbians. It was said he knew of a small peephole through which you could see into the girls' shower room. Goran also had his famous deck of playing cards, and these led to an argument with Frankie he thought about for days afterwards, walking the halls.

Goran never showed the entire deck, and Larry wondered if he really had a complete deck, or only a few cards. Usually he would show only one card, carrying it in a special small envelope which he was very guarded about.

The particular card he showed them, in the boys' room in a closed stall, showed the head of a woman. She had long, dark hair – how old was she? She was not a young girl – Larry guessed thirty, maybe even older. There seemed to be a slight film of sweat shining on her forehead, her hair looked damp.

The man in the picture was not visible, but only his heavy, thick cock, veins swollen, thrust half-way into the woman's mouth. Her head was turned sideways, so her thick lips showed, locked around it. Her eyes were closed, a detail that bothered Larry. The man, what could be seen of him, was extraordinarily hairy – "He's probably a goddamn Dago, or something," Frankie said.

The picture was disturbing, and looking at it made him feel upset and sad, as if he were seeing something he shouldn't. Later, he and Frankie had talked about it.

"It was ugly. That's what I think. Where in the hell does Goran get that stuff, anyway?"

Don Skiles

"Why was it ugly? A guy getting sucked off."

"What about her. The woman?"

"What do you mean – what about her?"

"I mean I don't think she was enjoying what she was doing. Her eyes are closed, for one thing. She's old, for another. She's sweating. Think about it. Where did they take that picture? How many other guys were there?"

Frankie grinned. "Sure – waiting their turn."

"She's not doing that because she wants to. That's what I'm getting at. The picture's ugly, Frankie. Bad."

Frankie had looked at him without speaking for a few seconds. "Whatever you say, Larry. Whatever you say. But she can bite me anytime."

"Bite me!" was a particularly popular saying – there was a new one every year – spreading through the school. Larry heard it often, called out in the halls by the lockers. Frankie said he'd seen it written many places, even on a fence post out in the country. But Larry found it a stupid saying.

"Look, Frankie – if that was acted on, then the person would be bitten, and I don't think anybody really wants to get bitten down there. Do you?"

"Come on! It's just an expression – nobody thinks that, what you just said…"

"Then why do they say it?"

Frankie looked at him for a minute. "You know, if I didn't know you better, I'd say you were really a devious

262

wise-ass. Really! And let me tell you something here. My dad was in the war, over in Italy, and he was in this city, up north, it's called Bologna? Like baloney – maybe that's where it comes from."

"He was in Bologna."

Frankie nodded vigorously. "Isn't that what I just said?" He leaned forward, looking around the hallway. "And you know what he told me, about in Bologna?"

Larry shook his head. "No. What?"

"Hah! The women there, they give the guy a blow-job and they use their teeth, up and down? And you know what they call that?"

"How would I know that?" Larry looked away, down the long hallway towards where it curved to the music room. He could hear faint singing sounds – probably the chorus class.

"*Rigatoni.* They call it a rigatoni. You know – like the big macaroni tubes?"

"Rigatoni?" Larry was puzzled.

"The rigatoni got ridges on it – ah, you know what I mean!" Frankie shook his head in frustration.

"...Bite me...the rigatoni..."

"There's an old university there, too. In Bologna. I think my dad said it was the oldest one in Europe."

Larry was still thinking over the rigatoni connection, and scuffled his feet absently, nodding.

"So think of that, huh? They got universities, they're older than this damn country is!"

"That's pretty old..."

Frankie nodded rapidly, in his manner. "Yeah. Old. Europe is old, that's what I think...and think of all the Dagos in Ralston! There's a lot of 'em."

The old Dagos – the Guineas – that's what people from Italy in the Lower End of Ralston were called. They were also called mackerel snappers, because they ate fish on Fridays, and Mickies, but he couldn't figure out the second term. You couldn't marry a Mickey, because if you did, then you had to agree to bring up your children to be Mickies, or else they wouldn't marry you... The Irish were Mickies, but they did not seem to have as many people who didn't like them, as the Italians, and they did not seem like they were from Europe. But they made damn good football players, good athletes in general, the Italians.

"They were on the other side. With the Germans. In the war." This is what Frankie always said, in explanation of the hatred of the Italians. But what side had the Irish been on? He couldn't recall reading about them in reading of the war. When he asked, the history teacher said the Irish were "neutral" in the war, but that seemed a hard thing to be. Neutral.

Of course, there were also the Hunkies, and the Polacks, but there weren't a lot of them in Ralston or on the farms in the surrounding areas. They were mainly down in Pittsburgh, and there were a lot of them down there, for sure. The guy who had owned the big garage, near where he had grown up as a child, uptown, had been a Polack, and his son had had fits. Seizures, his mother called them, they came from epilepsy. He could remember this boy, falling down by the kitchen table, and kicking his legs wildly...Billy Stanski was his name. He had been a big kid, too, even when they were only about seven years old. His father sold the garage, they had moved away. In the summer, when it was hot, Stanski's Garage had been cool and dark, smelling of motor oils and gasoline, cars parked in small, neat rows. A flock of pigeons lived in the big ceiling girders and there were huge rats, sewer rats his mother called them. One had killed their pet black tom cat, Nicky; they found the dead rat by the side of Nicky. Mr. Stanksi praised the cat, calling him "a hell of a fighter – those sewer rats are bad business." And he pointed at the dead rat, pushing it with his oily work boot. "Goddamn things, rats – what use are they?"

Why did he remember all this stuff? He wondered if other people did. If you remembered so much when you got older, it would be a great deal, maybe even a problem. Old people talked about the Great War, the First World War, the Kaiser. It seemed so far off in time he could not really imagine it. Yet someday, if he lived that long, even the Second World War, the Korean War, these would be as remote and forgotten and unbelievable. It made him feel odd to think that.

Or maybe he would write a book about some war to come (in some unknown part of the world that would be strange up until that point, like Korea), that he would take part in. Like James Jones and Norman Mailer. Some of his classmates would be killed in it, yet he would survive, and write the book of that war, and that book would be passed around in some school of that time.

And it was while thinking of that, "wool gathering," his mother called it, that he was approached in the library by Sandy Stevens, smiling, looking right at him. No mistaking that.

# 20

She asked him to the Hop, she asked to wear his sweater, he could hardly breathe as she stood close to him. The other kids passing by were a blur. All he could think about was the incredibly fine texture of her skin and the faint flush on it, in her cheeks, which made her even prettier if that was possible. Sandy Stevens. What the hell, what was he going to do? It would result in a massive foul-up, a disaster, he was certain of it.

The week of the Autumn Hop he couldn't concentrate at all in school. In practices, he screwed up so badly that Coach Barnes kicked him in the butt, which hurt. It hurt to have your ass kicked, it was true. In classes, he could focus on nothing for any length of time. Mr. Wadling, a young man wearing a badly grease-spattered tie and substituting in the algebra class, looked like a fish moving his mouth in water as he talked. He rapidly wrote, then erased, figures and equations on the board. They appeared to float in a watery haze to Larry. His brain would not function; it seemed stuck. He was thinking only of Sandy Stevens, who, amazingly, *he* was going to the Hop with. And Cameron Mitchell smiled at him, just at him, he thought. Certainly she knew – but Cameron, she probably wouldn't even go near the Hop. She was beyond that stuff... No, everyone in the whole damn school knew.

How had it happened? The event in the library, the sudden whisper in his ear and her so close to him that her smell enveloped him – what was it, something like vanilla, like a vanilla milkshake, but that couldn't be – it was some scheme of the various girls' groups you could come upon anywhere in the school, standing off to one side talking, always whispering in each others' ears. Cliques. They would be looking at you, some smiling as they did this. Sometimes, they would speak in unison suddenly – "Hi, Larry!" What were you supposed to do in reply to that? He would blush, they would laugh again, some holding their books over their mouths in a way girls had. Boys never did that sort of stuff. Someone, like Joe Labrador, might grab his crotch and say "Smoke a White Owl!" or try to cop a quick feel of a girl as she raised her books to her locker shelf. Larry did not do these things – his mother would be disappointed in him (as she said) – but in a grudging way he admired the boys who did these things, risked the punishments, even possible expulsion. They might get "Hambone" from Mr. Mazaroski, an ex-football player who wore double-breasted suits that looked too small and tight on his huge shoulders, "Want a taste of the Bone?" he would ask in a quiet, ominous, low tone of voice, glaring suddenly at somebody in his math- ematics class. "Yes. I think you do. Get up here, you little bastard!" He would lift the boy at the same time bodily from his seat, the boy's legs, his thin shins, banging hard against the desk. Hauling him, half suspended in air, to the front of the room, Mr. Mazaroski forced the boy to stand, facing the class.

"Now. Bend over. Grab your ankles, boy." He had retrieved the dreaded "Hambone" from his desk drawer. Now he suddenly slapped it, with great force, down on the desk, a fierce cracking sound that made everyone jump.

"Oh yeah! You hear that, don't you?"

Then, with no further words, he was swinging a quick stroke into the boy's buttocks, holding him at the same time by his belt so that he could not escape.

"One!" he cried out, as the boy's face froze in shock, reddened, his mouth trembling, his eyes already tearing.

"Two!" Straining forward, the boy tried to stretch away from him, rearing his head upwards, the neck muscles taut.

"Three!" The boy's head went down, and he gasped. "Jesus," he said, gritting his teeth. "Please..." The girls in the class looked down at their desks, hid their faces, looked away, or turned towards the back of the room, even though Mr. Mazaroski expressly prohibited this. Several boys glared at him, despite their own fear. The sound of the big paddle, with four large holes bored in its smooth surface to improve its striking pain, was terrible as it smacked into the boy's flesh.

Then he stopped, dramatically. "Do you want any more? Huh? Do you?" Mr. Mazaroski shook the boy like you would shake a disobedient dog, and the boy began now to cry openly, the one thing he desperately did not want to do, especially not in front of the girls. "Huh? Answer me, or I'll give you some more of it." He waved the paddle in the air. "Another taste, of the Hambone."

The boy shook his head rapidly. He could not speak, or was afraid to try.

"Yes, I didn't think you did!"

Those scenes made his classroom a feared place. Did Mr. Mazaroski enjoy what he did? He didn't seem to, although several students hinted that that was why he used "Hambone." Could someone really enjoy doing that? Was it allowed, what he did? No one seemed to know, and no parent had come to the school to complain.

But he did not want to think about "Hambone." He wanted to think about Sandy, and he was afraid to think about her, at the same, confusing time. The masturbation – the merciless erections ("A stiff prick has no conscience!") had become an overwhelming problem. The more he tried to resist, the more insistent the demand was, over-riding all his resolves. Goran had been no help, having now sold him several of the playing cards, which he'd hid in a wall crack in his bedroom, taking them out at night with a trembling hand. What if his mother ever found these things? He was disgusted with himself every time he looked at them. Yet he couldn't stop, or get rid of them, throw them into the burn barrel where they belonged. It was all Goran's fault! He was a slimy, low bastard, who belonged up on The Island, with the trash up there. He'd heard there were cases on The Island where fathers slept with their daughters, and brothers with their sisters. Or

raped them, if they refused. Nothing could be done about
it.

Sandy was a beautiful girl, and although it clearly had
to be impossible – maybe it wasn't? – she was growing
more beautiful day by day. But then this seemed to be
happening, overnight as it were, with a number of the girls.
Suddenly, they were not really girls anymore, but something different. He could remember sleeping in a tent, the
smell of the big canvas tent, in the Stevens' backyard when
they were in the fifth grade, and Sandy had already been
pretty, although he could not say so. Even then, being near
her had created an odd, trembling feeling in him.

Maybe it was the remarkable variety of her clothes. She
had an apparently inexhaustible supply of sweaters and
blouses – outfits, the girls called them. Some girls said
Sandy wanted to become an airline stewardess, a glamorous
job only very pretty girls aspired to. He could imagine her
as a stewardess, although he had never flown on a plane,
or even seen a real stewardess, except in movies. Talking to
her in class, looking into her blue eyes, he sometimes lost
his train of thought. How had she become so lovely? And
what could she possibly see in him?

In the boys' room, he looked in the mirror and saw
a worried boy. At least no obvious pimples, no hideous
blotches or rashes, blackheads, grease. Ugly things erupting
overnight like a wild fungus on one's face. The *Clearasil*
was working good. But he looked thin-faced, unfinished –
like one of the projects in wood shop, something like that.
She should be going to the dance with a junior, or even

a senior, although as soon as he thought this, he didn't want it to be so, he knew that for certain. He remembered clearly the incessant talk of these boys, in the boys' room, of how they had forced girls to do things, and how the girls had cried. That seemed to be good to them, too, that they had made the girl cry. Why?

In the line at the water fountain between classes in the morning, Cheryl Lake was standing behind him. Cheryl Lake. Cheryl was a knockout who had dated one of the Starting Eleven, but oddly she was not going steady with him, and in fact was famous for never having gone steady with anyone. For anyone but Cheryl, this would have been unthinkable – Cameron Mitchell might have gotten away with it, though. But Cheryl seemed to enjoy it. As he turned around and spoke to her, her dark eyes looking right into him, he thought probably the boy she was going out with did not have a clue. It was, he recalled with a jolt, Dick Atkins. She was Dick Atkins' girl! But compared to Cheryl Lake, he was just another football player, a strong guy who could run pretty good with the ball, straight ahead. And he could pass – *that* he could really do.

"He ain't got any moves at all," Frankie had complained. "Hell, he can't even juke when they give him the ball!"

She would finish him off, Larry thought, as she looked steadily at him. She would move on. He did not know clearly why he thought so, but Cheryl Lake was the type of girl who would marry a very rich man, somebody who – maybe even as they stood there in the water fountain line in Ralston High School – was already in college, a junior or senior even. He would wear dirty white bucks, Ivy League button-down shirts, drive a new car – a Plymouth, or a hot Chevy – his parents bought him, gave him. Cheryl would run over him, too. Even he did not know what was coming. He would get fat, die of a heart attack, and Cheryl would not give a damn. No. Cheryl Lake would never give a damn, he was certain.

At the dismal practices, other players on the JV squad had immediately - the damn school was a rumor factory! - heard about him going to the Autumn Hop with Sandy, and they ribbed him hard, snapping towels like gunshots at him in the shower room, slamming locker doors, yelling things about her, making obscene gestures, grinning. "I bet she's cherry!" one said. "Lotsa fun!" He found it hard to concentrate on working at practices now, too. It was affecting him constantly, the Sandy stuff, the day-dreaming about what it would be like. Why had she asked for his sweater? And that had been an embarrassment in itself, since he really did not have a sharp one to give her, only a gray crew neck that was not bad, but had no color, no look to it. It was plain, but it looked about as good as it could look when she put it on and wore it to school the week of the Hop. If only he could have gone to Scheer's, bought one of the neat cardigan-type sweaters there, or one of the brilliantly colored Orlon V-necks that some of the first string wore all the time, especially Dick Atkins. He wore them with a white tee-shirt showing under-neath, and it seemed the tee-shirt was always an impos-sible bright shade of white, like his teeth.

Seeing her in this nondescript gray sweater gave him an odd feeling, one he couldn't recall ever having. And again, who the hell could he talk to about how he felt? In history class, he stared at the old maps on rollers behind Dr. Traynor's desk. Some were frayed with use and age, probably far out of date. Some of the countries depicted didn't even exist anymore. A weird thought, that a country could cease to exist. At least, he found it so. Nobody ever asked about it.

The worst thing in the whole jumbled mess was that he'd begun to think he would have to quit the football team. He didn't belong, he didn't fit, he wasn't a *real* football player. It was a dispiriting feeling. Bonnie Evans' words haunted him.

This was what was really getting to him, weighing on him. To quit the football team was more than just quitting. He would be seen as weak, even a sissy, although his excessively light weight would explain it clear enough to some people. But people who played for a year, or maybe even two, and then stopped – that was bad, there was something in it that did not fit the way things were supposed to go. You were supposed to keep playing. If you stopped you were a quitter. He was even hoping, at odd moments, that one of the coaches would take him aside, have a fatherly talk to him, sort of like Coach Kowalski had done at the beginning, back in the Training Camp sessions.

If Carl would have come home, he could talk it over with him, he would have been helpful. And somehow he felt his brother would advise him positively, to quit

274

playing, to give it up. Except that he wouldn't use those words. He would find a positive way to describe it, show the good things that could come about from such a heavy decision. Quitting any team at Ralston almost certainly meant you'd have no future in any other sport either. He wanted to write Carl a letter about it, but couldn't.

At times like these Larry felt the lack of any father figure at all – even an uncle – a hard thing. He could not assess it clearly. Something important was simply lacking in his life, and he could realistically do little about it. It was the very feeling itself – or feelings, for they were different in range and intensity – that he felt unsettled by. Sometimes he felt a heavy sadness, a sense of futility, not just about the football team but all that was on the other side of that – getting through the rest of high school, going to some college, getting some type of work, a job, marrying somebody. He would have to make money, go to work daily, for years upon years. How did people do that, adults? Is that what happened, was that being adult? It was a grim thought.

His mother had never come to a game, as far as he could tell, although Larry thought it possible that she might have walked over to the field one afternoon and viewed practice, standing far away. In his mind's eye he could see her there, with the characteristic *babushka* wrapped around her head. All the older women, and even some of the younger ones, wore this scarf over their heads like that, tied simply under their chins. Why was that? Frankie said it was because of the Catholics, no woman could enter a church without her head covered. But that still made no real sense, until he heard in history class that the ancient cultures of biblical times looked upon women's undone hair as something dangerous, not to be idly seen. So women had to cover their hair up, even if they weren't Catholics.

His mother was having a hard time. She was getting older, it was less and less likely that any man would marry her. To be a woman alone, and getting steadily older, was a tough thing in the Ralston area. And there were a number of women in the category, since they seemed to outlive the men routinely. It was much more common to hear of a woman whose husband had died, than the other way around.

A neighbor, Mr. Franklin, had been interested in his mother. Or, at least, he picked her up in his car and they drove off to go to dinner at some place he knew, and liked, "up the road." That phrase meant north. "Down the road" meant south, towards Pittsburgh, the big city, all that that implied. The movie theaters there had thick carpets on the floor, and uniformed ushers and usherettes. But the drive-ins were doing damage to them. Everyone went to the drive-ins in the summer, and on into the early autumn, depending on the weather.

When Larry thought about the emotional life of his mother, it made him sad. What was she going to do? And what was he going to do? Having a father would have solved a large number of pressing problems for him; he would have learned to drive, he would have had better information about girls and all the stuff connected to them – or, at least, he could have brought this subject up with less discomfort. A father would advise him concerning college, too. He had already been badly damaged, in some fundamental way, by not having one, but this, too, he could not bring up, discuss, with his mother. It would be too much, even if he could. Maybe it could never be discussed. You were simply stuck with it, a fact. The famous "facts of life."

Boys who did have fathers had a basic confidence he lacked, a certainty. They seemed much more sure of themselves. Probably because they knew that their fathers had money, and there was no problem there. Larry was never sure that his mother had enough money, or even any money. It was in scarce supply, that was for certain. The matter of the Autumn Hop worried him, because there was a requirement for the boy to get a corsage for the girl. These could be quite expensive. What would happen if you showed up for your date without one, he wondered? Would she refuse to go out with you? You could always lie, and say that you had lost it, it had fallen out of the car and been run over by another car. You had dropped it, and it had been stepped on. But would you be able to say such a thing with a straight face? One thing was for certain, that he knew already, was that girls, somehow, knew when you were lying.

He could feel the effects of what had happened already in his life in his classes, and particularly in shop class, or IA, as it was supposed to be called, Industrial Arts. There was something funny about the conjunction of the two words to Larry but he never brought it up, except to Frankie when they walked aimlessly down by the river, skipping stones like they had when they were boys, kids, five, six years old. Now, with the arm strength developing, they could skip far out for a long way. What was that story about George Washington? That he could throw a stone across the Potomac River, something like that?

"If it was as broad as the Allegheny, he musta had a hell of an arm on him, old George. Think about it – he'd a been one hell of a quarterback, an arm like that on him. Eighty-yard passes... Like old Sammy Baugh, that played for the Redskins." Baugh was able to throw the ball from one goal line to other – 100 yards in the air, Larry remembered reading. Frankie shook his head. "Do you really believe that shit? You *do*, don't you? That cherry tree shit? I cannot tell a lie! Hey, I can!"

"It's nothing to brag about, that's what it means, Frankie," he'd said. That had shut him up, too.

"I say he's as bad as Guducci. Washington was a Dago, that's what I say. Hey! He had false teeth, too, it said so in the history book."

Mr. Guducci taught shop – the kids called him "Dago Frank." He lived in New Kensington, and some kids said his older brother was in the Mafia, the mob. He had thick, greasy black hair, and a long, hooked nose for which some other kids called him "Beak" or "The Beaker." Bandy-legged, seen from a distance coming down one of the long school hallways, he had an ape-like gait, so some referred to him as "Apeshit Guducci." His powerfully built chest and shoulders insured that nobody really messed with him. Mr. Guducci ruled his kingdom, the shop premises, with the proverbial iron hand.

Strange things happened in the shop room. Long, low, and broad, the room had very dirty wire-mesh covered windows ranging along its entire side. Larry did not like the place. Goran insisted chosen members of the football team fucked girls at night in this room. "I heard them," he said. "You can't make that up." In the previous spring, a boy cut off his thumb in the big planing machine. When Mr. Guducci asked him how he had done it, he had said "Like this," and proceeded to quickly slice off his other thumb, before Mr. Guducci could stop him. There had been blood everywhere that day; Larry still remembered it with a sickened feeling in the pit of his stomach – the idea of the kid slicing off his thumbs that way was like a bad scene in a movie, except that they no doubt would not be allowed to show it.

The shop room was really like a factory of some sort – was that what they were really doing there, preparing them all to work in factories? It was a mandatory class, for three years in a row. People made the usual "projects" every year – the gun racks for the house, these were really popular, along with varnished mounts for deer antlers. Odd sounds came from it all day long – banging, fierce, prolonged hammering, the ripping snarl of the big saws and planing machinery, and the jostling whoops of the students, some profane, yelled out into the hall as girls passed by. Some girls walked on the far side of the hall to stay away from the place. No girls ever took shop. Larry wondered if they would be allowed to if they asked. A far-fetched idea – yet why was it that none did? Many of the girls who lived on farms (Norma Sterns was a good example) could do everything the boys did – drive a car or truck, shoot a rifle and get their deer in deer season, care for the chickens and livestock, you name it – but no shop. They took home economics, which no boys took, although there had been a couple boys who had somehow ended up in home ec, a cause of a lot of jokes and laughter. Baking cookies. Which they then wolfed down.

Chryste Greene. She was a girl who some said had wanted to take shop. All kinds of jokes about her, but she was really a nice girl, with the misfortune to develop large breasts early, by the eighth grade – just like big-tittied Norma (as Frankie called her) except Chryste was pretty, with lustrous red hair and wonderful skin. What a problem breasts must be. You wake up, and you're growing, sprouting, these lumps… it gave him a queasy feeling. Hormones. The biology teacher said it was all hormones. "That's what all of you really are," he said, pointing at them like they were all specimens in a jar. "Hormones with legs." Hormones, that was what made you get the boner all the time. He could not believe how hard he got, sometimes he feared he might break himself or something. What did girls get that was like the boner? Nobody seemed to know for sure. He was afraid to ask.

It was all sex stuff. There was never-ending talk in the school about sex, and the big thing was the French Kiss. "Frenching" was big in the shop; one boy was even called "Frenchy," and he would stick out his tongue and waggle it, while the others laughed and hooted. It was something he couldn't have conceived of, and when he heard of how it was done, the details, he was amazed, and then wondered if he could ever do it. Basically, you stuck your tongue in the other person's mouth, and moved it around with their tongue. It was supposed to be very exciting.

"Swabbin' spit! It's hot, Larry. Hot!" Frankie Malone nodded his head vigorously. "It drives girls wild." He rubbed his crotch, like Goran would do.

There was another form of French he learned about unexpectedly, dressing in the locker room after practice one afternoon. He had taken a longer shower than usual. It had been unexpectedly cold – the sun was setting earlier, the mornings were darker, colder, too. There had been some white frost rime on the grass of the big field early in the morning, when he had walked up the alley to school; it looked beautiful, glinting in the sun, there was a different smell in the air from it.

Drying himself off behind a bank of lockers, he could hear two of the seniors talking.

"So you really heard about it – it's true?"

"No shit. She Frenched him. They were parking, on that dirt road up there, goes off the old dam road – you know the one."

"Goddamn! Frenched him… all the way?"

"That's what I heard."

Who was the girl? He did not hear – he dressed hurriedly, feeling uneasy, and for some reason, sad.

There were other sex acts discussed, in detail. Everywhere boys gathered. Hand jobs, in the balcony at the movie theater, or at the drive-in. Very common, apparently; many had experienced it. Paul Thorpe, who'd gotten Shannon Brunell and Kathy Ferris pregnant, was said to have received these especially. Some bragged of how many they'd had, kept a scrupulous count. Pecker tracks, incriminating, on the car seats. Stink finger. "Had three fingers in!" Scuts and pomps, a mysterious phrase he never found the meaning of – maybe he was mis-hearing it.

Then there were the things Larry thought must really come from Goran's deck of cards; it was hard to imagine kids actually doing them. The infamous Sixty-Nine – "the ultimate!" Frankie claimed. Or threesomes. This was usually two men and a woman – "gettin' it from both ends!" – but could also be two women and a man. There was talk of orgies in cabins out by the creek, with older people, adults, some who paid to watch. Larry didn't believe these.

But the talk bothered him increasingly, especially when he was thinking of Sandy Stevens. Would he French kiss her? Or even try? Would she? Was this what they had in store for them, in the future?

Too much was suddenly happening. The football season, accelerating towards its end already. Yet they had only just started. In the weekend Valley Daily News Sports section, before the Hop, a feature story ran about the Braddock football team, already picked to be in the Championship game. A large photograph, half a page, showed their starting eleven, lined up, ready to run a play. They were all black – Negroes. What were they like? – there were no Negroes at Ralston. He couldn't remember Ralston ever playing a team that had even one on its team. There had been one student a few years back – his father had moved his family to Ralston from Pittsburgh, it was said. What would that be like, he wondered, to be the only Negro in a school with no others? People called them "jigaboos," "shines," "chocolate drops". "Coons," Goran said, grinning and sticking his lips out. There were endless jokes about them, but Larry realized he did not know anything about them really. What if it came out that Ralston played Braddock, in the championship game, before Thanksgiving?

He had heard two basketball players discussing when they had taken part in a contest at the Tarkington field house, in Pittsburgh, a "shoot-off," for a charity event, a scholarship fund. Several Negro players had been there, from Pittsburgh area schools. The Ralston players saw them afterwards in the dressing room, showering. They talked about how big they were.

"I mean a *big* fuckin' dick!" The player measured with his two hands held apart, as in a fish story. "I tell you, you never seen a thing like that. Hanging down there... and this is not even hard!"

Larry had heard men at Sam's talk the same way, about experiences they said occurred in the service.

"Tell you what, you can say what you like, when it comes to the schlong, they got dealt a hand. And then some. I seen guys in the service, I tell ya, you wouldn't believe the size of it. Like a damn kolbossa, or a big cuke - and not even limber, either. They was girls - in the houses - they wouldn't service them, take them on. No – and I tell ya, I don't blame 'em, either. No way they was gonna have that thing rammed up into them. Like a fuckin' horsecock!"

Whatever the truth was – he had never seen a naked Negro man, or boy, there weren't any even in Goran's deck – it seemed odd that about all he had heard about them had been about such a thing. Whatever else people might say, they were damn good football players, that was certain. It was a fact.

# 21

Only in Mr. Turner's English class could he do much of anything. Things had become even thicker when Coach Kowalski called him into the coaches' office in the middle of the week, pulled open a door on a wall locker, and gave him a practice jersey, hanging on a hanger, telling him he'd earned it. It would be even harder to quit the team now. Then, on the spur on the moment, like a crazed man, he had gone to the library, where he thought he might find Sandy Stevens, and found her. And given her the practice jersey!

Mr. Turner's literature classroom was on the third floor, in a corner room, that had a view of the whole sweep of the River Hill above the Allegheny. The hillside was a constantly changing vista; turning from snow white to grey to rich green in the late winter and early spring, and now, in the advancing fall, it was brilliant with the autumn foliage, and the occasional tall evergreen prominent. It would have been good to have class in this room no matter what, but with Mr. Turner it was even more special. "A great teacher can change your whole life." Carl had said once. Maybe Mr. Turner was in this category.

He read poems regularly in the literature class, some-times at the opening of the class – at least one, almost daily. These were occasions when most of the twenty or so students in the room seemed to not pay much attention, as Mr. Turner read, sometimes walking around the room in his slow stride, sometimes standing by the big window, with River Hill framed in the background. Frankie Malone, oddly enough, liked the poems. He often asked Larry to read them again.

"You can read that stuff, Larry. You got a feel for it, when you read."

"I'm just copying Turner," he deferred.

Frankie shook his head emphatically. "Bullcrap. I know, I'm the one listenin', huh? And what about Bonnie? Evans? The smartest-ass girl in the class – in the whole school? Huh? Huh?"

Bonnie Evans. This was true, she had singled him out even in Mr. Turner's class, asking if he would read one of Shakespeare's sonnets. Embarrassed, he had declined, and Mr. Turner had read it again. It was one of the most famous, he said, sitting at the round table as he read, holding the book carefully, so that it was clear what he was holding, looking at, reading, was special, valuable.

"Sonnet 18. Right, then…

Shall I compare thee to a summer's day?

Thou art more lovely…"

It was the unexpected rhythm in the words, the conjunctions the words made, the sound, that amazed, captured him. The poems were all short – almost all. One day Mr. Turner announced he would read Walt Whitman, a poem he said was called "When I Heard The Learned Astronomer".

*When I heard the learn'd astronomer*

*When the proofs, the figures, were ranged in columns before me,*

*When I was shown the charts and diagrams, to add, divide, and measure them,*

*When I sitting heard the astronomer where he lectured with much*

   *applause in the lecture-room,*

*How soon unaccountable I became tired and sick,*

*Till rising and gliding out I wander'd off by myself,*

*In the mystical moist night-air, and from time to time,*

*Look'd up in perfect silence at the stars.*


After he read the poem, he paused, looking at each of them as if he was studying them, reading their faces. Larry, watching him do this so often, had come to the view that Mr. Turner was an unusual teacher, perhaps even better than good, but that most of the students did not sense this. Or worse, did not care. Teachers, by definition, were the enemy, like most parents, almost all older people. Ministers, principals, all of them. Coaches were included, to some extent, even.

"What – this poem. What's Whitman saying?"

Turner acknowledged Bonnie Evans' fiercely waving hand, which had shot up like a rocket, straight up.

"It's about school, isn't it? That what you learn in school, that can keep you from learning." Her face was flushed. Larry felt proud of her, which surprised him.

"Keep you from learning what?" Turner asked, running his thumb over the edges of the book's pages.

"More important things," she said, looking intently at him. "The most important things, he's saying, you *don't* learn them. They just are."

Bonnie Evans was suddenly slouched back, burrowing down in her chair, crossing her thin, small arms, which looked very weak, in front of her.

Mr. Turner nodded. "I see…anybody else have anything they want to say?" Even as he said it, everyone in the room knew – and he knew also – that there wouldn't be anymore said. Who could follow Bonnie?

Cameron Mitchell had asked him, that day, the Whitman day he privately called it, if he'd read any of Walt Whitman.

"I saw this picture of him, in a book in the library? He was an old man, with a big white beard." She smiled. "Looked like God. You know?" And she shook that thick, lustrous black hair, looking directly at him. He thought you could fall into her eyes and never come out.

"So. You like him – his poems, what Turner reads? (Cameron never said "Mr." or "Miss" when she spoke of a teacher – why was that? He wanted to ask her.) Tell me."

For some unknown reason, on that particular day, he had not dutifully answered the goddess's question.

"Why? Why do you want to know?"

That had brought a short pause, and then a different kind of smile, that he hadn't seen.

"Because I'm interested, Larry, in what you think."

Feeling already that he was getting out of his depth, he'd nevertheless answered her, noticing Frankie close by, waiting.

"I do like the poems. Yes. I like when he reads them to us."

"I hear you read them, too," she said quickly. "Is that so?"

He nodded. Some kind of sentencing was going on, girls were good at this. He looked over quickly at Frankie, who raised his eyebrows provocatively, the eyebrows clearly saying "Cameron Mitchell!"

"Sure. That's right. Cameron." He blurted out her name, and felt like saying "Your name is a poem," but this embarrassed him and he felt his face reddening.

She smiled again. How could somebody have teeth like that, too, he thought.

"A football player who likes to read poems. You must be the only one."

And before he'd realized it, he had said, "I'm not a football player. I –" He stuck there, and adding to his confusion, she laid her hand on his arm. Touched him.

"We'll have to read some poems. In the library?" Was she really asking this?

He nodded dumbly, his face now feeling mottled, as if by a strange disease, he thought, and she had smiled again and for a crazy second he thought she was even leaning towards him, as if they would kiss.

The autumn was almost gone, Mr. Turner said, and he read a longer poem, "Fern Hill," that Larry sensed was unusual, special, even for a poem. There was a sound about it, a movement, he hadn't heard in other poems read aloud. He looked out at the River Hill. Winter would soon arrive in the valley, already there were coal deliveries being made, the first of the year. There would be scrapple, and buckwheat cakes, made from a heavy grey stone crock out on the back porch, and the thick sausage patties he loved, with syrup over them. The first day of deer season would come, right after Thanksgiving. The creek would finally freeze – maybe by mid-December, and Ducky Estes and he would still go over to the old playground court to shoot some baskets, wearing gloves if it was really cold. He had a quick thought that Coach Pedjman should make his players wear gloves all the time, then they would become better ball handlers. It was like that school he'd heard about, up near New Castle, where the coach made his players dribble balls while running back and forth through a staggered line of folding chairs. They had had a championship season the past year. Or, it would be like Ty Cobb, who ran in the winter off-season wearing leg weights, so when he took them off in Spring Training, he was really fast.

The poet Dylan Thomas had been Welsh, Mr. Turner said. Maybe Wales was like Pennsylvania; coal miners, railroads, green trees and fields. Rain.

"Arcadia," Mr. Turner had said. "The Greeks called it Arcadia."

Meanwhile, he studiously avoided the library, even though he really wanted to go there, surprising Frankie Malone yet again, who said he was crazy, or worse, whatever that could be. Sandy Stevens was bad enough, but Cameron Mitchell was too much, she was like an Elvis Presley song come true, maybe even worse than Cheryl Lake. These girls weren't like Sandy Stevens. When he'd been a freshman, a junior girl, Karen Carlson, had lain out on the long library table in her skintight Levis. He'd gotten an erection and stood stupefied, unable to stop looking at the long, long sweep and swell of her legs and where they came together in the tight *y* of her crotch. Karen Carlson had lain there for what seemed a long time, and he was sure she knew he was looking. It was hopeless, the erection business, and girls like her did not help matters. He had slunk out of the side door of the library that day like a criminal of some type, hoping no one would see him. Karen Carlson was the Secretary of the Student Council, which was meeting that day in the library. Some senior boys called her "Erector Set."

His resolve was futile, as he knew in his gut it would be. "Trust your gut. It knows!" Coach Barnes would shout

out, punching himself violently in his own stomach. They had a practice drill where they all pounded on their guts. Cameron came up to him as he walked distractedly, staring at the floor yet again, through the hall towards his home room.

"Let's read, in the library? Remember?" Cameron always got up close to you when she talked to you; sometimes she seemed to absent-mindedly stroke her dark hair. You were quickly drawn in by her magnetism, pulled right to her. There was a warmth, a combination of scents of flowers and cinnamon and her. Sandy Stevens smelled like the cleanness of Ivory Soap, and he wondered how she could do that. And there was the Cameron hair, along with many other subtle body movements, almost like a slow dance. All this at the same time, a co-ordination making you feel even more awkward, intensely aware of your own clumsy, sweaty body. You were certain to commit some embarrassment – even fart, in your excitement – that would last for years. (Mr. Turner had read in English class about a nobleman in Queen Elizabeth's court, in Shakespeare's time, who had farted while bowing before her, and had banished himself for seven years or something like that.) Yet she could put you at ease, she had an uncanny sense, placing her hand lightly on your arm, laughing maybe. There was a definition of a gentleman in the literature book, as being a person who never made another uncomfortable.

So there he was then, with Cameron in the library on the second floor, almost before he knew it. Shanghaid, by

Cameron. If only it were like the library in Pittsburgh, the Carnegie, where there were rugs on the floor, and large, comfortable chairs, like in a house, a living room. The huge floor there had long tables, lamps with shades, not glaring fluorescent overhead lights.

It would be noted, soon, all over the school that they had come into the library together. He saw several girls look up – they missed nothing, the girls – as they tried to sit down quickly and quietly. Miss Vukovich, she of the impossibly long, curved legs, sat at her librarian's desk, commanding a full view of the long room. She smiled at them, nodding slightly. He wondered if she would get up and come over, and they would see her lithe walk, the glossy high heels she always wore. "Her *shoes* give me a stiff one," Frankie had said. "I'm sittin' there in the library with a stiff one. A boner! And I ain't the only one." He wondered, despite his best intentions, increasingly what Miss Vukovich would look like with her clothes off. Would she have the thick, dark triangle between her legs? If only somehow he could finagle her into initiating him into sex. He hadn't even told Frankie of this – except that he thought it very likely that he wasn't the only one with this dream. The older woman who would initiate you, show you how to do it all. "We'll do everything…" Everything. His head spun.

"*No Talking!*" There was a large scroll-lettered sign on Miss Vukovich's dark wooden desk. Another said "*Quiet, Please.*" Her desk looked like it had been in the school since the place was built. How were they going to read poems, then? He and Cameron? Even whispering was forbidden in the library, at least for any length of time.

Studying together in the library was almost the same as having a date with a girl – it was looked on that way, especially by the girls. It was true he'd often studied with Bonnie there, but everyone also knew that was different; he and Bonnie were smart. "Brains." At least, he thought this was the idea. But by the same token, no one would "study" with Cameron Mitchell. The idea, even, was crazy. Cameron didn't "study" in that way, or for anything.

With all this rocketing through his overloaded, burdened brain, he hardly noticed Cameron had a small stack of books on the library table in front of them.

"Let's look at these," she whispered so low he barely heard. They were at the farthest table from the librarian's desk, back near the far exit door. The green sign glowed above the door – why wasn't it red, he suddenly wondered?

He didn't want to look at the books – he felt he had already studied too much – he wanted to look at Cameron. So close, almost like a close-up in a movie, filling the screen. She was right next to him.

He took the top book. "Sonnets," William Shakespeare. "Old Shaky," Frankie had quipped. From Turner's class. The next book was an anthology of Modern Literature he hadn't seen before, probably out of the library. Then there was a thicker book – *Leaves of Grass*, Walt Whitman. Inside, on the frontispiece, was a picture of the poet. An old man, with a long white beard, like a prophet in the

Bible, Larry thought. Or even like God himself. There was another photo on the back, of Whitman "as a man of 37." That was old, but the poet looked young. He had a hat cocked jauntily on his head; no beard.

Cameron was watching him closely; he could feel her looking at him. Almost studying him. He shook his head, although he didn't know why. Where would this end? She didn't seem like a girl who read, and yet here were these books. She seemed to always have books with her. Did she keep books in her car, he wondered? Maybe she drove to secret places, different places she really liked, and read. He liked that idea – the image of Cameron sitting in her red '55 Chevy, reading. Maybe that place up on top of River Hill, she'd go there to get away and just read.

"What are you smiling at?" she said in a quiet whisper. "Larry?"

He shook his head, took the *Sonnets* and paged to the one he wanted, and gave the book to her. She looked down quickly at it, then up at him. Her face had become, in an instant, serious. He thought of a line of old poetry Turner wrote on the board, in an old form of English. "Thy eyen wole slaye mee…"

The sonnet was number eighteen. Since the first time Turner read it in their class, he'd read it many times, almost, by now, having it memorized. He was amazed at how much he liked Shakespeare, but he said little of his admiration, although he thought Turner somehow knew it. Kids would make gagging sounds, as if about to vomit, or make the motion of sticking their fingers down their throat if you mentioned Shakespeare's name. "Why do we have to read this old stuff?" was the continual complaint.

Cameron quickly passed him a small, neatly folded note. He opened it carefully, trying to make no noise at all. "He wrote 154 of these." That was all it said. But when he looked up, Cameron was smiling at him so that he smiled immediately in return. 154 sonnets. He was going to write down, in a flash, "And every one of them a touchdown!" give it back to her. But that was too cute. He couldn't do that, it wasn't sincere.

He heard the click of a male teacher's shoes coming back down the corridor – who could it be? No student would wear those clips on their shoes. Only adult men. It was so audible Miss Vukovich looked up from her desk. What was she reading? he wondered. She had a small book spread out in front of her. He thought the teacher was probably Mr. Mazaroski, with his double breasted suits, and crew cut. He was just out of college. The Hambone man.

Cameron was giving him the book back now, opened to another page. Sonnet fifty-five. He read it, and nodded. The full meaning of the poem was beyond him but just the sound the words made in his head as he read them was powerful and deep. Maybe you really didn't need to know "the meaning."

Now Cameron pushed over the Whitman book. He looked down – he didn't know the poem, it was a long one, it looked like, and he could tell by the page that it was the end of the poem. He read the lines

*I bequeath myself to the dirt to grow from the grass I*
*love*

*If you want me again look under your boot-soles.*

*You will hardly know who I am or what I mean,*
*But I shall be good health to you nevertheless,*
*And filter and fibre your blood.*

*Failing to catch me at first keep encouraged,*
*Missing me one place search another,*
*I stop somewhere waiting for you.*

*1855*

The poem dazed him, and when he had finished reading it, he remained looking down at the page. Then he saw Cameron's hand come across the table and onto the book, and rest there. Hesitantly, he put his own hand over hers. He looked at her; he felt his mouth was open, gaping, he must look stupid, but her eyes were fully on him, as if he was the only person in the room, and they were the only people there.

How long did that last, he wondered later that evening, lying on his bed in his room. The Del Vikings' great version of "Come and Go With Me" had just played, and the dj followed up with Jerry and Johnny's "Over The

Mountain." He felt the songs must have been written with him in mind, although he knew it could not be true. And the dj – he made a combination, a mix of the records, which was also a language, a poem even, if you knew the songs as he obviously did. But you had to know the songs. He wondered if Cameron was listening in her car. He wanted to be with her in that car so badly that he got up and walked agitatedly to the window and looked down, two stories, a long way, the old house must be sixty or seventy feet high, he thought, onto the tarred street below. It was sort of paved, but in the winter the frosts and then the rains of the spring, pitted and sloughed off the thin paving the town had put on it. He suddenly had an image of himself as a small boy playing "Pot" down on that street, in the early spring. When the ground would thaw, they'd dig a hole and throw marbles at it, and try to knock, or "shoot," others' marbles into the pot. You got to take those marbles you shot into the pot; the game continued until all the marbles were gone. Ducky maintained it was a game like shooting pool in the pool hall (which he'd never done), except you used marbles, and there was no cue stick to shoot with. You used your thumb, like a lever, to propel one marble into another. There was a lot of geometry to it, sighting the line that would result in the struck marble, or marbles if you were really good, to ricochet into the pot. (The size of the pot itself was a matter of negotiation; some made it quite small, and deep; others wide, so that it was possible for a marble to roll in and then back out.)

He and Cameron left the library together, after reading more Whitman – "When I Heard The Learned

Astronomer," one that Turner had first read – and a poem of Dylan Thomas's in the anthology, *Fern Hill*, that in some way made him think of Shakespeare and Walt Whitman combined together. Turner had read that one first, too. How many poems he had introduced them to – he was a fine teacher, and Larry was suffused with a warm feeling for the awkward teacher.

"Turner is a great teacher," he had said to Cameron as they walked from the library, in the hall. She had an algebra class, and he had a study hall, on "The Shelf." He wanted to hold her hand in the hall, but then it did not seem that was the thing to do. They were not "going steady," he and Cameron. She did not have his ring around her neck (Elvis had recorded a song "Wear my ring around your neck, To show the world..."). In fact, he doubted Cameron would wear anyone's ring, even one of the varsity players. He thought of giving her his white practice jersey, with the faint blood stains on it – he would be her knight! But he blushed even as he thought it, and she smiled as if she knew what he was thinking.

The rest of that day had been a haze for him, he often felt as if he had cotton around him, insulated. Who could he tell about these feelings, about what had happened in the library? Nobody. And what had happened?

As he passed outside the Problems of Democracy classroom, where he saw Mr. Ferris in a really sharp grey sports coat, sitting comfortably on the edge of his desk talking to Cheryl Lake, of all people, he noticed on the bulletin board that there was a newspaper story about the

Hungarian Revolution. But the Hungarians had fled, or
at least that was what he thought. Escaped; some had
been killed. The Russians had come in with big tanks,
right into Budapest. The pictures on television reminded
him of WWII newsreels at the Ritz, when he was a little
kid; there had been similar scenes of tanks in city streets,
firing; buildings crumbling, falling in billows of dust and
smoke, people fleeing, running, or just standing looking
dazed. What happened to these people? Were they killed,
or taken prisoner? Was it their house, their apartment,
that they were watching being blown up? He thought of
a tank coming down High Street, and then shelling their
house. It would not take much to destroy that old house;
one good shot would no doubt do it. But this would never
happen. Even as he was standing dithering in this thought,
Mr. Ferris looked out and saw him, smiled, and waved.
Cheryl Lake looked at him, too. He hurriedly went on
down the hall. He was getting strange, he thought, as he
walked, and would have to look out.

"They'll come get you in the flying saucers, Larry. You'd
be a good one to take," Frankie had laughed, making a
spooky sound, like in a horror movie. "You vill come with
us, earthling...do not resist. It is useless..."

Would the next war, then, be against the Russians, even
in Hungary maybe? Or one of those other small countries in Eastern Europe? And would that be his war –
and Frankie's, Ducky's, even Goran's? The whole damn
"starting eleven"? It suddenly struck him, there in front of
Ferris' door. That could be the future, right there.

# 22

Sitting in his room in the old house there on High Street, he was reading through a file he had collected of articles and stories, some transcribed from books in the library, about famous players. When he was still a kid, every August he'd eagerly awaited, and then thumbed through, the various glossy sports magazines at deNicchio's, by the train station, checking the football predictions. The Top Twenty teams in the country, the first team All American picks, the Heisman Trophy contenders. Howard "Hopalong" Cassady, a running back, from Ohio State, won the Heisman in 1955. Alan "The Iron Horse" Ameche had won it in 1954, he thought – also a running back. But it was odd that the Heisman winner didn't always star, or even play well, in the pros. Playing football for money must make a big difference.

The pictures of the players of "the old days," as he thought of them, already looked like they could be in some football museum. They looked funny wearing the odd tight-fitting leather helmets (which didn't look like they'd offer much real protection), and the lumpy pads they wore, which simply didn't look right. Their jerseys were often two-toned, something never seen in the current days, and the numerals on them were small. Even the shoes – they looked heavy, boot-like.

A story in a large book in the library had fascinated him and he had transcribed it. It was about the 1934 Rose Bowl, where Stanford played Columbia. (Such a match-up couldn't have occurred now, in 1956). The quarterback had called a trick play, a reverse/hidden ball play, which had won the game, 7-0. There had been such heavy rains before the game that the field was in extremely poor condition.

The article also noted that that the Rose Bowl, started in 1902, was the only important post-season game then. The quarterback had even been offered a film contract, but chose to go back and finish his education at Columbia. He said of the famous play, where the man who really had the ball ran easily into the Stanford end zone, that "seeing him there was one of the most thrilling sights of my life."

He had also transcribed notes about Fordham's Seven Blocks of Granite, the line they had in the mid-1930s. In those days, players went the entire game, playing both offense and defense. "Sixty-minute men," Coach Barnes approvingly called them. Notre Dame had had a line in the 1920s called the Seven Mules, who blocked for the famous Four Horsemen, who included Red Grange.

He was already old enough to remember recent legendary players – Blanchard and Davis, for Army, came immediately to mind. He had an intense memory of listening to the Army-Navy game when the great pair were at their height. He had been glued to the radio, rooting for the underdog, Navy, and their quarterback, who had the unlikely name of Reaves Baysinger. Navy had gotten down near the goal line, at the very end of a 0-0 game, but they could not score. Still, he felt they had won the game, against all odds, and Baysinger was a hero.

He wondered what had become of these famous players? Sometimes he'd see an old man at a Ralston game, and have a feeling that he was re-living a football season, a game, while watching. Maybe some played in the pros – he had read that these players received little money, maybe a hundred dollars a game – and some, no doubt, like Coach Rossi, became coaches. Football was their entire life. It was strange to think of that. He pondered it while walking over to the field for the Homecoming Game. The lights were bright, and there was a good crowd, and he could see the new, gleaming Chevys lined up, waiting to be driven around the field with the Homecoming Court riding in them, waving to the crowd.

But the game itself wasn't a great one. At half-time, Ralston led 20-0. The second string was already in, getting some letter – some "R" - time. It was looking like a game when even third stringers would get some of that letter time. There might even be a few, like the starting JV quarterback, Chad Lewis, who would get in enough time in this game, and in subsequent ones left in the season, to win a letter, become a three-striper by the time they were seniors. But no four-stripers, like Harry Gibb, were on the horizon, or even near it. Gibb was already out of the Clarksburg game in the second quarter, his uniform not even dirty, pacing the sidelines, his helmet off, talking animatedly to the other starters and the coaches. It was strongly rumored he would go to Pitt, and study pre-med.

Two Clarksburg players were injured in the first half, one with a possible broken arm, a serious injury. Ralston's players rarely sustained any injuries – other than the usual bloody nose, a cut mouth. But opposing teams did have players carted off the field, the wind knocked out of them often, limping off the field, trying to keep from showing the pain. You were not allowed, not supposed to show any pain in playing football. Was the lesson taught here – Coach Rossi often lectured them on looking for the lessons football taught – that in life you couldn't show you were in pain? Ralston had gained a reputation as a rough team – not a dirty one – but it wasn't something to be ashamed of. Coach Rossi, when asked about it, said it was probably due to their superior conditioning, and their crisp execution of plays.

Although he'd put on muscle, lifted the old weights he'd found way back when, was in the best shape of his life, he was still, in a word, small. Too small. He hadn't been picked to suit up for any varsity games. He thought it unlikely he would. If he was honest, and he tried to be, he had to admit he was losing heart, which Coach Kowalski said was bad. He was sorry he hadn't been picked for the Clarksburg game, because it would have meant something to run out onto that field where so many had played for however brief a time, maybe only a play or two, with the Ralston varsity uniform on. And it would have been noticed. He had "got in," had played with the varsity. Sandy Stevens would have noticed. Cameron – she probably wasn't even at the game. Driving around, somewhere, listening to the radio. Now, he doubted it could happen. The coaches missed nothing. He could feel football slipping away from him, like a pass slithering through clutching hands.

Watching Sandy Stevens march and twirl as part of the Ralston Band, he was still befuddled (his mother's word) that he was actually going to go to the Saturday night Hop with this sparkling, smiling, truly beautiful girl. Just – only – a sophomore. How could she be so beautiful? She was particularly vibrant out on the field at half-time, and although he knew she really could not see him standing in the crowd on the sideline, he felt she was looking right at him, and that was enough to knock the wind out of him. And what if he was playing in the game, what would that be like? Standing with dirt on his uniform, helmet in hand…What was he going to do? Complication had been suddenly put into his life; there was this whole business of the poetry readings with Cameron in the library. Everybody in the whole school no doubt knew about that now, since everyone noticed whatever Cameron did, or didn't, do. If he had been seen with Carol Bigelow, it would hardly have been worse. The game faded into insignificance, as much as any Ralston game could. He knew they would win anyway.

The second half proved him right. Clarksburg was a beaten team even when they came out onto the field after half time, you could see it in their slow running back onto the field and the uncoordinated plays they ran in their first possession, after receiving the kick-off. Ralston scored three more touchdowns, and the game proved significant only for the fact that the last two were scored with the third string quarterback, the JV, Chad Lewis, in the game. He was definitely a comer, he might be the next Famous Player to come out of Ralston, go to a Big Ten school, or one of the major independents – Pitt, Penn State, or the ultimate football school, Notre Dame. He passed for one of the touchdowns, and some spectators wondered when a third-stringer had passed for a touchdown before in a Ralston game; no one could recall offhand, but it would be settled at Sam's the next morning, for sure. Maybe it was "one for the record books" in that sense.

Even the famous half-time parade of cars from Amstead's Chevrolet seemed anticlimactic. The girls looked great in the cars – Cheryl Lake, the two cheer-leader twins (in one car) – but the steam was out of the game, and the Homecoming crowning, at mid-field, couldn't make up for this.

By the time the game was over, the stands were two-thirds full at best. It was at times like this, and with games like this, that the real action shifted to what was going on off the field, and so it was this night. The damp night air coming up the valley off the big river was getting pretty cold ( "Getting chilly!" people would say, smiling) and the usual fire – it was almost a ritual fire, a certainty on a night like this one – had been started in an old 55-gallon oil drum, back by the practice field. Where did these drums come from? Larry had asked a few people, like Pete, the old Swede at the gas station. He said he did not know, they were "just around. People find them – you know." He jerked his thumb behind him, as if to indicate where the drums came from; somewhere out there, in back.

This particular one had been sitting outside so long that one side was rusted through – raw-looking, jagged wound-like holes with fire licking through in several places, surging with the gusting river wind. At one game the previous year, with Allenwood, tires had been set on fire, but the police had come, the fire department. Thick, harsh, smoke billowed out, an ominous, ugly deep black color, especially with the sudden flaring of red-yellow flames in the heart of it. The oil drum glowed, pulsed, like an old fashioned pot-bellied stove.

Always the same people stood around these oil drum fires. There was Charlie MacGready, an older guy who wore a dirty, stained Pittsburgh Pirates cap, even in the winter time, and looked like he had never eaten a good meal in his entire life. You could often see him standing up in front of the bank, at the main intersection of Ralston, Fifth and Market, where he would remain for several hours, talking to anyone who came by, watching the traffic go through the big stop light there, with a smile on his face. There were others – even old Smick Smead, the fisherman from The Island, would show up at times. They were men who had no apparent steady job, and maybe never had, as far as he could tell. (Smick was said to be one of the last "commercial" fishermen working the river; they sold their catch to shops down in New Kensington and Pittsburgh, or to individuals who liked to have really fresh fish.) They hadn't got on at the mill or the brickyard or over at Montgomery Lumber company, where his brother Carl had had his first job. He never talked about that job, but Larry could remember him coming home (it was the middle of the summer, hot and humid days stretching out) covered in lime. He was an odd sight, and his mother worried about him. He sat in the bathtub for a long time each evening, and Larry wondered what job they had Carl doing at the lumber yard. Again, it was scary, thinking that that was the type of work waiting for you when you finally made it through school, graduated.

Larry wondered if they actually came to football games to mainly stand around the oil drum, talking. They talked in short bursts, rocking back and forth, sometimes spreading their hands out to the fire. Some stared into the drum with a fixed intensity – they seemed hypnotized by the dancing, jumping, flaring flames. Standing by the fire in the drum made you get heated through, and if you remained long enough, you would even begin sweating. The rival school bands blared away in the background, you heard alternating shouts and groans from the crowd, and sometimes isolated, odd single sounds - a bottle rolling down steps in the bleachers, a kid's balloon popping, or the disembodied voices of the cheerleaders, doing a cheer. Some of the men – it was almost all men around the drum – suggested they ought to do a barbecue, but that never happened.

The remaining crowd was flowing away by the end of the Clarksburg game, out of the gates, out into the surrounding streets, and you could hear the sounds of many cars and pick-up trucks – even a few motorcycles – starting up. Heading home. The really big event lie ahead, on Saturday night. The Homecoming, the Autumn Hop. It would be a long twenty-four hours to the next evening, he felt as he walked towards the field gates. He did not really feel like going back to the house, where his mother would probably be waiting, doing something around the brightly lit kitchen. He felt restless and even angry, he could not have said why. But it had something to do with a realization that already, at his age, he was always waiting for something to happen but he did not know what it was, and he was also, at the same time, afraid, nervous, uncertain. Maybe it would not happen, would never happen; no, he was one of those cursed with bad luck. Somehow the Homecoming Game hadn't been as important as he'd thought it was, and he did not know what to do with that realization. It felt wrong to have such a thought about a football game, in Ralston. He almost felt naked, in the cold late evening wind, now blowing in hard off the big river; he was shivering. Since he did not want to go home yet, he decided to walk uptown; a brisk walk would help him warm up. He thought of the oil drum, the fire would still be there, and even some of the old timers, no doubt, but he did not want to go back there.

Uptown – how funny the phrase was, since uptown was the intersection of Market and Fifth Streets, the place where Charlie MacGready always stood, and what was here was not that much, compared to real places like Pittsburgh, the Big City. In fact, uptown was, increasingly, embarrassing to him. There were the two brick banks with stone facades; they had been there as long as he could remember, and for much longer than that, probably. There was a Ben Franklin Department Store where one member of the current Ralston senior class had supposedly been caught stealing. So his nickname was "Klepto." The Ritz Theater, the town movie house, was one block down Fifth. The Ritz looked small, old; its marquee needed fixing. There was a house that somebody actually lived in down one place from the bank, with a small strip of vacant land in between. Who lived in that house? The dirty, yellowed venetian blinds were always drawn and he had never seen anybody come in or go out of the house. Yet you could see, at night, a thin strip of artificial light coming under the blinds. Somebody was in there.

On the other side of the mysterious house was what had once been a hotel for railroaders, his mother said. It had two stories, unusual for Ralston, and seemed to be tottering to the side, leaning over, getting ready to fall some night when people least expected it. Oddly enough, right across the narrow alleyway was the infamous Adam's Tavern, which stank of stale beer and the dried sweat of the many men who walked in and staggered out of its green wooden doors. These were chipped and dirty looking and made a loud slamming noise when someone did come in or out. Briefly, then, you could look in and see the long high wooden bar, with a few regulars seated on barstools, nursing a beer or maybe with a beer and a shot.

Did they like the taste of the stuff, Larry often wondered. Was it really that good? His father, he had liked the taste of it. Maybe. But he really did not know. His father had done most of his drinking, his boozing, his "tanking up, getting plastered," at the Eagles Club, down by the river park. It had a more selective clientèle, mostly members, and their friends. The VFW, also with members only, was in a big old wooden house directly across from the Eagles Club, and it was another famous boozing location. But his father was not a veteran, so could not go there. How had he avoided the draft? Larry did not know – maybe even then he was physically unfit – what did they call it, 4-F?

He often saw men reeling out of the Eagles in the bright middle of the afternoon, going down Riverside Drive, maybe even walking out the Dam Road, out to where some people lived on The Island. He walked up away from Adam's Tavern, towards the drug store, and across the street from it, the kids' hang-out, Peter's, where kids would play the juke box and talk. A few would sometimes push chairs and tables back in the middle of the place and dance, but Mr. Peters did not allow this often; he claimed it was against some town ordinance, and that the Burgess would have him arrested, or could suspend his restaurant license if he found out. The Burgess, an odd term, Larry thought. Not the Mayor. Vincent Lewis was the Burgess, an elected official, a very fat man Larry had seen only occasionally, coming out of his insurance office on the corner of Fifth Street above the bank. His enormous paunch slopped so far out over his pants that Larry had often wondered how his pants stayed up. And in fact he could often be seen tugging on them, pulling them up. Somehow, it was hard to imagine Mr. Lewis having anybody arrested for much of anything; he seemed harmless. And what was it that he did as Burgess? He had asked his mother, but she had simply said "He's like a mayor. The Burgess – it's an old German word, I think. He's the head person of the town, the leading person …" That really seemed to be about all she knew. Larry wondered if he got paid for being Burgess, but his mother was not sure if he did or not.

Peter's was crowded. There was a shiny cherry red '55 Chevy parked right in front of the place and the neon sign lights reflected off it so it glittered, gleamed. The image of Cameron Mitchell sitting in the Chevy, coolly playing the radio softly, came into his head – she was perfect in it. But she probably never came to Peter's, and this was not her red '55 Chevy. He stayed well on the other side of the street, in the shadows, but he could clearly see the kids packed into booths, laughing and talking. The front door was even open, with a couple of kids smoking ciga-rettes in the small alley on the side, back near the entrance to the Odd Fellows Hall. He wondered who they were – probably Bill Fleck was one of them, a notorious smoker who had even smoked inside a classroom in the school at times, and had gone down into the Boiler room where the janitor allowed him to smoke, although Larry did not believe this. Only teachers were allowed to smoke down there. You could smell it on their clothes in the class later.

Who did the Chevy belong to? Jimmy Caye? That was not likely, because he did not go to Peter's either - it wasn't his kind of place. No – somebody else, out of town, maybe even from Clarksburg? Whoever it was, the car was a magnet for girls. Goran called such cars "cockwagons." It was an odd idea – why would a girl be attracted, really, to an automobile? He couldn't figure it out clearly. Something about its power, its speed, it was a thrill, took your breath away, all that stuff from the ads on television and in magazines. They always showed a pretty girl in a new car, the guy at the wheel smiling. Perfect teeth. They always had impossibly perfect teeth. Nobody in Ralston had teeth like that.

The '55 Chevy was a very hot car to have. In the cherry red color, irresistible. He had ridden in Jimmy Caye's a couple times right after he got it and it was an amazing experience. Jimmy Caye wasn't a handsome guy at all – he wore heavy dark framed glasses and had a nose like a potato – yet they had attracted girls as if by magic wherever they stopped. When they went to the Eat N' Park down in Natrona, they'd come out to find five girls standing around the car, waiting... five very cute girls, too. The hottest car was a Thunderbird. But no kid could have such a car, at least not in Ralston. Or a Cadillac convertible, such as Elvis had. Somebody said he had twenty of them, something like that. How could you have so many cars?

The Pharmacy was closed up already, although he could see Mr. Thompson in the back. It was one of the sons really, the old man had had a bad heart attack the previous year and only was in the store occasionally. His sons looked just like him, carbon copies. They even wore small, neat moustaches, as he always had. Pharmacists – that was a good job, if you could get into it. It required a four-year college degree – Duquesne University, down in Pittsburgh, was said to have a good pharmacy school. What, though, did they actually do? Mixed up prescriptions for people, that the doctors wrote. So it sounded like they were sort of chemists. They always wore white coats, like doctors, or scientists. Even now, at night and with nobody in the place, the son had his white coat still on.

As he stood getting colder in the shadows by the pharmacy, three kids came out of Peter's and quickly got into the red '55 Chevy. It sprang to life, lights going on, a deep growling noise coming from it – it had shining chrome twin pipes in the rear, he saw as it did a U-turn, tires squealing, heading down Buffalo Street, towards the creek bridge and the long Hill Road, Route 128, that eventually led to Pittsburgh. Barenekkid Stroup must not be around, he thought – or they didn't care. If you had a car like that, it suddenly struck him, why would you? That would be the last thing on your mind. No, they were going somewhere else, maybe the roadhouse up on top of Mile Long Hill, or maybe even to Pittsburgh. In a car like that, you could go wherever you wanted. You could be just like James Dean, and people would believe you.

He knew he had to go back home, he did not want to go into Peter's – that would be strange – so he turned and went back down the alley running by the pharmacy, that ran all the way down to Buffalo Creek nearly. As he looked over toward Mile Long Hill, he saw the big lights illuminating the football field go out, just like that, and now it was dark down there, even darker because it had just been so brightly lit. There was a flickering light, though – the oil drum, no doubt. Some of the old guys would still be standing down there, spitting off to the side, shifting from one foot to the other.

He could still faintly hear the Chevy's pipes, heading out of town. It was another dead night in Ralston, as Frankie would say. Somewhere back up the dark hill that Washington Street ran steeply up, the steepest street in the town, a dog was barking, repeatedly. And then, across the river, he heard a train heading up to the Schenley Distillery. It sounded far away, but clear in the cold air, and he shivered in his jacket as he heard its whistle. What a sound that was! It was a sound you never forget... the Midnight Bummer. When he was a little kid, his mother used to say that, when a train whistle was heard late in the night. The Midnight Bummer. It sounded like the name of a song you'd hear on the radio, late at night, only you and the gleaming dial there, in the dark. "I ride that Midnight Bummer, goin' up the Pennsy line..." But there was no such song, he realized, even as he thought it, heard it in his head, walking down the dark, old alley he had walked down to home, the old house, since he was six years old, in the first grade. He and Frankie Malone had finally screwed up their courage, and asked the teacher, Miss Clemens, if they could kiss her. She kissed them.

# 23

The next night, Saturday, when he and Frankie Malone walked into the big gym, it had been transfigured. Even Frankie, for a few seconds, was stopped in his tracks.

"For God's sake!" He threw up his hands, grinning. "It's Paris!"

There was an Eiffel Tower perched over one basket, winking off and on, and an Arc de Triomphe, which you walked into the gym through, at the far end. There were wine bottles – how'd they gotten those? A sign read "Left Bank," and one of the art teachers, in a black beret and pasted-on black moustache, manned the main door.

The gym was already packed, and looking at it Larry found it hard to believe that just the previous evening a large number of nearly naked, sweating boys had been walking back and forth in its seats, and in and out of the locker rooms. Now it was totally different, and certainly smelled different, although the old, fundamental gym smells of sneakers, sweat, and floor wax and dust, were still there. But maybe the girls, the ever-creative girls, had sprayed the place or something. Or maybe it was just the presence of so many of them, looking like flowers in their gowns. God, they looked different, he thought. How they could change!

Sandy Stevens and Frankie's date Cindy Shaffer had already gone off to talk with some other girls they had spied as soon as they entered the big side door, that was put open completely, something rarely done. He and Frankie were left as if holding something in their hands, looking around, feeling already uncomfortable. The five-piece band hired for the evening was not yet playing, or maybe they were taking a break; instead, the sounds of Elvis Presley singing "Heartbreak Hotel" filled the gym. It was amazing they were allowed to play that, Larry thought, as he watched couples try to dance to the song, which wasn't really a good number to dance to. The Principal must be having a fit, somewhere. Even more than James Dean, Elvis was a threat, a rebel, a bad guy.

And when you heard his music, "Heartbreak Hotel" was a good example, it was clear Elvis was very different. You could not *not* listen – the twanging guitar, the piano that reverberated – and the voice. You were compelled to listen, he had something to say, you had to hear it. Many adults hated him, and Coach Rossi had become as angry as Larry had ever seen him when he had come on two boys gyrating, grinding their hips, imitating Elvis, in the gym while one of his records was being played over the PA in there. He had lectured them sternly, fixing them with his glare, his hard eyes, his hands on his hips. They had stood, heads hanging, looking anywhere but at him, ashamed. What were they ashamed of, Larry had wondered. Really?

"Heartbreak Hotel" was good, no doubt about it, all his songs, so far, were good. There was Fats Domino – "the Fat Man, cause I weigh two hundred pounds" – and Pat Boone, doing "Red Sails At Sunset." But it was the slow songs that really got into, inside you – ones like "In The Still of the Night," or "Earth Angel," or "Over the Mountain"; the rhythm n' blues ones, not the rock n' roll. You could feel these completely, in your body, and if you danced, even if you weren't that good at it – as he felt was his case, hell, how often had he really done it? – "slippin' and slidin'" with a girl across the gym floor to that music, you would melt together, inevitably, and feel you wanted to stay there forever like that, hardly moving, full of warmth, the lighted, suspended ball above reflecting twinkling "starlight" on the gym floor spinning on and on. Who wanted to go home from that? Those long, slow songs.

The girl's body imprinted on yours long after the dance ended. He could remember that even from the seventh grade training dances. That feel was special – a surprising firmness, it was always a surprise how firm the girls felt – yet a yielding softness like no other softness you'd ever felt. Some couples looked as if it could be impossible to get them apart when the song ended and they remained on the floor, still moving, very slowly, as if they would never stop, just glide around forever like that, around and around and around. Dancing with a girl there on the gym floor with The Penguins singing "Earth Angel" in the rafters, filling the place, was a dream come true – no, it was better than a dream, it was true. The girl's body was right there, almost visible in the gauzy fabric of the dance dresses, brushing and touching you and if you were able to pull her really against you, the erection came – instantaneous, embarrassing. But it felt so good – Goran was right, his famous call "Feels so good!" A hard-on. "I got a hard!" some of the boys would sing out in the showers, or point to themselves sitting in the classroom, or in the library, when Miss Vukovich would perform her maddening leg show. It was probably the most common scrawl in the bathrooms. Someone wrote above a urinal "Show It Hard!" Frankie would point out a girl, and say "Endless hard-on, I'm tellin' you!"

You could go on all night dancing like that, except for the fact of the hard-on. And, he wondered, incessantly, what did the *girl* think? For, as far as he knew, none of them ever said a word about, or even alluded to it, did not even glance down, but yet there it was, in some cases, with the bigger boys, noticeably sticking out, in a comic way.

Now they had put on "Young Love," a favorite, by Ferlin Husky, a country n' western singer who had a hit with it. Who was playing records? They must be in the PA booth, back by the principal's office, whoever it was. "Young Love" wasn't that good for slow dancing, either.

"Where'd the girls go?" Frankie asked, looking around. They were nowhere to be seen, probably swallowed up in the billowing clouds of chiffon – was that what the frothy dresses were made of? – that puffed up at every place you looked.

"They'll come back," Larry replied. He was still with the music, it made him think of being a dj, but he was also thinking about the irony of them now waiting for the girls. It seemed that was the girls' role, to wait. They had to learn that, waiting. It must be hard.

The Queen of the Hop, the autumn Queen, was not Cheryl Lake, or Cameron Mitchell – Cameron, he thought, was certainly not even at the Hop – but Brenda Morrison, a senior girl he really didn't know much about. She was blonde and pretty, with a great smile that everyone noticed. The King was Dick Atkins. This was fitting, he was the king of the football team, but maybe it was too much for such a successful athlete to get to be King, too. It would mean that he would have to squire Brenda around at the Hop, but he had not brought her, probably. So where was Cheryl Lake? The rules of these things were increasingly complex and intricate. Maybe he had brought her.

"Hey – did Atkins bring the Queen? What's her name?" Frankie asked, as if reading his mind. He seemed nervous, distracted, his eyes were wide.

"Brenda Morrison… Do you like Cindy?" Larry asked, mischievously.

"Up yours!" Frankie retorted, grabbing Larry's left arm and twisting it hard up behind him. "Up yours, man!"

Larry freed himself with a quick move, and straightened his jacket. The football conditioning had had its effect; in the spring, before Training Camp, the workouts, he couldn't have done that.

"No offense. Just kidding, you know what I mean."

"Yeah… you're just pissed because you can't play Mr. DJ, and spin the records. That's what you want. You'd rather do that, than be with her – Sandy. Or Cameron! Hey, what about the poems, and Cameron? Up in the library? Nutso case!"

He could not clearly recall when the disc jockey business had begun, but it was weird. It was an unknown side of him that just emerged. Maybe, as his mother claimed, he listened to the radio too much. It was an addiction, the radio, the night disc jockey show, from 8-12. He knew every record, and the opening of one he especially liked was enough to send him into an instant euphoria. Afterwards, he would feel deflated, like a flat tire going down.

The routine was always the same. He would pull down the window shade, he didn't want anybody passing by in the street outside to see him in his intensity. He wanted total concentration, to be in the music as far as he could be. He would turn out all the lights in his room, except a small gooseneck study lamp his mother had bought him; he left it on so she would not open his door, seeing no lights on. Often he lay on his bed, staring into the near darkness. He was not at all sure he knew how to dance – how did you learn, like you were supposed to? He would imagine he was dancing to the music, especially the slow ones. At those times, if he could have had any wish, it would have been to be a really good dancer, one of those guys whose confidence was visible as they moved around the floor with the girl held close. Their moves were fluid, smooth, natural, never any hesitation or, worse, stumbling or stepping on the girl's feet. Lurching around, he called it, and he made up a group, Larry and the Lurchers, a stupid name but he liked it anyway, and thought it had a sort of genius, even.

"Hey. There they are – over there, under the basket?" Frankie motioned with a nod of his head, and it was true; Cindy and Sandy were just emerging from under the basket – a place where he had often pivoted, faked, thrown a sharp hook. Two points!

"They probably went to the bathroom. Girls are always going to the bathroom, you know? Not to pee. The make-up!" Frankie patted his cheeks, and made a primping motion to his hair, simpering. "How do I look?"

Now the two girls were making their way around the perimeter of the floor, towards them, smiling and waving. Larry felt his stomach knot up. He did not have the faintest idea what would happen in the evening ahead. It was uncharted territory. He would have to dance with Sandy. It meant holding her close, so that she would be up against him, and he would feel the warmth, the heat, of her firm body, look into those eyes, and get the hard-on. It was like a disease. The prospect filled him with a churning confusion. Frankie claimed it was possible, a girl might let you, to press up against her so you would come off in your pants – but what kind of a thing was that? Horseshit, from the gym, the shower room talk. He did not want to do it, in any case, and certainly not with Sandy. He also realized he would have to tell Sandy he really did not know how to dance well; it would be very obvious, quickly. "I'm a slow dancer," he thought; he would say that. And how was he to get better at it? No sister to practice with like many guys did, and no brother, either, to show him the moves, give him confidence. You needed *confidence* to dance, above all else. He could not ask his mother – or Frankie. For that matter, he was not sure Frankie knew so much, either. Girls, of course, always knew how; they taught each other.

"Frankie!" he said urgently. "You *really* know how to dance?"

Frankie looked at him quickly, a fast flicker of fear passing over his face. He straightened his shoulders, looked across the teeming, shifting mass on the floor. "I can do it. No problem. I can do it." He swallowed heavily, as if he just drank something.

Who were the really good dancers in the class, the school? Cheryl Lake was supposed to be, but who would have the courage to find out, to actually dance with her? Cheryl Lake was said to go to college dances already. Gibby Davis, whose real name was Gilbert – he was good. He would dance free style sometimes in the auditorium at lunch hour, with a small radio that somebody plugged in, and that was against the principal's laws. He could dance, move, "juke," like the Negroes down in Pittsburgh were said to dance – a fluid, continuous, shifting sinuous movement of his body, with his feet amazingly keeping the beat. Larry desperately wished that he had some of that ability, even a fraction. The confidence. That was what it was, confidence. How did you get that? Maybe that was why he wanted to be a disc jockey – you didn't have to dance, but you controlled the whole thing, every move. The idea dawned on him with the force of a realization. Then the girls were almost to them.

"Holy shit!" Frankie said. "They're coming..."

The girls were beautiful in their dresses, and the boys at the dance, they were simply interchangeable pieces. What was going on was something more than what met the eye, and something that he would remember a long time into the future, and wish he could re-capture, because in its way it was perfect, even if he did not know a damn thing about really dancing, being smooth on the floor. Dancing – that was something that stood for, meant, something else, easy to see that. He was probably the only one in the place thinking that.

In the long seconds as they stood frozen to the gym floor watching the two girls approach as surely as the coming of the next day, Larry thought of the girls' marvelous inhabitance of the current fashions. Every girl in the gym had on a slightly different dress, of amazing colors. Some had straps and some did not; some were longer than others, some fit closely and tightly, others were like frothy foam surrounding them. The girls' seemingly endless knowledge of the latest styles fascinated him – where did they learn it, where did all these things – the ponytails, the rolled-up blue jeans (only to an exact two cuff length), the two-tone saddle shoes and the penny loafers, even the white rolled socks they wore, and the wearing of a class ring from your steady on a fine, thin gold chain around your neck – where did all that stuff start? Who started it?

Not that there weren't the same mysterious waves of styles among boys – oxblood, "spade" shoes one year, engineer boots the next, and now, blue suede shoes which were ruined in the first good rain. And the haircuts – the Balboa, the DA, the standard flattop crew-cut that a popular group was even named after, "The Crew Cuts." The Mohawk was the most extreme – Pecker Dolan had been threatened with expulsion for coming to school wearing one. It had looked fantastic, you could see it bobbing down the halls a long way off, and Pecker, a bad guy if there ever was one, had compounded it by wearing only a tight fitting men's white undershirt stained with grease. That was a change from the tight-fitting t-shirt with a pack of smokes rolled in one arm sleeve, that other greasers wore, along with tight, dirty Levis and engineer boots.

"I wonder how you'd dance in engineer boots," he said out loud, and Frankie looked at him, his mouth open.

"What?..."

The girls were there, and there was their perfume, each different, and before he knew it he was out on the dance floor. But not with Sandy. He was moving, somehow, around the perimeter of the floor with Cindy Shaffer, her red hair filling his field of vision. He felt strangely muffled, distant from himself, and realized that she was talking to him, going on as if nothing was happening. What was she saying?

"...some other time. Did you go to that dance? Last year? Larry?"

"No – no, I missed it... I was studying. For a test. In literature."

She smiled, and nodded. "You're a really good student. You'll probably get a scholarship."

He nodded in his turn, although he realized even as he did so that this was somewhat arrogant. "I hope to. I need one."

At least the latter statement was true. He would need help, a lot of it, and the probability of it was so low, in his mind, that he was beginning to let go of the idea of going to college, while holding onto it simultaneously, fiercely. He had to go to college. There was no question. Maybe he would dig graves at night – he had read about some guy in Pittsburgh who'd put himself through Pitt that way. Or so a newspaper article said. He'd written a book about it.

"Maybe I'll have to work my way through college. Dig graves. Or something." Why was he saying these things? The dance floor, over every inch of which he had dribbled basketballs endless times, seemed a totally foreign, large space in which he was lost.

"You could get a football scholarship," she said. "Those are full scholarships, too. And you're smart, you have top grades."

He thought what a kind girl she was, to say that. What was the record that was playing? "Earth Angel," The Penguins. Had they gone from one record to another, and he had not noticed? He was moving, his legs were working, he had not stepped on her feet, or her dress, yet. Cindy had made no complaint; he must be doing ok. But he wished, suddenly, she was Cameron, if only she was Cameron, with this record. Cameron Mitchell.

He was glad, though, when the record ended, and he could take Cindy to the side of the floor, and excuse himself. Sandy was at the opposite end of the gym with several of the other majorettes; they were huddled together in the way girls do. He already needed some cooler air, some quiet, and walked out the big double doors into the long hall outside the gym. He could see the steps off at the end, that led down to the new wing, where his home room was, and where the art and music rooms were. He ambled in that direction, maybe a back door would be open, maybe he would even leave the dance.

Walking in the semi-darkened hall of the school made it seem bigger, even unfamiliar. No one was in it, it was the complete absence of kids. As he walked away from the gym, he could hear the music fade. Rooms 115-116 – Art and Music. No home rooms in those rooms. The music room curved in an arc so that the chorus could sit in tiers to rehearse, with Mrs. Heald, who had taught music for as long as anyone could remember, but she did not seem old. She loved music, too. She had married one of her students, a much younger man – after he had graduated, of course.

Zeb Lewis, the mad saxophonist of the Pep Band, could be heard playing in the music room, too, at odd times, and there was some way that you could play records in the room and pipe them out over the school PA system, or so he had been told.

He was thinking about Zeb when he head her voice behind him. Cameron Mitchell. No mistaking it.

"Have you got a late class, Larry?" she said. Where had she come from, he wondered?

"I was just wandering around in here…" He did not know what to say, and felt his throat constrict dryly.

"It's kinda fun, isn't it? When no one is here." Was she at the dance? She looked, as always, beautiful, different, older; she looked like a lot of things he could not really define, but there she was, right in front of him, so close now he could smell her perfume, and see that glisten of her dark mane of hair – Cameron's hair, which she shook and flipped effortlessly. And now she was staring at him, a faint smile playing around her lips.

"Yeah, it is…" He nodded quickly, maybe too quickly. If anything, Cameron was even more beautiful in the semi-darkness of the half-lit corridor than in daytime. Or differently beautiful. She looked older, he could not quite place it.

"You're at the Hop, right? With Sandy Stevens?"

Again, he bobbed his head in a quick nodding. Why didn't he, why couldn't he, speak more easily? It was agonizing, this paralysis a girl like Cameron could cause in him.

"Right... I – just wanted to get some air. Kinda hot in the gym." He gestured behind him. "I went out the corridor door..." What was he saying? he wondered, even as he tried to say something.

She smiled, and started walking on, towards the steps, and then where the corridor curved, down at the end. She was dressed like Cameron dressed, always something different. She had on Levis, and some sort of short jacket that came only to her waist; it was a deep blue color that really set off her hair. Room 114 was down there. His home room; there the corridor curved, and the rooms he'd been thinking about, 115-116, weren't visible yet. He thought to say something about that, it was the only thing he could think of, but he knew it was stupid, and walked alongside her, wondering if he was gnawing his lip, if his deodorant had worn off, what did he look like to her? Maybe the EXIT door down there, at the very end, would be open, maybe even propped open, by Mr. Dempsey. Maybe he'd even be down there, smoking his pipe.

" I like the music room," he said. It was true, he did like it, even though he couldn't sing at all and so had no classes there. The same was true of art. He could not draw well at all, and had watched in silent amazement as George Dempsey, the janitor's son, drew free hand on large white sheets of drawing paper in that room – the shapes appeared out of nothing, with just a few deft strokes, lines, and some shading, cross-hatching. It seemed effortless, like a child playing intently. Dempsey had drawn a cardinal like that the previous winter, looking at a live one, brilliantly red, sitting outside on a barren snow-covered tree branch. He had the drawing in his room at home; his mother had asked with amazement, the first time she saw it, if he'd done it. It was the art room, too, where he'd watched silently as George sketched Cameron Mitchell, skillfully adding her '55 Chevy, and the front of Peter's, in the background of the sketch.

"Zeb Lewis plays there, all the time... you've heard him?"

He nodded, probably too enthusiastically. "Oh, yeah. A lot of times – you see him playing in the Pep Band? He really does it."

They were in front of the very room as he said it. Here it was like the rest of the school was gone, cut off, disappeared, and he liked that, he realized that was why he liked to hang around the wing. The big music room was completely dark. They both bent slightly, to peer in the glass-paned door, and their heads were close together, almost bumping. He could smell her, feel her warmth, and some strands of her dark hair brushed his shoulder and the side of his face lightly. He felt a little dizzy, and embarrassed.

"Strange... to see it so empty. Usually there's kids all over in there. And quiet..." Far away, he could hear the music from the Hop, slurred, faint.

Cameron looked down at the door handle. He had never been that close to her. Her eyes were large and changed as you looked into them; it gave him a strange feeling.

"Think it's open?" she said, and then, not waiting for him to answer, she lightly pushed down, and the door swung open, into the warm darkness of the room. She pulled his arm, bringing him in quickly; he had been standing stock still. What if the janitor saw them, or one of the chaperons?

" Maybe Zeb's here," she was saying, walking towards a far corner of the room. She hadn't turned on the light, and he thought he should, but remained standing, letting his eyes adjust. There was a large light on a high pole out behind the room, which shed light down into the room; all was pale and shadowy, even unreal looking, like one of those underwater films. It was beautiful, and he thought it was something he'd never seen if they hadn't happened to be in the hall at the same time, all of that.

"Zeb? Are you here?" she called softly. There was no answer, of course – Zeb never came to dances, as far as Larry knew, although he might come if he thought a neat band was playing. But none of the small bands that played school dances were really any good. They were made up of older guys, in their twenties or even thirties, who played the dances to pick up extra money. In their day jobs, they sold shoes or worked in the Alcoa factory; something like that.

"I doubt he's here," he said, looking around as if he might see him, in spite of what he'd said.

"No." Cameron motioned to him with her hand. "Come over here, Larry."

He swallowed heavily, and his legs suddenly felt heavy and uncertain. "Should I turn the light on, you think?"

"No." she said. "No light."

As if he were walking to his execution in a film, he went to her. She was smiling slightly, and as he got closer he wondered what it was all about, what was happening, and then she stepped to him, and put her hand lightly on his chest.

"Stop. That's a good place."

"A good place?" he asked.

"Have you ever kissed a girl, Larry – for real, I mean? A real kiss?"

Later he was to wonder what had kept him from turning and walking away, but he heard himself say, with utter amazement. "No. Not really. I haven't. I haven't... really. Kissed a girl..."

"Well. Here I am." And she moved close in to him so that she was inches from his face, and the light from the pole came through the mane of dark hair, which she shook very slightly. "Right here." She took his hand, and slid his arm around her waist, and then they were kissing.

Kissing Cameron Mitchell was like falling in slow motion off the Rocks, up the creek, where you went skinny-dipping in the spring and the most adventurous boys leaped off with a high, yodeling yell and plunged down, down into the cascading water of the deep pool there. Some said it was thirty feet or more deep. It felt like that high leap and then the slow-down of the deep water, the pull of it, so different. Her mouth was soft and warm, and he closed his eyes instinctively and leaned into her, and put his other hand up tentatively, even as he kissed her, to touch that hair. That hair. It was so soft and lush, full, that he felt himself breathe in deeply even as they were kissing, and the pressure of her mouth against his increased.

He was kissing Cameron Mitchell in the music room and far away the Autumn Hop was going on, and nobody knew it. She was kissing the side of his face and then his eyes, still closed, and then back down to his mouth again, and he wondered if there was lipstick, like on tv. They were stock still in the room. Outside he heard the wind come up, and a couple of trees that still had a good bit of leaves on them made that rustling night sound they made when the wind blew and he was laying up in bed at the house.

"Cameron." He said her name. "You have beautiful hair." He stroked it hesitantly, and she leaned into him. He could stay there forever, in the music room, forget the Autumn Hop, it now seemed in the distant past.

"Cameron." He loved saying her name, and she reached up and pulled him into another kiss. He shut his eyes, although he thought about keeping them open – an experiment, like in science. But this was not science, he knew that.

How long did that second, lush kiss last? That was the word that came in his mind afterwards, *lush*, when he was trying to walk back to the gym floor, knowing that Frankie and the girls would maybe be getting annoyed that he'd disappeared. Maybe even left, he would be capable of that, walk back down the alley home, maybe even stop in and see if Ducky was there in his strange little alley house. Why did anyone build a house right on an alley, like that, anyway?

He didn't know how long it lasted, but he knew he wouldn't forget it. He grazed her neck with his lips afterwards, and started to nuzzle up under that hair, but she pushed him – very gently – back.

"No. Have to stop. That's enough." Her mouth was slightly open still, and she was looking at him intently.

He wanted to lay down with her, he realized. It was the most natural feeling in the world. But there was nowhere to lay down; the floor was hard concrete. It was out of his mind as soon as it came in, though he thought too of her '55 Chevy. To lay down with Cameron Mitchell in that car – that would be something. He might never come back from that.

"I think you better get back to the Hop," she said. "Didn't you come with Sandy Stevens? She'll be wondering what happened to you."

"Should I tell her?" he said, before he was thinking straight. Why did he say that, and he started to shake his head. "I didn't mean that..."
Now Cameron was smiling. She shook her head slightly. "I don't think so. Do you?"

He agreed silently, and took a large breath; he realized he wasn't breathing, he was holding his breath all this time, or it felt like that. He closed his eyes, and opened them again. He doubted he could even tell his mother about it, what had just happened.

"Where are you going?" he asked. "I mean – did you come to the Hop?"

"Sort of, you could say that. Just to see what was happening. I was just driving around, in my car, and I knew the Hop was tonight… and so here I am."

It made sense, for Cameron. That she would go out and drive around – prowl around came into his mind – in that '55 cherry red Chevy.

"I'd rather leave with you," Larry said then.

She was going to say something, but they both heard a sound up the hall, as of a door screeching open, maybe the janitor, or some other kids who were messing around in a darkened classroom, like they'd just been doing.

"You better go back, Larry. OK?" And she quickly stepped in front of him, out the door, he followed automatically, and then she had neatly and quietly closed it, with a soft click. He wondered if maybe she hadn't locked it, too; nobody else could get in now. And nobody had been in, since it was obviously locked. She was a smart girl.

"See you," she said, and surprising him once again she moved back into the darkness at the very end of the corridor and out the EXIT door there, which he would not have thought was open. The janitor wasn't keeping things locked up, he thought, and even as he thought it,

Cameron was gone, out the back entrance, which was rarely used, except to bring supplies into the art room, 116, the last room on the wing. Gone, back to her car, no doubt.

She would drive off into the night with Bill Hailey and the Comets blasting "Rock Around The Clock" on the car radio, or The Platters singing "The Great Pretender" or an older hit, The Crew Cuts doing "Shboom!" It would be that station in Greensburg, WGBH, the one he listened to in his room all the time, with the blind down, laying on the bed, the room dark, just the glow of the radio dial, something he loved. He would hear his mother move by the door, stop, come back, and listen, then move on; he could see her shadow under the door from the hallway light. He spent more and more nights like that, too. Not studying, as he should. But school was proving somewhat easy, although he knew he could not admit that.

As he walked slowly back towards the gym, he thought what if he could call up the dj on that night show, and ask him, beg him, to play a request, a dedication/request, for Cameron, so she'd hear it as she drove somewhere in that Chevy, and know it was him that sent it out on the airwaves. Only they would know that, too. But he didn't know the station's telephone number, and he'd never heard the jockey give a request before on the show, so probably he wouldn't do it this time, either. Why should he? He probably got the same line every night from some listeners who wanted the same thing as Larry did now.

He got to the big doors back by the coaches' office, and they were closed and the music from inside was much louder now, with the scraping and rustling sounds of the dancers moving around the floor inside. What an odd thing to do, he suddenly thought. It was some kind of ritual, really, that's what it was. He would have to go back in and find Sandy, and dance with her some more – not that that was so awful, after all; he had a vision of her marching, twirling her baton, and her wonderful legs which somehow looked peppy, her legs had personality, yes, that was how he would have described them – and no doubt there would be dances with other girls in their frothy gowns, their Hop dresses that he heard cost as much as fifty or seventy five dollars. Seventy-five dollars. And they'd only wear them that one time.

If he was really different he'd leave and see if Cameron was still parked outside, waiting for him, to see if he'd come out, follow her. James Dean – he would have done that. He should have done that down there in the music room when she left, followed her right away, and then they could have driven off and parked somewhere and continued kissing, making out. Or talking – why did he think that? But he did, somehow he knew they would have talked, a lot. It could have happened. But here he was, going back into the gym, the Hop, and he felt suddenly like a kid. A kid.

He sighed heavily, and pulled the big door open, and a wave of heat and sound and smell engulfed him as he moved into the noisy gym. Nobody noticed him.

# 24

He was moving around the gym floor with Myra Hynes, was it? She was a nice girl, also a sophomore, in his literature class with Mr. Turner. She didn't talk much, had braces on her teeth, and he thought that might be why she didn't say much. He still wasn't really there. He could see a basketball laying up in the stands, just sitting there, and he could hear it, on the floor. That bouncing, thudding sound of the basketball. An unmistakable, sure sign winter was coming. The try-outs for the team were already underway in late October, right before Halloween, and looking in the window of the gym door from the long classroom hallway, you could see the players moving in the drills Coach Pedjman favored – the old, classic give-and-go, the dribbling in and out through a twisting line of folding metal chairs, the passing drills, practice at the foul line – shooting underhand, of course, like girls did. He would never change, and the team would never win.

He and Ducky would not be in the practices this year. They had opted out and would, at best, appear in the annual Charity Game, where the teachers played a group of students chosen for their ineptitude and sheer lack of any athletic ability, as often as not. The head cheerleader of the Pep Rallies, Charlie Hibbing, would play, and somebody from several of the student clubs, and the president of the senior class, too, Ron Sorenson, who wore heavy dark framed glasses and was tall and bony-looking. The game was meant to be funny – the teachers entering the gym exaggeratedly limping, a few awkwardly slinging along on crutches, stopping every five paces, some apparently tottering as if with old age and exhaustion, with their arms in slings, or their head wound in white bandages. One entered sitting in a wheelchair, with a portable oxygen tank wheeled alongside him; another had a uniformed (and well-stacked, as Frankie liked to say) nurse supporting him as he walked. One with his arm in a sling, would suddenly cast it off when he reached the bench, shaking it as if it were newly healed, raising it triumphantly.

How long had he and Ducky played in the old hard-frozen playground down in the Lower End, where dirty, frayed shreds of net hung on the rims of the baskets? Playing at night, their pleasure in it was so sharp and fresh, playing by light of the streetlights on Second Street, driving into the basket for a spinning lay-up, or flicking a hook shot from twenty-five feet out. Coach Pedjman did not care about their love of the game and would have been perplexed if told of their night games there. Maybe he should have driven around the town more at night, like the football coaches who were said to stalk the streets of Vandergrift and Monessen in the early evenings, peering in dining rooms and kitchens to see if there were any good-sized prospects eating huge plates of spaghetti there while their mothers watched them, beaming. Larry had read in a book up in the library about a coach from Notre Dame, in the old days, who would drive around the farm fields in the spring months, and stop and ask a prospect he saw plowing for directions. If the boy pointed with his hand, he was out, but if he simply lifted the plow to give the direction, he was a good prospect. And on the Ralston team, there was the big lineman, the left tackle John Curtis, who was said to do plowing on the Curtis farm, out beyond Slate Lick.

Somehow another song, by the Platters, had started, and he and Myra were still dancing. "This is a nice dance," he said, having to say something. Myra nodded. A nice girl.

What would Coach Pedjman have made of it, seeing he and Ducky driving and darting and shooting there, for hours, in the cold, with only the streetlight glaring nakedly? Probably not much, if he had noticed at all. A better coach would have sought the boys out, brought them into the gym. Or, even further, would have made a point of getting to observe their play, unobserved himself. He felt this was true, but there seemed to be nothing he could do about it, and it hurt him, angering him and at the same time making him sad, because it was an example of the thing he heard repeated so often, from his mother and from many others, that things were already determined, set-up, the way they were, and what you had to do was accept that.

What would Cameron look like without her dress, or her jeans, on? A forbidden thought he tried to squelch as soon as it came into his mind, an ugly thought, who could approve of such a thing? Goran's cards exercised their baneful effects. Earlier, as he had danced with Sandy, he imagined her suddenly shedding her dress, stepping easily out of it, kicking it aside with her underpants, and she would be – naked. He was going to hell, no doubt about it, and even Myra Hynes wasn't safe with the kind of monster he was becoming.

He had never seen a real live naked girl. Only these damn photos of Goran's, which were in any case not girls, but women, and women who were not that pretty even. But what would a really pretty young girl look like without any clothes on? Years ago, as a kid, he had gone to "The Rocks," a swimming hole further up from Mickey's Mill, and swum naked. Skinny dipped. But only boys did this. He had never heard of any girls even trying it – it was an unthinkable idea. Or, if they did do it, it was a very well-kept secret, known only to them.

And when would it be when he would see a girl naked? What would be the situation, how old would he be? He did not want to peep into the girls' locker room, as it was said some did (Goran especially, again, the evil bastard), and could do, although he really did not believe it. Some boys apparently were willing to risk possible expulsion also, by hiding out in the gym, and watching the girls undress.

Did girls find naked boys as interesting? *That* was a hard idea to get hold of; at least, he found it so. Would they like to look at a naked boy? Did they peep in the locker room? Did they play with themselves, as Coach Rossi distastefully put it, frowning? It was hard to imagine, but Frankie maintained they could do it easier than boys.

"You know when they're sittin' one leg over the other, and rockin' away like crazy? They're doin' it!"

In Sam's, it was maintained they were worse than boys. "Do it every chance they can… you ask me. You get a girl's got a hot tail, ain't nobody gonna stop her."

"Got to put out that fire. Bush fire!" another old guy cackled, one who'd been a barber himself, Jakie Fair, but he had retired, at eighty. Some said he was a hundred years old, and could remember the Civil War.

Carl Hamilton, a dark-haired, silent type of man was standing looking out the big barbershop window. His voice sounded like it came out of a well.

"A stiff prick…" he shook his head. "These days, they'll do anything."

"You got that right!" Everybody nodded, like synchronous puppets on strings.

There was not much that happened when he came back to the Hop, and this amazed him, for everything had happened in that interval down in the music room. But Sandy apparently hadn't really gotten upset that he'd stepped out, and Frankie was beaming and he thought maybe Frankie really liked Cindy Shaffer more than he let on. The music continued playing out over the gym floor, where couples circulated in a slow round, and as the evening wore on they became closer together, some almost one, fused, the boy enfolded in the gauzy froth of the dresses the girls wore. The music was something Larry felt strongly and dancing to it was almost too much, too intense. The music made you happy, delirious, full, and he thought that years from that night he would hear some record – maybe driving somewhere in a car, maybe even in another country, maybe on military duty – and it would bring him right there, to the gym, to this time and place. The music was a miracle, although the adults didn't like it, or said they didn't understand it, or that it wasn't really music, it would not last. Their music was the real music, that was music! Jazz. Larry couldn't get it, although the speech teacher had played a record for him with some jazz greats playing. The quality of the recording was uneven, and the teacher had told Larry that the secret of jazz was "they never play the same thing twice, not exactly the same. It's always unique, the improvisation. Every time." Jazz musicians didn't make the kind of money popular musicians did, though. Look at Elvis. He had heard a dj in Pittsburgh say that Elvis had turned down the unheard of sum of fifty thousand dollars for one concert. *$50,000!* It was a sum so large Larry couldn't really comprehend it. What would that much money look like, all piled up?

The thing was, he really now wanted to dance only with Cameron Mitchell, not Myra or Cindy or Sandy or other girls, as pretty as they undeniably were. But what was she up to? Some game, with him? Or with everyone? He was out of his depth with Cameron, and the soft, insistent kiss, the parting of her lips in the music room earlier, that already seemed like a fantasy, but it had happened. Cameron was quite capable of acting as if it hadn't, but he'd already been changed by it. And what was he now supposed to do about it? These were the games girls played, he was beginning to see. Maybe this was her game, her pursuit – to change people, see what they would, or could, do? Or not do.

Cameron's hair. That would be what he'd remember. You could die in it, and be happy, he thought. Who would she marry? Who would, in Frankie's memorable phrase, "be gettin' that. Every night." He could not imagine the man Cameron would marry, and he thought that if she did marry – and she almost had to, the way things were – whoever the guy was, he wouldn't know. In that sense, she was another Cheryl Lake.

He held up his end manfully for the rest of the evening, which seemed to get longer and longer. But he felt distanced from Sandy – he felt he was acting odd, but couldn't change it. Some of the girls had taken off their shoes, dancing in their bare feet, or stockinged feet. The boys grew heavy-lidded, moving slower and slower. Finally it was time to go, and the faculty chaperons stood up at the end of the gym under one basket on a small platform they'd hauled out of somewhere, and announced the Last Dance.

It had been decided, apparently while he was gone from the gym, that they would all drive down to Eat N' Park and end the evening there, and so they did, and the whole way there, as the girls chattered in the car happily, he watched the dark night slip by outside the windows, like in a movie, saying little, wondering if Cameron Mitchell might be there. If he was James Dean, it would be different. But he knew she wouldn't be. He would, always, be just missing Cameron. He lacked confidence. But when he thought of James Dean, it wasn't confidence he portrayed. He was uncertain, too, he did not know what to do. He wondered if he ever would know what to do, the move to make. He was not James Dean. For some reason, he thought of the red jacket Dean wore in the film, with the collar up. That had started a style, already. If he had that jacket, or one like it, and walked into Eat N' Park, and Cameron was there, she would notice. Her car was that color. But he did not think even Scheer's sold a jacket like that one.

# 25

After the music room, the evening was anticlimactic
– wasn't that a word Mr. Turner used, a lot, in the literature class? At Eat N' Park they had double cheeseburgers
and fries and the thick shakes they made there – it was
amazing how much girls could eat, something everyone
said was true, and it was. They could eat as much as a
boy, and more. The food and the long evening made him
feel heavy and he fought going to sleep in Frankie's car.
*That* would get around the school; fell asleep, with Sandy
Stevens. He imagined Goran cawing like a beaky crow in
the boys room, "Sure. She had her hand in his pants!"

But Sandy was a really nice girl. She talked about the
Hop, and how the gym had looked, she wouldn't ever
forget that, and included him by talking about the football
season. She didn't talk about being a majorette and yet
only a sophomore. She wasn't "stuck-up" – although she
had plenty of reason to be. He liked her, but the moments
with Cameron in the music room had changed, abruptly,
how he felt. He was confused in a way he'd never been.

Frankie Malone drove around with the radio playing
– the station from Greensburg, the four hours' show of
all the best stuff, the show he fantasized about being on

himself, his voice spilling out into a thousand cars like Frankie's, with a thousand couples making out. People would remember you, years later, as "that guy, the dj, that was on from 8-12." In an odd sleepy energy, they drove all the way down to New Kensington. But it was getting really late by then, and they didn't want to get into any trouble, even have the police stop them, maybe. That could happen. That was for the greasers – the guys with engineer boots and tight levis and the slicked-back DAs or some form of the DA. Maybe a Balboa... they always had a comb sticking out of their jeans hip pocket, like a badge. Or a switchblade. There was one of these he had heard of where the blade came straight out the end. The Negroes in the Hill District in Pittsburgh carried straight-edged razors, they said in Sam's. "They as soon cut ya as look at ya." They were not looking for any of that.

Sandy had sleepily cuddled up against him, probably more for warmth, because it was getting cold at night, nearly November, and there had already been a couple of light frosts. Sandy was a beautiful girl, and he felt protective of her. It was a great feeling, being with a girl like that, riding in the car. He thought he could do that for a long time. When they dropped her off, out at the Stevens' big house in the country ("Mock Tudor," his mother had said. "A wonderful house!"), he walked her to the door where the light had been, sure enough, left on, just as she'd said it would be.

They stood fussing at the door. The Hop was over. There wouldn't be another one now until the early spring of the next year, a long way off. Sandy looked at him, and he knew he could kiss her if he wanted to; he was even supposed to, almost had a right, it was the big moment, the climax of the entire evening – and they had already done this, hesitantly, in Frankie's car, Frankie eye-balling it in the rear-view mirror. It was a double date, so it wasn't fair to make out in the back while Frankie had to drive, with his date sitting pressed up next to him so close – he and Cindy might be an item, Larry thought.

"I better go," he said lamely, and he was actually looking at Frankie's car, back down the driveway hunched in the street like some kind of getaway car, they were going to go to Pittsburgh and do a job. The whole time they had been driving around "New Ken" and on the road back out to Sandy's he realized he'd been looking for that red '55 Chevy.

She touched his arm. "I had a really good time, Larry. Thank you." She leaned just a bit forward, he kissed her, a soft, warm quick contact; again, he was amazed at the reality of a girl, the feel and smell of them. She was very different from Cameron, that was for sure. And he knew that if he had not kissed Cameron earlier that evening, this kiss would be different. This was that bright, shining girl who looked like a spotlight was on her when she marched out in front of the Ralston band. If anyone had told him a week previous that he'd be kissing these two girls, Sandy Stevens and Cameron Mitchell, in the same night, he would have stared in disbelief. It reminded him of what Frankie said about Coach Barnes. "Played too long at Purdue without his helmet on, that guy."

Frankie did not have much to say, they still had to drop Cindy off, but Larry suggested they drop him off first. Cindy turned quickly and smiled at him.

"You got it, ace," Frankie said. "Your personal chauffeur service…"

His mother was waiting up. They went into the kitchen and she made hot chocolate for him. They sat at the kitchen table, where they had sat so often, he thought, more than anywhere else in the house. The lack of his stepfather was a presence, even now, everywhere in the house. They had carried his body down the steep upstairs; he thought the straining men would lose it, the gurney banging heavily. He remembered the look on his mother's face. Here, in this kitchen.

Looking around the house, it seemed to be aging, like his mother. The furniture was out of date, the sofa too overstuffed, people didn't have sofas like that any more at all. It was from the 1940s, long ago already. The cellar dusty, dark; a cave. Always a musty smell in the house. He kept opening windows to get air in and his mother kept closing them, invariably asking him why he opened them so much. He felt tired and did not say much; he wanted to go up to his room, lay in the dark, listen to the radio, look at the soft green light of the dial; it comforted him. Hopefully, he might get something good on it, maybe the wild guy up in Buffalo, or a Cleveland station. These days he didn't feel like he had much to say to his mother. She said, "Well, I can see you had a big night. We'll talk about it in the morning – if you feel like it, that is." He nodded, but he knew he would not feel like it. If Carl had been home, he'd have talked to him. But he was far away, in North Carolina. Camp Lejeune.

Up in his room he found nothing but crackly static on the radio, even the signal of WILY, down in the Hill District, coming in and out so that you didn't want to listen. He couldn't get Buffalo or Cleveland very well at all; some nights he could, and he'd never been able to figure that one out. "Atmospheric conditions," Calvin Harris, the president of Mr. Sweeney's Science Club had told him. "Didn't you know that affects the signals, from that far away? Even those big fifty thousand watt jobs..." 50,000 watts! That was beyond belief. Calvin told him there was a radio station far down near the Mexican border with Texas – it was actually in Mexico – a 50,000 watter that broadcast all kinds of crazy music continuously. Texas. That was further away than North Carolina. Furthest away was California. He could not imagine going there. His stepfather had a younger brother, Vincent, who lived in Stockton. What would that be like?

He stood staring out the window at the big, dark backyard spread out below. Down at the far end of the yard, where the alley ran down to Buffalo Creek, was the old smooth-barked cherry tree. His mother would make pies from those cherries every summer. They were sour cherries; birds loved them. He had picked them from that tree all his life. Under some strange inspiration, the previous summer he mowed the lawn in the backyard trying to make it look like a golf course, constructing little holes, narrow, curving fairways and greens. But the grass, cut so short around the holes and on the greens, died, burned a dead brown, and he was in some trouble with his mother to explain what he was trying to do. Nobody in Ralston played golf, except Sam, the owner of the barbershop, who took off Wednesdays to do just that at some country club down near Pittsburgh. Golf was for rich people, who didn't have to work and never had had to, but only played golf and then ate thick steaks in the clubhouse, drinking whiskey – cocktails – before doing so. He had read about it in *Look* magazine, where there were glossy photographs of them.

The recent summer – August, even – seemed so long ago now. And other than his training for Football Summer Camp, in August, what had he done, really? Day-dreaming it away. He would lie in the backyard, right down there, on a thin blanket soaking up his sweat, listening to the purple Motorola radio with the neat, modernistic-looking dial he'd been given when he'd turned twelve. He ran a long extension cord out from the basement that his mother constantly worried about. So much of the summer went like that – lying in the sun. Lying out even a couple of times in the middle of the football field in the middle of a hot summer day; that was something special. Ducky had put him on to that one – as long as you could stand it. The sun baked you, so hot your jeans became heated, and burned when you sat up. He had the impression of lying on a griddle. Ducky became nearly black. No one in the school had a tan like his. His mother thought that there was something odd about it. "I don't know how that boy can get *that* dark."

He got a deep brown, but not as dark as Ducky. It was an important ritual, you had to get as dark as you could, because in the early fall months you would wear a white tee shirt, as white as you could get it, with short sleeves, and the tan would look good, the girls really liked it. The football practice jerseys looked really great with a tan. The girls had gotten tanned legs in their summer, which looked unbelievably good in the short-shorts they wore, although these could not be worn in the school. Chaos would rule if they were. A girl in shorts like that, at the end of the summer, blinded you; you would walk into the wall, as some boys did as a joke. The short shorts were a torture, they looked so good. There was a goofy song out about them, even.

The radio, the disc jockeys, took him to another world, far away from Ralston. He was not sure what that world was, or even how to find it. Especially, it came out of car radios – it would exist powerfully in the red '55 Chevy, with Cameron Mitchell in it. Kids who had cars – usually their parents' – drove endlessly around on the hot summer nights, radio blaring. That was what you did, it was the thing to do, especially in the summer. Summer meant car radios, the music, the dj's voice in the night.

There was an inaccessibility to it, though, that frustrated him. In Pittsburgh, he had stood on the sidewalk outside a department store window – was it Gimbels? –

that had been enlarged so that a very popular dj, Jaye Henderson, could appear there "spinning his records" in public. The suave dj sat comfortably there, talking into the microphone, smiling and gesturing to the crowd outside, waving, an almost continuous set of smooth motions; his patter and the music spilled out onto the sidewalk and washed over them. He wore a suit that didn't seem to have ever known a wrinkle. Larry wondered how much that suit had cost, not counting the light blue shirt and darker blue tie he wore with it.

Jaye Henderson wasn't old, but he wasn't young, either. Larry had wondered if he was wearing make-up. It gave him a strange feeling, that sudden idea, that the dj would be made-up for his appearances, but it made sense, too; the lighting in the booth in the window was harsh. Maybe he should have worn sunglasses – that would have been very wild, he would have become, instantly, a "cool cat," one of the in-phrases, but he wasn't that kind of dj, he was not from WILY, the rhythm n' blues station in the Lower Hill District.

Jaye Henderson appeared god-like, safe, endlessly happy, with a job so marvelous how could it be a real job? Such a person never got dirty working, something every man in Ralston did, every day – it wasn't work if you didn't get dirty, that was a standard saying of wisdom. How did you get where Jaye Henderson was? That was a recurrent, nagging question Larry could find no answer to. Writing a letter to him would not be much help. But you couldn't be sure. In the eighth grade, he had written a letter to a morning network news television celebrity, Dave Garroway. Amazingly, he'd received a typed and signed reply. The letter urged him to continue to do well in school, and above all, to go to college.

The disc jockey was his King, especially in the summer. How many *hours* had he spent, lying on some towel or old blanket, the sun baking him brown, listening, in that other world? The one named Louis Barton, "Leapin' Louie!", who was on WILY in the evenings, was something else. His voice, his incessant going on, unmistakable and irresistible – you couldn't stop listening, no matter how long he went on. He played records by groups hard to find, or even know of. The Clovers. The Five Keys. The Cadillacs. He also played Bo Diddley, Chuck Berry.

"I'll be – heh, let's see, where will I be? *Yessir*, right here 'tis, I'll be in *Cheswick*, I know it well, I know all those people down there, the good folks in Cheswick, *yessir*, we've been there many times. You know that!! You know the place! That big roller arena – need I say more? And, hey! *Hey hey hey*! Ches-Arena! That's it, that is *the place*! I just think, I just think, I just think the *Baron may* have some very special *special* people with him – what night is that? – Monday night! Yeah! Come on down, then, come on down, come on down! *Down*! Ches-Arena, Monday night, baby, 8pm, we gonna be *shakin'* the joint down there real *bad*, something like this!"

The music swelled up, Bill Hailey and the Comets, doing "Shake, Rattle, and Roll". What did it mean – "Git out in that kitchen, roll my breakfast, cause I'm a hungry man!" Who was gittin' out in the kitchen? Not his wife, no. And "roll my breakfast?" Who said that, in the morning? There was a black man who sang the song before Bill Hailey, Big Joe Turner. He'd heard that on WILY, too. Turner's version of the song was better than Bill Hailey's, but Hailey's record was a big hit. WILY played what some people called "race" music. It was said that there were some records they couldn't play.

Frankie Malone loved this music. "You ever hear that one, 'Mary Had A Baby'?," he said. "The Midnighters? Or was it The Crows? And there's another one, they sing 'Jus a little bit higher/ Baby, my joint's on fire!' And 'Sixty Minute Man'? The Dominos? You can't play that shit on the fuckin' radio, man! Lose their broadcasting license, you know that's a fact…But somebody's buying those records, too. Else they wouldn't get made. And if you go hear them, like down at the Syria Mosque, somewhere, they sing it there. You hear it."

As the night got later – towards 11, 12 – Leapin' Louie, the Baron, played Chuck Berry, "Roll Over Beethoven" and "Maybellene", and Bo Diddley – "Bo Diddley, Bo Diddley, where you been…" And Louie would suddenly say weird things. Like, "Put it down! That pedal *down*, baby! Put it to the floor! We gonna let it rip! Yeah, yeah!" And he would play a Little Richard record, Little Richard who was more outrageous and wilder than even Elvis, or Jerry Lee Lewis. "Rip it Up" or "The Girl Can't Help It" or "Long Tall Sally". "Tutti Frutti." He would repeat a line from the song, chuckling, "Yes, the Baron got *everything* you need. Right here, baby, right here on WILY, and don't you forget it!"

Was it the very remoteness, the total inaccessibility, of Jaye Henderson's, the djs' world that appealed so much? That he wore an expensive suit, a shirt and tie, to work, and not just on Sundays, to church? His brother Carl hated suits and ties. He often said he could never stand a job where he worked at a desk, inside. He wanted to be a tree surgeon, a landscaper, but had gone right out of high school graduation, two weeks later, into the lumber yard, not even a break. Work was real, and you had to get used to it. Because it would be the rest of your life.

Somehow people like Jaye Henderson had escaped, that was it. And so had the Baron – Leapin' Louie – though he wasn't so sure about him, about *what* he had escaped to. He knew with a kind of desperation in his stomach he did not want to lead the "working" kind of life, but he could not see how to get to the life he did want, or thought he did. The djs had escaped the grinding work most in Ralston were fated to wear themselves out doing, making somebody else wealthy. The futility of these jobs bothered him, even frightened him. The lumber yard. The brick yard. There seemed no escape from it, it led nowhere that he could see. Few adult men lived to enjoy the retirement they sweated for, earned with thirty, thirty-five, forty years of hard labor; if they did make their retirement, they died within the year, often as not, as his mother pointed out over and over. Was she trying to tell him something without realizing it?

In the cold winter mornings, the winter right around the corner now, that was the worst. You saw them going off to work – some walking quickly, head down usually – to the train station in the middle of Ralston. Most drove cars – "the jalopy", or an old beaten-up rusting truck – leaving in that freezing darkness of the pre-dawn hours. His own mother got up for years – how many years? – at four am to make breakfast for his father, then stepfather, and then for Carl when he had started working at the Copley Lumber Yard.

Already this was his recurrent, abiding memory of them. Leaving in that cold time, plodding home silent by five or six in the evening, working a half a day on Saturdays, but it really meant most of the day. They came home dirty and tired and often said little, sitting in a favorite chair, sometimes falling asleep – "a little nap'll always fix you up…"

The supper hour was sacred because of this. It was like church. Larry felt it went far back, this taking of the supper – the eating, the quietness at the table, only the sounds of the knives and forks on plates, the smells of the heavy foods, the short inquiries. "No more bread?" "Milk gone?" Little was discussed at the table, eating was serious business, best done while the food was hot, or at least warm. Wives were rated by their cooking, too. The man whose wife was a poor cook, or worse, didn't cook at all - everybody felt sorry for him. To have a wife who was a bad or lousy cook, even if she was good-looking, was serious, bad luck.

He could recall tales of other kids sent to their rooms without their supper, a real punishment which horrified him; it had never been done to him. What was the point of doing that to a child? Was it "to teach them what the world is like," as some claimed? Why not teach them what the world could be? Something was going on, and it was about "work". It would be hard and probably injure you in time – people were often really worked to death, worn out like an old, used machine. What could you do? Did you have any other answer?

Sometimes he felt it would be better to be a criminal of some type, a crook. Once you had decided to be a criminal, – an outsider – you would be free, in an odd way. Maybe he would become a car thief – something like that – down in Pittsburgh. Or go to Philly, where he heard there were a lot of criminals, a lot of car theft. Why not? When he thought like this, immediately he could think of people who deserved to have their cars stolen, serve them right, too. They were always stealing from everybody else, they had the power to do this, the power that came with money. Pure and simple. Steal their damn car while they ate and swilled up at the country club. Rob them, as they robbed. Serve them right!

These thoughts disturbed him with their intensity. Now he lay down on the bed, in the dark of his room, only that radio dial glowing like a beacon from another planet or a spaceship. He lay there, how many nights had it been? How much time? Late at night, tossing and turning; and as sure as the sun would rise in the morning, the heated dreams, vivid imaginings of seemingly *all* the girls in Ralston High School. Some of the teachers, too... Miss Vukovich, the librarian, sitting perched up on the edge of her desk facing them, swinging one leg over the other, and then back again, the flash of stockings, the bare thigh up higher. She knew exactly what she was doing. Torturing them. Goran would get a hall pass and go to the boys' room, and pull off; come back grinning. Or at least, so he claimed... "Bashing the Bishop!" What did that mean, anyway?

He wondered if he was going crazy sometimes, if this was how you ended up crazy, committing other crimes, like rape, assault. In the morning, his pajamas stiff with dried semen, he felt soiled and desperate. And how old was he? Would it just get worse, he wondered, was there no relief, no hope at all? Was it the same for everybody? He would be weak in practice, and the coaches, they would all know. You couldn't fool them, the coaches. They knew what he was. A masturbator. Over and over again. Five or six times, sometimes. It was terrible.

What could he do? He seemed trapped, trapped in Ralston, that was it. The winter was coming on fast, there would be no lying out in the sun daydreaming then, and it crossed his mind that maybe that was already over for good. No girls in short-shorts, and he, he had to – do what? He stared at the ceiling, far above, dim.

"I gotta grow up," he heard himself say. "I gotta grow up."

One of the very first things he had to do was tell Coach Rossi he wasn't going to play football the next season. He had made up his mind. He had to do that. He dreaded the conversation with the coach, yet he wanted it to come, get it over with. The coach was a moody man, with a dark, fierce, sudden temper. He remembered an event that had happened not long ago, at the lunch hour, when Coach Rossi had entered the gym to find a group of students grouped around two seniors, the infamous Joe Labrador and Bill Frissen, a quiet guy who never said much. Labrador had been wildly gyrating, like Elvis Presley, as "Hound Dog" played from a portable record player the cheerleaders had. The two boys got more and more animated and Labrador proved he was a very good dancer, moving in ways that you heard about from the rock n' roll shows down in Pittsburgh, but nobody danced like that in Ralston. Coach Rossi plowed through the students and glared at the two, his face a mottled dark red. "That's disgusting!" he had said, after turning off the record player with a loud snap. "I never want to see you doing that again." Pushing Joe Labrador back so hard he nearly fell, he had then swept the group with his thick arm, a rigid forefinger pointing accusingly at all of them. His voice rose, his chest moving with the force of his breathing. "None of you. Not in this gym. Or anywhere else. That – that's just going to get you in a lot of trouble, that garbage!" He spat the last word out with a deep contempt, like a piece of bad food.

That was Coach Rossi at his most formidable. You were afraid of him, afraid of his wrath, his disapproval, his dislike. But it was stronger than that word. And only he could speak to him; he had to. And after seeing that scene in the gym, he knew it would be hard to do, like it seemed a lot of things were becoming. He would be branded a "quitter". Even if the coach didn't say it.

Playing in the JVs he had found football was not the game they had played in the muddy grass behind John Lowers' house in the Lower End, when fat Iggy Hill (who had moved away years ago) looked so red in the face, as he lumbered forward unsteadily with the ball, that they all yelled "Fire! Fire!" There, the game had gone on for a long time, and only stopped when they were good and tired, or they heard their mothers calling them to come in for supper.

Now the game was measured, and there was an outcome. "Football is life!" Coach Barnes would yell, lifting his arms in his fierceness. "Football is life, and it's time to get used to it." But he thought something was wrong with this, it was too pat, too simple, and he was worried that he thought that. He could not say it to Barnes, or Rossi, or even Kowalski, whom he thought might just understand what he meant. Life was more than anyone could say – and it certainly wasn't just a game, or a sport, like hunting or fishing, although the guys in Sam's maintained it was. It was more like the poems in Mr. Turner's class. But he knew he could not say that, either.

What if the coaches were wrong? Just wrong? He knew he was not supposed to think such a thing, that in doing so, he had already crossed a boundary, a dividing line, and there were many fewer people on the other side.

It was not what he thought he knew, either. Football was all right, it could be great, a special moment, or moments, something people remembered out of all the things that happened. A night in the fall, a game, a play in that game, when everything was in the balance, and how would it go? You *felt* that, that was the thing.

# 26

It rained on Sunday – a gray, cold day – and there was even some sleet. On Monday, the JV practice field was a mud hole, a quagmire, a boggy swamp. It looked lousy, sitting in the classrooms, looking outside; there was a light haze, a gray-white mist, up off the river and creek, laying down on the field. It would be cold and wet down there in that. He didn't like to think about practicing; it seemed futile, a punishment, even. After the first real hard frosts came and the ground began to freeze and then partially thaw, it would get even worse - and that might be that very week, because it was only about three weeks to the last game of the season, the game with Chester. That was in the second week of November, Armistice Day weekend. He could recall games from former seasons at this time of the year, when men started fires in the 55-gallon oil drum containers even before the game began, roasting hot dogs and marshmallows, holding the blackened things up for people to see.

One of the coldest games he could recall, back when he was a kid, maybe eight or nine years old, was played at an old field just up off the river, down in Springdale. By the beginning of the third quarter half the crowd had left, not being able to stand the damp bone-chilling cold any longer. His hands shook so much holding a cup of hot chocolate he'd brought back to the stands he spilled some, his teeth chattering. Some men sitting nearby talked about wearing women's nylon stockings to keep warm, like they did when deer hunting in December, up in the mountains. Both his stepfather and Carl had talked about that, so it must be true. People walked up and down on the side-lines, swinging their arms back and forth, and the players' breaths puffed out in large clouds, like the balloons comic book characters spoke in. He could not imagine what it would be like to actually be playing in such a game, and to play for the whole game or a good part of it. Tackling - a nightmare. Coach Barnes would like it, that would be just his style. His "meat," as Frankie called it. Maybe the exercise, the running, maybe it kept you warm. But there were the intervals, sitting on the bench on the sideline. Even his stepfather admitted it was cold that night, going before the game ended to the car and starting it up so the heater could warm it up, and they'd had the heater on the whole time they drove back home. He could remember the wonderful heat inside the car, thinking how good it must have felt for the players to take a hot shower after that game.

It was getting to be that cold time of the year, that time of the football season. Ralston remained unde-feated, untied. It seemed certain the Chester game, the last of the season, would decide whether or not Ralston would advance to the Championship Game down at Pitt Stadium, the day before Thanksgiving Day. Nobody talked much about this, though, not even the coaches, because it was felt it could spook things, jinx them - like no one talked about a pitcher having a no-hitter going in the dugout between innings, even though it was the only thing on everyone's mind.

People talked about the Autumn Hop already as if it had been a year ago. There were already some photographs put up in the hall, outside some of the home rooms – one was of Sandy Stevens and him dancing - and there would be pictures in the yearbook, away off in April or May, and they'd look at those and think how far back the Hop had been. It was over, and when he met Sandy before the Problems of Democracy class in the hallway outside, she smiled and waved her hand at him, and asked him if he'd seen the photos. Not much else, but they were standing in public, everyone no doubt noticing. Confusing, girls, though, he thought. He hadn't spoken to Cameron, although when they would pass in the halls between classes, their eyes would meet, she would smile. He would feel a rush of feeling that would make him think about it the entire rest of the day.

In the Problems of Democracy class, Mr. Ferris talked about the American Dream. They'd written an essay on what it was, or what they thought it was. Mr. Ferris often talked while looking out the window, looking away from them, looking over at the River Hill rising over the Allegheny, as if he wanted to head right on out of the window and over that hill, flying somehow, airborne. He talked in a soft, almost monotone voice, which oddly enough made you listen harder to catch exactly what it was he was saying. Frankie Malone thought he was "nuts." "They're all a bunch of fruitcakes, these teachers. Hey! That's why they gotta be teachers. They couldn't get a decent job – that's what my old man says, too."

Mr. Ferris was leaning on the small wooden lectern in the front of the room, looking at them. There was a sizable smudge of chalk on his jacket arm, but he seemed unaware of it. He wore no tie clip so his dark red tie hung down limply in two strands. It also had a chalk smudge on it. This was unusual for him – he must be feeling bad, something had gone wrong. Usually he was upbeat, and "neat as a pin," as Larry's mother would say. It was strange to see such a change in a teacher, but then maybe not.

"The lost dream…is that it? One of you wrote that as an essay title, you know? That's good…but what did we have that we lost? What is the American Dream? Television shows us the ideal family – a couple living in a nice suburban house, it's a ranch-style house, in the fall with the leaves down making it colorful, a two-car garage. A dog. A nice lawn. They had married each other, they were high school sweethearts, huh? You know anybody like that?"

He looked slowly around the room, but no one responded. He nodded.

"Two children. They have two children. Their son plays quarterback on the school football team, while the girl – she's a cheerleader. The father has a stable job, wears a suit and tie to work. The mother stays at home. A homemaker..."

He trailed off, staring again out the big windows.

"Now, you tell me. Is that out of date? Is that dream dead? Gone?"

Pinky Saunders shook his head slowly in the second row, but Mr. Ferris either did not see him or did not want to see him.

"Fireplace, in the winter. Marshmallows. Hot chocolate..." He heaved a large sigh.

Larry thought he knew what he was talking about. Did he want to live that way with Sandy? Was that what he was supposed to aim for, to get, to achieve? Go to college for? Would James Dean live in a house like that? In the movie they broke into an old house nobody was living in, and there was that scene where Dean lay with his head in Natalie Wood's lap, and Sal Mineo looked at them, his face registering a deep happiness; they were his family. There was even a fireplace somewhere in that scene, he thought. Would Cameron Mitchell live in a house like that?

It was not true, what he had said to Frankie at the Hop, that he had never seen a naked girl. Well, that was true, as far as it went, but he had seen a naked woman. A young married woman, Virginia Adams, who lived in the apartment in the bottom of the old Shultz house – right in back of Larry's house – that two widows owned, two very ancient women he thought were witches when he was a kid. The story was they captured little kids, and roasted them in their big black metal furnace in the basement of their old house, down by the creek, at the end of First Street, the last house on the street. When the old women opened their garage door, you could see the furnace, gleaming and shiny, with a big black opening in front, where they stuck you in to roast you. "Roast kid!" Frankie had yelled, startling the two old ladies, who always wore black outfits, even in the middle of summer. He had wondered if they were widows. But everyone said they were witches.

Mr. Ferris' voice was droning on, he was staring out the window again at River Hill, and it looked like there were a few – a very few snowflakes, was it? – floating randomly down.

He thought of her as Virginia Dare, the woman in a swim suit pictured on the pop bottles. There was also Virginia Mayo, the movie star, but he had never believed that was her real name. It was early in the summer, in June. A humid heat wave had settled down into the valley. He'd been coming home from a long walk down along Buffalo Creek, where it was a little cooler, watching the fishermen down there, none of whom seemed to be catching anything. Their carbide lights, the same as miners wore on their helmets, winked like large lightning bugs all along both banks. Down where the creek flowed into the Allegheny there were small clusters of them, almost like towns or villages.

He had walked slowly back into the town from the creek, thinking about reading, maybe late into the night again, the Sherlock Holmes stories which he had just discovered. Coming around the corner before their house, he decided to go in the back door, so as not to disturb his mother. There was a small alleyway, a short cut, and he saw a square of light from the window there. And then he'd seen Virginia Adams, and stood stock still.

She had come into the small kitchen, where there was a lamp on the table – that was the square of light he'd seen, the rest of the room was shadowy. She had a thin, gauzy bathrobe on – he assumed she'd just taken a bath, to cool off. Then, just as he turned away, she stepped out of it, as simply as that, and walked back across the kitchen, towards the sink. He saw instantly she was completely naked – a pale, translucent form moving in that kitchen. She was heavier than he'd have thought, but it wasn't a fattish, dumpy type of heaviness. She looked solid, firm.

He stood transfixed, not able to move, or even breathe, afraid she would hear, that even a sharp intake of breath would be audible. The small window was open, with a screen on the bottom.

Then she walked back from the sink, out of the shadows, carrying a small yellow peach, and before she stooped and picked up her robe and slipped it on again, he'd had a full view of her.

Mr. Ferris was going on still, now sitting on the window ledge, looking up in the sky. But Larry was remembering Virginia Adams' nakedness. The size of the nipples, reddish-brown and as large as half dollars. That, and the deep cleft between them. To his amazement, her stomach looked firm and soft at the same time. And below it was an ample, dark triangle, coming up further than he could have imagined. He had stared as if transfixed, even thinking that the intensity of his stare would alert her to his presence. But he could not have moved if he had tried.

She walked over then, and turned off the small lamp and went back into the interior of the apartment. To her waiting husband? What if he had come out, seen him looking in? He was sweating, thinking of that. But maybe her husband wasn't there. Working a night shift – didn't he work up at the distillery, and they had a midnight shift there? He had finally moved, and gone in the back door of their house dazed, sat at the table, not moved. His mother had come in and found him there. How long had he sat like that? There was a Pittsburgh Pirates' baseball game broadcast audible from somewhere. He hadn't told his mother about seeing Virgina Adams naked, he hadn't told anyone. But when he saw Virginia Adams after that, he felt a welter of confused emotions. He never went in the alley again that summer.

He did not catch, dreaming of Virginia Adams, what Mr. Ferris had wound up the Problems of Democracy class with, but he gathered, hustling out the door to his English class – but not too fast, because you wanted to be slow, and cool, show you really were not involved, so it was said – that he'd not said too much, but read a passage, a short one, from some book. But no one could tell him what the book was, or the author, either. It wasn't important, because probably it would not be on the test. This was always the reason things covered in a class were said to be important, or not important – the test.

His English class, with Mr. Turner, was coming up. He walked past the room where, early in September, Digger Hayes had had his eye put out, and when he saw the front row of desks he often recalled the whole incident. Digger sitting there, laughing and joking, a guard on the varsity squad, getting more muscular, it seemed, with each week. He'd been rough and strong in the tackling drills in August camp. He already looked like a small college player.

But Digger was no student. Even players said it would be hard for him to win any sort of good scholarship if he didn't straighten up and fly right in his academics that year. He was a senior, after all. It was time to get serious, quit his horseplay and "grab-assin' around." Coach Rossi gave him "The Lecture" in his office next to the gym.

It was a fast and furious session of horseplay, a flurry of activity at the front of the room. One of the varsity players had suddenly come in from the hallway and got Digger in a hammerlock. Digger, turning and twisting, kicked the desk, his face going beet-red. Mr. Turner, in charge of the study hall period, was nowhere to be seen. He would put a stop to it in short order, no question, he did not tolerate such things.

Then someone said "Turner! He's coming down the hall!" and everyone scurried to their seats, and the varsity player, Emilio Patrone, slapped Digger playfully and darted out. A quick, unnatural quiet in the room. Then, someone – and it was still not clear who this was – had yelled out "Hey, Digger!"

Hayes turned, grinning (Larry could still see this clearly in his mind), as a chestnut, beautiful in its burnished brown shades, arced through the air and struck him in the head. In his eye, it turned out. He fell to the floor, writhing and crying out, as Mr. Turner entered the room.

He'd had just a glimpse of Digger's inflamed eye as the school nurse led him from the room, in a silence broken only by his choked sounds of pain. His hands were shaking. It was obviously a serious injury, but no one had realized at the time how serious. Digger was not going to recover the vision is his left eye, the football season was over for him, and any football season in the future. In the fraction of a second it took for the gleaming, burnished chestnut to fly like a round dart through the classroom, his entire life changed.

When he'd told his mother about it, she recalled an incident in the early summer, right after school had ended. Two boys, hitchhiking, in front of the bank on Fifth Street – many people had seen them. They were picked up by a new Oldsmobile, driven by a young man, a young girl in the front seat with him; they were from Har-Brack High School, a large Double AA school that Ralston did not play against, a school that had over 2,000 students enrolled in it.

Five miles outside of Ralston, the car, doing over a hundred miles an hour, veered off a sharp curve into a farmer's field, catapulting through the air for seventy or eighty feet, according to two farmers who'd been driving a tractor in the field across the road, and saw the whole thing happen. All the occupants of the car were killed. It was said the young girl had been decapitated in the accident.

"Haven't you hitchhiked there, at that spot, before? In front of the bank?" she'd asked. He had. No question. Many times, going back to when he was barely eleven or so, getting rides out to Slate Lick and Paul Thorsen's family's farm. He and Paul had gone to grade school together, since the first grade. It could as easily have been him – and Paul, for that matter - then, picked up by the laughing girl and the young guy from Har-Brack. He had thought it about it for several days afterwards – what had they been talking about, just before it happened? Why did it happen? It was the middle of the day, they were not drinking – had they, then, just lost control, a new car, going too fast, misjudged the curve? Unfamiliar with the road?

James Dean had been killed in a car accident, too. To lose an eye was, in the scale of it, preferable to being killed in a car accident. But it was all at too young an age. In its way, the accident with Digger Hayes was more bizarre and unexpected, if such things could even be imagined, than the car accident; after all, car accidents were common and happened as a matter of course. It was all a matter of luck, whatever that was; the men in Sam's shook their heads and muttered "Bad luck, then. Too bad…"

Larry wondered if Mr. Turner had felt guilty about the incident. But there was nothing he could have done. Everyone who'd been in the room remembered it. Maybe they would never forget.

In the English classroom, with the big round table, Mr. Turner was pacing back and forth now in his slow, thoughtful way, the big red English book held open in his hands. He looked like a minister, reading like that. Always, he had a book; Frankie joked he'd probably been born reading one. He was talking of poets, writers, artists lost in World War I – all the way back then. 1914-18. It was hard to imagine such a time.

"Wilfred Owen. Killed the last week of the war. Listen to this."

He read a poem about a gas attack that contained the line "Gas! GAS! Quick, boys!" The poem was about "the old lie" that war was glorious, that it was good to die for your country in war. The photograph in their book showed a young man with a cropped moustache and his hair parted in the middle, something never seen now. The man, the poet, Wilfred Owen, had kind eyes, and although he had a uniform on, he didn't look like a soldier, somehow. Yet the book said he had been an officer, and a heroic figure.

"It makes you wonder – it makes me wonder, at least – what was the cost? In that war. In just one battle. How much great poetry, like this, did we lose? How many paintings? Great inventions?" Turner tapped on the thick book, looking at them.

That was a thought Larry had never had. It struck him with the force of a physical blow, this idea. All that was lost. Completely lost. That was real - much more serious than losing a game, for instance, something everyone was thinking about now at the end of the season.

Mr. Turner slowly turned some pages, and now read another war poem, also from the First World War. The poet was not as famous as Wilfred Owen, but the poem was similar to Owen's. It was called "The Rear Guard." The image was of a soldier coming upon dead men in a deep trench. Looking up from the page, he saw the milky sky outside, River Hill.

This autumn was almost gone, already River Hill was starting to get the special silvery-gray, bare look of winter, and winter would soon arrive all down through the valley. Already there had been coal deliveries, the first of the year. The food would change – scrapple, big buckwheat cakes made fresh from the cold stone crock sitting out on the back porch, the thick sausage patties he loved, with syrup over them. "A breakfast that'll stick to your ribs!" Buffalo Creek – had there really once been buffalo in, or by that creek? – would finally freeze, maybe by mid-December, and it would already be basketball season. Ducky Estes and he would go over to the playground court to shoot some baskets, wearing gloves if it was really cold.

"Dylan Thomas was Welsh," Mr. Turner was saying, looking out the classroom window. "Wales. It's a lot like Pennsylvania – coal mines, railroads, green trees and fields. Rain. A lot of rain... an old place." It struck Larry that Mr. Turner was a poet himself, hearing him say that.

"Arcadia," he said. "The Greeks called it Arcadia."

He could hear the Pep Band tuning up down near the music room – he could hear Zeb Lewis honking away – and Mr. Turner closed the book; the class was over. He smiled at them, and nodded. Larry had the feeling that they didn't appreciate Mr. Turner, or at least most of them didn't, even in this college prep English class. He had a master's degree from Columbia University, and not many of the teachers had master's degrees, at all. Sometimes Larry found himself wondering what Mr. Turner was doing in Ralston High School, or even in Ralston. But nobody at school knew much about him, or his wife; their life outside the school was private. Nobody was even sure where he actually lived. What would have brought somebody from Columbia University to Ralston High School, he wondered?

The day dragged – one of those school days that would never end. By the time of the afternoon session on plays for the JV, it turned out they were going to only do conditioning drills in the gym – the field was too sloppy (Coach Barnes must be disappointed, he thought) – and go over plays on the chalkboard. A "skull session". The Xs and Os of the plays on the chalkboard had an endless fascination for the coaches. They stared intently at them as at a riddle that if solved would disclose the location of some buried treasure. Some wrote them – Barnes, particularly – with a frenzied, slashing style, pointing at them as if they were revealing some great truth, some apparent essential fact of life, that must be learned. Others (Coach Rossi) placed them on the board as if writing a religious script, very meticulously – a word he'd learned from Coach Rossi. In fact, the Xs and Os authors could easily be distinguished, after a while, by the varying styles of their inscription and erasure.

The Xs and Os, and the long, straight, or looping, arrow-headed line showing the course of the ball, whether carried or thrown; all indicated real flesh and blood people, individuals, their inevitable collisions, and were maps of the individual plays – R46, SY2 – the quarterback barked out in the huddle, and Ralston's team ran, or those of the opponent, in the case of defensive strategies.

The players studied these diagrams over and over, learned them, committed them to memory. They were students, scholars, of football, with an intensity and devotion they never gave to their real school classes, and studies. Sitting in the "skull sessions", he felt outside the group. They received stern, finger-wagging lectures regularly on the sapping evils of smoking and "playin' with yourself." It had to be saved, to be expended then on the field, in the game, against the opponent, ferociously. There, this pent-up energy could be let out.

There was something troubling about this idea. Was sex also a violent act of domination, of crushing or running over the other person, "tearin' them apart," as Coach Barnes exhorted the defensive players?

"You rip that sunnavbitch's nuts off! You hear me? You let him know what he's got comin' to him when you hit him. Drive that bastard *down*! Right into the ground, you hear me? *Bury* that cocksucker!" He stamped and reared at them, his face mottled red, froth on his mouth.

This made him sick to his stomach. He simply did not have these feelings, he did not want to rip anybody's nuts off – why would you? – or drive them into the ground, bury them. These were all images repeated, over and over, in the language of the Sports pages' write-ups of games.

Football was continually praised there, and in assemblies when the coaches spoke, as fine preparation for life, for leadership, success. But what kind of leadership, success? He could not stop wondering about these questions. At the same time, he knew there was no one he could ask them to. They seemed to be a religious sin, heresy, blasphemous, as the preacher would say on Sundays, thumping the pulpit, the very Bible, loudly.

If you didn't play football, what did that mean, then? It seemed, at best, that you were less than what you should be ("a man"), and no doubt already, by self-definition, a failure. Maybe you were a "homo," as Goran cawed out. You were like the skinny guy in the Charles Atlas cartoon ad, who couldn't do anything about the bully kicking sand on him and his girlfriend, too. The one old man Krebs' exercise equipment was meant to help. You were weak – a pussy, as the varsity players liked to say. You probably played with yourself all the time, ruining your health, stunting your growth, giving you bad eyesight. You were a jerk-off, as they said. No real man did that; he forced the girl, at least to give him a hand job.

There was endless talk of these hand jobs – how many they'd had, who'd done them and how, graphic descriptions of "shooting a load," pecker tracks on the back seats of cars. Some bragged knowingly of blow-jobs, "head" or "Frenching." Then there was "The Hershey Highway" – "I had Carol Bigelow, up The Hershey Highway!" a scrawled sign in the boys room read. And it seemed these were especially the prerogatives of the football players.

As opposed to all this, he thought of something Mr. Turner had said in class, about why they were reading poetry. The students had complained about the reading, saying out in the hallway, "This is not *college!*"

"There are things, marvelous things, all around you, happening daily, if you can only see them. And if you see them, do you understand their significance? Are you wondering about that? Are you? Because these things are trying to help us, can help *you*, if you can recognize them. But, so often, you can't. You develop single vision, tracked inside your marvelous head, like a railroad train." He opened the textbook, and read a Whitman poem, "When I Heard The Learned Astronomer". Larry had already read it, with Cameron in the library and then one night at home, looking over at the big lights that were on over the football field.

Coach Rossi had said one time in a skull session that the Xs and Os were "poetry" too, but Larry was not so sure.

Digger Hayes was back in school now, and came religiously to the skull sessions, the coaches always welcomed him. He wore a white bandage strapped around his left eye, and told Larry that it would be "Christmastime" before it would be removed. Larry wondered what it would reveal – would the eye be gone, for instance? His mother theorized "They'll find him a glass eye – someplace down there in Pittsburgh, probably at the University medical school. They're not bad, after all. Better than no eye!" The thought of Digger Hayes with a glass eye was a strange one to take in. He was seventeen years old.

But he did not ask Digger about this, and watched as he moved off down the halls with a couple of the Varsity, they seemed always to be with him, laughing loudly. Digger had always laughed a lot, and now the players laughed with him, slapping him on the back, nodding their heads. He wore his letter sweater from the last year, and Larry noticed he wore it nearly all the time.

In the study hall, he was dreaming off, again. There in the balcony, "The Shelf". How far back it went, football. Back to himself and a gang of small kids who went in the early mornings of August, or on Saturdays, to dig the cleats out of the field, like football archaeologists, if they could escape detection by the custodians, or the fat policeman Stroup. These cleats were hoarded like prized marbles, they almost had a currency value.

They were kept on, or in, desks or chests in the kids' rooms, and talked about – who had worn the shoes these came off? They talked, in hushed voices, of the certainty of cleat marks on a player's body, like tattoos. To wear the cleated shoes would make one stronger, more powerful, ready to crash through the line, run a reverse, streak forty yards down the sideline, running a "clothesline", straight-arm the safety so his head snapped back sharply, and he grabbed empty air as he lunged and fell.

He had some of these found cleats in one drawer of the "study desk" his mother and stepfather presented to him when he was twelve, in the sixth grade. The top folded down to reveal narrow slots where you could put letters, papers, folders. It was a bit small to write on, if you had a book open, too. But it was solidly built and he had a satisfying sense of the desk being *his*.

How long ago had he found them? A few still had small pieces of dirt from the field in them. And whose shoes had they come from; how long ago? There was no way of telling. But they did seem like magical charms as he laid them out on the flat fold-down of his desk. He wondered if his mother knew he had them. What would she make of them? Probably give a familiar shake of the head, and smile in that special, knowing way she had. She knew him, there wasn't any question, although more and more he felt different, and maybe that she did not know.

# 27

A student in the junior class, Bill Scopes, had a death in his family – his father. This was rare in the school – any kind of death was rare, because the parents, generally, were still fairly young. But Scopes' father had suffered a fatal heart attack as he stepped down from the diesel loco-motive he was driving on a local run, up to Schenley and back. Bill was his only son; there was a much younger daughter, still in grade school.

"He was dead before he hit the ground," the doctor reportedly said. It was noted in the newspaper as a "massive coronary occlusion." Nobody probably knew precisely what that meant, but Scopes' father, Ray, was dead at 51. And at 16, Bill Scopes was without his dad, and would be for the rest of his life. Larry felt a kinship with him, because of that cold, hard fact.

He went with Frankie Malone to Revere's Funeral Home, which was the larger of the two establishments in the town. He had never been in the other one, Martinson's, which was nearly right across the street from the school, an odd place for a funeral home. It was smaller, somehow more like a house. Revere's was in a large, red brick style "mansion" – at least, they were called that in Ralston. It was much larger than a usual house, with a long, curving porch running all the way around the front of the house. It stood on a prime corner lot, set back off the street with a good strip of lawn around it (where there was a small, discreet sign, floodlit at night, "Revere Funeral Home"), and several tall, old oak trees. They seemed to have been there forever, and just got bigger and bigger with the passing of time.

He did not really know Bill Scopes – it was said that they had once lived on "The Island" – and so wondered if he should go to the viewing, as it was called. To go and look at somebody's dead body, lying in a fancy casket said to be very expensive. "It keeps out the water," his mother said. And nobody, after all, wanted to be seen as cheap. Frankie Malone said you could get a "pine box", but Larry thought it was probably not the case.

"They have laws about it. About how you have to be buried so your body doesn't decompose and contaminate the water, the ground..." He was sure he had heard something like this when people spoke of coffins.

"I heard that some of them, these coffins, cost a couple of thousand dollars. As much as a new car!" Frankie shook his head. "Waste of money, ain't it? Don't ya think so, Larry?"

Maybe it was. But Larry knew that the funeral was about, and for, the people who were still alive. They would be comforted, distracted, by the people who came to the viewing, at least some of them. He wondered about those cases where nobody came, or very few people. That would be bad, painful, for the family. They had to stand in the room where the coffin was, or in a smaller room just outside it, where they talked to people and received their condolences.

It was always pretty much the same, the viewing, although Catholic ones could be different, in that the deceased usually had a rosary wrapped in their hands, and there was a sort of kneeling bench provided by the coffin where you could kneel and pray. Sometimes a priest was present, too.

But Ray Scopes had been a Presbyterian, although apparently it was his wife who was really involved with the church, and went regularly. Inside the Revere Funeral home, in a softly lit room – they called it indirect lighting, his mother said - barely audible music played and there he was, the dead man lay in his coffin, surrounded by banks of bright-hued flowers, rising back behind the bier and arranged out around the sides. The funeral director and his son, standing near the door, respectfully greeted people who spoke to them. The Scopes family clustered tightly together, and occasionally one would walk in and stare at the coffin for a long time, or go up to it and touch the dead man's face. It gave Larry a turn to see that; he remembered how the face of his stepfather had felt when he'd touched it in his coffin. It was like touching a piece of wood – it did not feel like a person, and he had never forgotten it.

Nobody talked about the death of Ray Scopes much, although his mother talked about how he had driven trucks and trains during the war.

"He had three trucks blown out from under him, that's what they said…And then those trains. That was even worse. They were shot at by their own pilots! But he had been on the railroad since back before the war. You know, they gave those boys their jobs back when they came back, too. Nothing more than right. And now he's dead. Just like that." She was drying dishes with a red and white checked dish towel that was getting frayed around the edges, but she never threw anything out, and kept even string and rubber bands, wrapped in perfect round balls.

"But Ray… he was never right after he got back from the war. Like so many of them…"

His mother shook her head, and drew in a sharp, sighing breath.

At school, Bill Scopes was much the same, but Larry thought he must be in bad shape inside. Yet, as his mother had said, what could he do? He could not go around in the halls with red eyes from crying all night, or during the day. You couldn't do that; you just couldn't do that. So Bill Scopes had a few pats on the back, and a few "I'm sorry about your dad, Bill" said to him, him nodding. There was a card from his home room, which everybody signed. Larry wondered if he would keep it, and years later, take it out and read those names. Probably not. It would disappear, be forgotten.

"Life has to go on," Frankie said, quietly, but what was that to say? Yet it was true, wasn't it? It did go on. It was relentless. It wasn't going to stop for you.

One man walked back and forth, in and out of the funeral home. Several times he seemed to be almost laughing. But this was a nervous laughter. Larry found out it was Ray Scopes' younger brother, who lived in Philadelphia. The man ran his hand through his hair repeatedly, and looked distracted.

Digger Hayes came into the viewing as they were leaving. He was wearing a dark suit and Larry at first did not realize who he was, even with the eye patch. He had never seen Digger in a suit.

"Did you know he taught me how to drive?" Digger said. His good eye was red and moist. "He was a damn good guy…"

He did not know what to do after leaving the viewing. Bill Scopes had thanked him for coming. He felt better that he had gone. When he got home, after walking down the alley and stopping in to see if Ducky was home (he wasn't), his mother asked him about the viewing, who had been there.

"It's a good thing you went, Larry. I'm sure Bill Scopes will remember it. It's a hard thing, losing a father, at that age." She looked at him, and shook her head slightly. "But you know all about that. I don't need to tell you. Nobody does."

It was true. He did know, but he wished he didn't. When he had been standing in the funeral home, he had recalled his stepfather's funeral, the relatives who came whom he didn't really know, the way everyone looked at him.

A few days later, he was standing at the bank corner on Fifth and Market, when Cameron stopped to pick him up. There had been a café and lunch counter started underneath the bank, the steps going down were still there, that was called "The Bomb Shelter". It went out of business after a year or so but the sign still remained, with an arrow pointing down the stairs. It was a popular place to gather and hitchhike, as Larry could attest. He remembered the story his mom told him about some boys who were picked up here and had been killed in an accident outside of town. He had been wondering if their ghosts were still about that place, and when Cameron asked him how he was, he thought of telling her what he was thinking, but you couldn't do that, either. Not really.

"I'm going up on River Hill," she said, leaning over and looking at him. "And I saw you standing here." The long hair, the Cameron hair, he thought, tumbled around her face, and she looked like a magazine ad, sitting there like that. She was so beautiful driving the Chevy it was like they had been made together, the car and her. But if it was the way it was supposed to be, *he* would be driving, with one hand on the wheel and the other casually stuck up holding the side of the window. Like James Dean, he thought, as he got in and sat facing forward, wondering why she'd decided to pick him up, just like that. But the day was nice for late, late fall and he hadn't been up on River Hill for a long time.

The radio was playing softly, not blasting out. Little Willie John's song, "All Around the World" came on. He could go into a song like that almost from the first note. It was one he really liked, and he did not want to talk, but listen to it. Cameron seemed to realize this, and didn't say anything, but drove slowly over the Garver's Ferry Bridge – he had a sudden flash of when he was a small kid and his brother Carl dived directly off this old iron bridge, a smooth, clean arc flashing in the sun, something he became famous in Ralston for – and up the curving road out of town, past the one rocky, steep face of River Hill, where it seemed there was always water dripping and running. River Hill, where they would soon be running coon. Carl had done that, too. He had also found a champion coon dog thrown out in a box by the road a few years earlier. Captain. What a dog he was. He grew to be huge, with very large feet, and a great bay, but they did that only when they ran the coon. Did Captain live for that, he wondered? To run coons, tree them, be in that pack stringing out along the top of the ridge of the hill under the autumn moon, in the crisp November night?

Here he was, in a hot '55 Chevy, with a hot girl that the guys in the locker room made endless comments about what they'd like to do to, and he thought of a coon dog. Frankie would laugh a good one, if he told him that. But to hell with them. The night of the Hop, the kiss in the music room, that was somehow already over, that was not just past, but long past. He had told no one of it, and he thought probably Cameron hadn't, either.

There was an old road, half gone, that Cameron pulled off on; it led back up to near the top of River Hill, and Cameron steered them as smoothly as possible along this jolting, pot-holed, once-paved road. True, it had been re-surfaced with tar, probably in the summer, but the tar was already split and cracked. He knew the road from when he was a kid and Carl had brought him along on a long blackberrying hunt. Few people went up to the top of River Hill, and fewer went down the steep side of it. Carl had led the way – he was in his element there – to thick, lush patches of blackberry bushes. They would harvest, losing track of the time, until their hands were stained a deep black, their arms scratched, bleeding from the thorns of the wild bushes.

"I used to go blackberrying. Up here..." he said, sweeping his hands across, as they neared the end of the road, and Cameron slowed down. She turned briefly and looked at him, nodded.

"Not too many people come up here. You can't really get up here in the winter, matter of fact. Or, even if you did, you couldn't get back down." He was looking around at the dark trees. There were a lot of them, the woods were heavy up there. In some ways, it was a grim place when it was like this. Few leaves were left now. Those on the ground had no colors. Mr. Turner had read a sonnet of Shakespeare's, where he compared himself to a tree with few leaves on it. A wild idea came into his head to start reciting it to Cameron, but he stopped himself immediately. Better to not start babbling.

A month ago, the hillside was a blaze, like a fire, unbelievable shades of orange, yellow, scarlet reds, rich browns. It was one of the great sights of autumn in Ralston – River Hill in fall foliage, as they called it. (The school had once had a Fall Foliage Queen, but the Homecoming Queen had taken her place.) He thought of those leaves in Cameron's hair, for no reason that he could tell, suddenly. They would fall down slowly, and into the Chevy…The radio was playing the Crewcuts' "Sh-Boom", an awkward song that sounded like it had been manufactured, and yet it was "catchy", and had been not just a big hit, but Number One on the Hit Parade listings, for quite a while. The Crewcuts. They were actual, real guys; he'd seen their photo on the record jacket, the EP, in a pose as if they were harmonizing. Who were they, where did they come from? Probably college kids, from some university in the midwest, or something. Or maybe they were just singers who'd been made to appear like they were collegiate. Even Bill Haley and the Comets wore sports coats; he'd seen that in a photo in the Pittsburgh paper. So did Buddy Holly, who also wore glasses, which was really unusual. He could not think of another singer who wore glasses. He thought of Chuck Berry, or Little Richard, or Elvis wearing horn-rimmed glasses. It was impossible.

Cameron had stopped the car, pulled off to one side of the dead-end road. There really wasn't anywhere further to go, but he knew that if they got out of the car and walked about a hundred yards, a great view of Ralston would open up, the town lying down in the triangle between Buffalo Creek and the big Allegheny River, like it had been made there. Carl had shown him that, too.

"Bill Scopes' dad died…I heard you went to the viewing. You and Frankie Malone. The inseparables." She smiled. He wondered if they should, or he should, get out of the car. How did she know about the viewing? Well, she was Cameron, to start with. People told her everything, he had heard.

"He had a heart attack. Bill Scopes' father. Dead before he hit the ground – stepping down from the engine."

She nodded her head. "I heard that, too…Want to walk over and look down?" She motioned with her head to where the edge of River Hill was.

He nodded without speaking, he thought his voice might crack, it still did that, and at the worst times. Like now. They walked around the car, and toward the bluff of the big hill, the dead leaves crunching under their feet, a sound he particularly liked but could not have said why.

"What's your favorite time of year, Larry? Season?"

"Right now. Fall." He scuffed at some dead leaves, plastered thick near the edges of the old roadway.

She looked over at him – they were walking next to each other, but not too close. "Is that because of football?" she asked. Her voice seemed different to him than when they were in the school, but he couldn't figure how that could really be. Maybe it was the air, the unconfined space. The *acoustics*, Mr. Sweeney would say, dramatically throwing his hands up.

"No. At least, I don't think so. I'm getting ready to quit football," he blurted out suddenly, shocking himself even as he heard the irrevocable words, like a sentence, coming out of his own mouth. He felt dazed, light-headed. Why had he said that?

Cameron nodded slowly, and seemed even to slow her walking pace, although they were not going very fast as it was. "I can understand that," she said.

"You can?"

Cameron stopped and faced him. What was she, two feet away from him?

"You're not a football player, Larry. Nobody expects you to be, either. You should know that."

He looked away quickly, as if in embarrassment, then looked back at her. "No, Cameron, I don't think I am. You're probably right…" He had said her name. He saw that register in her eyes.

"So what are you going to do, then? Now that you've made *that* decision?" She resumed walking and he moved with a jerk to do the same, hoping he was not looking helplessly awkward, although this was what he felt like. Clumsy, awkward. Alone, walking with Cameron Mitchell, on top of River Hill. Impossible. No one would believe it.

"I have to tell Coach Rossi…"

She laughed, a clear, fine sound in the sharp fall air. "Send him a letter!" she said then. "Just send him a letter.

Slip it under the coaches' door." She stooped quickly, made a motion with her hand.

It was a shocking idea. He stiffened, hearing it, shaking his head. "No, I can't do that. I have to tell him. Face to face." He thought of the moment, seeing Coach Rossi's strong, darkly tanned, lined face under the ever-present baseball cap, as he tried to say it to him. In that office, next to the gym.

"Well…do it quick. Otherwise, it'll haunt you. Isn't it doing that now?"

He nodded, took a deep breath. They were into the last broken vestiges of the old road now, and now you could see through a thin scrim of wan trees – a few broken down, even – the triangle of land between the river and the creek and the town, Ralston, there it was, nestled down on it and spreading up the hill behind it, smoke curling out of some chimneys and windows flashing from the sun. They both stopped again, looking at it. From there, the most prominent feature was the big field, the tall lights on their stands that looked like scaffolding, the baseball diamond away off in one corner, almost as if tucked away deliberately.

"What are you going to do?" he asked. It was the only thing he could think of saying, and he realized it wasn't very sharp, but he wanted to know, he realized.

"There's a modeling school, in New York, that my mother wants to send me to. It's in a hotel, and you live there. In the hotel. Right in Manhattan." She scuffed the road lightly with her small dark-tan loafer that looked as if it was polished. Did girls shine their shoes? he wondered.

"Is that what you want to do? Model? Be a model?" He could tell as he said it, that he was implying she didn't want to do this, and he cursed himself mentally.

She looked at him for a few seconds, just a slight delay. "I honestly don't know..."

"Yes you do," he cut in, taking a breath. "You don't want to be a model. I mean, nothing against it or anything, I don't mean..." He shook his head, taking another deep breath. "Hell. What am I saying? I don't know anything about being a model, all that. New York – it must be a big deal."

She laughed again, cocking her head slightly as she looked at him.

"You know that a lot of girls like you, right?"

He felt the deep, hot blush spreading so swiftly that he thought it must be startling to see, and looked down at the road, then up at her. "No. I mean...I don't think a lot of girls – like me. Why should they?"

"Because you're sweet, Larry. And smart. And thoughtful."

He did not know what to say to this and looked away from her, out over the valley, down where Ralston was in an autumn haze, and then closed his eyes momentarily. When he opened them, he shook his head. "I'm as bad as the rest of them. So I don't believe that." He was thinking of the things guys said in the locker room about her, what they would like to do, what they would do, making a hard, thrusting motion.

She was right in front of him, close now. "I do," she said. It was like the music room. He realized she was going to kiss him, not at all what was supposed to go on. He began to move backwards but she was right there and instead he put his arms around her, met her kiss and felt that long dark full Cameron hair finally all around him, the root smell of her hair and the fresh taste of her warm mouth.

How long had they stood like that? he wondered afterwards. Not moving, but after kissing, and kissing more, just standing there with their arms around each other, and his head buried in that hair just as he had wanted to do so many times, watching her walk by in the hall or sitting in a class, or even far away, going up the street, away from the school. And she seemed to know that. How did she know that about him? He didn't feel awkward now, but uncertain. And then she had pulled back from him.

"I know I'm right. Remember what I've said...please." She looked quickly around her, as if she had just remembered something. "And we better get back down. People notice things like this."

With that she turned resolutely and walked towards the red Chevy. He would always remember how it looked sitting there, as if it had been watching and approved, if a car could approve. He nodded, although she wasn't looking now. Cameron was Cameron and walking back and he followed, got into the car. She had the key in and turned and looked at him intently, almost, he thought, fiercely. "You tell Coach Rossi," she said, and started up the '55 Chevy with a smooth, firm motion. He was still back there, deep in her hair, but he heard what she said. He watched in a haze now as the gaunt, dark trees peeled by, the sun flashing on them, and they went on down, then across the Garver's Ferry Bridge, where he lay back in the red seat, watching the green-grey girders flick by in the wan sun, and felt the big river pulling smoothly underneath. "Earth Angel" was on the radio now, and he felt himself going into the music, going deep. Carl, his brother, had dived off this iron bridge, and now he was riding across it in a '55 Chevy with a girl. A beautiful girl.

# 28

November. Already. Sleety weather for a day or so, premonition of the winter, when sports would move indoors. No hockey, although he could vividly remember pick-up games on Buffalo Creek, using stones and all sorts of stuff for sticks. One kid had a long, yellow pole for a stick. The other kids teased him, saying it was from a toilet plunger. Hockey must be played only in high schools in New England, Larry thought. Or Canada. He had seen a Pittsburgh Penguins game when he was about nine, part of a Lutheran Church group taken to the rink in downtown Pittsburgh to see the game. He had marveled at the speed of the players and the shaking of the arena – or so it seemed – when one of the defensemen checked a player into the boards. It was rougher than football, was his conclusion. And the players wore no helmets, either, or any facial protection. "Penguins", though, seemed a funny name for a team, like some Walt Disney movie team. Yet they were an old franchise, like the venerable football Steelers, one of the original eight teams in the National Football League.

In the locker room, Coach Barnes had put up, at the beginning of the season, a large brightly lettered colored sign, which he had the art teacher and her advanced art class make. Copies of this sign were in the Principal's office, and by the third or fourth week of the season, in almost all of the classrooms, except in Mr. Sweeney's laboratory, where he would not permit any signs, citing fire regulations and various chemical "dangers." Nevertheless, one appeared anyway on the outside door of his room. He took it down, and it was quickly replaced.

There was one in Sam's barbershop, where Sam could be seen in the big front window eagerly filling in the weekly score every Saturday morning. Adam's Tavern had one, and even across the river, in Garver's Ferry, they had them up, in a deli and a grocery store over there. One was found on the wall of each of the two town banks, and in the Ben Franklin 5&10. Of course, there was a very large one in Peter's, signed by all the starting varsity players, the cheerleaders, the majorettes, and the Great Leader of the Pep Rallies, Charlie Hibbing. An almost equally large one sat behind the soda fountains in Thompson's Pharmacy.

The sign, in blue and white lettering and trim, featured two columns, with "Ralston" above one, and "Opponent" above the other. In that column, there was room to write the name of the school, along with the Final Score.

| Ralston Raiders | | Opponent | |
|---|---|---|---|
| H | 28 | Glassboro | 0 |
| | 14 | Wilson | 7 |
| H | 35 | Clarksburg | 6 |
| | 42 | Lewiston | 14 |

| | | | |
|---|---|---|---|
| | 21 | Plum Twp. | 0 |
| H | 7 | Mansfield | 6 |
| H | 30 | Saxonburg | 13 |
| | 20 | Whitney | 7 |
| H | 21 | Sharon | 6 |
| | | Chester | |

An impressive record. Only two teams had scored more than one touchdown against Ralston; two had been held scoreless. This was attributed to the "rock-ribbed" (as sports columnists put it) Ralston defense, led particularly by the very players that Larry remembered vividly standing on the dusty practice field back in August; already looking determined, fearsome, serious in a way that he couldn't get at in his mind. They did not talk to players like himself, or even really notice you; if you happened on them going in and out of the shower, say, they looked right past you. The four-letter Harry Gibb at linebacker, Charley "Dago" Paretti at safety.

The offense was as impressive, scoring easily in most games, and in several, the second and third stringers logged ample varsity letter time in the third and fourth quarters, or the scores would have been higher. Coach Rossi did not hold with running up the score against a weak team – and giving the benchers playing time could only help the team, producing juniors who'd already lettered and were experienced players.

Every game on the schedule conjured up a different set of fresh memories. Larry was sure this was so for almost everybody in Ralston, not just the students. As the season progressed, each game was discussed over and over, the feats of the various players recited like already famous legends. Great players from past Ralston teams were brought up; comparisons were made of running styles, yardage, tackles, stamina and strength, and extraordinary, great plays – especially the latter.

Everyone had seen an incredible pass, an equally incredible catch, a fantastic block or tackle, an unbelievable interception or fumble recovery; plays the entire game hung or turned on; plays "blown", so that a game, and a season, was lost. A wet, muddy ball causing a crucial fumble, a dropped pass; a player saying later he'd momentarily lost the football in the lights' glare, the white haze above the field.

In the current season, as the chart indicated, the initial game proved typical. Ralston, with the two-week August Training Camp and its tradition of physical conditioning, ran over the inept Glassers like the proverbial well-oiled machine. "Those fellas up there," Sam quipped, "they're getting poisoned by all that glass, sure as I'm standin' here cutting yer hair."

The Wilson game had been different. Wilson was a much bigger school than Ralston, almost in the Double AA category, rather than Single A. Their teams had grown larger physically over the last few years, and with a new coach (who was a friend of Coach Rossi) they fielded hard-playing, skilled teams. "They do the basics well," Coach Rossi said in a sports page interview. "Block, tackle, run hard, play as a *team*. Football's a team sport, when it's all said and done." This was true of Wilson; they had no stand-outs at any position, although their quarterback, Jay Winters, already noted by sports writers, was only a junior. Wilson gave the Raiders a close, hard game, although the final score didn't reflect that.

In the Clarksburg and Lewiston games, Robert Henderson and Fred Lucas both scored twice. Those games were more memorable for the fine, crisp autumn evenings they were played on; a full-scale huge harvest moon rose over the Lewiston game, delighting the crowd.

And of course there had been the Autumn Hop, that now seemed to exist in a far-off mist. The kiss with Cameron, in the music room. For him, he knew the season had changed at that moment, that very moment, in that dark, warm music room – and he hadn't told a soul about it, either. It weighed on him almost as bad as the need to talk to Coach Rossi.

As the remaining games rolled by, the prospect of a possible unbeaten season loomed. At the end of the Mansfield game, the toughest game of the season, the Ralston players walked off the field looking, for the first time in the season, tired - looking like they could be beaten. People talked about it, but not much, and it wasn't mentioned in the school at all, since that would be bad luck, very bad luck. There was something about a team walking off the field after a game that was telling, though, and Larry hadn't seen Ralston players look like they did that night. They looked like the men coming off the shift at the mills, or on the railroad – their slow walk, their looking down, an older look, somehow, about them. Some didn't even take their helmets off.

Frankie Malone did talk about the game. "If Dago hadn't made that fumble recovery – hey, shit, they coulda beat our ass out there. Those fucking Vikings!" Larry had told him to get off of it.

"Sandy Stevens looked good, though. The half time show? Larry! What's going on there?"

He let it pass. A strain, a tenseness, had developed between them. He felt he was supposed to do something, say something, to Sandy but he couldn't figure out what it was, what he was to do. And who knew what was circulating among the girls' network of stories, rumors, notes passed in study hall or home room? That never stopped. He even wondered if she didn't know about Cameron, the music room. Anything was possible with the girls' network of spies. It could be that it was around among them that he had "been" with Cameron when they'd gone up on River Hill. That "been" could cover a lot of ground. And maybe that was what Sandy Stevens was waiting for him to do, to tell her? But he had nothing to say.

Coach Rossi gave a short speech at the Friday Pep Rally, and the players, especially the first string, looked dead serious. If they won the Sharon game, they had only to beat Chester – the hated Chester White Knights – in the last game. That would not be easy, Chester was never an easy game. But Chester had a spotty record for the year. Coach Rossi had spoken about that, too.

"It's a long season. Especially around about now, around about the very last games. Sharon, and then Chester. I know, I know," he'd held up his amazingly large hands as the crowd in the auditorium began to yell and some boo at the hated name. Joe Labrador barked like a dog. "People say they have a lackluster record. An uneven team. I would feel better—" he had paused until it quieted down completely – "I would feel better if they were undefeated. Going into that game."

By the time of the Sharon game, the season consumed everything and everybody. There wasn't much else in the town. The game sign appeared even in the Recreation Hall of the Catholic Church, and on the front door of the Lutheran Church over on the hill. Mr. Turner even spoke of football in his class. He said late autumn was the time when a poet was most likely to write a great work, a masterpiece. He even named the month.

"October. Golden October. The peak of autumn… the leaves make the air like wine…but none of you have drunk any wine. Or have you?"

Frankie suppressed a snigger, although Larry still heard it in its stifled form, a short snort; Frankie made it seem like he was having trouble with his nose, digging out a dirty handkerchief and pressing his nose into it. His eyes grinned over its top; he looked for a second like a bandit in a Western movie.

He wondered if Frankie would remember anything about the class, afterwards. He was increasingly taken with it – the poems, the stories Mr. Turner told about the poets and the novelists and the others of the various times they were studying. And especially his reading aloud. Mr. Turner insisted on this, saying it brought a dimension, the *sound*, that was inherent, vital, necessary in good poetry.

Bonnie sat enthralled in the class, her eyes wide, mouth slightly ajar at times. Larry wondered if she had a crush on Mr. Turner. Girls' crushes; these were different from the mad lusts of the boys, he felt. But what did he know, after all? Did the girls have the types of locker room/gym conversations boys had? Goran – and others – who'd snuck in the girls' room, maintained there were dirty pictures drawn there, too, and dirty stories written down on the stall walls.

"Right on the Kotex machine!" Goran claimed, while the others nodded vehemently. "They're worse than us!"

Turner linked football – athletics – to poetry. He read them A.E. Housman's "To An Athlete Dying Young" one afternoon. There was a light drizzle falling all day long making it misty in the distance, River Hill fading in and out of it. Soon, there would be mean, hard driving sleet, then advancing curtains of snow. The blanket of winter.

Larry looked around the classroom, as Turner stood reading by the wet, streaked windows. When he read like that, he had a look of absolute concentration and intensity, even like they, the students, weren't there, not in the room. His large, black frame glasses contrasted with his unusually pale skin, and black hair. Coal black, as his mother liked to say, about someone's hair.

Would any of them die young? It was difficult to think clearly about that, it was such a large idea. If it was even an idea. His own father and stepfather had died, but not young. And then there was always the possibility of a war. But no, there was something contradictory in thinking about death, dying, while young, because to be young was to be alive, above all else. Was that what the poem was getting at? He shook his head.

"...there's a poetry in the athlete. And that comes out in the game, the contest, the *physical* event," Mr. Turner said, looking now, Larry felt, right at him as if reading his mind.

"Yes." He looked at them, standing there by the window. "Yes... it's not expressed in words, it's not printed in a book. But poetry. Some great, no question. An 80-yard touchdown run...no question. Dick Atkins is a poet when he throws a pass...Robert Henderson, when he runs." He nodded, as if talking to himself, as if he had been convincing himself.

"What about this, then? Football games are rituals, too, and rituals are another way of saying poetry. Eh?"

Nobody spoke. The room was quiet, so much so that the hissing of the now increasing rain was clearly audible, and the low tick of the big wall clock.

"Football is a ritual where young men complete a celebration. But also a complaint. Over the dying of the year. It must be a very old game, then, and probably at some point they had a sacrifice. A big fire roaring. What do you think?" He pointed out the window. "Up on River Hill there, so you could see it for miles."

His face was flushed, his neck taut, you could see the big veins standing out, above the tight collar of his blue dress shirt. He sighed heavily. There was a faint sense of embarrassment in the room.

"Well. Let's hope Ralston goes all the way." He held up their book. "Let's talk over the rest of these that I assigned next class, then. OK."

People were in that strange drifting mode outside, milling in the halls. Hoss Fobbs, a known bad kid, who wore a Balboa haircut, had inked "Kill Chester!" on his right bicep, along with "Thunder" on one forearm. A lot of the guys strode in the halls trying to look mean and intense, as if they were going to play in the game against Chester. The girls were bright-eyed with excitement.

There were banners urging Ralston to "Go ALL the Way!" Goran had sniggered, grabbing his crotch, pointing at the banner. He wondered who Goran would marry. It was a grim thought, and he felt sorry for the girl, whoever she was. Maybe one of those girls that lived way back in the country on some run-down farm, sat on the front porch bare-footed, swinging in a swing in the summer, and just stared at you when you talked. He had met such girls. Sometimes they went barefoot all summer. Their eyes were strange. He wondered what they did, the stories about the barn, the outhouse, all that – like the incident with Gary in the barn earlier that summer. There was supposed to be a lot of incest in some of these families, like up on The Island.

"They're all inter-related, up there. You'd be surprised. That's the way those people are…" his mother had said one night when he talked about fishing up at The Island, in a place they called The Eddy – a large pond of trapped water from the Allegheny River that flooded easily and repeatedly in spring. In winter, people skated up there on The Eddy, with fires burning on the shore to keep warm. There were supposed to be huge carp in The Eddy, five or six feet long. Smick Smead told a story of being pulled in by one. He had wondered where these big fish went when the water froze.

He saw Sandy Stevens in her majorette outfit, hurrying down towards the outside door – probably some practice, or maybe the band? If anything, she looked even better than usual. Maybe it was just that he hadn't seen her for a while – and in school, two weeks was "a while," a long time. What had happened with her, and with him? It was Cameron, no question about it. He had done nothing, really. Nevertheless, as Frankie claimed (and Ducky seconded), "They always *know*." Even Bonnie looked at him oddly sometimes these days.

Coach Rossi was going into a classroom to teach one of his health classes, and he thought again: he had to tell him. Here he was, walking around the halls, and nobody knew about the decision he was going to make. Maybe Coach Rossi sensed it. People sensed a lot of things, he was realizing. Certainly Mr. Turner did. And the poets, they did – it was all about sensing, poetry. Was there any poetry in football? There was, he felt sure, but it was not something he could explain, and maybe it was something that never did get explained, not fully at least. Football. It wasn't supposed to be "poetry." The guys at Sam's would hoot at that one!

If he quit, talked to Coach Rossi, he would miss that whole life. He would miss football. He would miss the early autumn, the pick-up games that went on for hours – nobody kept score, and you could run like the wind – with the smell of cut grass in your nostrils, go home with your mother complaining about the grass stains on all your clothing, you couldn't get those out. To be able to do that, to feel that way in your youth, on into college, that would be poetry, he felt sure. Coach Rossi probably understood that, but he did not know if he could speak of it that way to him.

The Librarian, Miss Vukovich, was coming up the main stairs, he could hear her heels clicking lightly. Those great legs. "Built like a brick shithouse," they said. But the question was, how, just how, was a brick shithouse built? And why brick? He had never seen such a place, and he'd seen shithouses, many of them, even some with the cute little moon carved out on the door. Up where they had gone deer hunting, near Leeper, he'd seen a five-holer, a big shithouse. He thought of asking about the phrase at Sam's – but you had to be careful what you asked the old geezers in there, they could take things the wrong way easily.

Who was her boyfriend, he wondered? "Put your hand up there…" Goran said, licking his lips. Some other teacher, somewhere else? Maybe a steel worker, one of those muscular guys down in Blawnox? No. Not a steel worker. He felt sure of that. Goran speculated out loud one day how many of them in Ralston High School "beat it" – making a frenzied motion with his hand – thinking of her.

He was in the school, but what was he learning? And why did he have these incessant thoughts, couldn't turn them off, wandering in the halls of Ralston High School, which nobody knew about, or gave a damn about for that matter? Would Ralston beat Chester and go to the Big Game, to Pitt Stadium, only a few weeks away now? *That* was something.

"I'd like to fuck her," he heard Goran's voice hissing, sudden, in his ear, as Miss Vukovich rounded the corner of the stairs and came striding towards them. "Goddamn!"

School had become for him a welter of impressions, which he could never be sure of, never prepare for. In the study hall, where little was formally studied, a discussion had been finally interrupted by the teacher, a first-year one, who looked perplexed and bored; he would not last. What was he, a geography teacher? And the discussion; about argyle socks, which Larry secretly had a passion for but did not want to admit to. It would not do for a boy, a man, a young man, to admit to loving clothes so much, he thought. Yet he did. If he were rich, he would spend a fortune on clothes just to have them hanging in the closet,

the shoes lined up and ready, the sports coats in a row –
several rows!

But the argyle socks were like all the other fads of teen-
agedom. Where did they come from? There had been a
craze, down in some schools in the Valley, for white
clothes; pants, shoes – had the white bucks come from
that? He heard that that was what they wore at Penn
State, up in State College. Or did they come from out in
California, so far away – 3 days on the train – and if they
did, why? What was it about California that made that
happen there?

Los Angeles was where Hollywood was, and that made
sense. James Dean had started the whole fad of turning
up jacket collars. And just wearing the white tee-shirt –
that was James Dean, although others said it was Marlon
Brando. But no kid identified with Brando. He was too
old.

Frankie Malone said it was all rich kids' stuff. "That's
who it is starts alla that crapola. They got nuthin' else to do
but start fads, you ask me."

Maybe he was right, in the case of the argyle socks. They
were best worn with loafers, but were ok with other shoes.
They were cool with the spade-toed oxblood oxfords. Mr.
Mazaroski wore that style of shoe, with double-breasted
suits, all the time. How many pairs did he have?

It made Larry feel good to wear his argyle socks,
although Frankie ribbed him about being "a goddamn
clothes horse!" And Frankie reared up and neighed, like

one. But he did feel good just seeing them stacked neatly in his drawers at home. They were beautiful just to look at.

Argyle, Bonnie said, was Scottish, in Scotland; a plaid, a tartan. "That's where the name comes from," she announced. "Not California." But that was even odder. How had they gotten to Ralston?

Meanwhile, Frankie told him in the study hall of being picked up hitch-hiking by a guy who'd asked him if he'd gotten a piece for Christmas yet. "He said – they got some of these girls, you gotta *spoon* it outta them, there's so much."

# 29

The morning of the Big Game with Chester, Joe Labrador grabbed Norma Sterns' tits, from behind, as she reached up in her locker to get a book. Norma yelled, struggled, elbowing and thrashing like a steer in a rodeo, but Labrador lifted her right off the ground so that one of her penny loafers fell off. His face was red, he was puffing, he had a visible hard-on through his Levis. He knew he would be expelled, but he did not give a goddamn, squeezing Norma's big tits for all he was worth. She shook with the fury of their struggle, her face brick red, her feet banging hard into the locker wall. Nobody did anything, for this had been coming for a long time. Everyone just standing around, apparently idle, a few even kept on going, to class, and Goran, of all people, drank at the water fountain, as if nothing was happening. He wiped his mouth and stared.

Mr. Sweeney came flying out of his lab as if forcibly ejected by an explosion, and tried to intercede. But Joe Labrador had a vise grip on Norma Stearns, holding on, like the expression said, for dear life, and shook Mr. Sweeney off so that he, too, banged into the lockers with a loud, clanging crash. And maybe, too, Joe Labrador was afraid to let go, afraid of what Norma would do in that instant, that moment, before they were really separated.

It was a football player who saved the day. Dago Paretti yelled out in a hoarse voice "Let her go, you dumb shit! Let go of her. Goddamn!" and started threateningly forward. That did it. Joe Labrador snapped out of it, and with the slight relaxation, Norma was gone. She bolted down the hall towards the girls room, bowling over two girls in her path so hard that one flew into the wall, her books spewing in the air, while the other – Penny Robinson, a near-sighted girl who wore thick glasses eerily magnifying her eyes like an owl's – went "ass over gimlet," as the phrase had it (but what did it really mean?), with a thick thud onto the hard floor of the corridor by the swinging locker door. Her dark glasses broke into two pieces, the lens splintering. She screamed and started crying.

Afterwards, because it was the day of The Big Game, it seemed a brief incident. Maybe Labrador had planned it that way. He cared nothing about football, or the Ralston team, and had several times made a motion of masturbating when going by one of them in the hall. It was a shocking gesture, worse by far than if he had given them the finger. "The Holy Mystic Sign!" Frankie called it. "Perch on this!" What was the source of his contempt, Larry wondered? But he had never talked to him, and didn't know anyone who really had. Bonnie said he was "a psycho case, obviously." But was he?

"He just couldn't stand it anymore," Goran claimed. He smiled his thin, narrow-lipped smile. "Hard and firm.

Hard and firm. Yessir. That old cock, he don't give a good goddamn when he gets hard enough. A stiff prick has no conscience." It was one of Goran's favorite proverbs, and he said it slowly, with relish.

"You're supposed to think with your head, not your dick, you asshole Goran. He was halfway raping her. You can't do that shit. Jesus!" Paretti shook his head.

"Halfway?" Frankie said. But he was shaken by the force of it, as he told Larry, and wondered what Norma felt like. That surprised Larry, gave him a different sense of Frankie.

The planned monster Pep Rally wasn't affected. A small group of girls took Norma into the principal's office. There they remained. Soon the Pep Band was marching around the corridors, with Zeb Lewis honking as usual, and somebody pulling a small red wagon around with Digger Hayes sitting scrunched in it, yelling through a homemade paper megaphone. "Kill Chester! Kill Chester! Aaaargh!"

*The First String.* A huge banner, in blue and white, strung above the stage opening; somebody somehow got it onto the curtains up there. There were photographs of the starting eleven, as Coach Rossi usually referred to them, pinned on the banner, blown-up photographs. They were famous.

Larry could not remember an atmosphere quite like the one inside the auditorium for this Pep Rally. A hot, intense, singing energy; people's faces were flushed red, like adults who'd been drinking. The concentrated energy of teenagers, powerful, amazing. What would it be like at the game that night? And what if Ralston lost? He did not want to think that thought – "the thing" as some referred to it - but couldn't help it. It seemed traitorous, as if thinking it could make it happen.

Up and down the aisles in the auditorium now, a terrific commotion, they were pushing Digger Hayes in the Little Red Wagon. Ralston was going "to fix Chester's wagon!" a cardboard sign on the side read. Two of the cheerleaders joined in the pushing, their short skirts hiking up so their blue panties showed, gleaming. Some boys stared open-mouthed as the wagon rushed by. Goran, with a choice aisle seat, grinned, licked his lips, and slowly rubbed his crotch. "Fuck you, Goran!" somebody yelled, and he looked around quickly. "That big hairy-assed bitch. That one. Jesus!" somebody else yelled. Who was the hairy-assed bitch? Not one of the cheerleaders, that wasn't possible.

The assistant coaches began filing somberly in from one side of the stage, pushing aside the drawn-back plush red curtain. Coach Barnes had his lower lip thrust out and looked mean, ready for a fist fight. He would ask players, "You ever been in a fist fight, kid?" Coach Kowalski looked tired, and frowned. Already he had a crease in his forehead, between the eyes, from frowning. At least that was what Larry's mother was always telling him, not to frown and make that mark. Coach Rossi came last. They took their places in folding metal chairs set up on the stage. It was going to be one of those rallies, then; the coaches would speak, ending with Coach Rossi. The team would be introduced – the "Starting Eleven". After all, it was their last game as a starting unit. Glory was brief. It wouldn't do but to make the most of it, now. They had played a tie only one game; all the rest wins. Lots of players would get scholarships. They had played their best.

Cameron Mitchell. Sitting at the end of one row near the back of the auditorium. She noticed him looking and smiled; the smile sped right to him, it was for *him*, on a bright beam of light. Did Cameron really care about the game? Probably not. She was beyond football already. She seemed sitting in or on an island of calm back there. Would she even drive up to Chester for the game? Or would she instead "drive around," as the phrase had it. Listening to the radio, driving around. Little Willie John. Elvis. Bo Diddley. The Chordettes. The old Four Freshman, even. It gave you a feeling of power, he knew that.

There were certain stories about Cameron that he now increasingly heard. For instance, there was one that she was "going with" Dago Paretti. Maybe they'd been around before but he hadn't noticed them. Stories about things she'd done, things she did, things she would do. With "the Dago," in particular. He did not believe these stories – and the stuff that appeared scrawled in the boys room – but then he thought of the music room, that night.

The whole school, the halls, full of pulsing energy, milling students horsing around. Grab-assing, Coach Barnes called it. If you could see the whole building at that moment, the yellow brick building of Ralston High, built in 1924 or something like that, it would be vibrating with energy rays, like in a cartoon illustration. The swelling noise – the sound of school – was unmistakable. And that familiar school smell, unique, he was sure he would never forget it – sweat and girls' hair, and boys' hair cream – Wildroot Hair Cream – soap and restrooms and shoes and dust; wax and the steam heat radiator smell, since the big boiler was on now, for winter. The classrooms humid, steamy, the windows fogging over (the kids would draw or write on them), from now until early spring – late March, maybe, or early April. What a feeling that was, when that came – spring! A long way away, that time. He liked the school, and hated to think of leaving it. In many ways, especially since his stepfather's death, it had become his home. He could not tell anyone that, though; he wished he could. Who had the school for a home?

What had happened to Norma Stearns? Coach Rossi would make his speech at the Pep Rally. Norma would soon be forgotten, the two older women in the principal's office, his secretaries, would calm her down. Maybe now was the time to tell Rossi he was not going out next year, he was not trying out for the team. In the hurry of the day, it could be slipped in, quickly, suddenly.

It was a growing, heavy stone on his back, the pressure he was feeling to tell the coach about his decision. He had told no one, not even his mother; no one except Cameron. He wondered that other people couldn't see it. He was walking through the school halls staring so often at the floor that Frankie ragged him about "looking for the answer? It ain't there."

Coming around the corner from the main stairs, near the landing, he'd collided with Miss Vukovich, and putting out his hands instinctively, brushed her breasts. The softness! He was amazed. How could anything *feel* like that? She surprised him by smiling. He thought he saw a faint blush in her cheeks, and suddenly wondered how old she was. Twenty-four or five? Much older than he was. But maybe she had just put some rouge on, too. You could never tell.

Why not *just not go out* next year? Even as he would think this, his stomach churned acidly, and he knew he could not do that. No, it wasn't possible. He had to speak to Coach Rossi face to face. And no other coach, either. There was no other way.

If he could talk his dilemma over with someone, he knew he'd at least feel some relief. Bonnie would praise him and not understand. He didn't know what Frankie's reaction would be, but he felt he could not bring it up that easily with him. Once you brought it up, you had to finish it.

The thing was, it was not fear that made him feel he had to quit. And, as far as that went, he was not "quitting." The JV season was already over. For those not chosen to suit up for varsity games, there really wasn't anything left to this season; a few semi-practices, sad affairs.

He was in a sort of limbo. The previous Saturday, in a surprising move, he and Ducky had met Frankie Malone in Peter's. Nobody who was really anybody in the school would be caught dead in Peter's on a Saturday afternoon.

They had drunk cherry phosphates and had a sort of conversation with Peter himself, who seemed amused at them being there. What had that all been about? Nowhere to go, nothing to do. "Think I'll go home, play with myself for a while," Frankie had said when Peter had asked what they were up to. Frankie, of course, would say anything that came into his head.

"You boys seen that girl, riding around in that '55 Chevy?" Peter had asked them.

"Cameron Mitchell?" Frankie asked, pointing to Larry with a quick jab-like motion.

"Dark-haired girl..."

"That's her."

"That's some car she got. There was a couple of boys in here the other night, had one just like it. From down in New Ken..."

Now Charlie Hibbing bounded onto the stage and Larry thought he'd do one of the cartwheels the cheerleaders did – that amazing, vaulting arc. You would see the flash of the blue, or the gold, panties. But it was all right, it wasn't bad. At Hibbing's appearance, a huge roar – "The Ralston Roar," which he encouraged with his hands, like a conductor – swelled up in the auditorium.

Even Goran was red in the face from yelling. Then Charlie, again with marvelous hand gestures, shushed everyone down, even placing a finger before his lips. He walked up to the microphone on its stand, and tapped it several times, hard, so that it made a loud sound in the auditorium. The students laughed.

He pointed up at the balcony. "Hey! Can you hear me, up there on The Shelf?"

"Yes!" Came back a loud response, and the students began pounding their feet on the floor. Charlie let the sound raise, and quicken, and then, dramatically, held his hand up, and just as dramatically, it stopped.

"Are we gonna do it? Are we gonna BEAT CHESTER?" He leaped in the air, and the cheerleaders did, too, shaking their pom poms. The students cheered and whistled and yelled, and some isolated voices yelled out "Fuck Chester!" Charley held his hands up.

"This team, this school, we don't lose… We are winners! CHAMPIONS!"

A roar again. Larry felt suddenly that he wanted to leave the auditorium and go where it would be completely quiet. Maybe out in the woods, so that all you could hear would be birds, the wind in the trees. But you could not leave the auditorium. Especially not now. He felt weary, heavy, a traitor. He wished he could just leave, go out the front door of the school, and go down and walk slowly along the river. Skipping stones, like he and Frankie used to do when they were little kids. Sometimes, if you got a good one, you could get this flat skip on the sheen of the river's surface for six or even seven times. What made that happen?

Coach Rossi approached the microphone, the podium that had Ralston blue and white draped around it. He raised his hands, and the noise in the auditorium subsided so quickly it was like somebody had cut off a current. There was the rustling, scraping and creaking sounds of the students moving around in seats.

The coach looked somber. He looked down briefly, and then raised his head. When he did not have the baseball cap on, he looked older.

"I know that this is one of the biggest occasions for the school. But I don't want to talk about the upcoming game with Chester. No." He held his hands up briefly, palms outward.

"I want to talk about these players, these young men seated up here before you today. I want you to take a good, close look at each one of them." He stood sideways then, and the first string, the Starting Eleven, stared out at the auditorium, several blinking from the stage lights. All had short crew-cuts, except for Dago Paretti whose black hair shone in the lights. It looked oily. He moved uncomfortably in his chair, and looked briefly off to the side of the stage, as if someone was about to come on stage.

The quiet in the auditorium grew deeper. The coach stood silent, looking at the players, nearly all of whom began to move in their chairs. All were wearing their letter sweaters. Harry Gibb's had those four stripes, on the thick upper arm; it stretched tight on him. Would he take that sweater out of some closet, far in the future, and stare at it, and think of this moment, Larry wondered, watching the scene.

The coach turned back facing the assembled students and teachers. The auditorium was so full that a few were standing alongside the walls, although usually this was prohibited by the teachers. But some of them were standing there also now. It must be that everyone in the school was there. Even Mr. Dempsey, the janitor, was standing along the side, down near the EXIT door.

"You know…my wife and I, we've become close to these boys." The coach cleared his throat audibly. "Back early in the fall, back in early September, when we had the Parents' Night, I knew, I felt, that there was something special about this group. This team."

A few yells erupted, but quickly subsided, as people looked around to see who it was.

"I know that feeling. I've only had it a couple of times. Once was when I was a player myself."

A soft, uncertain laugh rippled through the crowd, and there was a quick, increased sound of people moving, shifting in their seats.

"I know – that was a long time ago." He nodded. "But these boys, up here now – I won't forget a single one of them. I know the other coaches won't, either. Whatever happens tonight, up in Chester there, I know that this group has given their all, every game, every minute, every play. They are already champions. Yes. Champions. And I want you all to remember that. Don't forget it."

The students erupted in a prolonged yell, a wild cry that was intense and truly shook the old building; Larry was sure he could feel the floor shaking. Feet were stomping. Coach Rossi stood stock still, then nodded his head, raised his hand above his head, and walked towards the side of the stage. At the same time, Charlie Hibbing bounded out of the other side, followed by the cheerleaders gesturing and beckoning for all to yell even louder, and the Pep Band crashed into "On, Wisconsin."

The players stood suddenly, and followed the coach off stage. They looked grim and intent.

Charlie Hibbing had grabbed the microphone in his hand, making it ring and then squawk. "Hey! Hey! Raiders, all the way! Hey! Hey! Raiders, all the way!" The chant was taken up, and boomed out in the auditorium. "Hey! Hey! Raiders, all the way!" The cheerleaders waved their arms in unison, and swayed as a group, leading the chant.

Hibbing leaped straight up into the air, repeatedly; it seemed certain his glasses would fly off, but they didn't. "Let's GO!" he roared into the static hiss of the mike. "Let's GO! GO, GO, GO!" And he ran to the edge of the stage where the steps were and began to come down them. The Pep Band's big bass drum began a heavy, repeated beat.

The doors were thrown open, and the outside front doors could be seen, also open, over the heads of the milling, yet orderly, students as they started a stomping beat in time with the drum, setting out on the Pep March.

They would snake through all the corridors and even some of the rooms of the building, around the perimeter of the old gym, while the Pep Band led them, with Charlie Hibbing and Donna Charles and the Wood twins leading. They'd even march through the library and Mr. Sweeney's classroom. It was a tradition. Game Night, a Big Game, was coming.

On that day, though, for some reason he didn't know himself, Larry sat in his auditorium seat and did not join the Pep March. A few students jabbed him playfully, he smiled, and the sounds of the march moved out of the auditorium, until he was by himself. He saw Mr. Dempsey, already in the aisle, with his big broom. It was an odd feeling, and for a moment he could see himself, a single, seated figure in the empty auditorium, while the sounds of the Pep Band and the students echoed off in the school corridors. Where had the players gone? he wondered. Finally, he got up and hurried out a side door; he would catch up with the march. It wouldn't be hard. Behind him, as he exited, Mr. Dempsey moved slowly, methodically, sweeping up the aisle.

# 30

The long, narrow yellow buses pulled slowly in and parked neatly in a close row behind the lit-up Chester playing field. Dalvey Field. Named after another of the Valley's World War Two heroes, this one a Medal of Honor winner killed on Iwo Jima. The high-raked, splintery bleachers, painted white and maroon (the Chester colors), stood in long rows along the sides of the field, lining it with a clean precision. There were a lot of buses - townspeople from Ralston had packed on them this time, and on the road they made a snaking caravan with cars, blowing their horns, the kids hanging out the windows hollering and yelling, waving Ralston banners, faces flushed with the excitement of this approaching climatic game. The Big Game. If Ralston could win on this cold November Friday night under the lights at Chester, they would go undefeated, claim the title of their section, and with it the opportunity to play in the Division II Championship Game in Pittsburgh in Pitt Stadium, the day before Thanksgiving. Probably against Braddock High. Or "Jigaboo High", as it was referred to in Sam's. "See, they all smile – blinds the other team!"

Pitt Stadium. He loved, if one could be said to love, Pitt Stadium although he had only been in it once (and it had been *empty*) on a school tour of the university and the Carnegie Museum of Art. The stadium was out in Oakland, "a ways," as it was always said, from downtown Pittsburgh, the famous city center at the confluence of the Allegheny and Monongahela Rivers, joining at The Point – the Golden Triangle. In fact, Braddock High School was named after the English general who the original fort there had been named after. In history class, they had read of Braddock's red coats coming through the dark forests of Pennsylvania. The book recorded a statement that at that time the American forest was so thick, so vast and dense, that a squirrel could have gone all the way to the Mississippi River without coming down. Now, fast traffic flowed around the old historic fort site, and if one of the original inhabitants of the fort had been brought back there, no doubt they would have been more terrified than by an Indian raid. Who could have imagined any of it – Pittsburgh itself, the modern Steel City, the huge stadium, the roaring fans, the game of football itself? It was weird, what you remembered from history classes, even if the teachers were boring.

He had not liked the Pitt campus that much, though. Penn State was better and was a better football school, some said, although Pitt was tough. Penn State was his ideal of a college campus. When he'd first gone there the previous summer, he had instantly felt he could easily stay there the rest of his life. There were long paved walkways lined with large, old graceful trees and seemingly unending green lawns, edged often with blazing beds of flowers. Then there were the college buildings themselves. Many in the famous Gothic style, but others plainer, older-looking, simple grey stone or white-painted brick. Covered in ivy. He liked to think of himself working in one of these, a professor, who wore stylish dark horn-rimmed glasses, sports coats with leather patches on the elbows, cardigan sweaters. And those neat, striped ties that he'd heard originated as university or school colors in England. Like the actor, Robert Young, in *The Halls of Ivy*. There would be a small fireplace in his office, and he would have a larger one in his colonial style white house near the campus – he's seen many of these kinds of houses there in State College. They too had lots of trees around them, and large green lawns, and some even had ivy growing on a side, or in front. He would sit in an old, cracked leather chair and read books, smoking a pipe and drinking tea. When he did this, he'd wear an especially old cardigan-style sweater, argyle socks, and smooth, buttery leather loafers. Wasn't that what a professor did, mainly, read books? What a life! It was even more remarkable than being a dj.

His mother had listened with an indulgent smile when he spun out this professorial fantasy to her. In fact, some distant relative supposedly had been a professor of Civil Engineering at Penn State, but not much was known of him except his name, Cecil, a name Larry felt an instant aversion to; it didn't sound like an American name. Cecil.

"When the winter sets in up there," his mother said, "it gets *cold*." She nodded to herself in a way she had. "Ten, even twenty below zero – how about that? You might change your mind…"

"I'll have my wife. To keep me warm." He surprised himself saying it. He had a sudden, quick vision of himself laying in a large bed with an old quilt on it. With Cameron. It was snowing heavily outside.

"Ohh, I see…" she said, nodding again. "Your wife – so you're going to get married, then? I thought you said you'd never get married. Be a bachelor all your life."

"Maybe…at least until I'm thirty."

It took time to get off the buses. They even had to drive to another parking site, further back from the field. The buses lurched and swayed over gravel and pot holes. Then, finally parked, the door slid open, and they stepped out into the night. For a game coming in the second week of November, it was not going to be that cold, he thought, feeling the air. By the end of the game, around ten o'clock or so, it'd be damp and chill – the heater in the car would feel real good. But you wouldn't be frozen, so cold that you were sick with it. Numb, to the bone, shivering uncontrollably. Really cold.

The newspapers' predictions worried him. "Ralston, by two touchdowns, or more." How could they be so certain? Anything could happen in a football game like this one. It was like a jinx, to call it that way. Chester was the clear underdog and Coach Rossi had often lectured on how it was better, and easier, to be the clear underdog. You had nothing to lose. It was when you had a lot to lose that it was tough. If Hunter, Chester's small but elusive running back, could be stopped – contained was the word used in all the sports columns – Ralston would win. It could be by two touchdowns. Or more. A rout…

Hunter. William Hunter. What a name. Small, compact, light, a half-back, whose sudden bursts of speed, elusiveness, and darting running style made him hard to tackle, to catch, before he'd reeled off ten, fifteen or twenty yards. He never seemed to really get hit hard, "smeared", by tacklers. Difficult to knock off balance or down, he would spin out of an apparent tackle, reverse field, reel off another ten yards, or a touchdown. He ran in an odd, quick, darting crouch, so low to the ground ("He runs like a goddam rat!" somebody at Sam's had complained) it seemed he had to fall at the next step. But he never did. One sports writer claimed he probably had exceptional peripheral vision. He could thus see tacklers long before they got to him; he could also see down the field more fully, widely. He could also pass effectively, so that had to be factored in. Hunter wore number 27. Some joked it stood for the average number of points he scored in a game. He led all Division II players in total yardage, and touchdowns scored, and was being courted by, it was said, over 100 colleges and universities. He wanted to go to Princeton – not a football school, although they had had a triple-threat All American, Dick Kazmaier, a few years back. They were one of the few teams left that ran a single wing offense, not the T-formation. Their coach, Charlie Caldwell, was famous for sticking to it. Larry had seen a photograph of this old coach, and thought he looked like a coach he would want to play for. He did not look like Coach Rossi.

On the radio on the bus on the way up to Chester, Perry Como sang "Ivy Rose" and "Magic Moments." He was an older guy, from World War Two really, but his voice was so smooth that it did not matter. His songs were popular with kids, big hits. What the radio, and the songs, did was conjure up white bucks and great sweaters, an escape from the grey dreariness of the worn-down, worn-out towns in the Valley, lost in some time fifty years back. Chester did not look much different. The houses leaned slightly sideways, some of the porches fallen down or even gone from the front of the houses, stairs in very decayed condition.

The thing was, in these towns, everything was dirty – there was a sense of never being able to get all the accumulated grit and dust and dark, black dirt out of the houses, their very paint. The streets looked the same. "Shabby" was his mother's word for it. He wanted to get out of it, all of it – the whole damn rust and gray-black colored shabbiness, the poorly built, shingled houses – so badly he walked for several hours, all around Ralston, out the Dam Road to The Island, ending up walking down the side of the railroads tracks, up on the Highgrade, out of town, where you could look back, and down, on Ralston. It already seemed history, finished, past. When he told his mother about these feelings, she smiled and said there would be a day when he would think of Ralston and want to come back to it. But he did not think so. He would like to go to Princeton, like the great running back Hunter, or Robert Henderson, the aloof one who seemed to know much more than all the rest of them and walked the halls of the school like he had an aura around him. Around school, he was supposed to now be "going" with Cheryl Lake, Dick Atkins' former girlfriend.

Princeton's team was called the Tigers. Their uniforms were distinct. They looked like those of old-time football from around the turn of the century, or even earlier, the era of Walter Camp, who parted his hair in the middle and wore a moustache. It was amazing to think of a football player with a moustache. The arms of the Princeton jerseys were striped, colored in orange, black and white, like a tiger. "Once a Tiger, always a Tiger," Frankie had quipped when he'd told him of his dream, and it sounded like something someone from Princeton would say. But neither he or Frankie had ever been there. It was somewhere in New Jersey. F. Scott Fitzgerald had gone to Princeton; Mr. Turner had noted that in class. Hemingway had gone to World War I, not college.

After unloading from the buses, he separated from the other kids, walking around Dalvey Field somewhat aimlessly. For some reason he couldn't pin down, he did not want to be talking, gabbing, to people during this game. It was too important. He stood watching as the two bands paraded onto the field, and then the two teams came running onto it, the Chester team bursting through a large red and white paper banner strung under the one goal post, just as Ralston did on their home field, and ran onto the field through a flanking line formed by the kneeling majorettes and cheerleaders. The White Knights! That was their team name. It was a damn sight better than Plum Township's – "the Farmers." Who had given a football team such a name?

Then, quickly, the referees were meeting with the two team captains – Harry Gibb for Ralston, and Hunter for Chester – tapping Hunter on the shoulder pads to indicate they had won the toss and chosen to receive. Now the noise rose in waves of sound, sweeping the field – did the players hear it, or were they in a kind of deaf trance with excitement? And then Ralston's kicker, Dago Paretti, booted a mean line-drive that the Chester fullback bobbled and nearly fumbled, but kept hold of, getting smeared at the twenty-five yard line by Harry Gibb and John Patrick and two others. The game – The Game – was underway. He decided not to even sit in the stands, but stood on the forty yard line, watching intently. He felt like he had radar vision.

The game developed then in a sort of state of suspended animation for him. So much was riding on it he wondered how the players could stand it. Constant, rising crescendos of sound shifted back and forth across the brightly lit field. A white mist, like a fog, already was forming above the field, from the big crowd's generated heat. As many as fifteen thousand people could be there. The mist made him think of a few years back when Ralston played a home game when it had snowed in the second half, a white curtain slowly, densely enveloping the field. Some had said the game would be stopped, but it wasn't.

Ralston scored first. An amazing play resulting from a fumble by the quarterback, Dick Atkins, who bobbled the snap, dropped the ball, chased it, and then scooped it up with a lunge, reversed his field, and ran straight down the sideline, sixty yards, for a touchdown. He ran right past Larry, standing on the forty – almost close enough to touch. Atkins looked frightened; that surprised him. Maybe it was just concentration.

The pattern of the game developed, and he walked back and forth on the sideline in distraction, watching it. Frankie and Bonnie were up in the stands. It would be warmer there, but he was absorbed in this game, one like no other, and didn't want to hear them talking about it, as they would. So he stayed where he was, feeling almost like he was standing on a very small island. Chester came right back and scored when they got possession, with Hunter reeling off stunning runs, although it was the fullback who actually scored. Then, after a series of ineffectual plays, then punts by both sides, Atkins threw a screen pass to Robert Henderson, who then threw downfield to Emilio Patrone, and he scored, running into the end zone holding the ball aloft with one hand.

When you actually saw Hunter darting through the line, or down the sideline – proving to be as good as he was said to be – it was hard to admit it but he was playing an outstanding game. Hunter, he realized, was one of those who was a King. It would be like that his whole life, no matter what. Football showed this clearly. Hunter was the King of Dalvey Field; he owned it.

How must it feel to have that much depending on you? Would you think about it, going back out onto the field? What would you carry with you? No doubt, in the huddles, the other players were looking at you. If you could somehow forget about all that, and just do what you practiced so often −"Execute!" as Coach Rossi said − you would be ok. You would play well. But to play outstandingly − he realized, watching Hunter shoot past Harry Gibb's outstretched arms, grabbing air where Hunter had just been − that called for being more than just "good." Good wasn't good enough, he realized, as the big crowd roared, and he began to think differently about Harry Gibb, despite his four letters.

He looked back and up, at the mass of fans in the stands, with the steam, that football game mist, rising high up into the lights so that it looked like a low cloud had settled over the field. Ralston would not win by two touchdowns − those damn newspaper predictions meant nothing, less than nothing. At least, not as long as Hunter was in the game. Just stepping onto the field seemed to change the atmosphere; he was that kind of player. Hunter's play made him feel older; he could not have explained it, but it did. He noticed the crowd was often oddly quiet when he ran, or came on or off the field, even though it was the home crowd, his field.

Did that fact, the famous home field advantage, have something to do with Hunter's mastery? That he knew exactly where he was? His deft, certain moves as he reeled off runs for chunks of yardage − 11 yards, 9, 14 − and then, with one swift motion that looked like he was throwing a javelin in track and field, threw a touchdown pass to the Chester right end, who loped into the end zone untouched, and, like Patrone, held the ball aloft with one hand for the crowd to see. When they wrote articles about him in the *Valley Daily News* – and there had been many this fall – they always talked about his "innate athleticism." Hunter also ran track and played baseball, and was so good in the latter, as a second baseman, that pro interest was said to be strong; he might be a Bonus Baby, and sign for some unimaginable sum of money ($50,000 a year was mentioned) with a major league baseball team – and never play football again. This could be his last game.

He wondered, as he paced the sidelines, whether others were thinking as he was. The mood of the crowd, what was it? He couldn't tell how he felt – maybe numb, suspended. The game was tied at half-time as the bands prepared for the half-time show, moving along the edges of the field. The big maroon and white busby hats of the Chester band nodded, swayed. The field itself was oddly empty for a short time then; the teams gone to the locker rooms for the speeches of the coaches. The famous locker room Pep Talk. As a JV, he hadn't really experienced Coach Rossi's talk, but it was known. Sometimes, it was said, he did not say much of anything, but simply circulated among his players, talking to them quietly, an arm around their shoulder, almost like a minister in a church. And football, after all, was church. No question. He did not need convincing.

The sharp, pungent smell of brewing coffee, steam rising from the refreshment stands, people wolfing hot dogs, dripping glops of ketchup and mustard or sauerkraut. Everybody looked happy, pleased. The school colors of both teams everywhere; everywhere the particular heavy smell of crushed grass and earth, the football smell, almost like when a farm field was being plowed. The night air shone in the big lights over the field. Dalvey Field. It was a special place for two hours or so on this Friday night. And then everyone would leave and it would just lie there, flat, empty, quiet, dark. It was strange to think of that. Every small town in Pennsylvania was like that, too. Perhaps only the first day of deer season, later on, was as predictable.

The big field, as he stood now looking out on it, could have been a place where medieval knights had just jousted, it was so churned up when you got this close to it. For a few seconds he imagined huge war horses rearing, the clanging crash of an unhorsed knight onto the turf. The vision was so vivid he turned around him, looking, then shook his head. He was reading too much of that historical fiction in the Readers' Digest Condensed Books his aunt received every month or so, and saw to it that he got thereafter. He was damaging his eyes, some of the regulars at Sam's said outright ("always got a book with you don't ya?"). There were the loud guffaws about making love with "Minny Fingers." That was bad for your eyes – you'd end up wearing those glasses that looked like Coke bottle bottoms. Sex, and football.

He noticed as the players left for the locker rooms that the linemen in particular were already splattered with mud; some had jerseys so smeared that the numbers were partially covered. This was especially noticeable with Chester's white jerseys. In Sam's they talked of how the Cleveland Brown's great quarterback, Otto Graham, never got his white jersey – he wore number 14 – dirty. Lou "The Toe" Groza, a tackle, never missed a field goal or conversion for them, either. Taking the snap from their great All-Pro center, "Gunner" Gatski, Graham threw impossibly long – 70,80 yards – passes that appeared to reach a height equal with the huge stadium's upper rim. They fell perfectly, softly, into the hands of a streaking end – Dante Lavelli or Mac Speedie, perfectly named - running full-out, not breaking stride. It was a beautiful thing to see. Larry remembered seeing a Philadelphia Eagles game on television where the end, Pete Pihos, running full-out like that, looking for the pass coming, had run directly into the goal post.

The huge crowd went silent. Pihos lay flat, unmoving, on the field. He had to be carried off on a stretcher. The force of the collision was unimaginable. How did players recover from something like that and go back out and play again? It was scary – but they were pros, they were getting paid. Still and all, something like that could cause permanent damage – a concussion, something that would not show up until years later, like with boxers. Or maybe Pihos would be able to show his grandchildren the pictures, everyone laughing. "Look at Granpa Pete! What a play!"

He finally got tired of wandering the sideline, and sat down in the front part of the bleacher section allotted to Ralston supporters. The Ralston band was just coming onto the field, Sandy Stevens marching proudly, stepping with such high lifts of her legs he wondered how she did it, maintaining her balance on that muddy field. To slip, to fall, a disaster. The band did not sound bad, but some of the Chester fans hooted, a show of bad sportsmanship that would be noted. The band moved around in some complicated marching maneuvers, the sort of thing he could see them doing often, looking out of a classroom window up in the school. He wondered if there were ever really bad mistakes in these formations, with some band member marching off alone in the wrong direction. That would be awful, but also very funny. Maybe a routine that incorporated that would be good. He saw Terry Malone beating the big blue and white bass drum that had "Raiders" on it, and thought that he would be the member to send off on the wrong way, while he kept pounding away at his drum. It would make a good scene in a film, he decided.

Sandy. Cameron. Sandy. No clear path in the situation – two of the most beautiful girls in the entire school. He would not know what to do, if it came to "that" with Cameron. Impossible…Thinking, as a matter of fact, was probably not going to do much good. He knew how he felt – or thought he did. But not sure. It was all confusing, the rushes of feelings, *his* feelings. He still had two years of high school to get through. It dismayed him to find himself in the situation he was in, distracting him continually, he couldn't keep his concentration, study, as he once had so easily. He should do something – but what? What was in his power? He could not really discuss it with his mother, who, sensing his distress, made his favorite foods more and more often, and joshed him about gaining weight, although he had not gained a pound, an ounce. He devoutly wished he could. That would be positive, but he could not, it seemed impossible. His mother even laughed and told him that he would come to a point in his life where he'd be trying to lose weight, that this was inevitable, although he didn't believe this. Adults, for that matter, were always saying how you would come to "realize" something when you got older. Why was that?

Just before the field announcer noted that the teams were poised to return to the playing field, he wondered if his mother was listening to this game on the Greensburg station. It was carrying a live broadcast. He could see the station's promotional banner from where he sat. She said she might, if she could stand it. So even she was involved with the whole thing. He saw Joe Labrador running in a zig-zag along the sideline, wearing a goofy-looking red hunting cap, and someone in the stands yelled out. "Hey Joe! Keep yer pecker up!" People laughed, and Labrador turned, paused, and then nodded energetically. But it was quite possible he'd be expelled for the Norma Stearns business. And what would he do, after that? Join the Army, or the Navy, probably if he could. Get out of Ralston.

Larry watched closely when the teams came back onto the field, lining up for the kick-off of the second half. It was hard to tell which team was more invigorated – or at least showing that they were. Ralston huddled around the coaches, compacting into a tight circle, then pressing their hands together, giving a large yell as they did so. The White Knights of Chester, as the PA announcer called them, jumped up and down, up and down, in a kind of fierce animated display of energy and determination. It would be impressive if a team remained silent, focused, methodical. That could intimidate an opponent.

Chester kicked off. He went back to standing, shifting from foot to foot, at his island at the forty-yard line. He would recall later, afterwards, that he would always remember the second half of this game. Robert Henderson caught the long arching end-over-end kickoff in the Ralston end zone and ran 101 yards (or so the paper reported the next day) for a touchdown – dodging, cutting back, reversing his field, using what blocks he got deftly – while pandemonium erupted in the Ralston stands. A touchdown! On the fucking kickoff! That was it, the game was over, they would run over Chester now.

But even as Henderson came off the field and the crowd roared and Coach Rossi gave him a congratulatory slap on the behind while the rest of the team gathered excitedly around him, Larry had the feeling that the game was not over. And it wasn't.

He was tired suddenly of the sidelines, so took a seat in the stands. He remained stationary in the stands for how long he did not know, as the game see-sawed back and forth through the third quarter. Ralston led, 27-21; the kick for extra point had been missed due to the holder,

Robert Henderson of all people, losing control of the slippery football, and not placing it down well. The main feature of that quarter – and well into the fourth – was the containment of Hunter, who repeatedly was punished with powerful gang tackles, two, three, four Ralston players riding him hard into the ground. Hunter also threw an intercepted pass, and fumbled on one run, sure signs that "it was getting to him."

Meanwhile, Ralston seemed stalled itself as a team. Maybe, as was said afterwards, it was the condition of the field which Ralston supporters said hadn't been maintained as well as it should have been, no doubt on purpose. But this made no sense since Chester's chief weapon was a running back. No – it was the weather that decided the game, if it wasn't Fortune. The biggest football game of both teams' lives.

By the middle of the fourth quarter, seven minutes left on the clock, no one had left. The refreshment stands were running out of food and everything else. Even the two bands did not seem to play as much, but to watch, intently. The majorettes' and cheerleaders' legs looked red and raw in the cold. They huddled together, their jackets on, looking worried, if majorettes and cheerleaders could look worried. There was a sense that something, something was still left to come, something was going to happen, this was not the end. This was a game of Destiny, truly a Big Game.

The teams were both tired by now. They had played their hearts out, and some of the players looked bewildered and dazed on the field, moving slowly. Many of the

Chester players' numbers were invisible, totally covered in mud. A fine sleety mist fell intermittently for half an hour or so, and many players slipped or fell as they tried to run, or cut back. Passing the ball seemed futile, or dangerous. It was the old type of football – a few yards each carry, try to get a hole, slip by, grind it out, as the coaches called it. Fundamentals, Coach Barnes liked to say, won football games in the end.

*"Character is reveled in the third and fourth attempts a person makes."* Early in the season, Coach Rossi had had that banner made and put up in the locker room in the gym. That banner came into his mind as he watched the play on the field which seemed to get slower and slower, the players obviously by now very tired, moving with the heaviness of that physical fatigue and the heavy, clinging mud engulfing everything and everyone. Mud was smeared by now even on the majorettes' pristine white jackets, which never were allowed to get dirty. The ball was covered in the greasy goo of the field, and runners held on with both hands, head down, trying for something. The coaches stood as close to being on the field as they could without getting penalized by the referees, who also looked tired, strained. Several slipped and fell on the field themselves in the second half, and were splattered with mud and grass stains like the players.

There were less then two minutes left on the clock and the sleety rain had stopped, when Hunter sprinted down the field on the left side, and the ball, dripping slime, fell, almost magically, into his hands – they had gone ahead, passed, what else? Hunter caught the pass, somehow evaded Harry Gibb, who was right on his tail, and then, for one last time, slipped – with some deft pivoting half step and juke – past the safety, Dago Paretti, who fell in the mud face down, his outstretched arms sending him sliding along like an odd sled rider. There was a thunderous roar from the Chester side as Hunter fell down in the end zone, then got up and walked slowly back off the field, still carrying the ball.

Larry knew that he would hold that scene in his memory for a long time - that arcing, awkwardly spiraling, dirty-looking football that already looked ancient, from another time period, falling through the dark misty night air, Hunter looking up expectantly, knowing that he was going to catch it, no matter what. It all ran like a slow motion sequence in his mind. He was numb with the shock of it, as if cotton had been wrapped around his head. He could see people around him staring in disbelief, looking around them; he could see the tears in the eyes of the majorettes, including Sandy Stevens, who stood with her baton dangling forlornly down; the tip of it too was muddy now. He had tears in his eyes, running hotly down the cold sides of his face.

The Chester kicker, using a fresh ball since Hunter would not give up the one he'd caught and carried into the end zone, put a perfect kick through the uprights, and the last few seconds of the Big Game ticked off with the Chester fans surging onto the field before he could get off a kick-off. People complained about that later. Who knew? It could have been run back for a touchdown. Not likely, but one would never know. Chester had won the game, 28-27. One point. One point. The 1956 season was over - suddenly, finally, forever - by one point. Ralston would not go to the big stadium down in Oakland, the University of Pittsburgh field. Harry Gibb and Dick Atkins and Dago Paretti and Robert Henderson and Fred Lucas had played their last game for Ralston, and now some hung their heads; Paretti threw his helmet hard into the mud, his face was smeared with it, and Coach Barnes grabbed him by one arm, putting his arm around him, talking earnestly to him. The cheerleaders stood in a sad little group crying, hugging each other. Their advisor, Miss Simmons, red-eyed, kept shaking her head. The Chester White Knights band played their school theme song, people milled around on the field thronging the Chester players, some of whom tried to come and shake hands with the Ralston players, a few even succeeding, their faces serious, intent.

The ride back home on the buses was stifled sobs from the cheerleaders, then outright loud bursts of crying. It hurt to hear them. He sat in the back of the big bus, listening to the diesel engine whine and hum, looking out at the passing dark landscape, the occasional light in front of a house by the road, then several small "villages" that looked bedraggled and even forgotten. Maybe they were. Who lived there? He had no idea, but it could easily have been Hunter, or one of the other Chester players. The White Knights came from a decidedly down-trodden area, even poorer than Ralston. The railroad had not gone through here; there were no major mills. Maybe in the past there had been a coal mine or two. It was like Blawnox, the oddly named town down near Pittsburgh, where they had made bleach in a big, white, block-long plant now closed, and people spoke of deformed people as coming from Blawnox. Or Cadogan, "Stinkville."

Something big had happened at the Chester field. He thought of how the players must feel, taking a shower, getting onto the bus, riding back to Ralston, as he was. Were they secretly relieved that it was all over? That wasn't a worthy thought. He realized he would never be a football player, when he reflected on it. They did not think that way. Could not…The coach, Coach Rossi, would be sitting stolidly in front, with his baseball cap on, and an old corduroy sports jacket he wore at every game, a talisman. His face would be like stone. Nobody would say much, if anything. They had lost, and it was irrevocable. The season was over.

Riding there on the wet road that was probably really treacherous, probably freezing in spots, black ice they called it, the whole school year had already ended. Back there at Dalvey Field, in those short few seconds when Hunter caught the muddy ball, scored the winning points. Everything else would be anticlimactic now, for the entire rest of the year. No matter how good the basketball team proved to be, what everybody was going to remember, years from now even, was this football team, the 1956 team, was the one that lost the last game. *By one point.* That only made it worse. Far worse. He was sure the players would remember it the rest of their lives. A long time.

He was clenching his jaw, he realized. He was beginning to feel really tired, even fatigued, and he realized he'd been concentrating. Focused, the coaches said. He had been focused, for sure. He thought of writing a letter to his brother Carl when he got home. That would help. He would describe the game, minutely. And he would describe how he felt about it as it progressed, how things changed. Even the temperature, the sleet, the mud.

When they finally got down Mile Long Hill (it was getting icy) and into the town, the buses dropped off everyone at the school, which sat silent and looked very cold. He walked back down the alley with Ducky, not saying much. The football field was a large black gap to their right; darker because down the alley there were no street lights or house lights, except the small front porch light on Ducky's house. As if by a cue, they both stopped, gripping the cold chain-link fence, staring at the long, black expanse of the field. The big lights were off, and he suddenly wanted to turn them on, flood the field with that special light. He wanted to hear that loud clang the big lights made when they came on, the jolt of the brightness flooding the field. But what good would it do?

Ducky went up the steep concrete steps to his small frame house and directly into it, without saying more than "See you…" over his shoulder. He walked down, and across Second Street past the gas station where a very weak light hung at the end of a frayed electrical cord in the back room. It had been there for years like that, and yet he knew that wasn't possible. "Some night that place'll burn down," Ducky had said several times.

His mother had already gone to bed. He went down in the basement, warm from the big furnace. He stood looking at Al's work bench, the tools, the power saw to the side that he had had a fear of. The kid in shop class who took off his thumb, blood sprayed on the wall high up visible later… How long he sat, down on the basement steps, he didn't know. He heard a slight tapping at the upstairs door, and his mother's voice calling his name and he walked back up, being careful to turn out the light. Al had always been careful about that. His mother hugged him. He just shook his head, he could not say how he felt, he really did not know. He climbed up the stairs to his room, thought of turning on the purple Motorola, but he couldn't. He lay on the bed without taking his clothes off, and that was how he woke the next morning, stiff and chilled, wondering if he was going to get a cold.

And so they had lost, and no one knew why, or what to do. That "thing" that no one wanted to think about. What *had* happened? And why? Was it the home-field advantage that Chester enjoyed, the known feelings, the familiarity of a field often played, practiced, walked on, its exact boundaries etched, indelibly imprinted on the Chester players' minds?

There was such a heaviness in the very atmosphere, the air, in the school on Monday morning that Larry wondered momentarily why the principal hadn't just called the day off, or at least the morning. There was a rumor that some sort of Pep Rally was going to be held, later in the week, but it seemed that would be a hard thing to do. Who would feel like it? He felt himself like the air had gone out of him, he felt weighted down, sad. The starting varsity players all had on their letter sweaters and moved somberly through the halls, looking straight ahead, not looking to either side, almost like they were marching.

# 31

Most of the leaves were down now, and the limbs of
the trees looked stark, bare and cold. Maybe a tree couldn't
feel cold, but they looked like they were. The air was hazy
and smoky; people were talking about how they had to
have the furnace on all night. Soon, they would stay on
for the winter. Ralston would be visible before you could
really see it, with the tall, billowing, floating plumes of
smoke going up from the various chimneys. He had seen
photographs in the history books of old Victorian cities in
England, almost covered in parts with dark, thick smoke
from the factories and the houses. There had been a terrible
fog in London not many years back, and then there had
been twenty people or so who died in Donora, a mill town
down the Monongahela, back in the late Forties. Smog. It
was the future, said Mr. Traynor in class one day.

Late in the night he heard the coon hounds running
up on River Hill – a sound you could never forget. He
had never heard a pig-sticking, but kids from the farms
talked about that, what a terrible sound that was, just like
a human being screaming. He didn't like to think about
that, and for a while he didn't eat bacon, although he loved
the smell of it frying on a cold morning, the sizzling,

popping sounds. It made his mother wonder when he didn't eat it in the morning, but he felt he couldn't tell her why. People thought such ideas were "odd."

The coon would be run, and then treed, and the hunters would traipse after the dogs, some of them already roaring drunk. Hopefully, none would fall into a hole, or worse, over the edge of River Hill. Finally, the coon would be treed, the dogs yelping, jumping in a frenzy around the base of the tree. The hunters would shine big flashlights – there it would be, its masked face peering down at what, to it, must be an awful, terrifying scene. And then they would shoot it, and probably it would not be dead, but it would fall, and they would let the dogs at it. That was the hunt, the coon hunt. The creature would be dead, finally.

In the English literature part of the school library he found an anthology of English poets, and in it, a poem by a poet named John Clare, called "The Badger." He could not keep from reading and re-reading the last lines.

*And then they loose them all and set them on.*

*He falls as dead and kicked by boys and men, Then starts and grins and drives the crowd agen:*

*Till kicked and torn and beaten he lies*

*And leaves his hold and cackles, groans, and dies.*

It startled him with a sharp jolt that poetry had, made him feel sad for the badger. He recognized in it the coon hunts up on River Hill – it was the same deep terror the coon must feel, being run, and then treed, with the lights shining in its eyes, the mass of barking, frenzied dogs at the foot of the tree, the red-eyed hunters looking up. Like the badger, it would die a painful death. What was the sense in it, he could not help asking, and did so in Turner's class to his astonishment, digging out the book and reading the poem. No answer came from any of the students, who stared at him. Some looked away, out the high windows of the classroom. Bonnie asked to borrow the book from him.

There was another meaning to the coon-running. They talked about it, some of the old timers, who had blackened stumps for teeth, ruined from how many years of "chewin' baccy, since I was a kid." *Red Man* – that was the favorite. Had the Indians chewed tobacco? he wondered.

"You know – they usta run a coon, that was a *nigger*. And they'd try to git in the river, the niggers, cause the dogs'd lose the scent that way... My daddy tole about it. Many times."

"Well – didn't they string one up too? Down in Etna there, under that bridge?"

"That's what they say...you know, (the old man would chuckle) that's how come they can run so fast. Runnin' from them hounds – you bet yer life!"

Now that the season had ended, everything was in a vacuum, waiting. Some basketball games had been played, early "exhibition games", but basketball was an indoor game and completely different from football. The loss of the final game to Chester remained like a stain, hung almost visible in the school halls and rooms.

In the championship game at Pitt Stadium, on a bitterly cold day (he tried to avoid reading about the game in the paper, but couldn't), Braddock defeated Union City, 21-7. Both teams had gone undefeated in the season. But who cared, at that point? It was also in the Sports section that Hunter, the Chester halfback, had accepted a scholarship to Duke University, a surprise. Now it was rumored that Harry Gibb might go there also. They would be teammates, then. Duke was in North Carolina, but he did not know much more about it, except that it really wasn't famous as a football school.

A light snow fell right after Thanksgiving, the first of the season. He enjoyed walking in it, seeing the foot tracks outlined in the clean, white snow. He had taken to walking around in the town at odd times again. He would leave the house, simply telling his mother he was going for a walk. She still cautioned him about going "down by the river" – it was a dangerous place; everyone had a fear of the big stream. He wondered if maybe some of the old Indian attacks told of – the scalpings that were so famous – hadn't in fact happened by the river as settlers got in or out of boats, or sought water, or fished.

Coach Rossi nodded to him if they passed in the halls, but just as often he passed with his head down, as if he didn't want to notice Larry. He had let the coach down in some fundamental way, and struggled with that feeling. He had tried to be honest, as honest as he could. The season was over, but Larry also thought that Coach Rossi must be re-living it, re-playing it. Was that what coaches did, perhaps all their lives?

The season was not really over. It would enter the school's history – the Ralston Raiders of 1956. Their team picture, with Coach Rossi beaming, standing beside them, would go up in the trophy case, with a small placard, "9-1". It would be featured in the 1956 Raider yearbook, and a copy of that would reside in the Library, upstairs at the school, for as long as there was a Ralston High. A great record, undefeated and untied. Until that final game. That one point. Not good enough; not a championship season or team; they would not have that to remember and come back to, twenty years later, for a grand reunion. All of the fervor, the fierce yelling at the Pep Rallies, the fantastic, springing leaps of the cheerleaders, the large crowds surging under the big lights on Friday nights, the long, snaking lines of yellow school buses full of singing kids – "Ninety-nine bottles of beer on the wall..." – the stories and front-page photos in the Sports Special on Saturdays in the newspaper – that was, already, completely past. It could never be done again.

Some players –Dick Atkins, certainly, who had had offers from nearly 100 schools already; Harry Gibb, Fred Martin, Dago Paretti, Robert Henderson– would claim full scholarships at a college, make the varsity, have their four years of college football. Yet there was no football like high school games, Larry felt. Why else would so many former players, like Lon Brueder, return, walk slowly across and around the field, sit by themselves in the vacant bleachers, staring out onto an empty field?

But it wasn't empty. There, as they stared, teams reassembled, the halfback broke free for a long gainer, the speedster end streaked down the sideline, the ball coming to his outstretched hands in unerring, amazing accuracy, he never broke stride, the safety falling in a last lunge at him, as the big crowd roared. There was a thrill – that was *the* word – in that not recaptureable. You could sit at the field and, even if you never played, faintly hear those sounds, coming and going. They were always there.

And yet they were gone. The high school player quite possibly would never be so heroic, in that way, again. The poem "To An Athlete Dying Young" was true; the whole thing of being young. His mother said "These are the best times, years, in your life, Larry. You'll see. You'll be old before you know it, looking back, and remember, and shake your head (as she did as she said it). You have it all, right now."

Could that be true? Was it just one of those pronouncements adults loved to make, staring at you intently, wagging a finger, nodding decisively. They knew, and you didn't. But you would find out. Experience was the best teacher, but on the other hand, why not avoid mistakes if you could? Maybe you couldn't avoid mistakes – your own, or others. He'd already made some with Sandy Stevens, hadn't' he? Some kind of betrayal, which Mr. Turner, when they were reading *Hamlet*, had said was inevitable. Choices meant mistakes.

When he looked at the big field, frozen now in an early winter with a light coat of perfect white snow already over it, he now knew he would never have those experiences as a player. He would not feel the ball slap sharply into his hands, hear the pounding thud of the pursuing defensive back's cleated shoes, his heavy breathing, another player cursing, the crowd roaring all around him, waves of sound washing over the bright lighted square space of Friday nights. Like some kind of jewel. He would not cross the white striped goal line, *score*, know that feeling. What must it be like? Something important had eluded him, some deeper sense of the game itself. Some deeper experience. Football was much more than a "game" but he did not understand it.

He would not meet a waiting girl, his girl, her bright pony-tailed hair hanging down over the letterman's jacket, too big for her which made her even cuter; the flushed cheeks, bright eyes, looking eagerly only for him. No one else. That couldn't be gotten back, either. You never got that special chance again. Two of you in the car, the upholstery smell, the light of the car, the warmth, the *songs*, the songs on the radio... You had been a hero. Almost a god.

General Eisenhower had been re-elected president. It passed almost unnoticed in the intensity of those last weeks of the season. He would be president until 1960 – a date that, although only four years away, seemed so distant. He might, if he found the money somehow, be near graduating from some college in 1960. Those players who'd won scholarships would be. And then what? What fads would be in – the bright neon colors of a couple years back? White bucks, but they had to be grass-stained? Buckles on the backs of pants, the Ivy League button-down shirt? What would their lives be like? Four, five years seemed an eternity (his mother liked that phrase) to him… He would be 22 years old.

He was standing on the next to top step, looking back down at the wide open space of the field. A clean, white expanse. It could have been a farm field, out in the country; Slate Lick, Cortez, Saxonburg. The goal posts looked odd, far away, like some part of a building left standing. They would accumulate snow once the wind dropped, and in the long dark December nights ahead, long icicles would hang rigid down from the crossbars. He could remember trying to jump high enough to break them off, he and Ducky and some others of the Lower End kids. The big, open field would sleep through the winter, and even then it would remain a virtually untouched space; kids would not drag their sleds across it, and only a stray set of dog tracks, maybe with their master's, that would actually cross it.

The huge, tall light towers, the tallest things in Ralston, would stand like strange, silent robots, until the first night games of the baseball season in late April. But it was never the same when the big lights were on for these baseball games. Somehow, they *looked* different, the light flooded out differently on the baseball diamond, the outfield, old man Garret's apple trees they had stolen from when they were kids, up on the steep hill behind right field. Old man

Garret, toothless, gimping out of his ramshackle house which had later burned down, killing him and his ancient dog, Penny. "You goddam kids! You wait'll I ketch ya. Sunavbitches! I know who you are!" But he didn't, his eyes were failing, too. He had lived in Ralston all his life. All his life!

Games were sometimes played in the snow, while the cover of whiteness was on the field. He'd seen such games on television – in Chicago, Cleveland, in Green Bay, which must be a terrible place to play, the temperature below zero in some cases. Frostbite. The players' breaths wreathed their faces and helmets like smoke.

Far in the one corner of the field, near a chain-link fence, sat two blocking sleds. He could remember Coach Kowalski "riding" on one of them, dust rising around it, as a straining player pushed at it. They were near the heavy frame where the tackling dummy had hung suspended, in that heat and dust and stinging sweat of August. He remembered Coach Barnes, the beet-red face, yelling "Hit 'em! Hit 'em!", the screech of the chain on the dummy's weights painful in the blistering afternoon. Now they sat abandoned – why hadn't they taken the sleds into the gym, or at least put them under the field stairs? But nobody would steal blocking sleds, that was for sure. They were useless.

Beyond the big field the town of Ralston looked exactly like a greeting card, a series of small streets and houses, smoke curling up out of the brick chimneys of many of them… Ralston - tired faces of the people, small streets, outmoded shops that would never be "modern."

The creek was not safely frozen yet, but there was ice along the edges already – it might be a long winter, they were saying up at Sam's. Maybe even the river would freeze over. Larry had never seen that; it would be something.

When he reached the top of the stairs, he turned and looked back down. The wind was blowing harder at the top; he wrapped his arms around himself to keep warm. There was a flapping noise, under the very top set of the stairs. A piece of the blue and white banner from the last home game – "Go Raiders!" "We Love You!!" He could see his breath, small, white streams, like he was smoking. The big field, far below now, almost like he was in an airplane – five turns of steep stairs. The bleachers on the far side looked odd completely empty and with snow on them. The field was completely white, his tracks as if never there. It was hard to imagine, standing there, the heat and dust and sweat of the August training camp. Just four months ago.

For a few minutes, he stood stock-still, like he was on a deer stand. He would not play on this field. The 1956 football season was over and football, for him, was over. Just like that. Although he was "just a kid", as Sam the barber liked to repeat so often, he felt something important had happened, and finished. He had crossed some line.

He could hear basketballs thudding inside the gym – practice. Unlike football, where you were completely encased in a uniform, pads and helmet, in basketball you wore very little. But in some ways, it was an even more physical sport because of that. He could see Mrs. Heald in the music room, and thought of the night of the Autumn Hop, so far back now, when he'd kissed Cameron Mitchell there. He'd never been the same after that. That had changed everything, everything. If he had a nickel for every time he thought of Cameron, he'd be a rich man – the old saying was true. When they passed each other in the school corridors, he could feel himself start to get red, like Norma Stearns. "She's not like other girls," he had answered to one of Frankie's endless jibes, and predictably Frankie had hooted. "Naw. Sure, Larry. Whatever you say." Frankie was getting to be a pain in the ass. The keister? Was that the word he'd heard somebody use? Frankie swooned in the hall. "Ohh Cameron!" he moaned, grabbing his crotch. "I got it hard for you…"

It would be quiet out in the corridors of the school, especially if you could get out there during classes. Particularly the long hall that ended at the upper end in those worn, hard concrete steps. The hallway even gleamed. Or was it like Frankie said? "You know what's the trouble with you. You like school! Now that's a serious problem, Larry. Do you know how serious that is?" You could hear the far-off factory noise of the shop class, a low rumble; nearer, the flushing roar of urinals in a restroom. But the space in the long straight corridor was empty now, free. He liked that, but couldn't have explained – at least not clearly – why. It did not matter *why*; that was part of it. It was a free space, like in the poems read in class, or even some instants in practice when everything meshed, and

459

you were certain it was right. Execution, Coach Rossi called it. Execution.

He turned again to look at the field. Snow flurries, coming down faster, thicker. Shades of gray, white, shifting screens of snow. The first real snow of the winter. It would be 1957, in a month. *1957.* The snow stung his face in the hard driving wind coming off the river, and he instinctively turned, hunched over, his collar turned up against the cold, damp, hard wind that went right to the bone.

He was starting to shiver but tried to stand still. He had walked aimlessly around Ralston and ended up at the railroad station, on top of the Highgrade. It, and the railroad tracks it carried, were little used now, compared to what had once been the case. And that was already within his own memory. People could catch a train as early as 5:00am, going down to Pittsburgh, stopping at most of the small towns in the Allegheny Valley on the way, although there were some trains that stopped only at New Kensington. He could remember being a kid and being there at the station – it seemed much bigger then – and it was Christmas Eve, and his aunt was coming up on the train from Pittsburgh. She would bring a raft of presents with her, and these were presents he knew he wanted to get, not the usual stuff, that you really didn't want. His aunt took real trouble to find out what he wanted, and got it for him.

They had, just to kill time, walked across the bridge to Garver's Ferry earlier in the evening, and even then it was turning colder, and there was light snow. His father had remarked that if it got under 15 degrees it wouldn't snow much, and if it really went down, to zero or lower, it wouldn't snow at all. Never did at those temperatures, he claimed, his breath steaming out.

Standing that evening on the old cement platform that functioned as the station for Garver's Ferry, they saw something they hadn't expected, or even thought to see. As they shifted from foot to foot to keep warm, blowing out clouds of breath, the snow tumbling in increasing amounts out of the dark sky above, they saw - really, they heard first – the *New York Limited*, the famous express train on its way out from the great city, going to Chicago, his father said. It pulled up and stopped there at Garver's Ferry, for what reason no one seemed to know, and he could see the faces of the people in the large windows inside the brightly lit train. They were having coffee served, and some men stood in the aisle smoking long, dark cigars. They were dressed in suits, with their hair carefully combed. A waiter moved among them in a white jacket and bow tie, a black man. "The steward," his father had said, pointing with a gloved hand. "See there? The steward. He knows what he's doing."

The train itself was sleek, curved, all smoothness, shininess, glinting silver. The cars were named, with large nameplates on them; the one in front of them was "City of Erie."

It was a Streamliner, a train such as he had only seen in drawings and photos in magazines, and he could not imagine why it had stopped in Garver's Ferry. Such a train was never seen in Ralston, where the passenger cars on the local runs were grimy, stained with rust, the upholstery faded. They were seedy, as his mother would say. Only the conductor got off the Streamliner, and went into a small shack at the far end of the platform that served as a place where railroaders and working crews could rest, apparently; it wasn't a working station, and you could not even buy a ticket there, his father said.

The stop was not long. Several people looked out from the long sleek car windows at him and his father, as steam hissed and rose in billowing clouds. Then, with a hypnotic smoothness, the long silver train glided into the falling snow, down the tracks, headed West. To Chicago, which, he had heard in Sam's, was the biggest railroad junction in not just the country, but the world.

After the streamliner was gone, they'd stood without saying anything in the falling snow for several minutes. His father shook his head wonderingly.

"It must be something. Ride in a train like that one. Ride in style! Yessir. Ride in style."

He had wondered if his father had ever been to Chicago. He wanted to ask, but felt he shouldn't, for some reason. Chicago, St. Louis, Detroit, Indianapolis, Cleveland – they were all to him pretty far away, and magical sounding places, the very names. How many had his father been to?

They had walked back across Garver's Ferry Bridge in the cold, saying little more than that it was "getting cold" – it already was cold – but he felt close to his father, and walked, that night, as close to him as he could.

# 32

Walking to school in the morning, he could see that the Christmas lights were already going up around the town. At Kathy Ferris' house, he saw a big tree in the front room, blazing with many lights, frosted with a load of icicles – but Kathy, he had heard, was at a home for unwed mothers down in Pittsburgh. It gave him a bad feeling. She was already very far away – much further than those thirty odd miles down Route 28, in the big city.

The night before, on one of his rambles, he'd seen the drunks in Adam's Tavern trying to put up a string of bubble lights inside, over the pool table, as he looked in through the side window. They saw him looking and leered at him. There would be Christmas lights draped over the goal posts, too, down on the field. There were still some leaves lying in a corner by the gym wall when he came in the side door. It had really gotten cold over the weekend. The leaves had a rime of frost coating them, and sparkled in the sun. He looked at them for a few minutes; they were grey and dark brown and twisted, crushed, shredded. Just a few weeks back they had still been on the trees and a bit earlier they had been green. In August they had probably wilted in the "dog days," the fierce heat of the days of the Training Camp, when everybody had a tan and the whole football season was out there in the future. "Before you, like a country you haven't seen." Mr. Turner, in his expansive mode, talking about the English course in those early fall days.

Now he had to talk to Coach Rossi. He had made his mind up – he had done this while swimming in the big pool down in the YMCA in Natrona Heights. ( In Sam's he'd inquired one day where the heights of Natrona Heights were, and where, for that manner, was Natrona itself?). An old-timer, Ed Moses, who was reputed to be half-black but nobody talked about it much, said "Think yer smart, don't ya? Tell ya what. They got the biggest goddam bottling plant in the country down there. Did ya know that, smarty-pants? Huh? All them goddam soft drinks, them different colors, and what the hell you think they put in there, to git them colors – huh? Right down there in Natrona Heights, that's where they do that. 24 hours a day." He had spat in the brass spittoon for emphasis, and hitched up his ponderous belly, from which his pants always threatened to separate. He wore no belt, but an old broad pair of frayed suspenders, like a farmer. Most of the old-timers like him suffered from ruptures, and wore trusses. Maybe they were in pain most of the time; that made them ornery. Moses liked the image of sticking someone's head in a can full of wasps. "That'd teach 'em," he would say, nodding grimly. "Damn right it would." But what would it teach them? Would it be like one of those things that football was supposed to teach you?

Like Ed Moses, Coach Rossi had a pocket knife that he would take out and twirl in his hand, back and forth between his forefinger and his big thumb, that looked like it had been broken once. In fact, his hands looked like they had been broken, or stepped on, and this was one of the scary things about him. All men in Ralston had such knives, or even deer knives, strapped in a leather sheath on their belt during the season, and worn while down by the creek fishing. A deer knife. And they all had Zippo lighters, although he doubted Coach Rossi had one, since he sternly forbade smoking to his players. It was as bad as the other – playing with yourself. Coach Rossi often laid the big pocket knife on a pile of file folders and papers on his desk in his coach's office; you could see it laying there. The file folders were different colors – red, blue, green, yellow, orange. Larry often wondered what was in them.

There were framed photographs in his office, too, which Larry wondered about – were they real ones? Red Grange, Ernie Nevers, Bronko Nagurski, Johnny Blood, the famous Steelers player from the 1930s. Elroy "Crazy Legs" Hirsch, the great Los Angeles receiver and Don Hutson, the "Alabama Antelope", the greatest end ever to play the game, it said in the history of pro football he'd read in the library, watching Miss Vukovich's legs. There was an older photo, somewhat blurred, of Jim Thorpe, the Indian who'd played at Carlisle. "Jim Thorpe, All-American", was printed in a scroll-like type underneath the photo. The greatest athlete in the world, who'd won a lot of medals in the Olympics and then they'd taken them from him. These were Coach Rossi's heroes, then. Probably he hadn't actually known them personally. Certainly not Jim Thorpe. But there they were, like gods. They were gods. There was even a town in Pennsylvania, over in the eastern half somewhere, named after Jim Thorpe.

During the football season, Coach Rossi and his wife visited players' families on weekday evenings, to talk and also, or so it was said, to make sure the player was keeping up Training. One of the Training Rules was that you would be home, studying, on weekday nights. So in a real way, at least during the season, for the Varsity players, the first string, you became family. He was close to his players, those who played four years or three years for him, there wasn't any question about it. Yet Larry felt he could never have been part of this extended family of Coach Rossi's. It was a painful realization he didn't completely under-stand. But he felt it, there was no question of that. He was one of those on the Outside, one who peered through the window into the coach's office, or the door, with *Coach's Office* lettered in blue and white on it.

He had rehearsed a speech, an explanation, many times. He didn't feel he could contribute to the team. He was taking someone else's place, who might be a better player. He was trying to play, but realized he really could not. He was too small, when all was said and done. Coach Kowalski had said in practice one day "If you weighed fifty pounds more, you'd be an All-American." He did have "heart." Even a few varsity players had said so. But he knew what he now had to do.

He had not told his mother of his decision, and he hadn't written to Carl about it, although he wished he had. The truth was that he was intensely embarrassed by it. It would rapidly spread around the school – that he was "not going out next year."

He had idled outside Coach Rossi's office so often he felt sure many had noticed it, and wondered what he was doing – maybe even guessed his intentions. Once, the Coach had entered the gym when he was sitting alone in the stands, looking at the gym floor and the rope hanging there, the mats tied up at the ends on the walls, into which basketball players sometimes smashed, having made a hard drive on the basket. It would have been the perfect time – seize the opportunity, execute! A coaching maxim – but he hadn't done it. He'd been thinking of Cameron, burying his face in her hair, and what kind of a guy was he to sit mooning in the gym thinking like that?

He imagined them driving somewhere, parking, the radio playing with that lush sound a good car radio had... making out. Nobody or nothing to stop them. How far would she let him go? And what would he do, if she "let him"? That phrase he'd heard so often in the locker room, guys hollering it out, "Did she let you? Huh?" Slapping a towel. He had heard so many descriptions of this, the only topic, relentless, of conversation. And there was the whole business of getting, having, rubbers.

Condoms. Frankie talked of this incessantly, and carried one around in his wallet, which he'd eagerly pull out and show. It was beginning to look bedraggled, and Larry wondered if it was still functional.

"So you gotta – see, you have *somebody*, to get 'em for you, or you have to buy them yourself. In the drug store. And the thing is, they have them behind the counter, and so you have to fucking *ask* for them! Shit! And then some of them, the druggists, they won't sell the goddamn things to you! Can you beat that?"

"Why? Why not?"

"Immoral. What do you want rubbers for? Huh? A kid your age. Only one reason."

"You could say you're buying them for somebody else. Your brother."

"Your brother! Sure! Try it. See if they believe you. Old man Thompson knows everybody who buys rubbers in the whole damn town. I'm telling you, Larry."

The only thing that gave him much relief, now that the football season was over – and for him it was already over for good, forever - was to think of escaping from Ralston High School, once and for all, going on to college. He hoped he would get into at least one or two places, and felt fairly certain he would. But how would he pay for it? The costs, especially living in a dorm on campus, were high. That thought, even, delayed him, for if he were able to somehow stick it out, keep playing, he could get some sort of scholarship through Coach Rossi's influence and help. But, of course, that would mean making the team at the college, and four more years of it. You would have to really like, love, football. And when he was honest with himself, he knew he did not. He didn't look forward to the practices, which some did, liking that more than any subject in school. With the games, he had somehow always felt outside of them, even when he played. No, there was no way he could convince himself. That was honest, the center of it.

What did he love, then? Poetry. And Cameron. He was in love with Cameron – *that* was the truth. Hopeless love. With Cameron Mitchell, and that hair. And the poetry they increasingly read together. That was revealing too – who would read poetry with Cameron Mitchell, when they could be making out with her? What kind of a guy was he?

It was a realization he could not name, like the one when spring finally came after the long cold icy winters, and you saw the first robin, or when you heard the unmistakable song later in the spring and early summer. Or those coon hounds, running in the late fall nights, up on River Hill, with the moon above it.

After the last JV game in November, down in the shower room, he had showered longer than usual, feeling that hot water ping on his body. The game had been played on the mud-soaked field and ended in a 12-0 victory for the JV. Over Chester, of all things. But he felt little elation, only relief. Coach Kowalski put him into the game three times, and his uniform was suitably dirty by the game's conclusion. He felt sure he had a pretty good bruise on his leg – a helmet hit from a fat kid who'd submarined on a play.

He could see, as they came in and out of the shower room after this game, how hairy some of the guys had gotten, just since the summer. Comparatively, he was still without that much sign of being a male, a man. Body hair – the chest, under the arms, of course, in the crotch. Was it the same with girls? He recalled some comment in biology class that girls matured quicker, faster, than boys physically. If he saw Cameron naked, would she have luxuriant hair, like her great mane? What a thought that was! This was what he was coming to.

The whole school, it seemed, was getting strange. Maybe only football kept it together, that goal of the championship. Frankie told him Goran had "jerked off" in one of the boys room, wearing a rubber, and then showed it to people. "Maybe next thing you know, they all get their dicks out and do it, too," he said, shaking his head. "That Goran's a sick bastard…"

Did Coach Rossi keep condoms in his desk for some of his players? Was it in this very office that Dago Paretti got the ones he used when he fucked Cameron, as the story had it, going around? But that was not a true story. He knew it was not… Why did he think of such things?

The word. The Word. Fuck – ugly. Yet, loitering around as he did, all sorts of garbage came into his mind. His mind was becoming the proverbial cesspool, a phrase the coach himself used in his health lectures. "Two hundred and six bones in the human body, what a machine, a marvel of engineering. And the mind – a cesspool!"

That day in early December, loitering like he'd been, Coach Rossi suddenly came around the corner, from the opposite end of the corridor, stopped, and asked him "Do you want to see me, Larry?" And so he had had the conversation.

Coach Rossi opened the office door, he went in first, noticing the smell of the office, the smells, for it was a complex odor of sweat, leather, wool and old coffee, and the wax from the gym floor. Dust, papers and books, and then a smell which he could only think of as the coach's personal smell, which was not a bad smell.

Coach Rossi indicated, with a gesture of his hand, a chair that sat facing his desk, which he simultaneously sat down behind. It was quiet in the office, and even calm. The coach looked at him expectantly.

"I just wanted – I wanted to tell you that – I don't think I can come out next year. For the team." There it was.

The coach leaned back slightly in his chair, which Larry noted was really a special chair, a much better one than most of the teachers had. It looked like real leather, very comfortable. He wondered if he'd bought it himself.

"I see." He nodded slightly, and picked up a paper clip, an orange one, from his desk, and looked at it, and then at Larry, putting it back down carefully. "Well. You know, I thought you might be thinking of this. And I'm glad you came to me, told me." He nodded affirmatively.

"So am I," Larry said hurriedly, then thought how that sounded, and looked down for a second. "I mean – I feel I have to tell *you*. The sooner, the better. Not that – I mean, not that I would be a player or anything that you'd be thinking about, for next year, I mean." He stopped; he was beginning to babble.

"Well, you never know. Things can change. People can change. At your age, you might put on thirty pounds by next fall, and be four, five inches taller. Be a terror." He grinned suddenly, and Larry saw the deep creases coming from his eyes, which made him look kindly, different. "And I've seen that happen…But you're sure about this, is that it? You wanted to be sure I knew."

Larry found he couldn't speak, and nodded his head energetically, not too much so, he hoped.

"I see. Have you told Coach Kowalski about this?"

Larry shook his head. "No. I haven't. Just you."

"Okay," Coach Rossi said, and then stretched out his hand. Larry realized he was supposed to shake it, and he did. The coach's big hand was warm, and larger than he'd expected, and his grasp was rough, like that of a working man, somebody who worked with their hands. A favorite expression in Ralston. Work with your hands. "Thanks for coming and telling me, Larry." He nodded. "I know it wasn't easy. To make this decision. But I think it's the best one, for you. And I want you to know I appreciate you making it."

Larry felt as if the air was going out of him, as if out of an over-inflated tire. He could not keep from sighing; he looked around, the framed photos, all of it. "Did you – did you know these players?" he asked, surprised even as he said it. "They're really – famous."

The coach shook his head. "Oh, no. I couldn't say that. I met a couple of them, once or twice. That was a long time ago, too."

Coach Rossi absently moved the big pocket knife slightly on a stack of file folders. Maybe those were college materials, Larry suddenly thought; information about scholarships. Letters.

"You planning on going to college, Larry?" the coach asked, looking at him. This close, his eyes were a deep brown-black, large and luminous. Squint lines around his eyes – squinting into the sun during practices. How many practices had he been to? Larry wondered.

It was the question, or one of them, that he'd dreaded. He could feel his face flush, get warm. He shook his head. "Well – I want to go. Yes."

"I hear you're doing well in your academics. *Very* well. Keep it up, that's the way to go. You could win an academic scholarship." He looked out over Larry's shoulder briefly. "You never know what can happen in life. Keep that in mind, will you?"

"I will," Larry nodded. "I will."

The coach nodded again, and then stood up. Larry stood up quickly also, stumbling slightly as he did so. The coach came around the edge of his desk and put his hand on Larry's shoulder – it was a gesture he'd seen a hundred or more times, with the coach and one of the players, and he felt suddenly good, more positive. Coach Rossi had never done that before. "What you did – coming here, to me, and telling me of your decision – this is not something that's easy to do. I want you to know that I know that. And I respect what you've done, and your decision."

They were at the door to the office, and Coach Rossi opened it, and smiled. When he smiled, he looked a different person. It was amazing, how stern and fearsome he could look, and then his warm smile. He held out his hand again, and Larry shook it, feeling that harsh roughness of his fingers and even his palm. Large hands. The better to strongly grip and throw a football. Larry shook the coach's hand, stepped out the door, and heard it close quietly behind him.

He would not tell anyone in the school about what he'd done. As he walked away from the office, he wondered if anyone had seen them in there, talking. After all, why would he, Larry Simmons, be in Coach Rossi's office? It was more likely that Charlie Hibbing would be.

How long would it take, then, for it to get around the school? Because it would, and people would say, even at Sam's, "Heard you're not goin' out next year, Larry. Is that right? Givin' it up, eh?" The rest was not said, of course, or asked. Why not? Are you afraid of getting hurt? Getting your mouth smashed? Lose a few teeth…What was that phrase of Goran's? *Pussy boy.*

There was also a phrase he'd heard at Sam's. Pussy-whipped. Many men were pussy-whipped, it seemed, in Ralston. It was not like it used to be.

In his rambling aimlessly, thinking about what had just happened, he found he was back around the other side of the gym, where a door was open, and he could see the tall rope swaying, dangling down from the girder, the one that had given him fits earlier in the year. Something for a PE class, probably. The gym seemed small suddenly, old. He looked across the floor and thought of how many things had already happened there for him. Maybe it was the most important room in the school, in an odd way. There was no escaping it – and its smells. He was sure he would remember the gym smell, especially, as long as he lived, and that as soon as he mentioned it, others would smile and nod, remembering it as exactly as he did. It was, he thought, like the smell of church, in its way.

In the far corner sat the small white scale on which the players had been weighed, back in August. The doctor had said to Larry, "Kinda light, you are, young fella…" He listened longer than usual to Larry's heart, shook his head slightly, and touched him lightly on the arm. "Okay," he had said, but Larry had wondered. Why had he listened longer to his heart?

He had not gained much weight in the season, although he'd certainly tried. He ate a pint of ice cream after supper religiously for a month, for example. His mother had done her best to aid and abet him, smiling as if she knew something he didn't, like the whole project was doomed to failure from its start.

Early that summer they had sat at the kitchen happily eating one of his mother's favorites, a half of a cantaloupe with vanilla ice cream scooped into it. He remembered a dinner where they had had fried chicken, done perfectly (not soggy or greasy) and sliced beefsteak tomatoes right off the vines, with iced tea and mint leaves (the way his mother invariably made iced tea). There had also been a chocolate cake. He had eaten until he thought he might truly burst. It was too good to be true, that dinner; all was perfect.

Then there had been those Reward Dinners, in Vandergrift at an Italian restaurant that had a huge electric neon sign – "Luigi's" – in green, with an arrow. They were rewards for selling a certain number of subscriptions to the Pittsburgh Sun-Gazette newspaper – he had been a kid then, and even skinnier, if that was possible. The dinner started with a small green salad, something he had no taste for – Rabbit Food, he secretly called it. Adults said they loved salads, but he felt it was some kind of lie they all told to get kids to eat salads, vegetables. He could not remember a single salad he'd really enjoyed.

But then the gears shifted, the wonderful smells began to waft out of the kitchen, and they were served large plates of steaming spaghetti in a rich meat sauce. Even his mother's spaghetti wasn't as good – or maybe this was equal to his mother's. Following the big plate of spaghetti was a sizzling platter with a T-bone steak on it.

He'd never seen the sizzling platter before, and the steak came smothered in mushrooms and butter, done perfectly. Every time he thought of those steaks his mouth watered.

After finishing the T-bone, he was stuffed, ready to throw in the towel. But, it was then announced with smiles, there was still dessert! This announcement, which normally he'd have welcomed, made him a little queasy, something he could not have imagined normally, when he was hungry all the time. And the dessert was home-made apple pie and ice cream. He had had to pass on it, knowing that he risked being sick if he tried eating that, after the meal he'd just finished.

Food. Another thing he thought about increasingly. Why was he always hungry?Ravenous – that was the word. Sausages and buckwheat cakes in the bitter cold winter mornings. He would remember it, he felt sure, as an old man, because the old men at Sam's were forever talking about how the food was "in their day," and how it was no good now.

"You take that goddamn syrup – that's what they call it, but it ain't nothin' but sugar – they sell in the store nowdays? Now, you couldn't buy any *maple* syrup, even if you had the money! No! Why, hell, you can't even find a sugar maple tree! But that's the only kinda syrup worth a shit, you ask me, with hot cakes and sausage…and the goddamn ham they got these days! You gotta wonder what kinda hog it come from. Or maybe it don't come from no hog, but they *make* it! Goddamn artificial hams, full a water, all that shit. Gonna poison all of us, fer damn sure."

How old would he live to be? Maybe not as old as them, if half of what they prophesied came true. In the English literature book there was mention of a man in England who lived to be 152 years old. He was brought to London, so people could meet and see him, and then he died shortly thereafter.

In Pittsburgh, in the big restaurants there, they were said to eat food that only the rich, whoever that was, could get. It was brought to them on a big cart, and then they sat it in front of them, and took off a silver cover. And there it was. But *what* was it? A bird of some kind? A steak, or a chop, or a roast, or maybe some big fish, one you never heard of, from the ocean somewhere. Maybe a lobster! And how would you eat that?

Maybe if he went to college in Pittsburgh, or some such place, he'd get a job as a waiter, and find these things out. He would serve the rich, take the cover off that dish, and watch to see the reaction of the rich person. Put a steaming turd on the dish. No. He was thinking like that increasingly, too – it was the effect of that bastard Goran and all that stuff he dragged around with him, and his stories, and his jibes and cracks. Goran was a smart ass. He would get his, too. Maybe they would pull him from a car somewhere out on a back road some night, beat the living shit out of him, and leave him in the ditch. That could happen. "Kick his nuts off!" as Coach Barnes would say. Or yell, "Tear his fuckin' nuts off!"

It was going to be a long two years to go, to finish Ralston High School, let alone think of college, and being a waiter somewhere. Maybe he would buy a red jacket like the one James Dean wore in *Rebel*. The collar turned up. A cigarette. That was a fantasy. Nothing could come of it. He had to knuckle down – "sharpen your knife," as his brother said. "Keep your gear squared away." Marine Corps jargon, but maybe it was good advice. He wished, for sure, that Carl was around much more, and they could talk. Go fishing. He was certain, in fact, that if he could go fishing with his brother Carl that a number of his difficulties would be solved. And they would catch some damn good fish, too. Keepers.

Actually, when he thought of it – and he had a lot of time to think, it seemed, these days, now that the season was over – Carl had shown him a great deal. Stuff he'd learned in the service. He knew how to spit-shine shoes now, how to hang his shirts, buttoned, in the closet, and he had tried his hand at pressing his own pants, with his mother smiling and shaking her head. And there were the argyle socks, lined up, stacked neatly in his drawer, along with his underwear rolled tightly the way they did it in the service. Keep your area orderly – squared away, there was that phrase. Carl told him there was even a room called the Orderly Room in the barracks. Men regularly went around picking up cigarette butts, scraps of paper – "policing the area," Carl called it.

On the wall of the corridor somebody had penciled – this was strictly forbidden, but it was hard to stop – a lop-sided heart. Inside of it was written "Deanna Long – Bill Short." Who had done that? There were no such students in the school, as far as he knew. So what did it mean? Who could tell? But people would snicker about it, nevertheless. And, soon, someone would add a crude drawing. A large penis, drops of cum dripping, falling. To such a drawing in the boys room, someone had scrawled "Drip, drip. Heh heh!"

If he ran into Cameron, he'd try to get her to go up to the library and read some poems. That, that would save him. He had even thought of trying to write a poem, but the very idea staggered him. When he'd talked with Cameron, she had said, "Write a poem about a blast furnace. The steel mill. Football, Larry!" But people didn't write poems about these things.

"*...and lots of curly hair, like Liberace.*" He caught a snatch of music – The Chordettes, someone playing a 45 on one of those little 45 players? The girls sat around playing 45s, endlessly talking, if they were allowed to. Pajama parties – one of the girls' clubs had put up some photos on a bulletin board in home room of a party. How could they talk so much? About what? Giggling, talking, giggling, talking. But that wasn't fair. What about the boys, grabbing the crotch and giving the finger, making the fart noises? Goran's cards. There was one that showed a man behind a woman who was licking another woman. He couldn't get the image out of his mind.

People were saying he went to the library so much to look at Miss Vukovich's legs. Probably true, too. He was far gone, there wasn't any doubt, in the girl thing. It was increasingly hard to concentrate, to think of anything but Cameron, or Miss Vukovich, or a hundred other images that flooded unbidden into his mind. Hard. Ho, ho! Frankie had laughed, pointing. The library was beginning to seem smaller than it had before, though. He had read in the newspaper of a library at the University of Pittsburgh with six floors. How many books would that be?

Red Grange. Ernie Nevers. Ernie Stautner, the Steelers' defensive star – they were always good on defense, the Steelers. He would think of these names, and others, as he walked around the echoing halls. Where had they gone to high school? He mother told him that until recently, many people stopped school at the eighth grade. That was hard to believe. A time when a high school diploma was out of the ordinary. *"Graduated high school."* "The day'll come", his mother said, "when a high school diploma will be as common as an eighth grade certificate was. And then, then it'll be a college degree."

He also thought of Walt Whitman and Shakespeare and Edgar Allen Poe – he had read "The Fall of the House of Usher," a really scary story, the summer before. Poe must have been a strange man. He was buried in Baltimore, had died "in the gutter." He wondered if this was literally true, the business about the gutter. He knew his father had lain in the gutter, in the mud. It was bad he'd come to that, but Larry didn't know what he could do about it. Maybe he would end up there, too, and find out what it was like.

Like father, like son. A bum. Many men in the Valley did, when all was said and done.

He was beginning to wander around the school like he did the town, he thought. The teachers would notice, and begin to ask him about it; why wasn't he studying? On the Bulletin Board outside the principal's office, they had put up some penmanship exercise papers. These looked amazing. The discovery, in grade school, that you could create beautiful letters and then words, and then sentences. Looking at the lined papers, he remembered the inked writing, the tracery of it, the feel of it, when it went well. It was like magic. Girls, usually, did consistently well at it; he could not remember a boy who had, although sometimes the teacher would display a boy's work. It almost always looked clumsy and heavy, thick, next to the delicate lines of the girls' work. But the boys had been better at making the Indian village teepees out of the brightly colored aluminum foil milk bottle caps – red, white and blue, with an occasional orange, although few chose the orange drink.

Next to the penmanship examples was a listing of some seniors who'd received early college admission letters. He did not really know some of them, except for those on the football team. Dago Paretti was going to Lehigh – a small college in the eastern part of the state. Didn't even know they had a football team. Thinking bitterly, Larry felt certain the Dago would flunk out after a semester or two. "A dumb ass," Frankie had said, although he looked around himself as he said it. Everyone knew Dick Atkins had decided on Duke. The university had had him down to the campus twice already, once with his parents. "It looks like some place in England – old buildings like that. Real green lawns," he said. But Robert Henderson wasn't going to Princeton – he would not become a Tiger. It wasn't known yet where he'd go. Harry Gibb had had an early acceptance, full scholarship, to Pitt, after all, not Duke. And the *Valley* newspaper reported that Hunter, the Chester running back, was going to Duke, so he and Dick Atkins would be teammates – "Blue Devils." At Duke, the football players lived and ate in a special dorm, and it was said that dates were lined up for them with girls there. Larry wondered if this was true, or just another rumor.

Fred Lucas. He was going on a full scholarship to Muhlenberg College, and it was the rumor that he and Holly Burris wanted to get married. He would stay in Ralston and work out at the brickyard, where his father worked. Larry hoped that this was just a rumor. He felt certain both Fred and Holly would end up unhappy if this happened. On the other hand, if Fred Lucas went to Muhlenberg, how could he play well, study, do all he'd need to do, if he was always worrying about Holly? And if they broke up? But that seemed impossible. Maybe not to adults, but anyone who saw them around the school, constantly together, or in Fred's '51 green Mercury with the windshield visor knew the scrawled notations around the school – "*Fred/Holly Forever.*" "*Holly/Fred True Love!*" – were real. They were in love. To break them up would be a terrible thing.

When he thought about the intensity of their feelings, the certainty, that was how he felt about Cameron. He was walking the halls in endless fantasies of her. It was like he was drunk, in a way. When he'd heard some guys horsing around in the locker room, suggesting things about her, he thought he would burst, smash their heads into the lockers, call them out. Cameron wasn't that kind of girl. But how did he know?

"They're all that kind of girl," Frankie claimed, as they'd sat outside the side door of the gym one day. "With the right guy. That's what I think. So don't put Cameron on a pedestal. But you're that kinda guy, come to think of it. Aren't you?"

There was a single sheet of paper next to the College list – he thought of the listings of who'd made the team, back in August, and the home room assignments. It had only one sentence. "Joseph Labrador has been expelled from Ralston High School." It was like a death sentence, or something. It was cruel to put it up; everyone knew it. The business with Norma Stearns had been too much. Joe would become a full-fledged greaser now, no doubt. "He'll be lucky to escape Reform School," Goran had said, uncharacteristically, as they stood at the urinal in the boys room. Above the urinal, someone had scrawled "What are you looking at? The joke's in your hand." But Goran looked worried. Maybe it could happen to him.

There was yet another list, about the class play, the Junior Play, already in rehearsal. So this must be an old list, and the secretaries had forgotten to remove it, or the drama teacher, Mr. Herbert, had kept it there. Mr. Herbert was a dramatic person. He made expansive, large gestures while he taught his Literature classes, and students loved to mock these, enact them after he passed by in the hall. Goran was good at this, surprisingly. Mr. Herbert also wore bow ties, which nobody in Ralston (except little boys with their first suits or sports jackets) wore. Certainly none of the other male teachers did. The class play was "January Thaw" and it had gone around school that there would be a real live pig that appeared in this play. How could that be, he wondered? What if it got loose, ran into the audience, squealing? Maybe that was intentional, though – part of the dramatic action. He knew nothing about "January Thaw", but thought he would go to see it, maybe try and get his mother to go, just to see this pig, see if it was really true there was one.

The previous year, in Spring, the play had been "Time Out For Ginger", which he had enjoyed. It had an unusual plot, about a girl who went out for the high school football team, and made it, which upset and confused her father. But he changed, supported her, ending up running around the stage wearing a raccoon coat, waving a school banner for her. When he thought about that play, it seemed it was actually more about the father than Ginger, who really had not appeared in the play that much. He had never known a girl named Ginger, and didn't know one in the whole town or surrounding area, either. "Time Out For Ginger" had been very successful – they had repeated it for an additional week – which was a big surprise to everyone. He wondered if any of the football team went to it. Or the coaches.

In Sam's, an old man from a farm "way out past The Corners", which was where Goran's family lived, complained that night baseball games were bad. "Just plain bad. They don't make no sense, playin' baseball at night! You ask me, that's when this country started to go to hell. Yessir!"

But nobody said that about night football games, although the game was originally played, must have been played, in daylight. He could remember childhood games of baseball going on into the buggy twilight in late Spring when you could hardly see the ball. Baseball. He had played in a game on a street in the Lower End once when someone hit the ball in a hard line drive that smashed through the window of a house behind first base. Everyone had frozen, as if in suspended motion, and then ran in every direction as the shattered glass fell out of the window.

His mother had taken to watching more television. She liked *The Halls of Ivy*, and tried to get him to watch it. Robert Young was the professor, and the campus looked just as Larry imagined a college campus should look, and must look like. Robert Young wore sports coats with patches on the elbows – sometimes he wore cardigan sweaters, and he had seen one episode where he'd had on a v-neck sweater. And he smoked a pipe. "All college professors must smoke pipes," his mother said. "They always show them that way. You never see one smoking a cigarette, do you?"

Larry could not say. He hadn't even really thought about it. It was a mark of his mother, her way, that she would notice something like that, which maybe nobody else did. Or if they did, they didn't say it. But maybe that was what people did when they got old. She was getting older, even as he did. Always ahead of him, of course.

Would she ever remarry? He somehow didn't think she would, although there had been a couple of men who'd taken her out on dates. He found it hard to think of these "dates," what they would be like. They went to some restaurant, usually, or this is what she said. Maybe a movie, down at the Manos in Tarentum – a big, fancy movie theater, painted in shades of blue and green. What did the name of the theater mean? Nobody seemed to know, or care for that matter. It was just a name, a movie theater, it didn't mean anything. When he'd pressed Frankie about it, he'd said, "That's typical of you, Larry. You just think too damn much. You probably are gonna die before you're thirty, like that guy told your stepfather you would."

He definitely tried not to think of his stepfather, and his father. But then he did. Was it fair that at 16 he'd had both? There was something wrong with it, it affected him, but it was definitely a topic nobody could talk about. He sensed that, sometimes, in the way people would look at him. As if he was a lost, sad kid. Maybe he was. Like James Dean was.

Some of his stepfather's tools were still gathering dust down in the cellar. If he used the old shower that he had put in down there, he inevitably thought of him, showering for long periods of time down there in the hot summer evenings, when he'd come home from work. Later, he would stand in his garden, wearing a white undershirt, playing the garden hose on the plants just at twilight, that time when the lightning bugs first started to wink on and off, and it really started to get cooler. "Cool off," people said, sitting on their front porches drinking iced tea, or maybe lemonade. Some drank beer, but not that many. Not in public; that was kept inside the house. Before television had come in, in the summer, they would sit like that and listen to the Pirates baseball games. Bob Prince was the announcer. The same reliable voice, like the newsreels. You felt like you knew him, although you wouldn't recognize him if you saw him. But the voice was unmistakable. It wasn't like the disc jockeys' voices, which probably could be replaced by other disc jockeys' voices.

The truth was he missed his stepfather's presence in the house. Even his smell – sweaty often, but often, too, fresh from the shower or bath. His mother said he was a "clean man." It was reassuring, he felt relaxed, even though at times he feared him, since he was not really his father. He missed Carl in the same way – Carl, who was down in North or South Carolina and probably would not get home on Christmas leave, according to his latest letters. His mother claimed Carl had met a girl down there. That's how she put it. Carl had said nothing of this in his letters, though.

Parris Island, South Carolina – that was where they put you through Boot Camp. He remembered Carl saying that out of 80 men who began training with him, only 54 finished. The others "washed out." The phrase bothered him. "Washed out." Was that what had happened to him with the football team? Was he a "wash-out"? It sounded like you were a failure, and made him feel heavy, bad.

He found he had walked around, through the corridors of the school, all those intense, familiar smells and the dusty light and the cracked floors, twice – at least. He felt odd, as if he wasn't really there at all. "Floating through it," Ducky would say.

The year was coming to an end. 1956. They were building new houses out along Route 28, near Slate Lick – where there had used to be only farms, barns and silos – for $12,000. A newly built house, outside Ralston a few miles north up on a slight rise, was said to be worth $30,000, an unimaginable sum to him. Hell, a new car was about $2,100. How would you ever get that much money?

Rocky Marciano had retired undefeated, after beating Archie Moore. 49 fights. The Brockton Blockbuster. It looked like the New York Giants, not the Cleveland Browns, would win the Pro football championship. The Steelers weren't even in it. The poor Steelers – he couldn't remember them ever having been in contention for the championship. Yet they were one of the original eight pro teams. He would have to check and see if they'd ever won the championship, the title.

It was becoming the time of year for topcoats. He'd never had one, he was too young to wear a topcoat. But they looked sharp. They were warm, too, much better than a jacket, since they reached to your knees, some even lower. Most were of nice wool; the best, advertised in the Pittsburgh papers (at Kaufmann's; Scheer's carried them, too) were of cashmere, which his mother said was too expensive to even think about. "But it would last you forever, a cashmere top coat..." she'd said, looking at him.

Something that was odd was that no man ever wore a hat or cap with a top coat, even if it was zero out or snowing heavily. No hat. You could see mens' heads when they came inside, covered with snow, melting, running down their face, their top coats stiff with snow, powdered like a cake. Why no hat? Nobody could say for sure when he'd asked at Sam's. The President, General Eisenhower, was completely bald and Larry wondered if that had anything to do with it. But he had seen photos on old record jackets from the Forties, showing men in top coats without hats. Maybe it started then.

Walking walking walking. Oh Cameron. That was what he found himself almost saying out loud, walking and walking and walking in the hallways of Ralston High School. If he thought hard enough about her, she would sense he was thinking of her and think of him, maybe even show up, magically. And this was the type of stuff Frankie called "bullshit." He thought again of Goran, snarling down the hall at another kid, his face twisted,

"Cogsugger!" Goran was no bullshitter, was he? You knew where he stood, what he thought.

"He'll end up pumping gas somewhere, you watch what I say," was what Ducky said, and he often said nothing, so you had to listen when he did.

"Nothin' wrong with that, is there? Pumpin' gas." Frankie retorted. Ducky made no reply, but shook his head.

As for him, 1956 would be the year he had tried to play football and learned he couldn't. Or wouldn't. He would be a junior the coming year, and then a senior. Graduating. Three years after that, he'd be legal – twenty-one. Out in the Big World somewhere, as his mother would say standing by the sink drying dishes. Where would all of them be, by then? All the football players, the varsity, the Starting Eleven? They would already be forgotten, even in Ralston. Fred Lucas, married with two kids and Holly getting fat, Fred working the midnight shift at the brickyard, getting off and hitting the tavern in the mornings before coming home, getting fat himself? The two girls that had gotten pregnant and gone down to Pittsburgh to have the babies which would have been taken from them? They couldn't come back, could they? They didn't allow that. Joe Labrador, a small time crook? Goran – Frankie suggested several times he'd publish dirty magazines and books. "A natural!" Would Coach Rossi still be Head Coach – would Ralston finally win the Championship, after all those years?

He was passing by the library again. Miss Vukovich came out the far door, stopped, and raised her skirt over her smooth, full knee, reaching up, adjusting her stocking. She saw him, he was sure, but she did not speak – simply lowered her skirt, and went walking off down the hall. He was stopped in his tracks, and his mouth was suddenly dry. He looked quickly around the hallway, feeling guilty – why should he feel that way? – but there was no one. When he looked back down the hall, all he could see was the top of her head, disappearing even as he looked, going down the stairs.

# 33

Right before school ended for the Christmas holidays, it snowed heavily. There was talk of the school closing – snow days – but they didn't do it. The principal stood smiling outside his door; the Christmas tree winked and glowed in the middle of the hallway directly inside the main front doors. Christmas carols came over the PA system each morning and at the lunch hour. The principal's two secretaries wore small Santa Claus pins, or reindeer, or plump white snowman pins. Every room in the school was filled with Christmas decorations made by the students. There were some great drawings of the comic book characters Archie, Jughead, Betty, and Veronica, celebrating Christmas. Had high school students ever really been like that? Still, the drawings were good ones. The football season was long gone now, although there were still some photos up of Fred Lucas running through the line at the Plum game; Dick Atkins, number 12, cocking his arm, the ball back, looking confident. But they already looked old.

The snow was deep enough for sled-riding and as soon as school finished in the afternoons he saw many smaller kids dragging their sleds towards the steep hill right in the middle of town, Hammer's Hill (who had Hammer been? Nobody seemed to know, although the regulars at Sam's argued about it when he brought it up).

He had once ridden his sled down Hammer's Hill and under a parked car, on a dare. This was similar to the challenge of having the train run over you, laying in the bed of the tracks. There had been one year when it had gotten very cold and stayed that way, and people tried to ride all the way down Hammer's Hill, out onto the ice of Buffalo Creek on their racketing sleds. To do that, you had to get a hell of a long hard run before you belly-flopped down on the racketing sled. Occasionally, when it got really icy, the sled would outrun the racer, and they would crash down onto the hard, frozen street. Only big kids succeeded. They became famous that winter for it. Rode right out onto Buffalo Creek! And the ice held. But lately he had wondered if these tales were true – he had never seen anyone actually do it, run out onto the ice like that. Ducky said he did not believe it, and had spat to the side when he said it as if to punctuate his statement. Then he had uttered one word. "Bullshit."

Maybe it was one of those stories like the one about the huge ten-point buck that was said to live up on the River Hill, but nobody had ever been able to bring him down, or even shoot him. But hunters swore they had seen him. In Sam's, many attested to his being there. "I tell ya, that's the biggest goddamned buck you'll ever see! Old Pete – the Swede – he said he started shakin' so bad when he did see him, he couldn't bring his rifle up steady to get off a shot at him…You see a deer like that, what'd you do?" When he had discussed this one year in hunting season with Carl, he had smiled and admitted he had never seen the big ten-point, but had heard of it from those who said they had. "That deer's smart. He's been around that long, he's clever." Lying in his bed later that night, he imagined that if the deer was shot they'd mount his head, his rack, up at Sam's. Or worse, in Adam's Tavern. He hoped nobody would get the big ten-point buck, but he never told this to anyone, certainly not at Sam's.

He made long walking expeditions around the town so much his mother asked him peevishly, "Don't you ever get tired of walking around like that? What are you *doing*?" He did not know, that was the truth. He had seemingly endless reserves of restless energy. He felt that in some way he was already visiting his past, but he was just a teenager, so how could that be? The town, Ralston, seemed on these walks to be getting old right before his eyes.

He'd go by the Ritz Theater, which he knew was old even when he was a kid. It was a very small movie theater. Here he'd seen films when he was five, six years old, fearing a taller kid would sit in front of him, or, worse, an adult. The screen towered above him, with huge, floating images, faces, on it. He felt like he was in church, but his mother had laughed when he'd said it.

One image he recalled for no particular reason he could understand, except that it was from World War II which had been everything when he was a small child, was an aircraft carrier, its huge deck oddly yellow, with a burning plane, slipping off over the side into the ocean. He had wondered if the pilot was still in it. Perhaps it had been in a newsreel; these he recalled vividly, especially the stern voice of the announcer, always the same man, and the stirring music. Then there were the "Selected Short Subjects," as they were announced. These were often short films about an inept, bumbling man who made continual errors trying to repair his house, or install something, and suffered the consequences. The audience laughed uproariously. These shorts were still running; fairly recently, they'd shown one of the bumbling man trying to install a new television antenna on his roof. Just as the man was about to make some particularly disastrous move – backing up towards the edge of the roof in this short – the announcer would yell out "Oh no!" Then, as the man proceeded to "do it," the announcer would groan "Oh yes!" It was always the same man who starred (if that term could be applied) in these shorts, and Larry wondered if he had ever made any other films? Probably as an extra, a bit player, Frankie had speculated. In any case, he was famous, in an odd way. As soon as the music of these shorts came on and his face was seen, the audience began to laugh and snicker. There was something relaxing about these little films.

At The Ritz he, and every other small boy in the town, had seen *She Wore A Yellow Ribbon* and went around afterwards wearing bandanas around their necks, while their mothers tried to get them off. Like the cavalry, they had run through the backyards and alleyways of Ralston, whooping and yelling, their bandanas streaming, slapping their legs like they were horses, and shooting off cap pistols. If someone had had a bugle, they would have blown that loudly, too.

And it was at the Ritz that he fell in love with the woman who was the mermaid in *Mr. Peabody and the Mermaid*, and with Deanna Durbin. Esther Williams, who always appeared in a swimsuit, was another passion, and the dark-haired Hedy Lamarr, in a film with the zany Bob Hope playing an inept detective, who spied through keyholes.

And for some reason he remembered the singer Mario Lanza, who he didn't like anyway, in a film called *The Student Prince*, where Lanza, in a tavern, roared out "Drink, drink, drink! Lift your steins, and drink your beer!" Why did he remember that? Maybe the continual masturbation was effecting his brain, already. He had not seen the great western, *Shane*, because he didn't like Alan Ladd. And for that matter he hadn't seen James Dean's first film, *East of Eden*, either. Nor had he seen Marlon Brando in *The Wild One*. But that might have been due to the fact that those pictures hadn't yet played at the Ritz. His mother said the Brando film was "violent," implying it was a dangerous picture to see. One thing he was sure of and that was that seeing James Dean smoking cigarettes in *Rebel Without A Cause* had got him to sneak up to the attic one night and light an Old Gold Straight, which set off a furious fit of coughing that alarmed his mother. But he had successfully kept her from coming up, where she'd have smelled the smoke. Later, he had had an interesting conversation with Frankie about how many actors and actresses smoked in movies, and if it would be possible to find a movie where nobody did. "Maybe a cartoon," Frankie had said. Then he'd looked at Larry, and said "You come up with the damnedst ideas. You know that? I can't figure you out sometimes, Larry, even though you're my friend. Probably my best friend."

"Neither can my mother," he had replied, and they both laughed loudly.

When he would walk by the Ritz when there weren't movies playing, in the daytime, it seemed as if it was already quite old, from another era. The marquee was small and worn with paint flaking off, and the light bulbs running around it were often burnt out in funny patterns that made him think of someone with missing teeth.

It gave him a bad feeling. If he had owned the Ritz, he would have had it repainted, put in new seats (softer ones), and gotten rid of the stale, moldy smells that seemed to always be in it. He would have stood outside the front doors greeting people as they came, too, and maybe even as they left, asking them how they liked the picture. Just like a pastor in church did.

After school finished one day near the end of the last week before Christmas, he stopped in at Mr. Turner's room, seeing him sitting alone at his desk reading a book. Turner asked him about that book of Thoreau's, *Walden*, that he'd given him earlier in the fall. Mr. Turner looked tired, there were large, dark circles under his dark eyes, and his skin was an unhealthy white color. "Fish belly," people would say, shaking their heads. "That's a bad sign, when you get that fish belly look." Turner seemed glad, though, to see him and waved him to a chair beside the desk.

"Just like college, Larry. You come and talk with your professor...you're going to like college." Mr. Turner already seemed certain Larry would go, but Larry wasn't sure at all, and lying in his room at night in the dark, he had stared up at the ceiling and felt his heart shrink at what lay ahead of him if he didn't manage somehow to go to college.

"Have you read much of it, then? *Walden?* I know – it's a tough book, an old style of writing. Nineteenth century. We don't write like that anymore. At all."

"I've kinda read – *in* it. Like, dipping into it. The first chapter's pretty long."

Turner nodded his head, smiled. "'Economy.' Funny title, for the first chapter in a book, eh?"

"How long did it take him to write it?" He had wanted to ask this; how long did it take someone to write a book?

"What do you think? Take a guess." Turner looked at him intently.

"I was reading some of it to Cameron, in the library – she said she thought it took him all his life."

Mr. Turner nodded, flicked a particle of paper off his desktop; a paperclip slid with it, making a tiny sound, then dropping to the floor. "You read *Walden*, to Cameron?"

"Just a small part. She liked it." Larry felt nervous talking about her, and realized that everyone in the whole school knew of their meetings in the library, their whispered exchanges. Reading poetry!

"Larry, it's great you read it to her. Yes…I admire you for that."

"Cameron likes reading. She likes literature. Poetry. Whitman. Shakespeare. ee cummings. The guy that doesn't capitalize?""

"You read cummings?" Turner smiled broadly.

Larry nodded, and looked to see if he could make out what book Turner'd been reading, but could not. "So how long did it take Thoreau? To write *Walden*?"

Mr. Turner was looking past him, over at the River Hill, which was covered in snow now. Some of it would be deep in places already, and there would be deer up there, those who had survived the two-week season just finished, when you could often hear the hunters' rifle shots throughout the day down in the town. Nobody had gotten the big ten-point, they'd reported at Sam's. He was free to roam his kingdom for another year.

"Nine years," Turner said. "Nine years. And he revised it seven times."

Nine years. In nine years, he would be twenty-five years old nearly. It was an inconceivable amount of time to him. Twice as long as you needed to get a college degree. A year longer than going all the way through to being a doctor. And that was just one book.

"He must have liked to write," he said on the impulse. Turner laughed softly.

"You could put it that way, yes." Then he walked over to the big windows, looking out, where it was rapidly getting grey, moving towards the early dark nights of winter time. "How old do you think he lived to be, Larry? Thoreau. Henry David Thoreau." He reached up and turned on a row of the front overhead lights.

Larry shook his head. The sudden lights made the classroom lighter as the darkness outside grew quickly. Some kids were still in the halls, calling out, horsing around, running loudly down corridors. A locker door banged loudly, someone laughed. "Smoke a White Owl!" a boy yelled. "I got yer White Owl, right here," another yelled out.

Turner came back from the window and sat on the edge of the old, scarred wooden desk, that was too small really for him to sit comfortably behind. When had that desk been new? Larry thought, looking at it. It was so old now. Older than he was.

"Forty-two. He was forty-two when he died. Not married. Maybe never even really had a girlfriend. No children. No property – no real estate to settle. Just the book. Just *Walden*, and a couple of others. But you know what, Larry?"

Larry was silent. He did not know. It sounded like Thoreau had had a sad life, to him, and he wondered why.

"He left this huge *journal*, that he kept daily for years... for his life. His whole life, Larry, this man...his whole life was writing. What he wrote was his life, you could say." Turner looked down, and shook his head. "He liked leading a huckleberrying party – that's in *Walden*. Thoreau said he liked that better than becoming famous – being captain of a huckleberrying party."

It was quiet now in the room where they sat, he in the chair and Turner on the edge of the old desk, while it really stared to turn dark outside. So quick, sudden, in winter. You could hear the soft, incessant hissing of the radiators. Out the windows now you could see some Christmas colored lights on around houses – red, green, blue, yellow, a few white even. One house had lights all around its edges, and even down the raised middle of the roof, and up around the old brick chimney. Some houses had holly all around their outside front door. He wondered where it had come from, that business about the mistletoe. The art room, next to his home room, had wonderful decorations, and some mistletoe hung up, that guys would try and get girls under. A few girls tried to steer guys under it, too.

And then Cameron was there, in the doorway, with her long shining lustrous black hair – it seemed longer than ever – and the lights from the hallway behind her in a halo. She looked so beautiful he thought his heart would stop, or break. Cameron.

"Can I come in? Is that ok?" A low, soft voice. Mr. Turner was somewhat dazed, too; Larry could tell. Rather than speaking, he simply gestured with his hand toward the classroom seats.

She sat down in the seat next to Larry, and he wondered if he would be able to say much with the force of her smile.

"I heard – I was just going by – I thought I heard you talking about Thoreau? *Walden?*"

Both of them nodded their heads vigorously. "We were doing that, yes, Cameron." Turner said. "Old Henry David. Himself. And his great book." He gestured at Larry. "This young man. Maybe he'll write a *Walden* of his own. Some day."

Larry felt himself blushing hotly, burning. He shook his head, looking down.

"You could, Larry. I think you could." Cameron shifted, facing him more in her seat and he heard the soft rustle of her long hair swinging around. She had a white tossle cap in her hand, and in that she would look even better, prettier. How pretty could she be? She was going to New York to become a model, and it was easy to believe it looking at her. Cameron was going to drive him crazy, he thought. It was terrible, the confusion of his feelings right at the moment, and when they left, whenever this was over, he would replay every second of it, and that would be even worse. There was nobody he could talk to about it either, not even Mr. Turner who he sensed felt there was something between them. What did he think? But it would be impossible to ask him. How could you do that?

"I couldn't write something like that," he said then, haltingly. "No…"

"You don't know what you could do, Larry." Cameron reached over and touched his arm. "You really don't."

Turner stood up from the edge of the desk. He really was a large man, almost bear-like. He ran his hand through his thick black hair and looked at it, as if he expected to discover something that would have the answer. "Being a writer, that's a hard one. But in Thoreau's case – you know, I don't think he set out to be a writer. Whatever that may mean. He really liked just living – raising his beans, fishing, looking at the ice on the pond in winter. You know what he really liked to do? And this is unusual, I think. Maybe the most unusual thing about him."

He looked down at them expectantly, like they were in his class. Neither of them said anything, looking up at him; he would tell them, for sure. He was the teacher.

"He liked to think. To just think, sitting or walking, out in the woods there, by Walden Pond. That's something most of us avoid, like the famous plague. Thinking."

"There's lots of ways to think, though," Larry said, surprising himself. As soon as he said it, he realized he did not know for sure what he meant, but he had said it. Cameron was nodding, looking at him.

"Sure. *Walden* is a record of that, isn't it? But it's very unusual for Americans to think. We *do*."

"This is turning into a class," Cameron said then, smiling. "But that's ok. Just the three of us."

It was warm in the room, and cold outside and dark, and Larry suddenly wondered if this would be what college would be like. The close, small intimacy – free discussion, no right answer. If it were like this, he would really like it.

Somebody had put a record of Bing Crosby on the PA system, and "Adeste Fidelis" rang out in the halls of Ralston High School. "O come all ye faithful..." probably the assistant principal, who was rarely in the building but always over at the main office that was located above a bank.

"Time to go home," Turner said, "To be continued."

So he ended up yet again walking in the hall, down towards the big double main door. But with Cameron, the girl he could not imagine being with and did not know what to do when he was with her. He felt rigid like a board, and somehow solemn, and wished he could banter and joke around, maybe even break into a little dance number, like he'd seen Gibby Davis do, the guy voted Best Dancer in the senior class. Or the halfback, Robert Henderson. He could really dance. Coach Rossi had even said that playing halfback was like dancing one time at a chalkboard session, looking at Henderson.

"What are you thinking, Larry?" she said as they went down the echoing stairs to the first floor. It was the question he'd already dreaded she would ask. He stopped in the bend of the high stairwell, and looked at her. The hair folded in against her face. God have mercy, he thought.

"You..."

She wasn't smiling and it felt like there were just the two of them in that place, the echoing staircase, and maybe if they were lucky they'd never leave.

"You are the girl of my dreams."

It was so quiet after he had come out with his confession, and then tried his best to not look at her, but he could not, that it was as if the school had closed and nobody was there.

Cameron slowly put her hand up, it was as warm as the air in the stairwell was cold, and touched his cheek. He could not have moved if he wanted to. He was rooted to the spot, now looking at her as if he would never stop looking at her. Her white tossle cap, which she'd had in her hand, lay on the floor between them, she had dropped it, and he thought he could not step on that, be careful.

And then there was the gravelly voice, booming out above them, the terrific racket of shoes on the stairs, coming down. "Cogsuggers, all of ya!" And Goran's voice, above, dulled by the stairwell, laughing with the cackling laugh he had that never sounded like a real laugh, but something else.

It was Bill Frissen, famous for having more pimples than anyone else in the school, his face a red blaze, who caromed off the wall as he saw them, his eyes wide, and then recovered his stride and took two stairs at once going on down around the bend, leaving a trail of sweat aroma behind him.

"Frissen! You fuckin' jerk-off!" Goran's voice echoed.

Larry bent down and picked up Cameron's white tossle cap, Frissen had not stepped on it, and handed it to her. "We better go. Before something else comes down here."

She nodded, placing the cap carefully on her head, tucking the long hair back, the white and black contrast like a magazine photograph. Like a model, he thought. The Bing Crosby record was still playing, with Bing now signing "Jingle Bells", which certainly wasn't one of Larry's favorites.

The stairs were wide and he thought how easy it would be to fall down them, although it never happened. Kids skidded, spun, teetered, lurched forward and backwards, and a tall, particularly skinny freshman, whose name he didn't know, had bumped down one flight on his behind, bouncing and yelling. And then holding his ass. He gained the nickname "Sore Ass" from his feat.

When they went through the big front doors of the school, they could see the light snow falling through the light cast up by the old iron lamps that stood directly outside on the lawn, flanking the door. They had been built when the school had, back in 1924. They were solid and sturdy, and Larry liked them, although he knew many felt they looked "old-fashioned." He was beginning to think he liked old-fashioned things, though. Thoreau was probably old-fashioned.

The snow was stopping and then starting again. When snow stopped, there was no sound, it just wasn't there, falling, anymore. If anything, if such a thing was possible, it was even quieter. Under the lights of the town, everything sparkled in it. He wondered if the old ten-point buck was sleeping now somewhere, hidden up on River Hill or out on the top of it in a big thicket.

He had walked Cameron to her red Chevy, helped her sweep snow off the windows. Then they drove slowly around the town, hardly saying a word. She hadn't turned on the radio, he was glad for that, and somehow he knew she was aware and glad too. There was only them, the car, the snow starting up again, spiraling out of the dark sky soundlessly, the ticking of the windshield wipers, the town being transformed in front of them. When they went past Peter's, they could see kids through the steamed windows but did not stop.

How long had they done that? It didn't matter. She stopped near his house, looming up in the dark, angles picked out with snow and the moon. For a moment, a few seconds, he thought he'd ask her to come in, meet his mother.

Instead, he got out of the warmth, that special car warmth in winter, and pulled his jacket collar up, walked a few steps towards the house, then back. He went around the front of the Chevy and Cameron put her window down. Her incredible face, looking up. He leaned down quickly, kissed her, then kissed her closed eyes which he could feel underneath his lips. The snow was coming down on both of them, maybe it would not stop. He could feel it in his hair.

A slow, lumbering car came around the corner and the headlights hit the Chevy. He stepped aside as it drove past, chains crunching.

"You better go, Cameron," he said, not what he wanted to say. Her white cap had slipped to one side and he thought he must have put his hand up to her hair.

"It's gonna get bad," he said, gesturing up at the sky. "It might not stop."

She sat there, looking at him, as if she would fix his image in a photograph. "Larry," she said. "Larry."

Then she nodded, and the red Chevy slowly pulled out, the window still open and he thought, "Maybe she won't close it," the tail lights fading into the snow at the far end of the street as she made that turn, down near the huge tree where Ducky and he had fixed a basket, now just a metal hoop, long ago, when they were kids.

He stayed there for a long time, watching the snow tumble down in the shaft of streetlight, covering him in a powder. He knew he should go in the house, old Mrs. Pearson, across the street, who saw everything, would see him standing still there and wonder. Maybe even ask his mother.

But he did not go in. He stamped his feet, shook the snow off his head, brushed his old hunting jacket Carl had given him, and headed off quickly towards the field. He didn't know why, no sense at all as they said at Sam's. It was close; it wasn't far to walk.

The big field was silent, stretching out into blackness at the far end, a hundred yards away, but some misty illumination even there from the Christmas lights strung on the far goalpost. The street gate was not locked; kids had probably vandalized it, messed with it. This happened all year, a war with ole Barenekkid Stroup, who vowed he'd get these kids, they would see, and then they would be sorry. But he never did, somehow.

He walked out to the edge of the field. Nobody in sight. A few faint halos and squares of light, up above in the school building. He walked out onto the field, the snow crunching in that special, unmistakable sound. A smooth, unbroken whiteness spread all around him as he stood where he estimated mid-field would be. No sound, once he stopped walking. He could see his tracks, out from the edge, the sideline. Turning slowly around, he looked at the bleacher rows he could barely make out, they had snow layered on them like a big cake. And then he walked back, in the tracks he'd made, and stood at the edge again. He could not have said why, but he felt a sense of relief. He looked out and saw his tracks fading into the dark and filling up even as he looked. In a half-hour or less, there would be no trace.

CPSIA information can be obtained
at www.ICGtesting.com
Printed in the USA
FFOW03n1743190914
7452FF

9 781938 349201